My Enemy, My Beloved

My Enemy, My Beloved

Karl Vanghen

NORTH STAR PRESS OF ST. CLOUD, INC.
ST. CLOUD, MINNESOTA

AUTHOR'S NOTES

My sincere appreciation to friends, authors, and acquaintances that helped me portray this story in a factual manner.

Special thanks to my wife, June, without whose help and encouragement this novel might never have been written

First Edition, September 1, 2010

Printed in the United States of America

Published by
North Star Press of St. Cloud, Inc.
P.O. Box 451
St. Cloud, Minnesota 56302

www.northstarpress.com

ACKNOWLEDGEMENTS

Joanne Englund, Writer's Unlimited

June Beck, Writer's Unlimited

Irving Killman, Traces

Charles Turner, Traces

Karl Heck, former Jugend member, German soldier, prisoner of war and coal miner

Robert Schmidt, Resident, New Ulm

Michael Luick, Thrams - Traces

Frank Sutherland, Mahtomedi, Minnesota

Marily Hesse, Librarian, Brown County Historical Society

Herbert Schaper, Resident, New Ulm

Patrick Eckstein, Resident, New Ulm

Gary Tiepel, Park Manager, Minnesota Department of Natural Resources, Flandreau State Park.

ONE

THE FEAR-FILLED IMPRESSION OF LIFE'S final moment infected Henrik Arndt like a sickness. Disillusioned and terrified amid the numbing horror of war, he drew on what little courage remained in his confused and petrified mind. But nothing, not even thoughts of home, could replace the horrible aspect of dying. The days preceding his forced march into Aachen were all but forgotten as he looked into the gruesome face of war through eyes drawn thin by smoke and the sickening breath-stealing stench around him . . . and he thought . . . I am terrified . . . and soon I will die.

Tired and hungry and restless from a night without sleep, he wormed his way across the shattered brick pile on which he lay, and as hope for living through another hour faded, he thought back on the events that had brought him to Aachen on that cold, miserable afternoon when death looked down at him from a sky twisted with smoke and fire and inhuman sounds; the noise of a world gone mad.

Drawing himself into as small a target as possible, he ripped the legs of his uniform. His lips stuttered. He twisted uneasily atop his vantage point, and waited, and waited, and waited.

Henrik had been thrust into combat just three weeks before shortly after the American army had launched an attack across the German border eight miles north of Aachen and had fought their way through six miles of the West Wall, the Siegfried Line. Defiantly, the defenders of Aachen had refused a surrender ultimatum that had then resulted in an intense artillery bombardment. Now, American infantrymen were entering the city in house-to-house fighting, and Henrik could do nothing but wait.

Depressed, lonely, and frightened, Henrik sprawled in the remains of the half-fallen building. The bricks that supported him were littered with an obscene tangle of furniture, glass, piping and wiring, and in shifting he inhaled the gritty, acrid scent of smoke, the reek of his own body, the choking dust, and the ever-present stench of decomposing corpses. He waited nervously, trapped in his own private horror, stiff with a fear that permeated his entire being. The war would soon come to him, from down the street, from around the shattered building that still spewed fire. How it would come, he didn't know. He knew only that it would, with all its fury and death and inhuman horror directed straight at him.

While compressing his mental pain to numbness, his crusted eyes peered out over the brick pile, over knuckles that were turning white against the cold barrel of the Panzerfaust 60, the anti-tank weapon pressed tightly against his side. He felt little of his body, the flesh and blood and bone that lay inside a uniform reeking with the stench of sweat and urine and fear. Choked with a dense feeling of disillusionment, he shifted beneath the raw wind that brushed across his shoulders, a wind that brought with it the distinct buzz of blowflies as they searched for the remains of dead soldiers. He felt discarded in a world gone mad, with nothing but his breath and scattered thoughts to sustain him, to connect him with a past that had already lost its worth.

Lowing his face to rest his cheek across his arms, he recalled the days when he played with his friend, Otto, in the hayfield near his home, when they were younger, when the world was at peace, when no one was concerned about dying, when they had ran and leaped across the fields like young deer, breathing the clear, sweet scent of nature, the call of their voices challenging the stillness. Then, just as the vision materialized into something resembling reality, a nearby explosion shook his body, and in an instant, the brief memory vanished. He trembled, and looked down at the bricks as if they were some sort of puzzle meant for him to solve. Then, in a moment of clarity, he realized that his eyes were unclear and watery. Quickly, he wiped the tears away, and as another explosion shook his body, he thought no more of hayfields and cool fall days, but rather of his precarious situation, and the likelihood that this might be his last day alive.

Henrik bit down hard on his teeth while struggling to maintain some semblance of courage. But courage was as scarce as warmth. He inched his way up the brick pile, and through the small burning slits of his eyes, he strained to see any sign of movement. In searching he caught sight of the Aachen cathedral, built in 786 AD by the emperor Charlemagne, whose remains still lay sequestered within its walls. Like many other structures in Aachen, the cathedral had not escaped the bombs and shellfire that had rained down on the city as the American army advanced steadily from their positions in Belgium just across the border. He was sure that even Charlemagne would not rest well this day.

Trying to swallow, he found only a dry lump in his throat. Lack of water and sleep had deprived him of his ability to function normally, except when it came to urinating where he lay.

Get ready, he told himself. Get ready. Soon they will come. Soon you will have to fight. Soon you will be either a hero or a dead man. If you don't fight you will be shot by one of your own countrymen. He had seen others shot, without a moment of pause, as fear scabbed their faces, the hunger for life already dead in their eyes. No, he would not be a coward. He would strengthen himself, now, before the enemy came, before the terror of battle overtook him.

Henrik's face quivered at the thought, and he shifted again as the agonizing whine of war approached him from the only street he could see. He thought he would die there, on the brick pile, filthy and hungry, with no one to mourn him, his body just another of the thousands that had fallen. Yes, he would die there, on the brick pile, as the result of one man's fanatic rise to power, this battle being only one of the many paybacks for his Führer's mad ambitions.

Now, ahead of him, the noise of the advancing army rumbled through the shattered streets, tightening his nerves, increasing his fear. To each side, and behind and above him, incoming ordinance rained death and destruction into every section of the city. To him, the end of life was only a block away, where the unmistakable sounds of battle intensified. To survive at all, he would have to kill the men who were coming to kill him.

As the bricks trembled beneath his body, he moved his tongue through the paste that coated his mouth. Tears ran freely across his cheeks. His jaw tightened; then went slack. His eyes, like those of a small animal, peered out across the pile, and he blinked to clear his vision. Gathering the last of his courage, he silently mumbled a verse from one of the hymns he had sung as a child. *Wenn endlich ich Komme, zu sterben. Nehmen Sie mich zuruckkehre…* When at last I come to die. Take me home. Then, as the noise ahead of him quickened, his eyes fluttered. Further down the cobblestone street, fire licked at a bombed-out building.

Henrik's head came up sharply as he eard an unmistakable rumble, Tanks! He scraped his booted foot against the loose bricks and inched his body upward, careful not to expose the Panzerfaust. His entire body quivered and for a moment he felt paralyzed and incapable of further movement. Drifting smoke blew over him. Calm yourself, he thought. You must be brave now. He eased himself higher and peered through a v-shape cleavage in the bricks. His heart pulsed faster. His breath stalled. He saw soldiers farther down the street, darting from building to building, taking cover, motioning, moving again, like the stiff little lead soldier figures he had played with as a child.

Americans!

Henrik stiffened, then allowed his body to relax. Instinctively, he slid farther down the pile. His breath came faster, to match the pounding of his heart. Then, in an attempt to calm himself, he rested, but only for a moment. He tugged the Panzerfaust tight to his body and glanced to his right. A short distance from him, another older Grenadier named Peter shifted across the refuse. He was armed with only a standard Mauser Karabiner 98k.

"Sie kommen," Peter said in a hoarse voice. They are coming.

Henrik's initial thought was: what good is a rifle against a tank? Then he gathered his strength, the last of it, and eased his way up for another look.

"Bereiten sie sich vor!" Get down, Peter grunted.

Henrik shifted the Panzerfaust forward and rested it on the bricks. Carefully, he snapped the sighting lever into position. The hastily taught routine he had learned back in the field drummed in his head: how to load, important precautions, how to aim and fire. The weapon had a range of 60 meters, so he would look through the vertical sighting hole marked 60. He would fire at long range in hopes of disabling the tank. Then he would get up and run. He had no other weapon with which to defend himself. He would have to get one from a dead man. Slowly, he disengaged the safety switch guarding the trigger. Then he scanned the warning message printed on the tube. *Achtung! Feuerstrahl!* Caution! Fire Jet!

Without delay, he reached for the single projectile tucked beneath his belt. The device was nothing more than a small rocket equipped with stabilizer fins that would extend after firing. Reaching up, he slipped it carefully into the chamber as the squealing sound of tank treads quickened. He rubbed a sleeve across his face, smearing sweat. He watched Peter aim his rifle over the top of the bricks. His hands began shaking, and he knew he would have to fire before Peter did, before the enemy pinpointed them. He clawed his way to a firing position and raised the Panzerfaust. As he leveled the weapon, the tank pivoted on its treads. Peter fired just as Henrik's finger touched the trigger.

The blast erupted right before Henrik's eyes, a bright blaze of light accompanied by a deafening roar that instantly numbed his senses. Immediately, he was thrown backwards, lifted as if by a mighty hand. He had no sensation of movement, only a terrible pressure pushing him upward, elevating him, and for a terrifying moment all sensation, thought, and emotion were sucked away by the compelling force. He was thrown backwards amid a shower of bricks and masonry. The Panzerfaust cartwheeled away from him. A profound ringing screamed in his ears, as he landed hard on his back. A shower of bricks, falling debris, glass fragments, particles of masonry and dirt peppered his body. His eyes fluttered and then closed. His ears rang with an incessant, horrifying din. He felt nothing, only numbness, as a dreadful silence settled over him.

Before he could react, before he could think, before he could move a finger, a numbing calm took hold of him, and as his body quivered, and as all sound was sucked away, he slipped into a moment of unconsciousness, and the war became nothing but a deep overpowering silence.

Slowly he came around, feeling life and numbness and pain all at once. His body seemed pinned to the ground, weighted down by an invisible force. Then, slowly, he realized what had happened, and he began wondering how badly he had been wounded. When he shifted, pain stabbed at his back where the bricks ground into his spine. Something like fire erupted in his leg. He gazed skyward, into the dark grey smoke that billowed above him. His body trembled sharply as the last of his energy released. He gasped, sucked dust into his throat, and then coughed.

Henrik remained motionless, trying to still his trembling jaw. Then it came to him. All the sounds around him were muffled. Sounds that should have been loud were mere whispers in his ears. He heard no explosions, no gunfire, only an unending ringing. He tilted his head and saw a tank creeping past him, chattering up the ground, its treads no more than ten feet from his outstretched arm. He tried to swallow and make a sound, but could not.. Turning his head the other way, he saw Peter sprawled face down on the ground, his head nothing more than red pulp. His detached arm lay a short distance away, its fingers coiled like a large claw. Have to move, he thought. Have to get up and get out of here before the Americans come. Groaning, he shifted on the bricks and rolled to his left, where the pain was less severe. He attempted to rise, but his strength was gone. His body jerked, hard. His face sagged onto the street, onto shards of glass and remnants of bricks. He sucked a deep breath, then coughed, felt grit in his throat. It is over for me, he thought. I am as good as dead. Soon they will find me, and then I will die. His officers had told him that the Americans would not take prisoners.

Then he heard a thumping sound. Mercifully, his hearing was returning. Soldiers were running past him. He could hear their shouts now, their steady footfalls, and the whine of an airplane somewhere above. I will be all right now, he thought. I will hear again. He saw a building to his right, just past Peter's body. A doorway, an opening, if only he could make it …perhaps.

Henrik began crawling slowly, toward the shattered building. Hard going. Pain roared through his leg and up the side of his face. He touched his cheek, his fingers bloodied. He probed his cheek, felt something hard just inside a gash on the side of his face. He trembled again. I am wounded, he thought. How bad? Will I bleed to death, here on the street? Then he worked his way up on one elbow and looked down where the pain was, in his leg. He saw nothing but his torn uniform, his skin black with dirt, and a redness there, but no blood. Again, he tried to crawl away.

After moving only three yards, a foot came down hard on his back, pinning him to the street. A voice came through the ringing in his head, loud enough for him to hear the words. "Get up Kraut. Now! *Stehen Sie auf*! Arms up!" Then the voice called out to someone else. "I got one over here."

Henrik heard the return call, and he stiffened. "Shoot the son-of-a-bitch!" He took a deep breath, and then shuddered. Would he die now, right here on the shattered cobblestones of the Aachen street? Darkness would come soon. He looked up at the soldier. "Don't shoot me," he pleaded, forcing his words, hoping he would be heard.

Then, again, the command, loud, demanding, *"Stehen Sie auf!"* as the bullet-end of a rifle jabbed him just below his ear.

Turning his head slowly, Henrick saw boots. The soldier had not shot him. His moment of panic gave way to hope. Perhaps he would live.

"Don't shoot me," he pleaded again. "Do not shoot. I speak English."

The rifle barrel lifted. Then, slowly, but with great effort Henrick rose to his knees. His vision blurred as he looked blankly at the soldier before him. "Don't shoot me. I am unarmed," he repeated, raising his arms above his head.

The soldier, a young man whose face was blackened, stepped back. His eyes appeared confused for a moment. Then he shouted, "Hey, this one speaks English."

The reply came instantly. "Get him on his feet. We might be able to use him."

The soldier nodded, stood back. He pointed the rifle at Henrik's forehead. "On your feet," he shouted.

Henrik understood all too well what he had to do. Slowly, but with great effort, he stood, wobbled uneasily, and then straightened his body. "I am wounded," he said.

"Where?"

"My face . . . and my leg."

The American looked quickly at the cheek. "Flesh wound," he said. "Looks like something slashed you."

"My leg also."

"Check it out. Hurry. I ain't got all day."

Henrik felt his leg where the pain was centered. No blood. He put all his weight on it, felt strength there, lifted it up, set it down again. He nodded. "I am all right there," he said.

The American stood back. His finger eased away from the trigger. He was a young man, not much older than he was. His eyes were dark, but his gaze bore straight ahead. He kept the rifle pointed at Henrik's chest.

"I am Volkstrum," Henrik said.

"What's that?'

"Conscripted. I am not a soldier."

"Then what are you?"

"A civilian, trained only a week ago. I was told to come here to fight."

The American looked at the bent barrel of the Panzerfaust, then back. His finger touched the trigger again. "You were gonna take out one of our tanks."

"It was my order."

The American curiously looked at him, sizing him up, questioning his statement, as if wondering what to do. Then, quickly, he reached out and frisked him, found no weapon. Then he reached into his own pocket and withdrew a soiled white cloth. "Here. Hold this on your cheek and walk back that way. Keep your other arm up in the air or someone'll shoot you." He pointed down the street to where another tank stood, its gun barrel pointed menacingly in their direction. "Now walk! Someone back there'll tell you where to go. You're now a prisoner of the United States of America."

"I understand," Henrik said, accepting the handkerchief.

The American sneered. "Good thing it was me that found you. I know a dozen other guys who'd have blown your head off. Now get the hell out of here."

"Yes. Yes," Henrik said, looking down the street to where the other tank stood. More men were running toward him, many of them darting from doorway to doorway, crisscrossing the street. From behind him came the rapid snarl of gunfire. Resistance. He moved slowly forward limping, testing his footing. His leg was firm but sore. A steady pain throbbed in his calf, like the worst headache he had ever had. With the handkerchief tight to his cheek, and his arm raised high above his head, he moved slowly toward the oncoming tank.

Henrik Arndt was now a non-combatant, a prisoner. For him, the war was over. He felt relieved as he walked, unsteadily at first, then faster as the pain eased. Slowly, his fear ebbed away. He thought: *I could be dead now, lying next to Peter. The old man hadn't wanted to fight, would have rather taught school. His wife of fifty years had died in a B-17 raid over Hamburg. His son had perished on the sand in Africa at a place called Mareth Line.* He breathed deeply as the Americans ran past him on their way to do battle with his stubborn countrymen who still refused to yield.

Soldiers gave him silent commands as he limped slowly through the streets choked with infantrymen, tanks, jeeps, and all the devilish equipment that accompanied an advancing army. He stopped where twenty or more or his countrymen stood in a tight circle guarded by a single infantryman armed with a machine gun. He fell in with them, and then eased the handkerchief away from his cheek. The white cloth had blood on it. He touched the wound, felt something hard there beneath his skin. The men around him offered no comment. They were silent; some with their heads bowed, either ashamed or afraid, some with their eyes to the sky watching the unchallenged airplanes that streaked over the city. Some were regular army men who were humiliated by surrender. A Waffen SS officer was the only one who held his head high, his chin thrust forward, appearing to be undaunted. He must be humiliated by his capture or his surrender, Henrik thought. Hitler would most certainly disapprove.

Henrik recognized a young boy about thirteen who had trained with him in the field before being sent to Aachen. The boy stood rigid, his arms tight to his sides to prevent them from trembling. The boy looked quickly at Henrik, and then was jolted by the sound of a nearby explosion. Henrik looked up as dark smoke rolled over the city, listening to the sounds of rapid fire, the howl of ordinance and the staccato of small arms from deep in the streets.

The pain in his leg sent tremors into his hip. His knee was sore. Soon, he thought, the knee would not be able to support him. I will fall, and if I cannot walk perhaps they might come and shoot me. Reason enough to fight the pain. Reason enough to endure the suffering. He ground his teeth together and tried to think of something other than where he was. Oddly enough, he could think only of trees, those in his yard, when the wind was up, when they moved like great billowing green clouds, dancing like beautifully crafted dancers swaying to an unheard symphony. For a moment, he forgot where he was, until the ground once again shook beneath his feet.

After about a half hour, a stern-faced officer came up and scanned the group. Without expression, he pointed, his hand moving rapidly. *"Marschieren Sie so!"* he said. March that way!

The prisoners turned, their boots scuffing on the roadway. They stepped off, some quicker than others, uncoordinated, their eyes fixed straight ahead to see where they were going. Soon someone counted cadence, and they quickly assumed a military manner, marching in coordinated steps down the shattered street. One of them quietly asked, *"Wo nehmen sie uns?"* "Where are they taking us?"

Someone else replied. *"Nur Spanziergang und is ruhig."* "Just walk and be quiet."

They were marched to an intact building, a one-story structure near the edge of the city, and ordered inside, the doors closing behind them. The room, once an office of sorts, held desks and chairs. It had been hastily abandoned, judging from the disorder. Papers and cigarette butts littered the floor, and the rooms smelled distinctly of smoke. The single broken window offered limited light. Outside, a guard watched them from across the street, his machine gun at the ready.

Utterly exhausted, Henrik slid down to a sitting position against a wall, scanning the room. No one spoke, but he recognized and smiled at the young boy he had seen earlier who almost immediately sat down beside him. Without saying a word, the boy leaned into his arm and cried silently. Another with blood on his face, sat just ahead of them. His features were almost mask-like, bereft of emotion. Some men whispered, but most were silent. Most found a place to sit while one sprawled on top of a desk. Words, wherever they were, seemed unimportant, mumblings only, all of them incoherent.

"My name is Henrik," he told the boy.

The young lad with a thin face, dark hair, and eyes the color of rust, replied, "I am Friedrich."

"I have seen you before."

"Yes, in the field."

"How old are you?"

"I am fourteen."

"Just a boy."

The young boy sniffled. "I was never a boy."

"Yes, I know," Henrik said. "In 1939, when I was twelve, Hitler made membership in the Hitlerjugund compulsory. I was a boy then, until it came to that."

Henrik's father had fought to keep him out, but he was rebuked by those who thought him disloyal to the great cause, and so Henrik was forced to join the Deutsches Juntgvold, a junior branch of the Hitler-Jugund movement. He received his Hitler youth registration book, his black shorts and brown shirt, and with hundreds of other youths at his side, he spoke a solemn oath to serve the Führer for the remainder of his life.

He went to the camps for training, and marched beneath the black flag bearing an eagle and swastika, and held his head high as did all the others, despite his discontent. However, it didn't take long for the officers to see that he was weaker than most, finding it difficult to keep up with the rigorous, physical exercises. He tired easily. He cried at times, though he tried desperately not to, and despite the constant prodding and jeering of others, he always fell behind, and often did poorly at his lessons. He was shouted at, struck down, beaten twice by the more physical boys, and was finally cast out of the order and branded unfit for service. Back home, his father steered him away from the Nazi doctrines and taught him other, kinder disciplines from the bible, and from his heart, for he was a gentle man who seemed to know where Germany was headed. As a result, Henrik was never brainwashed in the hate camps, where disciplines were strict, and war was spooned out to them like a dreadful aphrodisiac. He had led, what some would call, a sheltered life. When the panzers rolled into Poland, his father told him that hell was about to reveal itself. His father had been right.

"What will happen to us now," Friedrich asked.

"We will be taken to a camp, I think. We are no longer combatants."

"Then what?'

"We will find out when we get there."

"I am frightened."

"Don't be. The war is over for us."

The boy was silent for a while. He was almost asleep when an explosion rocked the building. Instantly, he groped Henrik's arm. When the blast gave way to sporadic machine gun fire, the boy asked him. "How did you come to be in the field?"

"The field, yes. It seems like such a long time ago."

"Tell me," Friedrich said.

"It is not much of a story,"

"Then just talk to me."

Henrik tugged him closer so he could whisper in his ear. He did not want anyone else listening to what he had to say.

"I was working in an armory until just a month ago, twelve hours a day. Then one day the bombers came. I was in the bomb shelter when they leveled our factory. When I came out all I could see was fire and wreckage, as if the entire world was burning. Flames consumed everything. My mother, who was with me, cried and wrung her hands. My father, who was also there, cursed God for bringing Hell to us."

Henrik paused and offered up a short, silent prayer. Within moments, fatigue crawled through his body. He felt a surge of sadness, or was it relief, inching its way through him like the movement of a centipede.

"Go on," the boy muttered.

"Two days later the SS came and rounded up every able-bodied man they could find, boys younger than me, and white-haired old men, grandfathers mostly, and wounded men from the hospital who could barely walk or carry a gun. They didn't take my father because he was ill."

It was painful for Henrik to recall those days, but he went on because the younger boy prodded him to do so.

"As you know, they banded us together with remnants of the army, and called us Volkstrum. They rushed us into the field. You were there. You know what it was like. They gave me a Panzerfaust 60, the single shot dispensable anti-tank weapon, and the rank of Grenadier. I was made to be a private, a civilian made soldier in three weeks. And you?"

"They gave me nothing more than a pistol and a canteen, a bread bag and mess tin with not much food. I was also a Grenadier."

"I had a uniform frayed at the cuffs, and with an elbow missing. Clothing that had once belonged to another soldier."

"They gave me only this," the boy said, touching his coat. He was wearing a fatigue jacket over his civilian clothing, and a cloth cap.

Henrik remembered the day when they had gathered in the field, waiting for their final orders. The American army had breached the Siegfried Line and were nearing Aachen. It was up to them to defend the city, along with remnants of the regular army, those still capable of fighting. Reinforcements would come, they had promised. Hold the enemy off until they arrive. Then you will be withdrawn. Everyone knew the words were false. Everyone prepared himself for death.

"Friedrich." He shook the boy but saw he was sound asleep on his shoulder. Henrik heard coughing in the room, shuffling, some snoring. Someone farted. Others rustled as they tried to find comfort on the floor. He had not eaten a bite of food in thirty hours. When darkness came, the room was like the inside of a cave.

An SS officer then stepped up onto the top of a desk, and in German loud enough for everyone to hear, he said. "*Achtung*, I must remind you, that even though we are prisoners, we must still be proud. We are all German soldiers, and are expected to act accordingly. The oaths we took must burn again in our hearts and minds. I expect all of you to be obedient to your captors, but stalwart in your loyalty to the Fatherland. Now we sleep. Tomorrow we will march with our heads high and our hearts proud. *Heil* Hitler!"

The response was muted, not as emphatic as the officer had wished it would be.

"I said, *Heil* Hitler!" he repeated.

That time he received the appropriate response.

Henrik Arndt fell asleep, although the bombardment continued throughout most of the night.

Two

New Ulm, Minnesota, October 1944

I N THE SMALL RIVER TOWN OF NEW ULM, nestled on the heights above the Minnesota River in the south-central quadrant of Minnesota, where beer and polka bands and celebrations were legendary, the citizens received the ongoing war news with a calm but dispassionate joy. Many of the town folks were of German extraction, immigrants mostly. Some had arrived in America just before Europe had been swept up in Hitler's fiendish hand. Scores of residents had relatives in Germany, and many harbored strong memories of their homeland. Some looked upon the war with a split allegiance. But although their minds still retained visions of the Fatherland, their hearts prayed for the American boys who had breached the Siegfried Line and were now fighting on German soil. The war had taken away the best of them, and hearts were heavy. Most everyone in town knew of someone in the service. With two wars being fought at the same time, one in Europe and another in the Pacific, hope for an early victory seemed unattainable.

As if to augment the news from Europe, work had been ongoing for some time at the abandoned CCC camp south of the city. Those who kept tabs on such things indicated that it would soon become a prisoner-of-war camp to house a contingent of Germans coming up from Algona, Iowa to join the small band of Mexican laborers already stationed there. Brown County was short of labor, and manpower was needed to keep the factories running at full output in the towns of Gaylord, Winthrop, St. Peter, Sleepy Eye, and New Ulm, and to assist the many farmers of Brown County with harvesting. The news of their impending arrival was met with uneasiness and concern, emphasized by the war news pouring in from Europe. Despite their Germanic ties, many in New Ulm disliked the prospect of having young enemy soldiers living in such close proximity with them. Unfortunately, they had no choice but to go along with the government decree.

The farms outside the city, those of vital importance to the war effort, were situated on some of the most favorable soil in Minnesota.

Among those who derived a living from the soil were the five hearty people of the Sommer family, who lived about five miles outside of New Ulm. The eldest of the three children was a sixteen-year-old girl named Elsa. She had arrived there with her father and mother, her brother David and her sister, Corina when she was only five years old. None of the children could remember anything but life on the farm.

Elsa had been farm reared and toughened by weather and labor. Even so, throughout her youth, and by following the example of her parents, she had acquired a belief in God as strong as faith could make it. She thought often about the boys in uniform, innocents caught up in a maelstrom of horror. War news always saddened her, and for that reason it was seldom discussed at the dinner table.

On the day following the historic breakthrough of the American army into Aachen, Elsa Sommer drove into New Ulm from her father's farm to keep a dentist appointment. A cavity had cost her a night's sleep. She was tired, both of mind and body, and nervous at the aspect of facing the nerve-jarring drill, her most hated instrument.

The weather was balmy for August. A light breeze drifted through the street, ruffling the American flags fixed to some of the streetlights. She was about to enter the building when the sound of a horn caused her to turn.

Across the street, an unmarked bus had pulled over to the curb, the driver seeking directions from someone on the sidewalk. The gray bus was much like a military vehicle, dull and unobtrusive. She thought nothing of it and was about to turn when a man thrust his head through one of the open windows. His voice carried easily across the street.

"*Hagen Fraulein. Sie einen Kuss fur mich?*" The statement was followed by a flurry of laughter deep inside the bus.

Elsa knew German, having studied the language in school, and her parents still spoke it at times, if only to keep it fresh in their minds. The man in the bus had said: Miss, do you have a kiss for me?

She stood quietly, her arms at her sides. Locked in a sense of bewilderment and in an extended moment of thought, she knew she was gazing upon the first contingent of German prisoners on their way to the new camp down by the Cottonwood River. As her curiosity bloomed, and as she failed to show any sign of moving on, others in the bus crammed around the window. Their smiling faces formed a circle of sorts, and they were laughing. One of them pointed to a beer sign outside a tavern, which caused an even greater outburst. Elsa was somewhat confused. Instead of being somber and withdrawn as she expected prisoners of war should be, they were gay and uninhibited, smiling and in high spirits. Surprised, but curious, she stood quietly, somewhat transfixed at their antics, until the moment the bus drove on.

A woman standing nearby turned toward her and remarked in a rather impudent voice. "Well, what do you think of that?"

Elsa shrugged. "I don't know. It seemed as though they're happy to be in Minnesota."

The stranger sneered and shifted her purse. "Prisoners of war have no place in our town," she said. "We'd all be better off if they stayed in Iowa."

Elsa's reply quickly. "They didn't appear to be dangerous at all."

The woman shrugged. "Even so, just the thought of having enemy soldiers so close gives me the willies. I hope they're wrapped up good and tight. I, for one, don't want them roaming around our streets."

Elsa didn't like the woman's insensitive manner. In fact she thought her quite rude. "My father said they won't bother anyone. They're here to help the farmers, and to work in the factories."

"Well, they can help us better by staying down in Iowa. I'd like to see them all shot."

The woman's nose went up as she walked away, leaving Elsa to wonder what sort of home she had grown up in. Certainly, it had not been like her home, where reasoning, good manners, and good will were served with the food. Certainly a bus-load of German prisoners would be no threat to a town like New Ulm.

The pain in her tooth throbbed again. She pressed her cheek. Yes, the dentist.

The diversion had almost made her forget the ache. Putting the POW incident aside, she turned and climbed the flight of steps leading to the black, leather chair, the drill, and the much-hated spit bowl.

Elsa thought no more about the German prisoners that day, for autumn was nearing its end, and there was still work to be done in the fields and garden patch behind the house, chickens to feed, hogs to attend, cows to take to pasture, milking, sewing, canning, and all the other things connected with a farm existence.

Occasionally, when work was at ebb, Elsa would spend time with her friend, Erica. They would talk about their friends, and gossip about the girls, and sing the new hit songs of the day, and reminisce about school and the New Year to come, and discuss boys, who were somewhat mysterious and daring in the mix of life. And occasionally, when they were aroused by some unknown spirit, they would discuss sex and what it would be like to love a man, for neither of them had lain with one. They were both virgins, although Erica often made it appear as if she was a woman of the world.

The trees had already lost most of their color, preparing for winter. The days usually ended with a welcomed coolness. The crickets had completed their nightly serenades. The harvest moon was full and bright on the land. The fields had given up their bounty. Papa and David had brought down their first rack of pheasants to be cleaned and canned before the frost set in, before the winter snow laid down its white fleece.

Elsa was back in school, and her routine had changed with studying taking priority. She was with her friends again, the girls and boys who shared her life. October's days were shorter. The preparations for winter had just begun. Soon they would wait for the inevitable snowfall.

Elsa Sommer faced life head on, not knowing where it would take her.

THREE

Aachen, Germany, October 1944

ENRIK AWOKE THE FOLLOWING MORNING, stiff and sore from his wounds. The first thing he noticed was the silence. He opened his eyes and saw most of the men, their voices low, were gathered in small groups. He heard no shooting, no explosions. It came to him then that the fighting had ended. He shook Friedrich, who was still pressed tightly to his side. When the boy opened his eyes, Henrik said. "It is over. The fighting is over."

They moved and rubbed their eyes and stood up. Others looked at them but said nothing. Then someone near them asked, "What do you think of this? "

"I think it is over," Henrik said.

"What will happen now?" Friedrich asked, moistening his lips.

Henrik repeated what he had said the night before. "We will be taken to a camp. Hopefully there will be food there, and shelter."

"Maybe we will sleep tonight in a potato field," someone said.

"Or maybe in our graves," someone else said.

"No. They will not kill us. We do not kill their prisoners, and they will not kill us."

"The Geneva Convention says we will be treated fairly."

"Piss on the Geneva Convention," someone remarked. "Give us more weapons and we will show them who will be masters of the world."

"Shut up," someone else said. "We will take our medicine."

When more of the men awoke, they spoke louder about what would happen. The superior officer said they would be taken to a prison camp where they would be interrogated, where they would be held, what it would be like in an Allied prison camp. Friedrich held close to Henrik's side.

"I am hungry," Friedrich said.

"They will give us food soon. The Americans are not monsters."

"How do you know that?"

"Because I have known them. My Uncle was an American."

Some of the men turned toward him, silently questioning his statement.

"Excuse me," Henrik said. "I have to find the bathroom."

"There is one over there," someone pointed.

Henrik found the bathroom in the office's hallway, though nothing there worked as it should. The room was full of papers the men had used to wipe themselves, and the water in the bowl was a dirty brown, full of urine. The room stank of human waste, enough so as to make one vomit. It was a horrible situation.

Before they could vent much of their antagonism, four American soldiers came through the door and herded them into a small group. One of the men was a Lieutenant. He was young and stern looking. He stood up on a chair so everyone could see him.

"Your army has surrendered," he said in German. "We will take you out now and you will fall in with the other prisoners. We will march out of the city and into Belgium where you will be moved to a place of safety. There you will be inspected and interrogated, and given food and shelter. You are prisoners of war, and will be treated as such. You need not fear your captors. We will care for you under the rules of the Convention. You." He pointed to the commanding officer of the group. "Take command of these men, and follow us."

Upon command, they were ushered into the street and marched to a wider street where thousands of others waited. When they were all in line, Henrik and Friedhelm became part of the 5,600 German prisoners-of-war that marched out of Aachen four abreast, leaving the destroyed city behind.

They walked most of the day, across the border into Belgium, down the long roads where trees were beginning to shed their leaves, where the raw winds gave way to a warmer afternoon, where the wreckage of war became prevalent: bombed towns, broken equipment, refugees everywhere, some of whom cursed them; others turned their heads. Some would have shot them had they been given the chance.

Conversation in the ranks was limited. Each prisoner was alone with his thoughts. Henrik heard laughter once, far back, and he wondered why anyone would laugh. He saw the American army, coming on, more and more of it, like a wave upon the land, and he thought: we will never stop them. There are too many. Germany is defeated.

Friedrich walked at his side, never faltering. They had walked only a mile or so before Henrik began to limp because his knee had swollen. Pain crept slowly toward his hip. He tolerated it for a long while, until they rested.

"I will be back," Friedrich said. Then he ran off, somewhere, without saying where he was going. Henrik thought he was going to look for a latrine. When he returned in about fifteen minutes, he was carrying a piece of wood, offering it to Henrik. "Use it for a crutch," he said. "It should be just about right for you."

"Where did you get this?"

"There," he pointed. "Over there, by that barn."

The barn was nearly level with the ground. Henrik took Friedrich around the neck and pulled him close. "You are amazing," he said. "You must stay with me. Maybe next time you can bring me some food."

They both laughed. The war was becoming less and less of a concern for them. Later in the day when the sun slid into a bank of gray clouds, they were marched into a field where they were given raw potatoes and carrots to eat, and a limited supply of water to drink. A latrine was gouged out of the ground by a bulldozer while a bullhorn announced that the field would have to be their bed for the night. Tomorrow would be a better day, the bullhorn said. They would have shelter, and more food. Interrogations would begin. They would be given ID numbers, and instructions. The bullhorn went on to say that anyone with wounds could report to the tent at the edge of the field, the one identified with a Red Cross, to be examined.

Henrik immediately took Friedhelm by the shoulders. "I will go to the tent and have them look at my leg. You wait there, by that fence. I will return soon, unless you do not want to wait for me."

"I will wait for you. I will stay by the fence."

"Alright then. Wish me good luck. We will go on together when the sun comes up."

Henrik went to the tent and waited in line until motioned inside. There, he stood in front of an officer, a middle-aged man with a round, stern face and piercing eyes.

"Your name," the officer demanded.

"Henrik Arndt. I am Volkstrum."

The officer nodded. "Where did you learn to speak English?"

"From my Uncle Alfred, when we lived in Langbroich. He was an American."

The officer smiled. "He was a good teacher."

"Yes."

"And why did your uncle teach you English?"

Henrik cleared his throat, hesitant to reply. "Because he said I would need to speak it someday before . . ."

The officer questioned the hesitation. "Before what?"

Henrik swallowed hard, turning his eyes aside. "Before Germany ruled the world."

"Did you believe him?"

"I think not. My father was not one to . . . accept the Nazi doctrine as being appropriate for a Christian."

"Then you are a Christian?"

"Yes."

The officer moved closer to Henrik. "Let me see that wound," he said. The officer inspected his face and his leg, and then stepped backward. "You'll go a field hospital tonight. We'll remove the shrapnel from your cheek, then cleanse and dress the wound. Two days, three perhaps. No longer. As for the leg, rest should be adequate. Then you'll join the prisoners for the train to Cherbourg."

"To Cherbourg?"

"Yes, to Cherbourg, in France."

Henrik paused before speaking, "I have a friend waiting for me, back there." He motioned toward the crowd of prisoners. "Can I bring him along?"

"Is he wounded?"

"No, he is not wounded."

"Then forget about him. They will be marched out tomorrow. If you want to go with them and take your chances with that leg, then go. Otherwise, you're going to the field hospital."

Henrik's eyes widened. "Where will I go from there?"

"I'd say you were lucky. You'll probably be sent to America as a prisoner of war. There, you'll see why your Uncle Alfred was wrong in thinking that Germany would rule the world. I think you already realize that your father was a wise man."

"Thank you," Henrik replied.

The officer pointed. "See the Sergeant over there. He'll take you to the vehicle. Good luck, Mr. Arndt." Then the officer snickered. "I wish I were going with you. I've been away from home far too long."

Henrik looked back at the huge crowd of prisoners. Darkness was already heavy on the land as the sun was about to slip behind the horizon. Most of the men were sitting down. Some had already found a place to sleep. Overhead, a squadron of fighter planes screamed low to the ground, headed toward Germany. He heard the rumble of cannon in the distance; saw the horizon glimmering with flames.

"Good-bye Friedhelm," he said. "Good luck to you. Maybe some day we will meet again."

The ride to the field hospital took about twenty minute, though it seemed much longer. He rode with another German soldier whose arm hung in a makeshift sling. They didn't speak, nor did the Sergeant who drove them hell-bent down a darkened road, guided only by moonlight. A cigarette dangled from his lips. His sidearm was positioned on his left side, away from tempting hands.

The field hospital was set in a small clearing, eight tents in all, rectangular structures covered with canvas. Huge red crosses were displayed on their sides and roofs. The two men were ushered into one of the tents where several other German soldiers lay. The corpsman, a tall, slender man with a face hardened by war, spoke to them curtly in German. "You're going to do exactly as you're told, when you're told to do it. I will accept no criticism, no complaints. We're going to look you over, and treat your wounds, and when you're well enough we'll release you to the rest of the prisoners. Now you just say, yes sir, and you'll be taken care of right well."

The two of soldiers said, "Yes sir."

Henrik was taken to a cot where he was stripped to his shorts, laid down, and covered with a single brown woolen blanket. His entire body was examined for shrapnel wounds. The orderly found a piece embedded in his cheek, removed it, but left two other smaller pieces there, explaining that they would work their way out in time. Going in to remove them would cause more problems than they were worth, he said. They also found a small piece of metal in the flesh just above his knee. After they removed it, they sealed him up with surgical tape. Then they gave him a drink of water and told him to rest.

More prisoners came in later that night, one with a severed hand, another unable to walk. Henrik was not concerned about them. He rested on his back, beneath the blanket and gazed at the tent's ceiling as it rippled under the pressure of the wind. He though of his parents who were somewhere in Bergheim near the foothills of the Eifel, the low mountains that arose from the Erft River basin. If given enough imagination, he could almost smell the clean air and the aroma of the fields in summer, and if he closed his eyes and concentrated hard enough he could almost see the bright blue sky and the green fields and the house where he lived. But then the noises would come; the coughing inside the tent, the movements outside, the sounds of engines, the occasional drone of an airplane above the compound, the sounds of muted voices, or an occasional scream of pain from one of the nearby cots, and the visions would disappear. The question persisted. Where was he to go now?

The officer had told him he was going to be sent to America. No, that did not seem probable. Why would they send him to America? Europe had enough space to hold the prisoners, enough space even in Germany, or France for that matter, or Belgium. Why would they send him across the Atlantic in a ship that might be torpedoed by one of Germany's own U-boats? But perhaps that is why they would send him there, in hopes they would be sunk, giving them nothing further to worry about, giving them reason to blame Germany for the loss of its own men. A ship could be sacrificed for the right reason. Many ships had been lost in the Atlantic. One more wouldn't matter. He trembled a bit, thinking about the cold waters, and what might happen there in the middle of a hostile ocean.

The man next to him was just an arm's length away. He hadn't said a word since Henrik had laid down beneath the blanket, but now he stirred and glanced over at Henrik and asked in a soft, almost commanding voice. "Where are you from?"

Henrik turned and scrutinized the man. He was older by ten years perhaps, still young but aged by war. His face was a blend of anger and sadness. His hair was dark, shaved in several spaces to reveal small wounds. Henrik did not want to talk to him, but he sensed a need to reply. "I am from Bergheim," he said.

"In the North Rhine, Westphalia," the man confirmed.

"Yes."

After a moment of silence, Henrik assumed the conversation was over, but then the man whispered, "I am from Koblenz. Have you ever been there?"

Henrik waited a moment before replying. "No, I have not been there."

"Then you have missed one of Germany's most beautiful cities. You must see it sometime, when this is over, when we have achieved our victory."

Henrik thought that the man is an officer, or else he would not talk of victory. Both of them fell silent for a several minutes, and in the silence Henrik thought about the hundreds of planes that came daily from the airfields in England to drop their massive bombs on the Fatherland. Many cities had perished. Berlin also. Some said Berlin was nothing more than a graveyard. Others, depending on their fervor, said it would never be taken, that the Reich would rise from the ashes. Henrik did not think anything would rise from the ashes. Perhaps Koblenz was not so beautiful any more.

The man in the next bed spoke again, softly, but with fervor. "I will never give up fighting. I was shot, here, in the side, and in the leg, and their grenade exploded right in front of my eyes. You can see my face. It is cut as if a butcher had used his knives on me. I have already begun to walk again, but I will always have a limp to show the world that I fought for our cause."

"Your fighting is over," Henrik said.

The man took a deep breath, to emphasize his reply. "No! It will never be over. I will not give in to them, no matter what they do. I will always live by our creed. Blood and Honor."

"You are Jugund, then?"

"I was Jugund, yes. Now I am Waffen SS. I am Hauptmann Arnold Schmidt."

Henrik fell silent again. So, he was a Captain, and a proud one at that. He thought then of the millions of young men just like him who had taken the oath of Blood and Honor. How many of them were dead now? How many graves, marked and unmarked, held their bodies? He remembered the parades through the streets, the flags bearing swastikas, the crashing boots, the proud set faces, all alike, as if Hitler had given them all the same features, young boys with nothing on their mind but power, boys who would report their parents to the Gestapo if anything was said against the Fatherland. He remembered the day they had sent him home. He had been disappointed then, ashamed and saddened. But now he was glad they had sent him home. He was fortunate, not to have been a part of their insanity.

"I was in Poland," Hauptmann Schmidt said. "There the enemy fought our panzers with horses and with old weapons that were useless against us. We crushed them in less than two months. They were nothing against us, our blitzkrieg."

Henrik disliked the conversation. He wanted to tell the man to close his mouth, to sleep, or to talk about something else, perhaps about farms and mown hay or horses, but he remained silent. He closed his eyes briefly and tried to envision his home again, but nothing materialized. Other things occupied his mind. He thought only of the following day, and the one after that, and the one after that, not knowing where they would take him.

Schmidt began talking again. "If you could have seen... "

"Why don't you just be quiet" Henrik interrupted. "I want to go to sleep now."

Just then, as if to further stifle the Captain's conversation, the corpsmen carried in another man on a stretcher. He was moaning and holding his shoulder. Nothing serious, Henrik surmised, just another wound. He turned his head away and closed his eyes, and within minutes he was asleep.

The following day they examined his wounds, covered them with clean, new dressings, returned his second-hand uniform, and stood him on his feet. Two days later they took him from the field hospital with three other prisoners, the SS officer from Koblenz included, and placed them on a bus. They were driven to a rail junction as the sky turned gray and rain began falling. There, he and hundreds of other German prisoners were herded into dirty, smelly passenger cars that stunk of bodies and sweat and cigarette smoke, and from there a train to Cherbourg, to await a ship that would carry them to America.

FOUR

New Ulm, Minnesota, October 1944

PRETTY SIXTEEN-YEAR-OLD ELSA SOMMER, with her wheat-colored hair, stood about five-foot-six. Her sincere eyes were soft and explorative, and her expression was always one of absolute determination. Her chin-up attitude was like her mother, Clara's, who dominated the farmhouse with a kind but stern attitude. Throughout the years, she had acquired many of her mother's traits. She was soft-spoken, yet firm in demands, warm-hearted, yet solidly unyielding in a dispute. Her posture was straight up, straight ahead, and assuredly female, crafted by a rural upbringing that included a strong faith, a helping hand, and firm, moral discipline. Her figure, well developed for her age, had turned many heads, though she never flaunted her god-given attributes. Calm-tempered and sensitive, she could handle most every problem that came her way. In effect, she was a born decision maker, careful thought being her best advocate. She loved music, art, flowers, surprises, close friends, and unimagined opportunities. Her mother said she was a flower that bloomed all year long.

During the summer months Elsa would wake to the soft cooing of the morning doves and the gentle touch of breeze through her open window, and, as a matter of habit she would pull the shades down to keep the house cool. During those idyllic days she would work as a man did, sweating beneath the warm sun to take what she could from each hour. She would bring the men their lunches, and would sometimes watch the rain line creep in on the edge of a storm, and hurry back before the downpour came, horizontal at times with a stiff wind behind it, all the while remembering the tornado that tore through their field a quarter mile from the house on that terrible day when it ripped their neighbors' barn apart.

Or, when she wanted to be alone with her thoughts, she would read from her favorite books while lying beneath the huge green ash tree up near the grove, or beside the Russian olive trees, during those solitary moments when she was in between chores. And she would sometimes watch the clouds, and pick at the Indian weeds and the switch grass, the Big Bluestem and Timothy. And on occasion, when her mood was right, she would think about boys, and dream about romance.

But summer was gone. The trees had lost their leaves and now, naked, their skeletal branches hardly moved an inch in the chilling breeze that skimmed across the land and over the bluffs where the gray-watered Cottonwood flowed. The sky was rarely blue now, having turned sullen and dreary, cooling itself for the oncoming winter when snow would blanket the quiet land and the world would shrink somewhat while preparing for spring.

Elsa was back in school now, in her junior year, having celebrated her seventeenth birthday with cake and candles and family. She had received a new white blouse with an embroidered collar from her mother, and ten dollars from her father, to do with as she pleased. Her sister had given her a small book of poetry and a kiss on the cheek. Her brother presented her with a bag of hard candy, each piece wrapped in cellophane. David had begun the birthday song. He liked to sing. Papa said he might become an entertainer some day like Nelson Eddy, if only the world would recognize his talent.

On one of the warm days, Elsa was on her way home from school, headed toward the bend in the dirt road, beyond which stood her father's farm, the two-hundred-eighty acres he had cultivated and grown crops on ever since his father, her Uncle Clifford, had purchased the property back in the late eighteen-hundreds from a man who wanted to satisfy his yearning for California. Friday had arrived, and she looked forward to the weekend. She enjoyed the solitude of the farm, working with the animals, doing her chores, helping her mother with canning, spending time on the porch with her sister, or pitching in to help milk the twenty head of cattle, when her father ordered it done. Sometimes she and her sister would watch the sun go down, and if it wasn't too cold outside, they would wait for the stars to appear as the sky darkened, and talk of things that interested two young girls. She scuffed to a sudden stop as she heard a shout behind her.

"El, wait up."

Elsa sighed. It was Kenny Hecht for sure. His voice was intense and heavy, as if he were a lot older. He always called her El instead of by her full name. Most everyone at school called her El, although she didn't prefer it. She turned to see Kenny Hecht striding fast toward her, his arms swinging in time with his rapid steps. His right arm went up, and he waved. "Wait up," he called. He twirled a piece of rope in his hand as he walked, as if it was a propeller. He was dressed in black pants and a flannel shirt, adequate enough for the autumn day when the temperature hovered around fifty degrees in the afternoon. His booted feet scuffed through the dirt, spreading gravel. He slowed down as he approached her. A brief smile crossed his face as he spoke.

"Been hoping to see you. I looked for you after school but you'd already left."

Elsa's right shoulder rose slightly. She didn't want to appear disinterested by his presence, even though she was a bit perturbed. "I was in a hurry to get home," she said.

"Chores?"

"Yes. I'm helping my mother put up chicken for the winter."

"Doesn't sound like much fun to me."

"It's necessary," she replied, turning away from him, resuming her walk while looking at the roadbed.

Kenny settled in beside her, slowing his pace. He kept his eyes on her, even though her gaze was elsewhere. Then he cleared his throat, and said rather boisterously. "How about goin' to a movie tomorrow night?"

She didn't change stride, or her expression. Yet she knew before she spoke exactly what she'd say, so it wouldn't be misunderstood. "I can't," she replied simply.

He twirled the rope. "Sure you can. Saturday nights are usually always open."

"Not tomorrow."

"Why."

"Because I promised my mother I'd help her."

Kenny stepped out in front of her, walking backwards while looking at her face. He grinned. His teeth were wide and somewhat yellowed behind his smile, and he still had that boyish smirk that characterized his shyness. "I bet she'd let you go if you asked."

Elsa shrugged and looked at him straight on. "But I won't ask her."

"Why?"

"Because I promised?"

Twisting the rope nervously in his hands, he asked, "Wouldn't change your mind then, even if I begged you?"

"No."

"Not even if I told you "Laura" was showin', with Gene Tierney and Dana Andrews? I know you like Dana Andrews."

She smiled as a way of hiding her frustration. "Not even then."

Kicking at a stone on the road, Kenny sent it sailing into the ditch. Elsa could see the disappointment on his face, a blend of frustration and regret. "You're one stubborn girl," he said, falling in beside her again, swinging his piece of rope. "I don't suppose you'd come to the football game tomorrow, either."

"Guess not."

Kenny moved in right alongside her and took her hand. She didn't repulse him even though it annoyed her. He seemed intent on continuing his pursuit. She had gone out with him only once before, to another movie. Afterwards he had driven his father's 1939 Master de Lux Town Sedan, two-door Chevrolet down near the river where he had parked, and there he attempted to expand their relationship from one of just friendship, to one of desire. He had kissed her twice, the second time more passionately than the first, and had tried to pull her closer. But, acting on her moral fortitude, she had silently repulsed his advance by easing him sternly away, leaving him wanting more of something he could not have. Making love, for the sake of satisfying a craving, was not her idea of companionship. She knew the consequences of run-away passion, and she had made a pact with herself, her mother, and God, that she would wait until marriage to give herself to the man she loved. Commitment would come later, and when it did, it would last forever. She knew right off, after that second kiss, that Kenny Hecht was not the type of man she would want for a husband, or even for a boyfriend. She had vowed that night never again to go out with him

Actually her desires were elsewhere, to another boy named Carlyle, a tall, slender, Jimmy Stewart type who didn't pay much attention to her. Carlyle lived across the river, closer to town, and although she tried repeatedly to capture his attention, he politely declined and went about his business with an ever-present smile on his face. They were friends of course, but their association never went beyond laughter and conversation and kidding, or an occasional touch that was given only to express a statement. Carlyle didn't have a steady girlfriend, though he could have had many. He was known to pal around with Billy Mattson, another boy who had just about everything it took to snare an unsuspecting girl. Carlyle was just the kind of boy she would wait for.

Kenny's thumb moved nervously across the knuckles of her hand. "I wanted to take you out for a specific reason." he said.

She nodded. "Yes. I think I know why."

"No, you don't. I told you before I apologized for my actions the last time. I know I was a bit forward. But I learned my lesson."

"What is it then?"

Kenny swallowed, grasped the piece of rope in both hands, tugged on it, and lowered his head. "George Keen and I are going to sign up."

Elsa paused and turned toward him. His declaration had a calming effect on her, and as its meaning churned her emotions she took a long, thoughtful look at him. Just then, his expression changed from calm to serious. At that precise moment he looked older than he was, more mature, because the decision he had made would impact his life forever.

"You're not serious," she said, her brow creasing.

"Yeah. We're goin' in next Monday."

"Why?"

"Because the war's almost over. Hell, Elsa, we're almost into Germany, and the Japs are on the run. If we don't get in soon we'll miss all the fun."

"Fun?"

He twisted the rope tightly in his fists. "You know what I mean. I want to get in a few shots, just to do my part. If we wait we'll only wish we hadn't."

Elka shook her head. She recalled instantly the images of newsreels, the boys fighting amid explosions and death, the dead lying still, the bombs, the.... "You're a fool," she murmured

"No we ain't. Lots of guys are going."

"But you're too young."

"Don't matter. We can lie about our age. Hell, the army will take just about anyone they can get. They won't care how old I am, as long as I can hold a rifle."

Elsa turned and looked across a cornfields where shocks still stood. The sun was about to slip behind a mantle of gray clouds. Suddenly she felt a chill, not from the wind, but from her emotions. She had read the newspapers, had seen the newsreels, had heard about Bataan and Guadalcanal, Tarawa and North Africa, Sicily, and the landings on Omaha Beach, had heard about the thousands of young men who had sacrificed their lives, and it pained her to think that Kenny and George Keen would soon be in uniform. For all the glory they hoped to earn, they could end up dead in a country not of their own.

A tear glistened in her eye. "I'll go to the movie with you," she said.

"You will?"

"Yes. You can pick me up at six o'clock. I'll be ready."

Beaming, Kenny tossed the rope into the ditch and did a quick tap dance on the road "My God, you just gave me some real good news."

She looked at him, plaintively. "You're impossible."

Kenny took her hand and pressed it tightly. "No, I'm not. I'm just a guy who wants to do the right thing. I love my country, Elsa."

"I admire you for that. Now let me go. I've got canning to do."

"Six o'clock," he stated.

"Yes, six o'clock."

He whooped aloud as he turned on his heels and ran back toward the crossroad.

T HEY HAD WATCHED THE MOVIE, her hand in his, and she had cried silently at its sensitivity and its beautiful music, and the lyrics of the song, so melancholy yet poignant. She had settled close to him without seeming improper. As she watched the film she thought of him in some foreign land, facing a vicious enemy, with chaos all around, and she wondered what he would do when confronted with such violence, such inhumanity, for he was not the type who would take pleasure in bloodshed or brutality. Oh, he hunted, to be sure. Everyone did, rabbit, fox and deer, for food and furs, and for the thrill of the hunt, for the camaraderie. But war would be different, a life or death situation so gruesome in scope that the mind alone could not comprehend it.

When the film was over they went to the car. He opened the door for her. "Do you want to go for a soda at the drug store?" he asked. His voice had an element of hope in its expression.

"No," she said simply.

So he got in the car and drove back toward her home, along the dark roads with no moon or stars visible in the night sky. As they approached the river she said meekly, "Don't take me home yet."

His head turned. He was silent for a moment. "Where do you want to go?" he asked.

"It doesn't matter," she replied.

Turning at the river road, Kenny drove down to where a car could park, and there he pulled onto a short path near the riverbank and turned off the lights. The river was silent, a dim stroke of gray in the darkness. Nothing moved, nor were there any sounds. The world was at rest. They sat still for while, looking at the ghosted trees that had a sense of loneliness about them,

"I'll leave the motor running. If the heater doors aren't open far enough just reach down and adjust 'em any way you want." The hot water heater was situated beneath the glove compartment on the passenger side.

"It's just fine," she said.

He turned on the radio as Bing Crosby began singing "It Had to be You." He smiled, turned to her and said softly. "My sentiment exactly."

Elsa knew he was trying to be romantic, but her mind was elsewhere. She didn't want romance. She just wanted to talk to him.

"How did your mother take it, when you told her you were enlisting?" she asked.

"Well," he said simply. "She cried a bit. She didn't want me to go. She tried her best to talk me out of it. But my dad, he understood. He was in the American Expeditionary Force in World War One, but he didn't see any action. Maybe if he'd done some fighting he would have tried to steer me away from going."

"Lucky for him."

"Yea. Even though he didn't fight, he always kept the war to himself."

Elsa didn't like war talk, and wished she'd never mentioned it. She looked at his face and said nothing for a while. He just looked out through the windshield as if looking into another land, as if seeing something he'd never seen before. Then he said offhandedly. "My brother, Sherman wished he could go with me. But he's only thirteen. I want to help end it before he reaches sixteen. I'd hate to see him go in. No one else knows we're going except George Keen."

George Keen was a neighbor boy of his. By the next afternoon the entire county would know. "We won't be graduating," he said. "We just want to get out of here before the winter comes. We both hope we'll be sent to a warm place, perhaps Hawaii, or one of the islands we already took back from the Japs. The enlistment officer said we could select our war zone, so we chose the Pacific. The days are warmer there."

Then the conversation ebbed. The only noises came from the heater and the shifting of their bodies. He took hold of her hand and drew it to his chest. She could feel the beating of his heart. The radio played softly, this time with an appropriate song, "I'll be Seeing You."

"I want you to know something," he said. His words seemed to hang in the air like a vapor. Not hearing a reply, he continued. "I feel strongly about you, Elsa. I always have. Right now you only know me as a football player, as someone who likes to rough it up now and then, or as someone who really fouled up the first time I took you out, which is something I'll always regret." He cleared his throat, looked out toward the river, then back at her. "Actually I'm a shy person, and right now I've got a world of words inside me that just don't seem to want to come out."

Elsa moved closer to him and placed her head on his shoulder. He's going to tell me things, she thought, things about him I do not know, things he wants me to know before he goes off to war, hoping I will remember them. Then he will want to kiss me, and hold me close, and perhaps . . .

Kenny's voice interrupted her thoughts. "When I'm gone, I want to write to you. Is that okay?"

She nodded, felt emotion like a breath of sorrow, a feather-like flow of sentiment rising within her. She was so taken by his simple statement that she could not reply.

He bit his lip. His eyes were melancholy. "Will you answer my letters?" he asked.

Clearing her throat, she replied meekly. "Yes, of course I will."

Kenny sighed as if grateful for the answer, and for a moment he looked out the window at the river and breathed deeply as if forming words he was hesitant to speak. Then he shifted toward her and found her hand and squeezed her fingers in his grasp. Her cold fingertips warmed in his calloused palm.

"I'm glad you came tonight," he said, clearing his throat. "I wouldn't have wanted to leave without saying good-bye. I won't be at school on Monday. George and I will be heading out early. My folks still don't understand, and maybe you don't either, but I just feel as if . . ."

He never finished the sentence. She leaned over and kissed him hard on the lips, and then his arms came around her and pulled her across the seat, and he crushed her in an embrace. For him, it was the answer to a passion he had kept inside himself for months, not knowing what to do, or how to do it, fearful that she would never want to see him again. For her it was a release, a time to give of herself, to create a memory he could take with him to continents unknown.

On that first date, Kenny had gone beyond kissing. He had taken her breast in his hand, and had drawn her skirt up high, and when his hand drifted onto her thigh, and when his passion had reached its height, he said he had a rubber in his pocket. He begged her to go all the way. It was then that she eased him away, and asked him to take her directly home.

As they separated, he peered into her eyes as if seeing a dream, and her eyes conveyed affection.

"I think I love you," he whispered.

She shook her head. "Don't say that, Kenny, you know it isn't—"

"But I do. I really do. I have for a long time."

"You're just saying that."

"No. No. You have to believe me. It's why I want to write to you. I want you to wait for me."

She eased back, putting space between them while still clutching his hand. "You have to understand. I can't make promises."

"I know. I know. There isn't someone else, is there?"

"No."

"Then I've got a chance?"

"I can't say. Who knows what tomorrow will bring."

Without another word, he eased her back into his arms and held her for a long time. She felt a tear against her face. She pulled away and brushed his cheek with her fingertips and kissed him again. Then she felt his hand against her breast. Slowly, without wanting to hurt him, she eased it away. "I think we should go now," she said.

He nodded apologetically. "I didn't mean—"

"Shush now," she ordered, placing her finger across his lips. "It's getting late. Mother will be expecting me home soon."

"Please, Elsa. I . . ."

"I said it's okay. I promise. I'll write to you, provided you let me know where you are."

"I promise. I'll let you know."

"Look," she said suddenly, pointing at the windshield. "It's snowing."

The first soft flakes of winter brushed against the glass, dancing in the slight breeze that rippled the surface of the Cottonwood. They watched for a while, hands together, her head on his shoulder as if to create a lasting memory, something he could take with him across the ocean.

"The snow is beautiful," she said,

"Not as beautiful as you," he replied.

They watched as the windshield turned white. Then he started the car, turned on the wipers, backed out onto the road and headed toward the farm, humming.

On the way back home, she wondered where life would take him, and where life would take her, and, if indeed, anything would come of the letters each of them would send and receive across thousands of miles. The war would change him, for sure. War always changed men. But whatever happened, their lives would go on. And she would keep on writing. The letters would give him a connection to things back home, to keep him going through the hardships of battle. When, and if, he came home, he might be a totally different person.

He turned at the mailbox and drove down the short road to the house. The yard light was on. The snowfall had covered everything.

"I guess I won't see you again, at least for a long time, "he said.

"I guess not."

"Then, it's good-bye for now."

"Yes. Thank you for a nice evening. I enjoyed the movie, and being with you."

He grinned, nodded a bit, and then kissed her lightly before she got out of the car. Slowly, as if he didn't want to leave, he swung the car around, waved briefly, and then drove away.

Elsa stood in the soft snowfall and watched the car disappear into the night. Then she turned and went into the house, and climbed the stairs to her bedroom. That night, before she fell asleep, she felt a deep remorse because a friend was going off to war.

FIVE

Crossing the Atlantic, November 1944

WHILE HENRIK AND THE THOUSANDS of German prisoners waited the arrival of a ship to take them to the United States, he began the process of registration into the POW system. He was assigned a serial number designating the command in which he was captured, in his case the theatre of operations in Europe. A second symbol denoted the first letter of the enemy country, G for Germany. The final number denoted the order of entry. He was temporarily billeted in Forte de Roule, a nineteenth-century fortress set into the foothills of the rugged Contentin Peninsula.

The ship, a converted cruise liner, arrived a week later, a three-stacker painted army gray, dull and unobtrusive. Someone who knew the ship said she was the Empress of Scotland. The Germans filed aboard under the watchful eyes of American Military Police, and selected German officers and NCOs who were assigned to enforce strict military order. Some five thousand were crammed into spaces originally designed to serve only 1,173 passengers.

After boarding, Henrik took quarter in one of the converted state rooms that had been stripped of all its former décor; no color, no fancy furnishings, only bare walls and a single porthole that offered a view to starboard. The only furnishings were eight hammocks. He claimed the one strung nearest the door. They would all share one bath, several bars of soap, four towels, toothpaste and brushes. One of the men remarked, "We are no longer prisoners. Now we are on a ocean cruise."

"But we are leaving our homeland," another quipped.

"Yes, to America, to see how our enemy lives, to see how badly we have crippled their cities."

"I have heard that the women there are beautiful," another said.

"The women everywhere are beautiful."

"We will not have a chance to meet the women. They will not come to a prison camp to see the men who have killed their sons and husbands."

"Then we will have to wait until the final victory to see them."

"When the war is over."

"Yes. When the Fatherland is victorious."

One of them chuckled.

Henrik crawled into a hammock that was already discolored with signs of wear. He drowsed for a while, half awake, half asleep, while attempting to retain visions of the past, memories now vague and shambled. Then, amid a slurry of voices, he drifted into a restless sleep until the ship's announcement system urged all prisoners to read the rules and instructions posted in German on the inside of the cabin door. He listened as one of the other prisoners read them aloud.

Six hours later the vessel got underway with a violent churning astern. Henrik and hundreds of other men jammed the railings, many bidding good-bye to France with catcalls or curses.

"Good-bye, you fucking Frenchmen."

"We will get you next time for sure."

"After the next war you will all be speaking German."

Their voices rolled like a hateful chorus over the dirty water where the remnants of sunken warships reared their steel carcasses above the oil-slicked surface. Then, as the vessel moved into open water, its massive weight began a slow rocking. Its engines reverberated through the decks and bulkheads like a giant clearing its throat. Henrik's legs and arms trembled as the ship sought deeper water. Soon the vessel shuddered with the ocean swells, and where there had been no wind before, now it came at him directly across the bow. Within an hour the French coast faded away and the only sounds were wind and the throb of engines and the eternal sea folding away from the bow.

Henrik had never seen the ocean. He had only imagined what it would be like from pictures he had gathered of navy ships and submarines belonging to the Third Reich, dreadnaughts and U-boats, photos that had spoken silently of honor and sacrifice and eventual victory, but nothing of death and misery. Inwardly he was somewhat frightened of water, but not on the first day when the ocean was calm and the clouds were no more than clusters of cotton gathered near the horizon. They left the coastline under cover of two American fighter planes, Mustangs, from the looks of them, but soon the aircraft veered away and they were alone, without escort.

He leaned on the rail for a while, in line with dozens of other men, until one of his roommates came up and stood beside him. He was a young man with blonde hair, no older than he, but bigger, wearing the same uniform. At first they looked at one another without speaking, forming thoughts. Then Henrik turned toward the sea, as the other man spoke.

"It is beautiful, no?"

Henrik shrugged. "It is water. We will cross a thousand miles of it."

"Without protection," the other man noted.

"It is no matter. We are not a warship. I do not believe our U-boats will sink us. They will know who we are."

"How would they know?"

"Perhaps by the signal flags we fly. We are not the first ship of this kind to cross, and we will not be the last. Before the war is over, there will be many ships like this crossing the Atlantic."

"So you think we are losing the war, yes?"

Henrik stiffened. He knew it was dangerous to answer questions, especially when they were contrary to Nazi doctrine. A loyal Nazi would never think the war was being lost. But the man beside him was not an officer. He appeared to be a lonely boy, just like himself. After the brief pause, he decided to take a chance with him. "I would agree. I was captured in Aachen. I heard it was the first German city to fall."

"I was shot in Belgium."

"Then we have something in common. We have done our duty."

"Our duty, yes."

Henrik gazed out over the water. "We are safe now. That much I know."

The blonde warrior held out his hand. "My name is Emil Dryer."

"And I am Henrik Arndt."

They shook hands and continued their guarded conversation. Behind them, the decks swarmed with prisoners, all of whom wore German uniforms, most of which were faded and rumpled, torn or dirty or stained with blood. There were men from the Luftwaffe, and the artillery, and Panzer divisions. Some were officers. Most were enlisted men, common soldiers who still believed in the Reich. Some were deeply tanned from the African campaigns. Those with pale faces were the submariners. Some had their arms in slings. Others had bandages covering their wounds. Some laughed, some smoked, and some spoke of their combat experiences, and bragged about how many men they had killed. Others said nothing. They were the ones who stood apart, solitary figures who gazed out at the sea, thinking of wives, or children, or events in their lives they wished they could live over again. And perhaps if one were to look carefully, some were tearful, caring not if their comrades saw them cry. Others guessed about their fate, or what would become of them for not having fought harder, or, if they would ever see their homeland again once they were behind barbed wire.

The first meal that night consisted of potatoes and stewed plums, with ice cream for desert. Most of the men ate. Some did not. Seasickness had already begun. Except for the port and starboard running lights, the ship remained dark throughout the night. Only a sliver of moon gave light to the Atlantic. Henrik remained on deck until the night chill sent him to his quarters. He slept poorly, tossing throughout the night while trying to relive memories of better days. He remained in his hammock until the sun was well up, until he was aroused by voices and curses. Several of the men abhorred their condition until they were reminded that the cabin was much better than lying in mud, or listening to the constant roar of artillery, or starving while awaiting food that seldom came.

Taking his turn at the sink, Henrik then went out onto the main deck, into the cold morning air. The sky was a steel gray color, the sun a mere blur behind a sheath of darker clouds. A stiff wind raked along the starboard side, slicing over a blue-black sea feathered with whitecaps. He went to the rail and watched the horizon lift and fall, and felt a wormlike uneasiness in his stomach. Within minutes he vomited over the side. Another man, nearby, shook his head, then stumbled back against a bulkhead where he slid down and buried his head between his arms.

Henrik did not eat breakfast that morning. Someone told him that if he would lay horizontal he might be able to avoid seasickness, so he spent most of the afternoon in his hammock, thinking of home, and wondering what life would be like in a strange country

He took a saltwater shower the next day. Fresh water was conserved for cooking, and for the crew. Then he joined others on deck for a quick inspection, where they were issued clean underwear. They were told to wash their clothing in the shower, or put them into a clothes net fastened to a throw line and drag them in the ocean, but for no more than four minutes lest the salt water turn them to rags.

By the third day the weather changed. A brilliant sun rose over undulating waters not choppy enough to form whitecaps. The only sound on deck came from the blowers, the throb of the engines, and the swish of the sea washing against the hull. Some of the men began playing shuffleboard. Another group selected willing participants for boxing and wrestling exhibitions, which were to take place in the empty swimming pools.

Henrik avoided going below decks where the passageways always held a distinct scent of vomit. Conditions there were usually crowded, men squeezing past one another, tempers short, occasional bursts of anger, and fights when the anger turned hostile. The American Military police maintained discipline, enforced by German officers and NCOs who kept behavior in check. The men who became abusive, or who disobeyed the rules of order, received a dressing down along with confinement to quarters on bread and water. Those who followed the rules were given cigarettes, writing paper, and a selection of books to occupy their time. The prisoners ate the same food as the crew. They all ate well. Many slept on deck, topside, beneath the dark sky festooned with stars, as they had in combat, but without the noise, without the fear.

Because of inadequate ventilation, the interior of the ship was normally hot. As a result, men lounged everywhere, against the bulkheads, or on the decks. They wrote letters, played cards, or threw a bundled-up sock that substituted for a baseball. And they exercised. The boxing matches began on the fourth afternoon when the sun was highest; men shouting, cheering, and encouraging the combatants with raillery, jeering when they didn't fight. On some days only one match was held, on others, three.

Henrik watched on occasion, but most of the time he read a book he had selected from the ship's library, *Eine Frau des Geheimnisses, A Woman of Mystery*. He was reading on the deck one warm afternoon, his legs outstretched, his back pressed against a stanchion, when a booted foot prodded his leg. He looked up, squinted in the sunlight, and immediately recognized the man standing in front of him, his hands on his hips, his cap pulled down tightly to his forehead. The man was Hauptmann Arnold Schmidt, the officer who had occupied the bed next to him in the Belgian field hospital.

"You are the man from Bergheim," the captain said smartly.

Henrik rose quickly to his feet and saluted him sharply. "Yes, I remember you, Hauptmann. It is quite unusual that you would remember me."

The captain grinned. His eyes narrowed as if to commit Henrik's features to memory "I make it my business to remember."

"Then we meet again, only this time under different circumstances."

"Yes, quite different."

Henrik tried not to squirm under the captain's continuing stare, his eyes the color of cobalt, a hard, cold discipline there, the steadfast gaze of the SS.

"As I recall," the captain went on. "You did not give me your name."

"My name is Henrik Arndt," he replied sharply.

"Ah, a good German name, one that bears remembering."

Henrik remained silent.

"And are you enjoying your ocean voyage, Henrik?"

"It is different, sir."

A brief grin. "Yes, different. We are prisoners now, no longer able to fight. We must now do as we told by order of our enemy."

Henrik swallowed. He said nothing. He continued peering directly into the captain's eyes, for fear of a sharp reprimand should he look away.

"Are you speechless, Henrik? Have you no comment on what I have said?"

Henrik cleared his throat. Strangely, he did not feel intimidated by the officer. He felt as though he could speak freely, so he did. "I believe the Americans are no longer our enemy."

The captain's mouth tightened. "And why do you believe that they are not our enemy?"

"Because they feed us as they are fed. We are non-combatants now."

The captain stiffened. "You are wrong. As German soldiers, we must never surrender."

"We have already surrendered, sir."

"In principle only. We must never surrender our honor."

Henrik stood at ease. He could see others out of the corner of his eyes, standing there, watching, and waiting for something to happen. The captain also knew they were there because his eyes darted quickly from left to right, seeking an audience. Then he said. "Perhaps you have not heard that there was an attempt on our Führer's life."

At last, Henrik thought, someone brave enough to put an end to all this butchery. "I did not know," he replied.

"Traitorous officers, all of them. But they failed. Their bomb was ineffective against him."

He waited for a response, but Henrik remained steadfast at attention, his features unmoved, his eyes riveted. "You see," the captain continued, "he's indestructible."

The captain turned then, and looked at the men to his right. Immediately, they dispersed, as did those on his left. Satisfied, he turned back to face Henrik, who had relaxed but did not move.

"You are a young boy yet," the captain said. "Tell me, where did you surrender?"

"At Aachen."

"Yes, I remember now. Ah, like so many others who did not have the nerve to continue the fight."

"I was Volkstrum," Henrik replied, as if telling him that would make a difference in the conversation.

"And were you in the Hitler-Jugend?"

"When I was younger."

"And?"

"I was released."

"Why?"

"Because I was unfit."

"Ah, physically incapable, I expect. Too bad. You might have aspired to something greater than the Volkstrum."

The captain relaxed slightly, and then looked skyward, into the sun, as if receiving a blessing. He shifted his weight. "You must come to the boxing match tomorrow afternoon. I am fighting a man from Berlin, someone of my rank, so he will fight as my equal. I intend to win. I always win against those who challenge me."

"But, your wounds, sir."

"Ah, they are healing well. If they open again, they will heal again."

"I will be there."

"Good." The captain hesitated momentarily while forming his question. "Now tell me, will you stand firm against our captors once we reach the prison camp?"

"What do you mean, sir?"

"Will you obey them? Or will you resist their orders?"

"I will obey them, sir."

The captain pressed a forefinger to his lips. "Or course you will. You will become like a sheep in their pen. Is that so, Henrik Arndt?"

"I expect it is, sir."

The captain grinned sagaciously while forming his next question. Then, quite deliberately, he said. "And what do you think of Germany now?"

The question took Henrik off guard, but only momentarily. Stiffening, he replied truthfully, the only way he could. "I think Germany is now a country without a soul."

Henrik knew the moment he spoke that he had said the wrong thing. The captain took a deep breath, and then looked directly into Henrik's eyes. The words he spoke came slowly through tightened lips. "Is that what you believe?"

"Yes, captain. It is what I believe."

"Then there is no hope for you."

"I have nothing further to say, sir."

The captain sighed. "Of course you don't. You will be led by the ear, and you will listen to what your captors tell you, and you will become someone who is hated by those who still believe in the Third Reich. Do you remember what our Führer said? If not, I will refresh your memory. He said, anyone who is not for us, is against us. I think perhaps you are one of those who is now against us. So I think I will watch for you, Henrik Arndt. If we are fortunate enough to be placed in the same camp when we arrive in America, I will make sure that you do not become a sympathizer."

Henrik released his breath. He realized in an instant that he had placed himself in danger. His truthfulness had made him a marked man, and there was little he could do to reverse himself. The captain, although a prisoner of war himself, still had powers. He could still command men with a snap of his fingers. Many would do as he ordered, without question, without hesitation.

Henrik made one final statement. "I answered your questions honestly, sir, as you wanted me to. I am still a German who loves my country."

The captain grinned. "Ha! Time will tell how much you love your country." He turned his head toward a group of men who were laughing. "But now I must go. Many things demand my time. A pleasant day to you, Henrik Arndt."

The captain clicked his heels and raised his hand to his shoulder in a quick salute. "Heil Hitler, my young Volkstrum soldier."

"Yes, Heil Hitler," Henrik replied.

Then the captain turned and strode off toward those who had been telling jokes and laughing. They parted as he approached, and he walked through them as if he were Hitler himself, his head straight to his destination, his posture erect, his stride slow and deliberate Everyone knew who he was. As SS, he demanded, and received, respect.

So what would happen now? Henrik knew only one thing. He would have to be careful, very careful of what he said, and to whom. There were thousands of ears aboard the ship, and he knew many of them would be listening to every word he spoke.

The following day, the captain fought the officer from Berlin, in the empty swimming pool surrounded by hundreds of shouting men. He defeated his opponent in the second round by feinting a left, then pounding his right fist into his belly, and smashing him again with a second left to the chin. As the final count was given, and as his opponent squirmed on the floor of the pool, the captain strode quietly around him, his arms raised high above his head so everyone could see the SS blood-group tattoo inscribed in gothic lettering beneath his left arm. Now everyone aboard knew Hauptmann Arnold Schmidt.

Chili and bread. Pork patties and potatoes. Hash. Eggs with bacon. An occasional apple or an orange. The meals seemed to improve as the ship moved closer to New York. Henrik began gaining weight.

Days in the sun. Nights beneath a blanket of stars that stretched from horizon to horizon, the moon growing larger, streaking the ocean with its cold light. Cooler breezes. Boredom. Books to read, when they were available, all printed in German. The Americans had thought of everything to bring as much comfort as possible to an otherwise monotonous crossing. He began writing letters home.

There was a day when one of the men leaped over the fantail and was lost in the churning wake. On another day a man went mad. He threw anything he could get his hands on, yelling and screaming, cursing every foul word that came to mind, his eyes red and wild, like a cornered animal, with an indescribable loathing only nature could explain. Crazy out of his head. He was subdued by a half dozen others and dragged away to sickbay.

The men ate, and slept, and walked the crowded decks, and gazed monotonously at the endless expanse of water. Occasionally they saw other ships some distance away, another freighter, or a warship. They would watch for porpoises and flying fish as they skimmed away from the bow. Nothing to do, but wait. Henrik spent a great deal of time at the railings. He saw much of the sea. The sun bled through the canopy of clouds. It flecked the ocean with scattered light, refreshing the water, warming the chill. The seas were dark in places, and a stillness lay upon it as if a hand had quieted its restlessness. There was a resonance of holiness on its surface, for it was all deep green and blue and laced with yellow light, and there was silence upon it which was beautiful and impressive and overpowering. The ocean had a newness to it, a beauty he had not seen before. It was opaque and shadowed, with an intensity that drew all color into its depths.

Some days he would lay on the deck with his eyes closed tightly, not quite awake, pretending that his eyes were open so that he could glimpse the first shred of land sprawling beneath the vast overhead of clouds. Then he opened them slightly and saw a corner of the blue sky with perhaps a cloud or two moving above him, and the familiar idyllic sun merging toward them as if wanting to hide. And when he closed his eyes again he heard familiar sounds, the call of his mother across a golden field, the squawking crows soaring in circles, and the wind rustling against autumn leaves. He was astonished whenever he opened his eyes, to see only sky and cloud. Then there came a day when he knew they were close to ending their voyage. Birds appeared in the endless sky, and he could almost smell wet fields and earth, for land had a scent of its own, a denseness about it, different than that of the ocean.

The time has come, he thought. Soon they would enter New York harbor and he would touch foot on a new continent. He had waited, and prayed, with few hopes and less illusions, because the things he really wanted were quite impossible to achieve. He wrote letters to spend the time, and to make the war seem remote. He wrote to his parents, not saying what was on his mind, but hoping they would remember things of the past as he did, not wanting them to think he was suffering. He wrote simply, knowing the letter might be censored. After all, there were regulations. He did not mention the war, or his wounds, but concentrated instead on shipboard life, and what he observed, and what he ate. He told them only that he was being treated properly. And he mentioned how quiet the ship had become;strangely silent at times as if no one were aboard. Voices were kept low, and the men were less active Most everyone had said what they intended to say, nothing more, nothing less. Instead he tried to recall the moments of his youth, the idyllic times before the war, the laughter and the hope, not mentioning the inward fear that had always devoured optimism like a silent beast.

Nights ended and days began, and with the passing of the sun and moon there was soon a rush to the railings because land had been sighted. Henrik was there, on the starboard side, pressing to see the first images, the rising terrain, the outline of cities. And as the shoreline became more defined he felt free again, free of his cage, free of the ship that had become a menagerie of boredom and routine and seemingly endless waiting.

His friend, Emil Dryer, had pressed in alongside him, his face gleaming with a smile. "Look at it, Henrik. America. Did you ever think you would see it?"

"Never."

The ship slid slowly through the Verrazano Narrows, its engines growing silent, its wake shrinking, as if she was in no hurry to make port, as if purposely hesitating to give the prisoners a chance to absorb the moment. There was a silence aboard, a strange stillness, because for some it was the beginning of a new and peaceful phase of their lives, for others it was a time to silently express hatred for a country that had pulverized their own fair land to ashes. For others, it was a deliverance from war.

Emil pointed. "There. There. See. It is the Statue of Liberty."

Henrik could see it now, vague and diminutive beneath the backdrop of New York. Somehow it struck a note of comfort inside him, knowing there would be no bombs or artillery or machine-gun fire to interrupt an otherwise peaceful day.

Someone behind him, who had also seen the statue, remarked. "It is an abomination. They talk of peace, yet they bomb our cities. She should be holding a saber instead of a lamp."

As they neared Manhattan the loud speakers told them to prepare for debarkation. They docked late in the afternoon at the North River Terminal directly at a pier, saving hours of guarded madness had they been ferried from ship to shore. Even so, they still had to endure hours of waiting until they were allowed to disembark.

As the sun settled low behind the city, they approached the gangway toward the waiting buses. "Well. Here we go," Emil said.

"Yes," Henrik replied. "Here we go." Then, as he descended the gangway and stepped foot on American soil, he uttered silently to himself, the words, *Bist du beir mir*, Be Thou near me, for he was then in the country of his enemy, with an uncertain future ahead of him, and the days, and months, and possibly years ahead, seemed to him, then, like an eternity.

SIX

New Ulm, Minnesota, November 1944

ELSA SOMMER STOOD MOTIONLESS in the root cellar, shivering slightly from the penetrating cold that had worked its way through the long coat she was wearing, the coat she used for farm work. She had graciously responded to a request from her mother to get a jar of canned pickles and another of chicken, amid the hundreds of glass containers stacked on the wooden shelves.

Her grandfather had dug the root cellar deep into the small hill crowned with elms and oaks, offering a partial windbreak from the north winds that screamed down from Canada or across the flat plains of Dakota, all the way from the Black Hills. The canned food was their lifeblood through the long and often bitter winter, during months when temperatures could plummet to twenty degrees below zero on days when the snow could top three feet in depth, when the wind blew fierce enough to force the snow through the gaps in her bedroom window and dust her top blanket with a white powder, making the room so cold she could see her morning breath.

Elsa's grandfather had told her about snows that were deep enough to bury a man standing upright, snows hard enough to support horses. She had never seen snow that deep, or that firm, but somehow she didn't doubt her grandfather because he had been an honest man. Grandfather had died three years earlier of old age, and by possibly working far past the time when he should have stopped. But then, no one stopped working on the farm, despite the hardships. He was ninety-three when they buried him in the town cemetery alongside his wife, Aunt Sarah.

Elsa placed the jars into her coat pockets, one in the right, and the other in the left. Then she turned and walked outside, closed the wooden door, made sure it was latched, and followed her footsteps back toward the house. Beyond the house, the morning sun glowed dimly as it prepared to take refuge in a spread of gray clouds. A flight of geese squawked above the weather-beaten barn; one of the last flights heading south before the heavy weather set in.

She walked slowly, the jars bumping against her hips. It was Sunday, a traditional day of rest, except for farmers. At the moment, her brother David and sister Corina were in the barn milking the Guernsey cows with the help of her father, who was probably bringing hay down from the loft. Chores still had to be done.

After breakfast they would all climb into father's 1941 blue Studebaker Commander and ride into town to worship. Father had bought the car just before the war began. Now he drove it as little as possible because of gas rationing. He, like everyone else, supported the war effort. As for Elsa and her siblings, they bought war stamps at school and did their best to scrounge up whatever metal they could for the frequent scrap drives. Already, they had cleared out most of the junk from the barns, the sheds, the grove and the ditches, and were hard pressed to find more. Thanksgiving was over. Earlier that month President Roosevelt had been elected to his fourth term in office. As she approached the house she heard a cow lowing from the barn.

The house had been repainted just before the war. It was now a light gray with white trim, replacing the aged and peeling paint that her grandfather had applied twenty years earlier. The windmill still brought up water, for both the house and the cattle, and Papa routinely changed the gear oil once a year. They had only two horses now, Wiggins, a chestnut mare, and Clem, a draft horse that had long since forgotten its role in life. The others had been replaced by a Farmall tractor. Wiggins and Clem were used only for riding and for bringing in the cows on occasion, or during harvesting. However, because of their broad girth, and a strong desire to trot, the bareback riders sometimes slid off, occasionally landing in mud.

The farm had been modernized to suit Papa's needs. The country was headed into a new era, having just emerged from the Great Depression, and Papa was still a bit cautious about spending. The only sad thing was the war. It dragged on horribly and without letup, sucking all the young men into its maelstrom.

Elsa entered the house, shooing a kitten past the screen door with a well-placed foot. Mother Clara smiled as Elsa placed the jars on the large, round oak table that had previously belonged to her grandparents. The table had several leaves that could be added whenever company came.

The kitchen was the largest room in the house, containing a sink with two pumps, one at each end. One pump brought in drinking water from the well, through underground pipes. The other drew up soft rainwater from the cistern just outside the pantry window. Occasionally, during the winter, the pipes from the windmill would freeze, which was why Papa always mounded the run with dirt and a foot or two of snow when it was available. The house had no indoor plumbing, but it did have a wood burning stove, and a wood box that Papa had made out of scrap lumber. It normally held wood gathered from the grove, but most of the time they burned corncobs. The stove provided hot, quick, free heat that radiated throughout the entire house. It was the kids' job to gather corncobs from the hog lot for fuel whenever they ran short of coal, which was not always available due to wartime shortages. Wood was seldom a problem. The severe storms most always pushed down a weak tree or two. All they had to do was clear it from the grove, saw it up, and split the wood. Warmth from labor.

"Erica called," her mother said without stopping her work.

"What did she want?"

"She asked if you would call her later, after dinner. She and her mother were going into town."

Erica Pauls was Elsa's best friend and classmate. She lived about a mile away, on another farm, up near Preacher's Grove, as they called it. She and Elsa were as close as sisters, even though Erica was precocious, always attempting to emulate the Hollywood movie stars. Flirting with the boys was her favorite past time. Erica had a steady boyfriend, Willard, and she was known to occasionally have a drink or two, and a cigarette at times. Her boyfriend smoked a wartime brand called Sano, a cigarette with hardly any nicotine. Yet, even with all her fanciful boldness, Erica remained a virgin just like Elsa. Both of them realized how a pregnancy would disgrace either family. Erica had fought off more than one boy in the backseat of a car, Willard being no exception. Willard had told her once that Erica had eyes that could stop a bird in flight. Actually, it was Willard who had been stopped in flight. He hung around her like a kitten at the cream separator. Elsa knew in her heart that Erica would turn away from him without a second thought, if not before the school year ended, then certainly after graduation. He wasn't the type she wanted to marry.

"It's getting cold outside," Elsa said.

"I think there may be a blizzard coming. There's heavy snow in South Dakota already."

"I hope not." Elsa removed her coat, fluffed it, and then hung it on a peg near the door. "Where's Corina?"

"Upstairs, taking a bath. Papa and David took their shotguns and went down by the slew, hoping to get a goose or two." Corina was obviously bathing in the large, round bathroom tub that was serviced with well water, and warmed with boiling water from the stove.

"I saw some flying south on my way in from the root cellar. I didn't hear any shots though."

Elsa took a chair and began peeling potatoes. Before she had finished, Papa and David came into the house, each carrying a Canada goose.

"We got two," David said proudly.

"Ain't many more flyin'." Papa concluded.

Mother looked back over her shoulder to where Elsa was seated. "Looks like we've got some pickin' ahead of us," she said.

Elsa and her mother were usually the ones to clean and prepare whatever wild game Papa and David brought into the house, pheasants, ducks, squirrels or geese. They were careful to remove all the pellets lest they crack their teeth on one while eating. Fortunately they didn't have to gut and skin the larger game animals. Carving, cleaning and preserving venison, or pork, or beef was a job reserved for the men of the house.

The men dropped both geese on the table, then turned, and without saying another word they left the house and headed for the barn. Papa was a man of hard flesh, lean and muscular, with a mouth that resembled a strand of wire. Dark skinned and often whiskered, except on Sunday when he shaved. Sometimes he moved with a gait that appeared he was uncomfortable. His footsteps, boot hard and set with authority, gave him a definition that required the respect of others, especially his children. He was usually clad in bib overalls, stained from the fields, bleached by the sun. Throughout the year, except on days when the summer sun was its hottest, he wore a flannel shirt. He seldom spoke while he worked, but when he did it was with authority. He gave orders only once. Compliance was mandatory. Still, he was not a taskmaster. Inside, he had a heart as big and as compassionate as God could give to a man, especially one who showed such deep respect for his wife and children.

The day went on as it usually did, patterned by years of routine, and when the chores were done, and the sun slinked down behind the barn into its cold bed, and the outdoors became as quiet as day a could be, they prepared to eat the evening meal. They washed up and changed from their work clothes into something more suitable, and sat down for dinner.

Supper was always served in the dining room, on another of Grandma's old oak tables. The table was always set with a linen cloth, white candles, napkins in brass rings, and flowers when they were available. Papa's place was at the head of the table, facing his wife. David always sat at his right, closest to his father. Corina and Elsa bracketed their mother. They all sat still, hands folded as Papa lifted his napkin, tucked it into his shirt at the neckline, and cleared his throat. "Are your hands clean?" he asked. Obediently, each of the children held their hands up for a cursory inspection. Satisfied with the cleanliness, he nodded. No second washings this night. His strong voice came again, "Now fold them and thank God for your blessings."

The prayers were usually brief, and when they were over Papa smiled and started the food around, usually thick meat sandwiches, sauce, fruit on occasion, sometimes pudding, or a pie for desert. As usual, Papa began the conversation. "I saw Mr. Hecht at church this morning. He said his son, Kenny, and the Keen boy, were enlisting tomorrow. Do you know anything about that, Elsa? I know you were with him last night."

"Yes, I was with him. We went to see a movie."

"And did he tell you he was going in the army?"

"He did. They're leaving tomorrow."

Clara nodded. "It's a shame that so many young men are going to war."

"I'm going in when I'm old enough," David put in. He liked to mingle with the conversation whenever possible. He was a tall boy, energetic and yellow-haired, a lad of fifteen who tried to emulate his father at every turn, a hard-working, dedicated farm boy who knew all the swear words, but guarded them cautiously when working alongside his father.

Papa was quick to reply, his voice crisp, "You're not going anywhere. You got a farm to take care of. Farming is more important now than ever before. Our troops have to eat. Besides the war will be over by next year."

"How do you know that?" Corina asked.

"Because we've got 'em on the run. Our boys are almost into Germany."

"Kenny wants me to write to him," Elsa remarked, prompting Corina to giggle.

David teased. "Elsa's got a boy friend. Elsa's got a boy friend."

"I do not," Elsa replied. "He will need letters to cheer him up, and to let him know that everything's okay back here. It's patriotic to write to a soldier."

"It's a fine gesture," Clara replied.

"There's still a lot of fighting to do in the Pacific," David stated.

"Enough talk of war," Papa said. "It's all we hear these days."

Corina said. "How can we forget? It's all around us. Gas rationing. Scrap drives. War bonds. No nylon stockings. Blackouts in the cities. The newspaper is full of it, and it's all you hear on WCCO. It's never ending."

"No complaining now," Papa said. "We got it good, despite the war. We're back to serious farming now. It's not like it was some fifteen years ago, when the farmers left their crops to rot in the fields because the cost of harvesting was more than the crops was worth."

"Your father's right," Clara agreed.

Papa grunted. "You kids don't know how bad it was. You were all just babes back then. Out on the prairie, when the dust storms blew in, some farms got buried up to their windowsills with topsoil. And when the black rollers came in from the west, they left nothing behind 'cept dead rabbits and birds, and barns drifted up with six feet of dirt."

"You've told us that before, father," Corina said.

"I suppose I have. I suppose I even told you that people sold pencils and apples on the streets over in Minneapolis because they had no jobs and no money."

"Yes. You told us that, too."

"It's a good thing Roosevelt came along." David chimed in.

Papa turned his head and looked hard and long at the boy before speaking, letting him know that his head was filled with knowledge, and that his eyes reflected the seriousness of his thought. "Roosevelt done a lot of good things with the WPA and he saved the reputation of the New Deal, but he wasn't the reason our country is what it is today."

"What was, Papa?"

"It was the Germans that did it. As soon as they started warring, it put us back in the production business. And when everybody was working again, our farms became profitable. Yea, if it wasn't for Hitler, a lot of people might still be sellin' pencils in Minneapolis, and standin' in breadlines."

"You're just saying that because we're German ourselves."

"No. I'm sayin' it because it's true."

"But the war is terrible."

"That it is. War's are the curse of mankind."

"Maybe this will be the last one," David suggested.

"No, my boy. They will go on and on until there ain't a one of us left. Our kind had been fightin' every since we first learned to carry a stick in our hand."

"Enough of war talk," Clara said. "Let's eat our dinner and be glad we have it."

Elsa ate quietly, thinking that perhaps tonight Kenny would be eating his last good meal for a while. She expected that army food wasn't the best, and that after he finished boot camp and was sent overseas, he'd have nothing by K-rations to eat, and some days not even that. She hoped he wouldn't be going to the Pacific. The war was so bad there. So many islands, so many dead. She hated to think what it would be like when they invaded Japan. Kenny might be right in the thick of it. She wished now that she would have said something romantic to him, something he could carry with him in his heart and onto the battlefield.

"Elsa. You've got cream separatin' to do after dinner," Papa said.

"I know. But I have to call Erica."

"Erica can wait until your chores are finished."

"Yes, Papa."

The milk was usually separated at night so that Papa could take it to town in the morning and sell it at the creamery where they made butter from the cream, and buttermilk for Papa, and plenty of cottage cheese that the family mixed with grape jelly. Cleaning the separator was a job she did not like. Not only was it was messy, and smelly, but the area was usually teeming with cats who wanted their portion. She had to hurry to wash the separator down because if left unclean overnight, the milk would sour on the metal discs, making the job all the more laborious and unpleasant the following day. Callling Erica would just have to wait until she was finished.

Elsa went out to the barn when the sky was hard-black and cold, when the stars gave off light in a thousand glistening strands of brilliance, quite like a massive tiara set for a queen. The moon was a sliver, no wider than a thin blade, hovering alongside the barn roof as if seeking shelter. Ahead of her, the barn light glimmered in the dark, lighting her way across the yard. The night chill crept along with her, keeping pace.

The farm scent hung in the air, unchanged by wind or season, sweet, yet pungent with the dry smell of hay and the trace odor of cows and chickens, and hogs that fed on corncobs and whatever garbage from the kitchen. The scent was everywhere, whatever the season, in the yard, the house, the acreage, and in the clothing they wore, but it was part of their life, essential to survival, and she thought no more of it than she would when smelling a newly blossomed rose in springtime, or the fragrant touch of perfume behind her ear. She finished her chores in less than a half hour and then, and with moonlight resting on her shoulder, she retraced her steps to the house. With her days' work complete, she received permission to call Erica. Settling onto a chair situated a scant six feet from her mother, she lifted the receiver from its hook, dialed the number and waited patiently through six rings. Then, a click.

"Hi, Erica. This is Elsa. Mom said you called earlier. What do you want?"

Erica's voice was excitable. "I was wondering what you were doing next Friday night."

"Nothing that I know of. Why?"

"Well," she replied, pausing slightly. "There's the pumpkin-patch dance at the school gymnasium."

"So."

Erica cleared her throat. "I was talking to Carlyle today. He wants to ask you to be his date."

Strange, Elsa thought, and a bit presumptuous on Carlyle's part. She had never thought of him as being reticent, not to the point of shyness. Her opinion of him had always been to the contrary. Her jaw tightened. Her answer formed quickly. "If he wants me to go to the dance, he can ask me himself."

Erica's reply was a bit restrained. "He was just searching, I think. He wanted to know if I thought you would say yes. Maybe he was afraid you might refuse him, so he wanted me to run interference."

Elsa had always thought of Carlyle as straightforward, not someone who would go around her to get an answer. His sneaky way of asking her to the dance left a sour taste in her mouth. Her reply was crusty with disappointment. "I might go, provided he's got enough common sense to ask me himself. Why I never thought he'd . . ."

"Shall I tell him to call you?"

Her answer had already formed. "No! If he can't ask me in person, then I won't go. Why the nerve of him, calling you instead of me. I think it's very inappropriate, and I wouldn't be afraid to tell him that, straight to his face."

The telephone clicked just then. A voice on the line interrupted, "I want to use the telephone." Party lines were such irritable things, when anyone can listen in– and when you never knew who of the twelve families on this free-for-all line might be listening in.

Elsa replied. "Is that you, Mrs. Harris?

"Yes, it is."

"Just give me another minute. This is Elsa. I'm talking to my friend. I'll be off soon."

No reply, just a click of indignation.

"I'm back," Elsa said.

"You know Carlyle. He's a bit bashful."

"He doesn't appear to be. I've seen him with other girls. He always has the upper hand."

"What you see isn't always what you get."

Elsa sighed. "This is nonsense. All this time I've been hoping he'd ask me out, but he never has. Now, when he wants to ask me out, he goes about it like a little kid, like someone who doesn't even know me. It's enough to make my blood boil."

"Well, don't boil. I'll tell him to ask you face-to-face at school this week."

"Save your breath. I probably won't go now, even if he does ask me."

"You're being stubborn."

"You know me."

"Guess I do. But c'mon, we'll have fun. I'm going with Bradley. We can make a foursome out of it."

Elsa's lips tightened. "I'll see. No promises."

"What do you mean? You've always wanted to go out with him. Now's your chance."

"Not like this. I don't appreciate his back-door approach."

"You're just playing hard to get."

"No, Erica. I'm just being sensible."

"Okay. Anyway I'll talk to him."

"I'll see you tomorrow. I think Mrs. Harris wants to use the phone now."

Elsa hung up, looked toward the curtained window, sighed, and then turned to her mother. "I suppose you heard," she said.

Clara paused at her work, darning stockings. She smiled. "It sounds like you've got a bit of a problem on your hands."

"No," Elsa replied, shaking her head. "I don't have a problem at all. Carlyle's the one with the problem."

"For what it's worth, I think you did the right thing."

"Mom, you know I'm a lot like you. I don't appreciate it when people beat around the bush. I like them best when they come right out and say what's on their mind. Imagine, Carlyle talking to Erica about wanting to take me to a dance. I think it's downright unforgivable."

"Will you go if he asks you?"

Elsa looked up at the spiral of flypaper spinning beneath the light. It had just snared another victim. Fitting enough for a fly who didn't know in which direction it was headed. "I don't think I will."

Clara smiled and resumed he work. ""Put him down easy, young lady."

Elsa snickered. "I'll put him down all right."

SEVEN

Algona, Iowa, November 1944

DURING THE CROSSING, THE CONTROL and well-being of the prisoners had been the responsibility of the Army, but once ashore prisoner supervision was transferred to the Quartermaster's office.

Their processing took several days, during which time the prisoners and their clothing were properly disinfected and their meager possessions returned. Then came more hours of waiting, and endless hours of boredom. Many of the prisoners asked questions, but the answers were usually vague. Military Police, most of whom spoke German, escorted them through the prodigious bureaucratic maze that included the interrogation of those whose value had somehow been overlooked during their first screening.

Eventually, when the waiting and the wondering had reached an unbearable level, Henrik and Emil, and hundreds of others, were transported to rail coaches and loaded up, two to each bench seat, and after security was provided, and their passage inland assured, the train pulled out of New York City into a bleak, sodden November night as dark as night could ever be. Their destination was a place called Algona, Iowa, right in the center of the country, fifteen hundred miles from any shoreline.

Despite the seemingly endless process, Henrik had been impressed by the efficiency of the operation. The disembarking, delousing, and questioning had gone off without incident as had the slow, but deliberate processing of thousands of prisoners. Fortunately, he had been billeted on one of the first trains headed west. Once on board he sat in a hard leather seat that didn't recline, nor did it offer comfortable sleeping. Still, it was far better than the filthy boxcars he had occupied from Belgium to France, those dirtied with animal feces, blood and the lingering stench of dead bodies.

Fortunately, his friend Emil Dryer had stuck close to him during the entire process, and they had been able to acquire seating next to one another on the train. Exhausted from the day's activity, Emil fell asleep almost immediately, snoring contentedly for the first two hours.

Being the more curious of the two, Henrik sat facing the window as they slipped past station after station through the darkened hills of central Pennsylvania. Even as he awaited the first blush of daylight, he didn't think of himself as being a prisoner. Rather, he imagined himself on a grand adventure that would bring him full circle after the war ended. He knew that someday he would return to Germany. When the sun finally did overcome the darkness he was sleeping, until Emil nudged him with an elbow.

"Henrik, wake up! Look. America!"

One of the men opposite him remarked. "Look at what?"

When Henrik opened his eyes he saw rolling hills, brown and gray and dusted with snow, not unlike the hills of Germany during the same season of the year. He raised his head and rubbed his face, and saw a road running parallel with the tracks He saw cars traveling in both directions, and trucks, many trucks. Behind them were fields, dormant in their winter coats, and occasionally a farm, red barns and white houses, and cattle and horses standing in the fields, and occasionally a town, houses and stores and churches, all untouched by war.

The soldier sitting opposite Emil tried his best to distance himself from the man sitting next to him, to prevent their bodies from touching. All were awake, their eyes searching about, scanning the outdoor scene, or sweeping over the car full of prisoners, most of whom were silent. Henrik was fortunate to have a window seat. For a while none of them spoke, but they did look down the aisle at other faces, unsure of their situation, unsure of what to say. They were all young men. The oldest of them, the tallest one who wore a field cap, was perhaps twenty-five, no older. His unkempt whiskers looked like dirt on his face.

"They are taking us through on a longer route," the man opposite Emil said, his voice low but distinct. "They won't allow us to go through the cities, where the Luftwaffe has raised a little hell." The soldier was a young man, slightly older than Henrik. One could almost see the patriotic fervor on his face, the way his mouth tightened, the way his eyes sparked, the condescending sneer on his lips.

Henrik disliked him almost at once. He would not become involved with this man. Discreetly, he clenched his fist. He had seen his kind so many times before, and he wanted no more of them. Still, he felt compelled to reply. "There has been no Luftwaffe here," Henrik said. "Our bombs have not touched American cities."

The man glared at Henrik. "They would not waste their bombs on these small towns. Wait until we see a city. Then you will see what they have done."

"You will wait a long time," Henrik replied. "We have all seen New York. It looked quite intact to me."

The upstart soldier wore the rank of Gefreiter, a lance corporal, and now he looked long and hard at Henrik, his eyes heating, as if determining what he should say. "Who are you?" he said at last.

"It is none of your business who I am. We are all going to the same place. We are all prisoners here. It is your choice, to be what you were in Germany, or to be a new man. As for myself, I choose to be a new man. I will make the best of my situation, whatever it is."

The lance corporal shifted in his seat and sat up straight, his back pressed tight against the backrest to make him look larger and more important than he was. The man next to him, a private, shifted over to give him more space. "You speak like one of them," the lance corporal said.

"No. I only speak the truth. You will see. There have been no bombings here."

"Be quiet," Emil whispered. "You will get yourself in trouble."

"I see what I see," Henrik replied. "I am not blind."

After years of strict discipline and never-ending propaganda at the hand of their own officers, some of the enlisted men were slow to accept the differences in culture between Germany and America. The brainwashed ones could look all day at the countryside and not see the extent of its peaceful existence. They were blind to everything except the Nazi principles that had been drilled into their heads. They were, and would always be, combatants in the Führer's great and invincible army.

Henrik looked past the lance corporal and saw the armed guards stationed at each end of the car, machine pistols in hand. They had been told before boarding the train that no one would be allowed to stand. If anyone had to go to the bathroom he was to raise his hand. One at a time. No exceptions. Pee in your uniforms if you have to, but no exceptions. Hands were raised almost constantly. They went, singly, to the toilet, or used the opportunity as a chance to stand up for a while. When one would come back, another would go.

"They think we are still school boys," the lance corporal said.

"Aren't you a bit curious," Henrik replied, "to see what America is really like?"

"No, I am not curious. We will see only barbed wire. Whatever you see out the window will not be available to us. You dream if you think otherwise."

"Henrik," Emil said, nudging him with an elbow. "Hold your comments to yourself."

Henrik looked out the window again at the farms, at the broad fields, at the hills rolling endlessly to the horizon. He thought again of his own farm in Germany, when it had looked much the same, when he could walk the roads and run in the fields, and listen to the whisper of the nearby stream as if it were a voice talking a different language. But so much for memory. Silently, and with hidden resolve, he began preparing himself for the ordeal ahead, when he would take a silent stand against those who still found glory in war, those puppet men who were still imbued with the pledge of blood and honor.

Henrik wondered how many men the lance corporal had killed. Perhaps many. Perhaps none. Perhaps he was a young nobody who just wanted to be important, or perhaps he was so infested with Hitler's lunacy that he would never see the light of a new day. Men like him would never understand the inherent dignity of freedom. Men like him were the reason Germany was now being pounded to dust. Henrik ignored the man as much as he could, but whenever he looked over at him, he saw his eyes upon him. And the eyes were filled with hate.

Food was distributed soon enough, on platters piled high with sandwiches, served on paper plates. The men who served them were black. One pushed the cart loaded with food. A second man followed, pushing another cart stacked with paper cups. He filled the cups with coffee.

"Look, Henrik," Emil said. "Negroes." Neither of them had ever seen a black man before.

Most of the prisoners stared blankly ahead while the stewards worked their way down the center of the car, handing out their sandwiches and coffee. Both of the Negroes were dressed in white aprons. One wore a high-collared sweater beneath his apron, the other a plaid shirt. Both had gleaming white teeth and wide, white eyes, and smiles. Their skin was glistening clean. One of them, the man with the sandwiches, paused for a moment. He peered down at one of the prisoners, one who was staring at him, and he said, "What ya all lookin' at. Ain't you never seen a real human being before?" He spoke in English, of course, surmising that the German would not understand him. Henrik was perhaps one of the few who knew what he was saying.

Then the black man looked up and flashed his broad, white teeth again. His grin gleamed like a sword blade. "Got some food for ya all. Best food in the world. Made from good old Georgia roosters, and some of them good lookin' Alabama hens." They worked the aisle slowly, careful not to drop any of the sandwiches, steady with the coffee. For some of the prisoners, it was the first time they had tasted coffee. It was not a strong coffee.

Then the man in front, the larger of the two, stopped and scanned the prisoners for a few seconds before speaking. He addressed them in German. "Bet you didn't think a black man could speak German. Well, I got a surprise for ya. We's educated." His body shook as he laughed. He turned back to the coffee stewart and whispered something, then laughed again. He continued talking to the prisoners. "When you get done eatin' just open the window and toss them paper plates out onto that good old American soil. Bet you thought that white stuff out there was snow. Well it ain't. It's paper plates and cups, that's what it is. We done hauled thousands of you through here already, and we got thousands more still commin'. How's that for winnin' the war?"

The stewart continued laughing and passing out the sandwiches. Then, as he approached Henrik and the others, Henrik heard him talking in English again, low and somewhat indistinctly, but comprehensible.

"Now, I may be talkin' to you all, but I ain't about to get marshmallow friendly, if you knows what I mean. Guess maybe some of you know what I'm sayin', and if you do, well, that's okay, cuz I'm speaking for all of us on this side of the ocean. Truth is, we still remember that you's the same bunch of murderous bastards that killed many of our boys. And you didn't give a rat's ass about bein' civilized when it came to honorin' women and children." He paused, snickered again, then chose additional words. He continued. "But we's the forgivin' kind. If we weren't, I wouldn't be givin' you this specially brewed coffee for you to wash down that elegant chicken. Ha, ha." When they reached the far end of the coach, both men turned and retraced their steps. His voice had a snicker in it. "Now eat up," he said. "Cuz you still got a long way to go. Hell, we ain't even in Ohio yet."

After they left the coach, Emil turned to Henrik and asked, "What did he say?"

Henrik looked at each of the men seated opposite him. He decided not to tell them the truth. The lance corporal would certainly vent his anger if he did. So he said. "They were talking about the good sandwiches and coffee they're giving us. They said we still have a long way to go. If you know where Ohio is, then you know where we are."

And so the hours passed, with nodding heads, and raised hands, and snoring from those who chose sleep instead of boredom. Henrik and Emil exchanged seats for several hours so Emil could view the countryside, so he could see the blizzard of white plates and cups piled against the side of the tracks. So many plates. Had that many prisoners passed this way? How many camps had been built to house them?

The prisoners sat straight up, cramped together, fitful, their tempers on the edge at times, with someone always complaining. A young soldier with a good voice sang German songs for a while until someone else told him to be quiet. There were mumblings, some laughter on occasion, jokes being told. When night came on, they slumbered, half asleep, half awake, as the train rocked in an endless motion, the clicking of steel wheels more pronounced in the darkness. They passed through a city, its lights ablaze in the darkness, its factories floodlighted, its roads carrying traffic at whatever the hour. The lance corporal knew the truth, and said nothing about the city. Seeing was believing.

Food was passed out again, sandwiches, fruit, apples or oranges, and round chocolate covered candy bars with peanuts. The wrappers said, Nut Goodies. Diarrhea began. Indigestion. More hands raised. The toilets were overworked. At times the train stopped to take on water and supplies. They were sometimes idle for an hour.

The land flattened out on the third day, revealing broad farms and groves of trees and a blue sky yawning to the horizon. The guards were switched every four hours. None of them ever spoke a word. They were always stern and alert, unlike the stewards who brought food, those who delighted in carrying on a banter completely alien to most of the prisoners.

One who knew his geography said they were in a state called Illinois, the place where Abraham Lincoln was born. Henrik knew of Lincoln because his uncle had told him. He also knew about the War between the States, how the country had been ripped apart by people of varying opinions. And he knew about the West, the broad, endless prairies and mountains where the Indians once lived before the white man came and pushed them off their land, and enslaved them the same way they had enslaved the blacks that had been shipped over from Africa. His uncle had told him many things about America when he was a small boy, some of which he still remembered. He also remembered the things his officers had told him when he was in the Hitler-Jugend. They had painted a very different verbal picture of America, contrary to his uncle's stories. Americans, they had said, were gangsters and slave owners, and they were selfish and spoiled and incapable of victory, and that their victory in World War One had bankrupted the country, and that the people were starving under the rule of an inept and crippled President who knew little of the world.

But now he was seeing America for himself, and he found it grand. Of the two conflicting stories he had heard, his uncle had been right. Henrik knew there was much to learn about America, and he was ready to be educated.

Then, on a cold day, when the sky was the same color as the snow, and when the wind blew hard in from the west, they arrived in Iowa, at the place named Algona.

EIGHT

New Ulm, Minnesota, December 1944

THE TEMPERATURE HOVERED SOMEWHERE around ten degrees as Elsa peered through the school bus window toward her destination, the New Ulm Public High School, the old brick structure that had been recently renovated by the Public Works Administration. The WPA had added a new combination gymnasium and auditorium to the building to update its usefulness. The original structure still housed the old, outdated below-ground gym beneath the library. The dance on Friday night would be held in the new gymnasium, on the basketball court. She felt uneasy, clouded by indecision. Carlyle would be awaiting her arrival. His thin, smooth face would be beaming a broad, arresting smile along with his practiced Hollywood persona, the image all the girls admired, including her.

Her best friend Erica Pauls nudged her with an elbow. "Are you excited?" she asked.

"About what?"

"About seeing Carlyle. I know he's waiting for you."

Elsa was in no mood for word play. She was still disappointed about the turn of events, especially Carlyle's off-handed conversation with Erica. But why did it bother her so? Pride? His inability to face her directly? Her melting desire? She shrugged, as if totally unable to command her decision. "Big deal," she said. "He can wait all week as far as I'm concerned. And, for what it's worth, I don't think I'll be going to the dance with him, or anyone."

Erica's face blanked. "You can't be serious."

Elsa turned to face her. "Well, I guess I am. You might call me stubborn, but I believe I've lost my attraction for Mr. Hollywood. He can ask Pricilla. He's been bumping shoulders with her for weeks now."

"No, he hasn't."

"He has. I'm not blind, Erica."

"He's like that with everyone. It's just a habit of his."

Elsa shrugged. "Well, anyway. We'll see what happens."

Erica snickered. "I thought so. Deep down you're weakening. My guess is, the minute you start talking to him, you'll melt."

"Oh, stop it."

Damn, she hated being goaded, that irrational sprinkling of annoyance that always added pressure to her thoughts. For as much as Erica was her friend, she sometimes annoyed her to the point of anger. She was like a little kitten sometimes, scratch, scratch, scratch, an annoying little kitten with sharp claws that backed off only when its opponent was about to hiss. Elsa peered out the window as if to place imaginary distance between the two of them. She had heard just about enough of Carlyle's intentions. Erica must have sensed her resentment because she leaned over to talk to someone else across the aisle, leaving Elsa to her own machinations.

The bus slowed, then stopped, and simultaneously the students stood up and shuffled forward, pushing and shoving and wisecracking their way toward the open door. Elsa cradled her books in both arms, and in a somber, yet auspicious mood, she stepped out into the snow and shuffled across the slush toward the school. Inside, she gave a passing glance toward the statue of Joan of Arc. She grinned. Someone had given the Saint a charming new appearance for Christmas. Lipstick had been carefully applied to her lips.

Elsa did not see Carlyle until third period, between classes. She had looked for him after first period, hoping to satisfy one of the two imagined voices that had whispered to her during class. One had said: Give it to him good, he doesn't deserve you. The other had responded by saying: Hold on. Give him a chance. It's all just a misunderstanding. Devils in her ears. First one, then the other, creating a mood of indifference that had begun to anger her.

As she was walking down the hallway Carlyle quite unexpectedly tapped her on the arm. "Hi Elsa," he said. With a soft touch of his hand he drew her aside.

As she awaited his usual, sweetened pitch, the two devils inside her head made their last second suggestions. Then, at the moment she looked into his wildly pleasing eyes, her resistance crumbled. For a moment she was uncertain whether to talk to him, or ignore him. For whatever the reason, she chose talking. "I can't stay long or I'll be late for class," she said, shielding the disappointment she still felt regarding his phone call to Erica.

His eyes brushed across her face as if to examine her every feature, while avoiding every flaw. Then he peered directly into her eyes as if to melt her. "I want to ask you something," he said.

"What?"

Carlyle's voice was as mellow as the call of a Morning Dove. "Will you go to the dance with me on Friday night?"

Elsa hesitated. Her reply seemed to float on an endless sea. She weighed her answer carefully for she knew it could be the beginning, or the end, of a long-awaited courtship. This was perhaps the last chance she would have to satisfy her desire for the boy who had occupied her thoughts for the past six months. All she would have to do was agree. Simple! One word and she could be danced and possibly romanced, on a night just four days away. A strange sensation slinked across the back of her neck, presenting a nervousness she had not anticipated. Her legs trembled.

"Well?" he asked anxiously.

"Yes," she blurted, as her negative thoughts evaporated. "Yes, I'm sure I'll be able to go."

He frowned. "You don't sound sure."

"I am. I am." She turned toward her classroom. Everyone had entered. "I have to go. Let's meet after school. How about Eibner's for a soda? But I'll have to get a ride home afterwards."

"I'll give you a ride." He had a car, an older model Ford. He was one of the few students who had a car of his own. It was common knowledge that his father gave him just about everything he wanted.

"Yeah, Eibner's. I'll skip basketball practice. See you there about five o'clock. Is that okay?"

"Yes, okay. But it'll have to be quick." She smiled meekly, so as not to appear overly pleased.

"Good deal," he remarked, as his grin broadened.

She turned then and hurried into the classroom, slid into her individual desk, and watched her red-haired teacher walk to the door, to close it silently in respect for its place in the order of things. The teacher was a hard one who showed no favoritism. Thirty-six-years old, and always attired in a colored dress, never black, she demanded respect, and always received it, or grades would suffer. She was strict on discipline.

Elsa sat silently, totally absorbed in thought. She had about eight hours to reverse her decision, eight hours to decide her future with Carlyle. At four thirty she would walk down to Eibner's, the combination ice-cream parlor and bakery where many of the kids hung out, and over a cherry-coke she would begin a relationship with him, or end it before it began, by merely reversing her decision.

How long had she waited for Carlyle to make a move? Six months? Perhaps longer? Time actually didn't matter, because now it was gone and only the future remained. She was at one point giddy with the thought of being with him, yet somewhat apprehensive of failure if he thought her unsuitable. What would the date be like? Would he be demanding of her, in a sexual way? Would he, like Kenny, tell her that he had a rubber in his pocket so she wouldn't get pregnant if she yielded? Or would he be a gentleman? Certainly on the first date he would want nothing more than a kiss, or perhaps not even that. Would she be disappointed either way? Would he be something different than she imagined him to be? Would he . . . ?

The teacher had given the class an assignment, and Elsa hadn't heard a word. The girl next to her was already paging through her textbook. Oh, my Lord, she thought. What sort of predicament have I got myself into?

Classes would be exceptionally long that day.

THE BUILDING THAT HOUSED EIBNER'S WAS one of historical significance. During the Dakota Uprising of 1862, some of the non-combatants, mostly women and children who hadn't fled to Mankato, found refuge in the basement during the two attacks on the city. Fortunately the building had survived, as had its occupants.

As Elsa entered the front door she felt beleaguered, as had the non-combatants during the uprising. Her conduct toward Carlyle would be simple. She would let him do most of the talking, and at some appropriate time during the conversation, based on his manner and interest in her, she would decide to either attend the dance, or politely refuse. Whatever her decision, she had practiced her prepared statements over and over. Even so, she knew that when the conversation began, the statement would go the way of the wind on a blustery day. *Oh my*, she thought, *can anything be more confusing than this?*

To begin with, Carlyle was twenty minutes late. She had drank a cherry coke and had gazed into the mirror until she was tired of looking at herself, and had rehashed the event several times until she had dulled it. When Carlyle finally did come in, he had a smile on his face and an apology on his lips. By then her tension had all but crippled the anticipation.

"Sorry," he said, shaking his shoulders to ward off the cold. He zipped down his jacket. "I got delayed. Couldn't help it. But here I am."

There was that smile again, attracting her like a hummingbird to nectar. He eased onto the stool beside her, near the end of the counter, and began talking like a radio announcer trying to peddle an unseen product. "I told the coach I couldn't practice today, that I had an important meeting to attend. He said he wasn't interested in my reason. He wanted me to stay and shoot some baskets, to get ready for the game on Saturday with Sleepy Eye. In fact he insisted that I stay. A player doesn't refuse his coach, unless he wants some bench time, and I don't want anything to do with a bench."

Trying to appear disinterested, she blurted out, "I thought you might have stayed to talk to Shirley." Shirley was his latest plaything, a short, tangle-haired, perky little girl that was as limber as a monkey when it came to cheerleading or back-seat romancing.

Carlyle grinned. "Shirley and I are on the outs."

"Oh."

"Want to know why?"

"No."

"Well, I'll tell you anyway. She took a liking to Brian Hellman, that tough German kid that plays football. Hell, he ain't any good. I think she just wants to make me jealous."

"Well, are you?"

"Me? Jealous? There are too many other opportunities for me to be jealous."

Elsa turned the empty cola glass in her fingers, drawing it through the wet ring on the countertop. "Is that what I am, just an opportunity?"

He nudged her shoulder. "Oh, come on, Elsa. You know damn well I didn't mean that."

"Then what did you mean?"

"Well, the truth is, I've been lookin' at you for a long time, wondering if maybe I had a chance. I saw you with Kenny lately, but now he's headed off for war, so I thought maybe, just maybe, I could take advantage of his absence."

"Kenny and I are just friends. He asked me to write to him when he's away."

"Are you gonna?"

"Sure."

"I hope he's not too late to kill him some of those goddam Germans."

She shot him an irritated glance. "I'm German, in case you didn't know."

He had overstepped his bounds, and he knew it. He bit down on his lower lip as if he wanted to bite the words. "I didn't mean anything by it. I was talking about our enemy, the krauts over in Europe that are killing our men. Hell, Elsa, I didn't mean all Germans. God knows, this town was founded by 'em. They're as thick as sheep in the springtime. C'mon, forget I said anything about 'em."

She nodded as if to throw off the remark, but deep down she resented the comment. She also disliked the swearing he had used to emphasize his dislike for Germans. She didn't admire a boy who swore. It wasn't polite, especially in the presence of a woman.

"What nationality are you," she asked.

"Well, my father was English, and my mother was Swedish."

Elsa looked at him critically, then turned and smiled at Amy Keller who was busy behind the counter preparing a malt, and too busy to smile back.

Carlyle exhaled rather loudly, then reached for her empty glass, turned it, and said, "Do you want another cherry coke?"

"No. I've had enough."

He looked casually over her shoulder at some other kids down at the end of the counter where laughter had erupted. He waved at someone. A prize-winning smile brightened his face. A moment later he switched his attention back to Elsa. "You're short on words today," he said. "Have I said something to offend you?"

"No. It's nothing. I haven't felt well lately. I must be coming down with a cold."

"I don't care if you do have a cold. I still want to take you to the dance on Friday. How about it?" He reached over and took her hand, then scribed a random design on her palm. "We'll have a good time."

His hands felt cold and inflexible; farmer's hands, to be sure, those that had been formed by toil and weather. He squeezed her fingers slightly, but she felt no emotional connection to him. His manner wasn't at all what she had expected it would be. Those many moments, when she had admired at him from a distance and had wondered what his touch would be like, had been mere fancy. She had actually willed herself into in his arms on several of those days, had felt his embrace, and had imagined his kiss on her neck. She had always imagined Carlyle to be a prince who lacked only regal clothing and a crown.

Suddenly his hand pulled away. He stood up and walked away from her without saying a word. He strode over to one of his teammates who had just entered, slapping his friend on the back. They talked while she sat alone, gazing at the back-bar where the glasses were stacked, where the mirror reflected her image, and at that moment she felt neglected. Within moments, her impression of Carlyle faded to insignificance. She waited patiently, toying with her glass, trying to decide if she would go to the dance. When he returned minutes later, she had already made her decision.

"Well," he said. "How about it? Will you go to the dance with me on Friday?"

She smiled coyly. "I have to go now. I'm late already. My mother will wonder what happened to me. By the time you drop me off at home, you'll have your answer."

"No!" he said jokingly. "I want it now."

"Do you always get everything you want?"

"Yea. Most of the time.'

"Well, I guess you'll just have to wait this time."

"It's unfair."

"It's also unfair to keep a girl waiting while you talk to one of your friends."

He tossed his head. "Oh, that. Are you going to use that against me?"

"I just made a comment."

His expression wrinkled with mock disappointment. "You sure know how to keep a guy guessing. Well, come on, let's get you home," he said, holding the door open for her.

He began talking the moment he entered the car. "I never thought Kenny would join up. He didn't seem like the type of guy who'd want to go off and fight. I always thought he was a sissy. He never played well at sports. He always stood in the background, you know, away from the crowd. I wonder what he'll do when he sees one of them krauts comin' his way. You wouldn't see me joining up. If they come and get me, well then I'll go, but not till they come rappin' on my door. Why would someone give up his freedom to go and fight? It doesn't make sense to me."

"We're fighting to preserve our freedom."

He shrugged. "Yea, I guess so."

"Besides, Kenny's just being patriotic."

"Yea. So he goes in and gets his ass shot off. Not me. I got more sense than that."

"Well, I think he's very brave."

"Brave, hell, he'll probably turn ass and run soon as he sees a f-ing Jap."

Elsa looked out the window at the snow-covered landscape. At that point she just wanted him to keep his mouth shut. She didn't like his bravado, his unwillingness to view the world through other eyes, and she certainly didn't like his cowardice. What had she seen in him anyway? He wasn't at all what she had expected.

Suddenly, and without warning, his hand was on her knee.

"I shot fourteen points against Mankato last week. The coach says if I can do it again we might just beat Sleepy Eye. Do you go to many of the basketball games?"

"I've only been to one."

"One! Hell, Elsa. You gotta do better than that. Why basketball is the best game in the world. It takes a lot more skill than football or baseball."

She held onto his hand, afraid that it would work its way up her leg. "I should really go to more of the games."

"And I think you should go to them with me. I know with gas rationing and all it's kind of difficult to get around, but we usually go in a bus, and sometimes we squeeze in some of our classmates. I bet I could get you on."

"It would depend on what my parents say."

His fingers tightened on her knee. "Why, hell, just tell 'em you're going. I can pick you up. What do you care what your parents think. We'd have a great time."

Carlyle talked on, mostly about himself. After a mile or two he removed his hand from her knee and she settled back into a more comfortable position. She saw the lights of her farm across the field even before they arrived, and by the time he turned and started down the dirt road to the yard, she had concluded that Carlyle was nothing more than a flash in the pan.

He swung the car around and pointed it toward the road. Before she could reach for the handle he asked her the final question. "Well, are you going with me to the dance?"

She hesitated; concerned that she might hurt his feelings. But then she recalled the many conversations she had with her mother about pride and responsibility and dignity and humility, and she knew Carlyle did not measure up to any of them. She formed her reply while looking directly at him. "Carlyle," she said, "thank you for asking me to the dance. Although I really haven't danced much, I think it would have been a good time. But I can't go with you."

"Why?" His expression was one of disbelief.

"Because I'm not the right girl for you."

"No," he replied, continuing his pursuit. "You are . . ."

"No, Carlyle. Please, don't persist. It's not going to work."

"Well, I sure had you pegged wrong," he said.

"I guess you did. I hope we can still be friends."

"Of course we can. Yes. Definitely. Always. Friends, yes." He shrugged. "I guess that's that."

"Yes, that's that."

"Well then, goodnight, Elsa Sommer."

"Goodnight, Carlyle."

As Elsa stepped out of the car, he sped off, scattering dirt. She thought: he couldn't leave fast enough. Now what would be said of her? Surely he would tell his buddies something far short of the truth, like, Elsa Sommer is a narrow-eyed prude, as cold at an Arctic winter. She gazed into the sky and found temporary comfort in the darkness. Then she turned and entered the house.

NINE

Algona, Iowa, December 1944

THE PRISONERS WERE DRIVEN BY A fleet of Army buses to the compound at Algona, a sprawling 227-acre complex surrounded by two tall barbed wire fences topped with three strands of wire, creating a no-man's zone between the inner and outer fences. Guard towers, all manned with machine guns, stood at intervals, each one capable of sweeping the entire camp with searchlights.

Upon arrival Henrik was lined up with the other prisoners for inspection. Their meager belongings, photos, shaving kits, slippers, mementos, letters and other personal belongings were arranged at their feet as they stood at ease. Then the guards came and inspected the belongings and read their letters. All were examined from head to foot. The guard who came down Henrik's line talked to nearly all the men in fluent German. He was an older man who walked with a slight limp. When he came to Henrik, he examined his papers, and then said. "Where are you from, soldier? How old are you?"

"I am from Bergheim. I am seventeen."

The officer nodded, and then looked at his cheek. "You have a wound there," he said, touching the cheek. "Where were you wounded?"

"In Aachen."

The officer nodded. "It will be okay. Whatever remains in there should work its way out by next summer. Welcome to America, soldier."

The politeness of the officer surprised him. Perhaps it would not be as bad in America as many of them expected. Before the day was over his personal effects were returned. His small amount of currency was placed in an envelope bearing his name and identification number. It would be held for him until the war ended. He was told that he would receive negotiable canteen coupons for work performed that was to be used as currency in the camp PX. He was allowed to retain his uniform. He could wear it inside the compound. Then he was issued one belt, a pair of shoes, two pair of cotton trousers, four pairs of socks, two wool trousers, four pair of drawers, one pair of gloves, four undershirts, one wool coat, one raincoat, one overcoat, and one wool shirt. All shirts, undershirts, jackets and coats were marked with bold PW letters on the back, and on the sleeves. Trousers and shorts were also imprinted across the back and below the belt.

When the processing neared its conclusion, he fell in line with hundreds of others and was officially welcomed by the camp commander who introduced his staff. They, in turn, explained camp regulations, precautions against fire, maintenance of sanitary conditions, dental inspections, and rules governing the length and legibility of letters to their families. Then, after being forewarned about the penalties for escape, they were dismissed to locate their bunk assignments. Henrik's destination was Barracks Number 27. In all, thirty-eight new prisoners accompanied him to Number 27.

The last shreds of daylight vanished with the low, red sun as the searchlights went on, crisscrossing the camp like long searching arms. Henrik and the others reached their building with hunger burning in their stomachs. As they entered, they were greeted by others. The man who grasped Henrik's hand was tall and slender. His hair was straw colored, his eyes a sharp blue. His hand gripped hard. His voice was mellow, but with a crisp cadence. He spoke to all the new arrivals.

"My name is Richard Horst," he announced. "I am from Berlin, and I will be the one who will tell you about your new home, and to make you feel comfortable here. Come in. Come in. Soon we will eat. Our lights will go out at ten o'clock every night. Tomorrow, we will get up at six-thirty and eat breakfast at seven. Then you can come back here and shower. Cleanliness is required. After breakfast there are many classes you can attend. You can even learn English from a Special Projects Officer who uses chalk and a blackboard. We eat again at twelve-ten. Afterwards you can read, or learn to play an instrument, of which we have many, or you can study whatever you wish until five. Then it is supper between six and seven. Until ten we are allowed to spend time together. Then it is to bed again."

His keen eyes roamed through the gathering to judge their attentiveness. Then he continued. "Life here is one day to the next. Welcome, my friends, to Algona, Iowa, and to strict regulations, which on some days are not strict at all. We have a guard whose name is Porter Bekins. He comes from a city named Fargo, which is in the neighboring state of South Dakota. We wrap him around our fingers."

He paused, looking at the total group with an instructive gaze. Then he nodded. "Work this time of year is slight. Sometimes we help build roads, or cut down trees, or roof barns, but that is always when the weather is cooperative. Now, in winter, we stay inside because of the cold. But to keep us occupied there is always laundry and kitchen work. When your name comes up for one of those tasks, you will willingly comply. Sometimes the snow here is very deep. Believe me, you have not seen cold until you have been here for a while. For a diversion, we have a building where you can play table tennis and chess. Or you can take up boxing or handicrafts. And if you are an actor you can take part in our theatrical performances. In the summer-time we play soccer. Yes, we have everything, except telephones and women. Un-fortunately, they are outside the fences. Now go and take a bed. The selection is yours."

The group dispersed. Henrik chose a bed close to the door, away from the shower room. The bed was narrow, but adequate. Henrik pushed down on the mat-tress. "It is a good one," he remarked as Richard came up beside him.

Richard put out his hand. "Yes, they are much better than lying in the mud of a battlefield. You can put your personal belongings in the box, there, at the foot. I sleep next to you. I hope we will become friends." His eyes softened as his voice quieted. "Some of the men here call me a neutral, which is someone who is neither pro-Nazi nor pro-American. But, like most of us, I have done my part for the Fa-therland. I was captured in Sicily. Now we come together in America, where we all try to make the best of it."

Henrik nodded, delighted that Richard was not among those who shared a rabid dislike for America. "I will be your friend," he replied.

"Ah, before I forget. The man who directs the camp choir is from Aachen. His name is Johann Bresseler."

"I was captured in Aachen."

"Then you must meet him. Do you sing?"

"If you call braying like a mule, yes, then I sing."

Richard laughed. "Bresseler will not want you. I think you will wash dishes then."

They both laughed. In those minutes when coming together meant everything to a newcomer, Henrik relaxed to the easy banter and the friendliness shown to him by another of his countryman.

Richard gestured. "Put your things away. Then we will go and eat. The Geneva Convention says we must eat the same food as the American servicemen, but tonight we might have non-restricted meat, either beef shanks, flanks and livers, salt pork, or bellies and feet. But do not grimace. Our German cooks do wonderful things with whatever they get. Ha, wait until you taste their rye bread and sauerkraut. Cer-tainly, it is better than we had when we were chasing the British. Come, I will show you the cafeteria. Then you can sleep."

Henrik was quick to reply. "You must meet my friend, Emil Dryer. He is from Dresden. We met on the ship coming over from France. But we were separated during the indoctrination. I don't know where he is now."

"We will find him. He cannot go far here, unless he likes to climb barbed wire or get shot at again. Trust me, Henrik, we will find him. Follow me. My stomach is crying."

They ate meat loaf and scrambled eggs that night, amid the constant banter of hundreds seated at the tables. Henrik looked for Emil, but could not find him.

"Don't worry," Richard said. "Tomorrow we will locate him. Now eat, and ask me some questions. You have much to learn about our life here. As for the food, the quantity we receive is based on the extent of our activity. We get the required calories, but not so much as to cause waste. We have our own gardens and bakery. Good food, Henrik. You will not starve here. We have officers' quarters, barracks with latrine and showers and laundry tubs with hot water. Also, an administration building for each company, and indoor and outdoor recreation facilities. Do you play soccer?"

"No."

"Too bad. In the summertime we have good sport."

"I will learn."

"Good. We have three thousand men here now. Maybe you can try out for one of the teams. There are ten now, I think. In addition we have a hospital and good doctors and a church. I, for one, am happy to be here, and not in a Russian camp. Life is good here, much better than in the German army." He looked to his left to where another prisoner was busy talking. Then he whispered close to Henrik's ear. "We must be careful what we say here. There are SS around, and they listen closely to every word. Last week a man died in his bed. Authorities said it was suicide, but we know different. The SS have ways of taking care of traitors. So, you see, Henrik, you must watch what you say."

"I am not political," Henrik replied.

"Then you must be careful. I don't know your passion, but I think you are too young to have been caught up in the storm."

"I was released from the Jugend, for physical reasons. The Volkstrum swept me up just before the fall of Aachen. I was wounded there."

"Then stay clear of the officers. They are insolent and insubordinate to their new authority. Some still brag that they had been chosen to have intercourse with the female SS for the production of superior children, but we know better. Many of the elite walk around here like they are the supermen they profess to be. They are anti-Christ. Non-believers. They believe only in Hitler. They refuse to believe that we are losing the war."

"I will be careful. Neither I, nor Emil will want anything to do with them."

"I will point them out to you." Richard chewed his food heartily. "Some refuse to work when they first come here, so they are denied food. But most start working after just ten days or so. Some of the harder ones have held out for a month or so, surviving on bread and water only. Then, when they have had enough, they are put to work tarring roofs. Some have bragged about almost starving to death on the Russian front, living on leaves and roots and sometimes potatoes they dug out of the ground, so they say this American punishment is nothing at all. They are braggarts. Some still speak of the *Endsieg*, the final victory, and how this country will be used after Germany has conquered it. I do not think so, Henrik. They call the Americanized soldiers traitors, or deserters. Sometimes they exact punishment on those they feel are no longer dedicated to the Third Reich. So be careful, Henrik. They are everywhere."

Henrik nodded. "Tell me. Are there any more camps than this one?"

"I believe there are more, over thirty I have heard. Some from this camp, the anti-Nazis, have been transferred to other camps, to help the farmers with their harvests. Most of the others work in the factories."

"And here?"

"There is a canning factory nearby, and many farms. We do what we are told to do. We are paid ten American cents for every hour of work. The money is placed into our private accounts. I will tell you more about that later."

"Tell me about the farms."

"The farms, yes. We have shocked up the oats and pulled weeds, cut hay and stacked wheat. It is hard work, but good work outside the wire. Some farms are better than others. Some of the farmers treat us poorly. Some days we work in the heat and they give us only warm, dirty water to drink. They are ones who have sons in the army. But they are few. Some of the good ones have even invited prisoners to eat dinner with them. Ha, most of them are Germans themselves. When we work on the farms we are usually up by five to wash and shave and have breakfast before reporting for work. But now it is winter, and we have time on our hands. We will be working in the canning factory."

"And me?"

"You are new. You will not be working for a while. You will spend your time being indoctrinated, and then they might hand you a snow shovel and say, get going before the snow covers you up."

"It will not be so bad."

"Wait. You have not seen snow like the kind of snow God makes in Iowa. And, oh, by the way, we have a newspaper that prints camp news only, formatted and printed by the prisoners. It is named the "Drahpost." We are not permitted to see the outside newspapers or listen to the radio. But we learn what is going on from those new prisoners, like you. But, eat! Eat! There is more where this came from. Eat, and get fat."

After dinner Henrik and Richard walked outside into the harsh evening where only the floodlights roamed. At least they were better off than the surrounding farms that had no electricity. They paused momentarily at the fence and stood silently, looking out over the windswept plains, dark to the faint horizon. The stars glistened like jewels in the night sky, and for a moment Henrik felt small and unimportant, for he had no idea where life would take him. He could see no trees beyond the wire, only snow-covered prairie.

Richard spoke. "Sometimes in the summer we hang our laundry on the wire. The wind dries it quickly there."

Henrik didn't answer him. He was, in a strange way, at peace with himself. He had left the war behind. The killing and the madness and the horror were slowly losing their place in his memory.

"There is a road there," Richard pointed. "In the summer some of the girls come from the nearby town just to look at us. Sometimes I wonder what is on their minds. Perhaps they would like to come and see us, to get a taste of good German meat, if you know what I mean. I expect the best of their men are gone. What do you think, Henrik?"

"I think maybe they only want to see the animals who have tried to rule the world, those who have killed their men. Now they are so lonely they want to spit on us."

"Is that what you think?"

"I don't know. We are here, behind the wire, and they are out there. We will probably never know what they think of us."

"I have met some of them on the farms. None of them have spoken to me. They look at us with curiosity. Ah, but so much for them. Tomorrow we will find your friend. And on Sunday there is church. Do you go to church?"

"Yes, I am Lutheran."

"Then I will accompany you. Now, you must be tired from the day. Perhaps you would like to clean up, and write a letter. There is paper and pen in the barrack."

Henrik nodded. "Yes, I would like to write to my mother and tell her about the first day in my new home."

Richard placed his arm around Henrik's shoulder. "I think we will be good friends. I am glad you came here."

Slowly Henrik and Richard walked back to the barrack, chatting all the way. By the time they arrived, Henrik was tired. He took a quick shower, and then sat down at the table with paper and pen, and he wrote:

My dear parents. I am here in America, at a large camp. I am well treated and am eating my fill. I pray you both are doing well, despite the hardships you must be facing. Hopefully the war will end soon. When it does, I will come home, and we will begin a new life. It is snowing here, and the weather is cold, but we are warm inside. It seems that the wind is always blowing. Tomorrow I will learn more about this place from a friend I have made, a young soldier who is from Berlin. He will, as they say over here, show me the ropes. I pray for you both, and wish you safety. Before long it will be Christmas, so I will light a candle for you. God's blessing to you both. I will write again soon. Love, Henrik

TEN

New Ulm, Minnesota, December 1944

PAPA HAD CUT DOWN A SMALL TREE from the plot of land behind the barn where the spruces were planted. He planted two every year to make up for those he had taken, and now the plot had near thirty trees of various sizes, one always perfect for Christmas. Sometimes a neighbor would come and offer to pay him for one, but Papa always gave them away. It was the thing to do at Christmas, he said.

Three weeks ago they had trimmed the tree with tinsel and small bells and cookies mother had made. David added pheasant feathers from the birds he had shot, and Elsa and Corina always made popcorn strings. They placed a star on top, one grandfather had made from cardboard and glue, painted white and adorned with goose down. It was old now, but cherished, and so they used it as a remembrance of him.

They had an old windup Victrola in the living room and 45rpm records filled with Christmas music, including the jolly new song, "All I Want for Christmas Is My Two Front Teeth," and the tender one, "Have Yourself a Very Merry Christmas." They had cookies galore and candy canes and hard-shell nuts that Papa broke open with a nutcracker. Mother made hot cider, and the axe blade always met the neck of an old tom turkey.

On Christmas morning, before church, they opened their presents. There was always clothing, some home made, and candy for everyone. The children had all they could eat, and laughter filled the house. Papa did his impersonation of Santa Claus by wearing a long cotton beard and horned-rimmed glasses while waddling through the room with a pillow tucked beneath his overcoat.

After breakfast, they went to church. A new snow had fallen, and the countryside glistened with diamond light. After church the children went sliding down the hill behind the barn near where the spruce trees grew, and afterwards, when they were tired and in need of rest, they gathered near the kitchen stove and rubbed warmth into their arms and then settled down in the chairs for hot cider and cookies.

When they were all gathered together, David made an offhanded remark that turned Elsa's head. "I wonder what the prisoners are doing today," he said.

Papa puffed on the pipe and swirled the smoke away with a wave of his hand. "They are probably celebrating just like we are," he replied.

"But they're Nazis."

Papa shook his head, slowly, the way he always did when expressing an opinion. "No. I've heard that most of them are not. The ones here aren't hardened to Hitler's doctrines. They're peaceful men, so much so that one of the local pastors has set up services for them on Wednesdays and Sundays. And I hear that they've carved an altar for themselves, built with donated lumber. Furthermore, one of the Catholic priests has found them a piano. No, David, they aren't without God in their midst. They're no trouble to anyone."

"They've been seen skating on the lake, "Elsa said.

"Yes. They've made skis and skates in their own workshop. They are industrious men."

"Where are they working now that winter's here?" David asked.

"In Sleepy Eye, at the packing company, and in town at the brick and tile yards." His eyes moved to intercept their attention. "I have spoken to one of them."

Elsa leaned for forward, her curiosity aroused to the point of breathlessness. "Tell me about him. What was he like?"

Papa puffed on the pipe again while slowly forming his reply. "He was no different than us. He was a young man who was hesitant to talk at first. I was with Elmer Frough when the German boy came in. He stood aside at first, until Elmer began asking him questions. Then he became comfortable with us, and he opened up a bit."

"What did he say?"

"Not much. He told us how they had fixed up the grounds, and painted the buildings, and made a clubroom for themselves. He said he played the concertina, and that they were quite comfortable here. He said he worked mostly in the cannery and that he carried his own lunch every day. He had even plucked chickens. They ride buses to and from work every day. He thanked us for being considerate of them. I thought it commendable of him,"

"Then they aren't so bad," David replied, as if questioning.

"They're men who have been through a terrible war. Most of them, I trust, are glad to be here, away from the fighting."

"Some of them have even been seen walking though town," David remarked.

Papa puffed again. "They're not locked up. The fence around their camp is unfinished. They can come and go as they wish, but mostly they stay where they are. They know their place."

"They give me the chills," Corina said.

Elsa sat up straight, shoulders back. "I would like to meet one."

Corina was shocked. "You can't be serious."

"I am. Papa said they're just like us. They're German just like we are. They don't go around shooting at us."

"But they're the enemy."

"Not any longer. They're prisoners, far away from their homes."

"I would run if I saw one," Corina replied.

"Not me," David boasted. "I want to see one, too.

Papa leaned forward, his pipe clamped tightly between his teeth. His eyes roamed over his children. "Enough!" he said.

The children were silenced. It was the last time they talked about the German prisoners until they went out to the barn just before nightfall to bring down hay for the cows. Corina and Elsa went into the loft. David stayed below to service the animals while Papa milked. Corina couldn't wait to bring up the subject.

"I can't believe that you want to meet one of those prisoners," she said. I think it's unpatriotic."

"You can believe what you want. As for me, I don't think patriotism has anything to do with it. We brought them over here. We gave them a place to live and food to eat, so what's wrong with wanting to be friendly."

"Well," Corina replied. "My teacher said these men should not be our guests, because just a few months ago they were shooting at our own boys, and now they receive treatment much better than some of our own soldiers. It isn't right."

Elsa rested on her pitchfork. "I don't think your teacher has any right to give her opinion about things when she's in a classroom."

"Doesn't yours?"

"No, she doesn't. She talks only about our subject and nothing else."

"Well, my teacher knows what's best."

"I don't think so. Why these men are not much older than I am. They aren't the German supermen that we read about. If they were, then why did they surrender?"

"Maybe because they were cowards."

"Of maybe because they were just sick of war. Did you ever think of that? How would you like to lie in the mud, and eat nothing for days, and get shot at every time you moved?"

Corina paused for a moment and thought about what Elsa had said. "I guess maybe they were frightened."

"Probably more than frightened. I think they were terrified."

Elsa pitched a forkful of hay down the chute, prompting a command from below. "Hey, hold it up there. Give me a minute."

Corina leaned on the pitchfork. "I would run if I saw one," she said.

"Not me."

"What would you do?"

Elsa shrugged. "I don't know. The only time I saw one was when they first came to town. One of them shouted at me from across the street."

"You never told me that. What did he say?"

Elsa laughed. "He asked if I had a kiss for him."

Corina's mouth sagged open. "You're kidding."

"No, really. They were across the street, in a bus."

"How could he say that to you? Oh god, that's…that's horrible."

Elsa giggled. "No, it isn't. I thought it was funny."

"Did you answer him back? What did you say to him?"

"Nothing. The bus pulled away. It was the last I saw of them."

"Did you tell Papa?"

"No, I didn't tell anyone, and I don't want you to tell anyone either. It's our little secret. Can you keep a secret?"

"You know I can. I'm no snitch."

"More hay." The command came from below.

The two girls looked at one another and giggled, and as Elsa stabbed the pitchfork into the hay, Corina remarked. "I think you're way too romantic for your own good." They laughed and finished their work, walking hand in hand back to the house until it was time for Elsa to clean the separator.

ELEVEN

Algona, Iowa, Christmas 1944

IN ALGONA, THE CHRISTMAS CELEBRATION had ended. The festivities had been held in the magnificently decorated hall where a profusion of hand-painted coats of arms representing German cities decorated the walls, making it appear as if it were a castle on the Rhine and not a prison camp in the middle of a strange country. Apples and nuts, gingerbread and cake were served in abundance, and they all ate and drank as if it were the first food they had ever tasted. The German Red Cross provided gifts of every kind, all wrapped in festive paper. They had sung old German songs, "Eidelweiss" among them. During coffee, Santa Claus came in amid a great fanfare to hand out presents to the prisoners as if they were children. Old Saint Nicolas was played by the stoutest of all the prisoners. Some of the prisoners even sat on his knee and caressed his beard amid hoots of laughter. Henrik received two volumes of Gothe's "Faust," and Emil a picture frame. Richard received a box of chocolate candy and two precious letters from home. The candy was devoured in seconds. The camp choir sang familiar German folk songs that misted many an eye, and the band played waltzes and music from operettas. Some of the men danced together, bringing forth roars of laughter and catcalls from the onlookers. The Christmas tree, donated by the town of Algona, was large and fully decorated with paper chains and lights and ornaments fashioned by the prisoners. A man in full uniform recited poems by Gothe, Schiller and Eichendorff. A record played music by Beethoven, Schubert and Handel. It was inevitable that each of the prisoners, during moments of silent recollection, remembered the celebrations back home, when they had set out the nativity scenes and had sung "O Come All Ye Faithful." Those in attendance were all Christians. Those who were not spent Christmas alone, in the barracks, with only the walls to keep them company.

At nine o'clock, filled with food and drink, and brimming with contentment, Richard, Emil, and Henrik put on their long coats and caps and walked outside beneath the moon. The Milky Way was smeared like diamond dust across the sky, so dazzling that it could have brightened the snow-covered landscape all by itself. The freshly fallen snow was bluish beneath the night sky. With no wind, the evening was still, almost comforting in its silence, serene except for the cold that touched their faces like an unsympathetic hand. They walked side by side, not saying a word. Each of them would remember the party in a different way, for the memories it had restored in their troubled minds, or for the happiness that had recalled a photographic picture of life back home.

Richard was the first to speak. His breath fogged in the air. "I remember, as a boy, my mother used to read Eichendorff to me, when the house was still."

Emil replied. "Eichendorff, yes. He was a fine poet. I also read him."

"I knew him also," Henrik put in. "My uncle encouraged me to read him, and sometimes we read together, out loud, to the rest of the family. They were good times."

"Did you memorize him?" Richard asked.

Henrik hesitated while his mind picked at words and phrases once so vivid to him. "Some, yes. I know a verse or two."

"Then give them to us now."

"Here?"

Emil nudged him with an elbow. "Yes, here, while we are still warm."

Henrik looked into the sky, and for a moment he remembered the nights he and his uncle used to sit together beneath the dim light and read, his uncle's arm around him, the book open in his lap, his emotional voice expressing each word as if it were, in itself, the total of the work. And then he would ask Henrik to read, and he would try to emulate his uncle with tone and passion while waiting for him to breath deeply with the grandeur of the words and to say at last, "That was so glorious, you are a wonderful reader, more, Henrik, more."

The three of them slowed their pace, and as Henrik assembled the once-familiar words, the others waited patiently. He looked at them. He could see memories etched in their eyes. Then Henrik spoke, remembering the once-delicate words that had been spoken so artfully to his uncle. "It was as though the sky had silently kissed the earth," he said, hoping to echo Eichendorff exactly as he had when wrapped in his uncle's arm, "So that it now had to dream of sky in shimmers of flowers."

"You know it," Richard said, slapping Henrik on the back.

"Yes, thank you."

"Do you know more?"

"I think I could remember, if I try hard enough."

"Come, then. Give us another verse."

Henrik was about to speak when a figure approached them from a nearby barrack, silhouetted by the broad beam of a searchlight. He walked rapidly, his arms swinging, his stride brisk. An SS officer for sure. There was no mistaking his collar patch. As the man came closer, Henrik recognized him immediately. It was Hauptmann Arnold Schmidt, the same officer he had met in the Allied field hospital in Belgium, the same man who had dressed him down on the ship. The three had no time to change their direction.

Captain Schmidt stopped short, and stood as straight as a hard oak board, his head slightly raised to one side. "Good evening," he said, extending his arm. "Heil Hitler."

The response was hesitantly crude. Only Emil and Richard mumbled the same words in response, their arms raised in a feeble salute. Henrik did not speak. He held his arm tightly to his side. He knew what to expect. The captain would not back away from an opportunity to chastise, not even on Christmas Eve.

The captain looked sharply at Henrik, his eyes thin with reproach. "Why do you not honor the Führer?"

Henrik didn't hesitate for a moment. He looked directly into the captain's eyes and spoke with sincerity. "Because I am on American soil. I, like you, am a prisoner here."

The captain looked queerly at Henrik, as if to test his own memory. "You are here only as a visitor," he declared. Then his eyes tightened with a nod. "I know you," he said. "Yes, you are the one I met in the field hospital, and again on the ship. You are Henrik . . . Henrik Arndt. Am I right?"

"Yes, that is my name."

"And I remember something else about you. You said Germany was a country without a soul. A terrible thing for a German soldier to say, don't you think?"

"I was not a soldier. I was a Volkstrum, a civilian made soldier."

"Ah, an honorable rank, if served properly."

"You might think so."

The captain took one step back, and looked at them critically. Then he spoke to Erik in an almost sneering manner, with fire in his voice. "You are his friend, yes?"

"I am."

Then he turned his eyes to Richard. "And you. You must realize that this man is not what one would call an honorable member of the German Reich. He does not respect the Führer. He stands here on the soil of his enemy and speaks with a traitorous tongue. If he were in Germany now we would have a remedy for his disobedience."

There was no response. The three stood as if frozen to the ground.

"So," the captain continued, "You are all quiet about this. Well, then your names please. And if you do not choose to give them to me I will get them from someone else."

"I am Oberschutze Richard Horst."

"And I am Gefreiter Emil Dryer."

The captain glanced quickly at Henrik, then back to the two. "You should not be seen with this man. He is unworthy of your friendship."

"He is our friend, sir," Emil replied.

"Ah, a friend." The captain looked off into the sky. His lips tightened. Then he turned back, slowly, to face them again. "You must not associate yourselves with this man. That is an order. By his actions, and with his tongue, you can see that he is not a friend of the Third Reich."

Emil stiffened. "We will try to change his thinking, Captain."

"And do you think you can?"

"Yes. He will listen to us. We are close, he and I."

The captain nodded. "Then you have a task ahead of you. I will see you again, and you." He tapped Henrik on the chest with his finger. "Sometimes a change of scenery can alter a man. But this land, this cold and desolate place, can only make you think of the Fatherland, and how beautiful it is. America, she will not look the same after we get through with her. When we are marching down her streets, then you will realize how strong and how magnificent the Third Reich really is."

Hauptmann Schmidt moved forward then, on a direct path between Henrik and Emil. Emil stepped aside to allow his passage.

"Goodnight," the captain said. "Remember. Christmas is only one day in the year. The rest belong to our Führer." He walked on, with a stride as bold as the Waffen SS troops that had goose-stepped through the streets of Berlin, when their black boots had crashed against the stones and their eyes had the glimmer of defiance in them, when their souls were etched with hate.

"Who does he think he is?" Emil remarked.

"He is what he thinks Germany must always be."

Richard nodded. "Germany is over."

Henrik stepped between them and placed his arms across their shoulders. "I think maybe you should stay clear of me."

"No!" Emil said immediately. "He has only limited power here. I will do as I wish."

Richard stepped back and looked directly at Henrik. He gestured passionately as if addressing a great audience. "Do you remember what I said that day we first met, in the kitchen, when we were eating our first meal together. I warned you about the SS. There have been deaths here, and although the authorities say they are suicides, we know the men were murdered by the likes of him. The SS still has power here. I say, Henrik, do not put yourself at risk. You must treat this captain like the man he is. If you must raise you arm to him, then do so. I would hate to see them put you in a grave. Be wise, Henrik. Someday this will all be over and we will return to Germany. It is better now to bow to someone like him, and take what you can from this place."

"He is a remnant of the past," Henrik said.

"Then keep your opinion to yourself. If you insist on being disobedient, then I must stay away from you, although I do not agree with him."

"No," Henrik replied, taking his hand. "I do not wish to lose you as a friend. If I must, I will say Seig Heil to him, if that is what he wants."

"Now you are being sensible."

Henrik clenched his teeth. "I am as much a German as he is. I would say I love my country more than he does. He can see Germany ruled only with power. I can see it ruled with compassion. My God, how can he be so blind?"

"He is so filled with blood and honor that he cannot see the truth of what is happening to Germany."

Henrik looked toward his barrack. "You two go on. I am going back to write a letter, and to sleep if I can."

"I will come with you," Richard said.

Emil shrugged. "Then I will go to my place, and maybe think about the song, "Old Parents Home" where the village ends, where the mill wheel turns by the brook, and where scented flower lie. You see, I too can remember the songs we used to sing when I was a boy. And tomorrow I will go and see the Lagersprecher, the camp speaker, to see if he can get me transferred to your barrack. Do you have room for me there, Richard?"

"We have two empty beds."

"Then I will do it. Perhaps soon we can all be together under one roof."

Henrik pulled them into his arms. "Goodnight then. I had a good time. I will be a good boy from now on. The next time I pass the captain I will not be disobedient."

"Goodnight, Henrik," Emil said. "I wish you well."

On the way back to their barrack, Henrik and Richard didn't say much. All that needed to be said had been said, and they approached their building with a sense of calm, neither wanting to begin a conversation. Inside the barrack, they shook hands and went each to their own bed. Henrik sat with two others at the center table. No one spoke as he wrote the letter to his parents. Then as the lights went out, he lay down on the bed, and for a long time he peered at the ceiling rafters, visible one minute, dark the next, as the searchlights prowled outside.

In moments of deep reflection, he longed to see his mother, and to have her hold him as she did when he was a child, and to hear her say: A mother is blessed to have a son like you. As he remembered, tears came to his eyes but he didn't bother to brush them aside. They trailed down his cheeks and onto his pillow, and for a long time he held his sobs deep within his chest so as not to arouse the others around him, some already snoring, others shifting. Muffled words came to him from the far side of the room.

"Mother," he said silently, praying that somehow his words would reach her across the thousands of miles separating them. "I promise you. I will not do anything foolish. I will do what I must to survive and to someday return to you and Papa. We will walk again down the long road and listen to the birds, and hear the brook whistling to us. And I will help rebuild what has been lost, and we will start a new life together. If God is listening to me, I ask him to bless you both, and to provide well for you. Keep me in your hearts, and find a way to survive this madness. One day I will come home. I promise you. Good night dear Vater, dear Mutter. I love you both."

Sleep came easily that night. As his eyes closed he drifted into a world of memories.

TWELVE

Algona, Iowa, January 1945

New Year's Day came and went, and life in the camp became a dull routine. Henrik was sent to the canning factory for a week, and then he spent several days in the kitchen, and another shoveling walkways. He went to the dentist following a nagging toothache and after taking x-rays, a German doctor pulled his tooth, behind the cheek where the shrapnel was imbedded, metal particles that were now beginning to work their way out. He watched a German movie that same evening. When time permitted he continued his friendship with both Emil and Richard.

Within the camp, there were educational classes, lectures, studies, and discussion groups available. One could even enroll in correspondence courses with any of fourteen educational centers across the country. The prisoners could select basic courses in reading, writing, geography, mathematics, languages, music, arts, history or literature. The courses were taught by the prisoners and by authorized civilians who were approved by the camp commander and the Provost Marshal General. Henrik chose to enter a class in mathematics, which had been one of his strongest subjects in Germany.

Henrik behaved himself so as not to fall victim to discipline. The prisoners were strictly managed by regulations stated in the articles of the Geneva Convention, and the camp commander could admonish or reprimand anyone, either orally or by written letter. Prisoners could also be punished by having their privileges withheld, or their pay discontinued, or by assigning them to extra duty, hard labor without confinement, or overtime work not to exceed four hours a day. Maximum disciplinary action could be as lengthy as thirty days confinement, including fourteen days on bread and water. Prisoners could also be tried by summary court martial, the sentences not to exceed thirty days in duration.

Henrick also spent considerable time in the library and reading room, where many German books were available. The war news came only by word of mouth, from those working in the factories, or from relatives who were allowed to enter the camp twice monthly for brief visits. As word of mouth penetrated the wire, they learned that American forces had landed in the Philippines. They also learned that the Battle of the Bulge had ended, that the German army had been driven back behind their border, and that the President of the United States, Franklin Delano Roosevelt, had been inaugurated for his fourth term in office. In all, the news was met with mixed emotions. Some thought the reports were nothing more than pure propaganda. But better than half of the prisoners knew the truth of it, that the war would end with Germany's defeat, and when it did, they would be allowed to return to a devastated homeland just in time to prod through its still warm ashes.

Much of his first letter from home was censored. However, enough of it remained to tell him that his mother and father were all right, and that his cousin, Arnold, was somewhere on the Russian front. They were thankful that he was in an American prisoner of war camp, a safe place to be, and they wished him well, with love and respect. He kept the letter in his footlocker.

His friendship with Richard and Emil continued, and he was not bothered by Hauptmann Schmidt, though he could still sense the animosity toward him whenever they passed one another.

On January twenty-seventh of that year, the Russians liberated a small town on their push toward Berlin. The town was named Auschwitz. What they discovered there would stun the world.

Thirteen

New Ulm, Minnesota, January, 1945

ELSA HAD FINISHED IRONING THE CLOTHES her mother had washed. Even though the REA had run electricity to the farm the year before, they still had not purchased an electric washing machine. Instead, they used a gasoline-fired one that stunk up the kitchen. Elsa was always afraid it would blow up in her face. They still heated water in an old teakettle for the big copper washtub, and although mother talked repeatedly about switching to modern conveniences, the old equipment sufficed, and would, until Papa thought it best to purchase new ones. Elsa pressed clothes with an old flat iron while waiting for a plug-in electric model. They were penny wise and prudent, a practice that had been passed along from their grandparents. The old kerosene lanterns were still kept within arms' reach, just in case the wires went down in an ice storm, or were blown over by a tornado, or were hampered by other unpredictable acts of nature. Papa was sometimes slow to adapt to new things, except when it came to farming, which was why he purchased the tractor, a new red Farmall, gleaming and noisy.

Near noon, Elsa had received permission to go into town to the "New Ulm" theatre, with Erica, to see the film, "To Have and Have Not," starring Humphrey Bogart and Lauren Bacall. She had freshened up, had slipped into her jeans and blouse, her bobby socks and tennis shoes, and had applied a limited amount of lipstick before Erica drove into the yard in her father's Ford.

"Enjoy yourself," mother said as she left the house.

Elsa pushed aside the old flat iron they used as a doorstop, and stepped outside. The day was pleasant, warm enough to thaw snow. Water dripped off the icicles hanging from the roof, and the path to the barn was nearly clear. It would be muddy if the weather remained above freezing, but everyone knew it wouldn't. Snow and cold would come again. In Minnesota spring didn't come around until April, if then.

Elsa opened the car door and slid into the warm interior. "Hi, how are ya," she asked, nudging Elsa with her shoulder.

Erica pressed the accelerator. The car bolted across the yard. "Are you ready for a good movie?"

"I am. Bogart. Yum-yum."

Erica laughed. "Does he warm your thighs?"

Elsa appeared shocked, when in fact she really wasn't. "That's nervy of you, to say a thing like that."

"Well, does he?"

Elsa relaxed, and then laughed. "Well, maybe just a little."

Elsa was not a prude. Although her moral standards were high, she often thought of sexual liaisons, and what it would be like to actually sleep with a man, to feel him against her, to touch him there, and for him to touch her, to enter her. She would dream occasionally of passions so vivid that she would wake up warm and excited and unable to get out of bed until the feeling passed, until the trembling in her thighs had settled down to where she could stand. When she was in the barn loft by herself, there were times when she would lay down on the hay and close her eyes, and place her hand between her legs and believe it was someone else caressing her. At other times she was actually hungry for a man, for someone to hold her, to ease the tedium of everyday existence, and to bed with her at night. Her body was full and desirable and she needed someone to satisfy the passions that grew stronger with every season, with every month. It didn't help when she saw the animals mating in the barn lot, when the bull sensed the need to satisfy its passion.

When the movie was over the two of them stopped briefly at Earl's for a cola. They talked for a while with two of their friends, and then got back into the old Ford.

"Are you in a hurry to get home?" Erica asked.

"No, why?"

Hesitation. "Well, I thought we could drive down by the lake. I saw some of the prisoners skating there yesterday." She turned toward Elsa, her eyes wide with anticipation. "The road is open. Do you want to see them?"

The thought of seeing the prisoners up close sent an immediate wave of excitement across Elsa's shoulders. She felt that tremor again, the song of desire, the resonance of its first notes. She also thought the suggestion was a bit bold, and perhaps dangerous. Seeing them at a distance was one thing, up close quite another. If they were seen, they might be judged as being promiscuous instead of just curious.

"Well?" Erica prodded.

"I don't know. It's just that…"

Elsa interrupted. "Who's to know?"

"But it's a bit bold."

"Sure it is. That's what makes it exciting. Or are you hesitating because of your silly morals? My God, Elsa, we're not going to crawl into bed with them."

Elsa's expression was one of mild exasperation. "Don't be so crude."

Erica giggled. "Sometimes I think I know you better than you know yourself. I know what goes on in that mind of yours."

"Oh, do you?"

"Yes. I know for a fact that you'd like to experiment with sex."

"This isn't about sex, it's about prisoners of war."

"They're just people," Erica said.

"Our enemies."

"Not any more."

Elsa sighed. The foolish discussion would get them nowhere. Erica had the car. She could do whatever she wanted, and right then and there she wanted to see the prisoners. Elsa remembered how her own curiosity had peaked the first time she saw one of them in the bus, that day she went to the dentist, how uninhibited they were, how one of them had asked her for a kiss.

"Okay, let's do it," she blurted."

Erica wiggled in her seat. "My pants are hot already."

"But we won't go near them, promise?"

"I promise. There's no harm in looking? We'll only stay a few minutes."

Elsa's last shred of resistance faded. "Okay. Let's get on with it."

On the way to the lake Elsa wondered what the German prisoners were really like. Were they the horrible creatures many of the town folks described them as being, or were they average men, like those who worked and played and lived free. She had never lost the vision of the young man in the bus who had called to her. Quite often she would find herself thinking of his jovial voice coming across the street, his blonde hair lifting with the wind, waving in time with his hand. He had appeared to be like everyone else his age, not at all like a goose-stepping monster or a brutal killer as they were often depicted. She was curious, and the thought of seeing one of them up close fed her imagination.

"Aren't you a little bit nervous?" she asked Erica.

"Gosh, no. Beverly Porter actually talked to one of them. She said they were as normal as anyone, friendly in fact."

"What did they say to her?"

"Not much. Things like, hello young lady, how are you today. She couldn't understand some of the things they said because she didn't understand German all that well. She said their dialect was somewhat different than the one she had learned in school."

"Where did she see them?"

"Down by Lake Flandreau. They were wearing their work clothes, you know, the ones with the big PW printed on the back. They were just walking along minding their own business."

"Aren't they locked up?"

"Not really. There's a fence, but it isn't complete. They can walk right around it. Beverly said they're trustworthy and not dangerous at all. And she said they're cute."

"The one I saw in town was cute, I think. I didn't get a real good look at him."

"You haven't forgotten about him, have you? Come on now, tell the truth."

"Yes, he was cute, handsome almost."

Erica laughed. She steered the car into a wide turn. "Just wait 'till you get close to one. It'll make your thighs ache."

Elsa slapped her on the shoulder. "Don't be so crude."

"Just wait. You just wait."

Erica drove carefully until they came to the dirt road that cut down through a ravine, curving toward Lake Flandreau, which was formed by a small dam that had backed up the Cottonwood River. Hemmed in on one side by trees that surrounded the old CCC camp, and on the opposite side by an embankment, it was now a picturesque place for boating and fishing, or just plain relaxing.

As Erica pulled the car into a turnoff, Elsa strained forward, anxious to see if anyone was there. Yes, there were four men on the lake ice, two on skates. Almost immediately she felt nervous, the way one gets when entering forbidden territory. She leaned forward to peer through the windshield.

"There they are," Erica said, easing the car to a stop while leaving the engine running.

Elsa giggled. "Oh, my gosh, I can't believe we're doing this."

The men on the ice turned to face them. The ones on skates paused momentarily. Another in a long coat pointed their way. They all looked toward the car, and one of them raised his arm and waved.

"Wave back at them," Erica said, nudging Elsa.

Elsa appeared shocked at the suggestion. "Are you kidding? No way. It wouldn't be right."

"Go ahead. Nothing bad is going to happen. We're just being friendly."

"What if someone saw us?"

"Who's going to see us? Nobody's here but us and them."

"Someone from the camp might see us, a guard maybe."

The men on the ice continued skating. One of them pushed off and made a wide arc near the opposite shoreline and then headed straight toward them.

"Oh, my God," Elsa breathed. "One of them is coming."

Erica giggled. "He's all yours."

"What do you mean by that?"

"He's curious, just like we are. So go ahead and talk to him. I know you want to."

"Shut up." Elsa trapped her words in the mittens she was wearing.

The POW hesitantly approached the shoreline. He looked in both directions before setting his gaze on Elsa's passenger window. He was a good-looking lad, narrow at the waist, slender as a young tree, with keen eyes, and a thin layer of whiskers as gold as ripe grain. He waved at them, cautiously it seemed, and in that first, delicate moment, when their eyes met, Elsa lost all fear of him. He drifted to a stop, stood quietly on his skates, and planted his hands on his hips. His smile was gracious. She rolled down the window just as he spoke.

"Kommen sie schlittschuh mit uns." he said, spreading his arm wide in a welcoming gesture.

"What did he say?" Erica asked quickly, demanding an answer.

Elsa responded, her voice soft but reserved. "He said, come and skate with us."

Erica squirmed in her seat and just about swooned behind the wheel. "What do you think? Should we join them?"

"Absolutely not," Elsa responded. "I wouldn't do such a thing."

The German had turned to face the others who approached him slowly from across the pond. "Oh, my god. Here come the rest of them." Elsa said.

The boy on skates grinned, and then motioned to Elsa. *"Kommen,"* he said. His broad smile was tranquil and mesmerizing.

Elsa leaned back in her seat, her shoulders tight against the backrest. Her reply was slow in coming, but even though forced, it was direct. She shook her head. "No," she replied. *"Nein."*

Now all four men looked at the car and smiled. They nudged one another in hopes of continuing the conversation. Then the one who had spoken turned and bowed slightly toward the car as if performing a courtly gesture. *"Vielleicht nachste zeit,"* he said.

"What did he say?" Erica demanded.

"He said . . . perhaps next time."

"Elsa shook her head. "Why wait until next time. Let's go now."

"I said before, no!" Then her voice heightened. "Oh, my God, there's a car coming."

A car was coming in behind them, approaching on the downgrade. Erica glanced quickly in the rear view mirror, and without delay she tapped the accelerator and moved expediently away from the riverbank. Immediately, the man on skates threw up his arms in despair and pushed away. Elsa cranked up the window as fast as she could. The oncoming car turned into the compound as they sped up the ravine.

"We did it," Erica laughed.

Elsa's heart was beating rapidly, and her eyes widened as she turned toward Erica. "Oh, my God, to think that they actually spoke to us."

"It was incredible." Erica gasped. Then catching her breath, she said. "He was cute, wasn't he? I just wanted to get out and hug him."

Elsa waved her hands excitedly. "I couldn't move. I was glued to my seat."

"You were mesmerized."

"Me? You couldn't even talk. You just sat there."

"You were the one next to the window."

"I couldn't say a word."

"If I'd have been sitting where you are, I would have. I wouldn't let you have all the fun?"

"You're no braver than me."

"Why didn't you get out and skate with them."

"Because a car was coming."

"Excuses! Excuses!"

A half-minute of silence brought a relaxed stillness to the car's interior. Elsa sat with her back straight, her hands cupped in her lap, her eyes dead ahead in an effort to calm the nervousness that had resulted from the heart-pounding experience. So, she had seen one of the enemies up close, a German soldier who might have killed an American during combat, or perhaps even Elsa's Uncle Barney who had been in the army for years, who was last known to be fighting in Italy. Her thoughts scattered, then arranged and rearranged like a shuffled deck of cards. One thing was clear; her impressions of the prisoners had changed during that brief moment of contact, and she no longer thought of them as frightful and sadistic monsters that were intent on devouring the world. The one who had spoken to her had been gracious, friendly, and winsome, with a dash of old-world refinement in his manner, unlike the local farm boys, or their male counterparts in town. She wondered what it would be like to place Carlyle and the German side by side, to compare their appearances, their manners, and their tact in dealing with women. Then she took a deep breath and exhaled it slowly and remembered that the chance meeting, regardless of whatever impression it left behind, would never be repeated. She did not think she could ever summon the courage, or the inclination, to see them again. Better to leave the pot

unstirred. Better to forget the incident. Better to go about her business without another thought of the blonde-haired lad who had asked her to skate with him.

"You're thinking about him, aren't you?" Erica said.

"You are, too," Elsa blurted.

"Yes, I am. He was handsome."

"I didn't notice."

Erica laughed. "Oh, yes you did. You can't tell me you didn't have a hot flash
or two just looking at him."

Not wanting to appear prudish, Elsa replied, "Well, maybe just a little."

Elsa response was hurried. "Want to do it again sometime?"

"No. Not again."

"Why not?"

"Well, for one thing. Father would have a fit if he ever found out. If you want
to see them again, you'll have to go by yourself."

Little more was said on the way home to drop Elsa at the farm. As Erica was about
to drive away she smiled and said, "Sweet dreams. I bet you won't sleep well tonight."

When Elsa entered the house her mother had a chicken ready to pluck for
Sunday dinner.

Supper that night consisted of Spam sandwiches on freshly baked bread, beans
and Jell-O salad. The wind picked up outside, and before the meal was over snow
began swirling across the porch. A hard wind came in from the west. KSTP warned
of an impending blizzard. Papa pulled all the shades and told the kids to get ready
for a loud night of screeching and blowing.

Later, Elsa went upstairs to use the "slop jar," their slang for a commode, a
large pot made out of heavy metal and coated with white enamel, complete with a
sturdy cover. They had a three-holer out back, in an outhouse twenty-five feet from
the kitchen window, but no one was about to face the wind and snow on such a
blustery night. For wiping they used pages from the catalog, or peach wrappers
when it was fruit canning season. Elsa preferred the peach wrappers. They were
kept in a bushel basket within easy reach. How she longed for a home with indoor
plumbing. All Papa could say about that was, next year, maybe next year. She went
to bed as the wind played a three-note symphony. Corina was already asleep.
Dressed in her flannel nightgown, Elsa tunneled beneath the thick woolen quilt,
her nightly cave of warmth. She adored the comforting bedcovers. She found her
dreams beneath them, those moments in elsewhere, when thoughts came to life in
images so vivid that she remembered them clearly at the moment of awakening.

On that night, when the wind howled, and the bare branch of the elm scratched against the house, and when the room was illuminated only by the whiteness of the snow outside, she crossed into the realm where dreams were fashioned. She was on the pond, skating. Her body twirled like a ballerina, her arms outstretched like wings as her fingers caressed the breeze, her eyes momentarily closed so as to capture the moment in sensation alone. She was weightless in the world of imagination, her body smooth flowing and light of foot as her skates touched the ice, leaving not a mark on its surface. The breeze on her face was warm and caressing and for a moment she felt as if she were a butterfly in flight.

He was there, then, touching the tips of her fingers with his own, and in that second of sheer wonder, an all-enveloping comfort encased her with a sense of wonderment, a dream within a dream. They circled on the ice; long, graceful sweeps of motion that brought her close to ecstasy in a world of diamond-dusted snow and majestic blue sky and trees flecked with frost. His face was a metaphor comprised of imagination and disbelief, a fascination so idyllic that she paused her skating just to look at him. Strangely, she saw no features, no soft, receptive eyes, no smile that could stall her breathing. She saw only an image of light, a combination of brightness and being; a boy who could have been . . . anyone.

Elsa awoke then, gasping, wanting desperately to return, but knowing she could not. Shadows moved overhead like specters across the ceiling, images cast by the snow and the tree and whatever else moved within the core of the storm. The wind breathed indistinguishable words as it rattled the window casings. She felt tears in her eyes, memory pearls she called them, those fashioned by imagination and wonder. Instantly, she rubbed them away, realizing that she had forgotten to draw the shade. Silently, she eased out from beneath the covers, grasped the ringed cord and drew it down. Instantly, the room darkened. She hustled back to the bed. The bare floor chilled her feet. There, she rolled to one side beneath the comforter and bunched the pillow tight around her head. She remembered what Erica had said as she had exited the car. "I bet you won't sleep well tonight."

Elsa closed her eyes as a thought played in her head. Would she ever find a boy that she could love? Could it be that he was waiting for her, somewhere, dreaming the same dream, this very night? No. The thought itself was impossible, the wish only a thing of dreams. But someday–perhaps, just perhaps their paths would cross, and she would know, as sure as the sun rose, that he was the one she had been waiting for.

Or was it too improbable even to consider?

FOURTEEN

New Ulm, Minnesota, February 1945

THE BLIZZARD LASTED A NIGHT AND A day and another night, drifting the roads, choking the city, rendering movement all but impossible until the plows came out on Monday and slowly cleared the roadways.

Elsa did not go to school until Tuesday. Her classroom was only half full. She sat in her usual desk, third from the front, second row in from the door. She thought it strange that two of the girls had turned to look at her without saying a word, offering no explanation, no remark. One of her good friends, Neva, had passed her without as much as a nod, and for a while she seemed to be a stranger in the hallways. She was in her study period, writing a paper for English class, when Carlyle came and sat next to her. She thought his presence strange, because he had avoided her ever since the night he had sped away from the farmyard leaving her standing flatfooted in the dark.

"What have you been up to?" he asked straight out. His expression was smug. He appeared to be irritated

She shrugged while maintaining a discreet distance. "Same old stuff, school and work." She appeared disinterested. She caught the drift of his cheap cologne, a scent that made her want to sneeze.

"Well, I heard you were doing something a bit out of the ordinary."

Her jaw tightened. She shifted to look at him. "What do you mean by that?"

"Well, I heard you were down by the river, playing up to some of them German bastards."

Elsa's lips tightened. She looked around quickly, to see if Erica was seated nearby. Immediately, she drew back in her seat while trying to appear smaller than she was. A fire of discontent burned in her throat. So, that was the reason for stares and silence. The entire school knew about it.

"Where did you hear that?" she asked vehemently. Her eyes tightened with scorn.

"Doesn't matter. I just wanted to know why you were down by the Cottonwood shining up to those Nazis."

"They aren't Nazis."

"Then what the hell are they? Far as I know, they're all bloodthirsty murderers who rape and slaughter Jews, and burn their bodies in ovens."

Elsa's cold stare drove at him like an Arctic gale. She knew immediately what his intention was, to pay her back for refusing his invitation to the dance, to belittle her, and to brand her as an enemy sympathizer.

Instead of shrinking, Elsa drew her shoulders back and went on the offensive. Her reply sizzled. "What I do is my own business, not yours."

"I guess when you start talking to our enemies, it becomes everybody's business."

Her eyes blazed. "Just shut your mouth, Carlyle."

He went on, unaffected by her anger. "Someone saw you talking to one of 'em from inside Erica's car, like you were sneaking around, or something."

The car that had passed them. Of course, someone had recognized her. Her first instinct was to varnish the truth, to soften the accusation, but a stronger influence prevailed. She would not provide no fuel for his fire. "It's none of your damn business what I do."

"Now you're getting feisty."

Her expression was one of pure anger. "You keep it up and you'll see what feisty is all about. Now why don't you just leave before I make a scene."

Carlyle shrugged. "I was curious about why you were talking to those chicken-shit POWs who've been shoved into our community. Hell, I thought you had more sense than to go pussyfooting around with murderers."

She turned on him then, ferocity burning in her eyes. "Listen, Carlyle. For your information, we didn't go there to pussyfoot with anybody. Erica and I were returning from the movie when we saw them skating on the pond. One of them came over and began talking to us. There's no harm in that."

"Returning from the movie? Hell, Elsa. You gotta go out of your way to get down to the lake from the movie house."

Her reply exploded in his face. "Why don't you just run off and leave me alone. I'm tired of looking at you."

He moved forward to within inches of her face. "What you did is called fraternizing."

"What I did is called being friendly."

"Well, I don't like it."

"Frankly, I don't give a damn if you do."

A slow burn escalated through Elsa's body. She was about to burst when Enid Rousch, who sat two seats ahead of them, turned her head to witness the altercation. Elsa scowled at her until she turned away. So, the entire school knew. She would now be branded as a sympathizer. Even so, this was no time to raise her voice. Even if the entire school did know about their escapade, she would not make a fool of herself. She calmed herself, turned back to Carlyle, and softened her reply.

"Now you said what was on your mind, so why don't you just go. I'll settle my own problems in my own way, fraternizing not being one of them."

Carlyle shifted. "I just don't want you going down by the river any more."

Elsa gasped. "What business is it of ours, or anyone's for that matter?"

He twisted his fingers into a ball. "It's my business, because I make it my business."

"What?" Her reply turned Enid Rousch's head again.

"What are you looking at?" Elsa snapped.

Again, Enid looked the other way.

Carlyle spoke softer, fidgeting with his fingers. "When I learned about you and Erica talking to those Germans, I got angry."

"It's my business. Not yours. Now stow it!"

"It's just that I don't like to see you doing wrong."

Elsa sat back and closed her eyes. His confession soothed her somewhat but the ember still smoldered inside her. Carefully, she formed her reply. "I appreciate what you're saying, Carlyle, but the fact of the matter is, I don't want you butting into my affairs. And for your information, if and when I do not talk to the POWs again, it's because I would rather talk to them than talk to you. Now you can go tell the entire class, or the entire school for that matter. I am not disloyal to my country, nor do I have any animosity toward those German prisoners who just happened to be sent here."

Carlyle shifted away from her, putting distance between them, his eyes narrowing. She could see disappointment there. A bit of anger sparked at the edges. "Okay," he said. "I get the story. I'll keep my distance, and you can go to hell. I wouldn't want to be seen with a Nazi lover anyway."

"You haven't heard a word I've said, have you?"

"I've heard enough."

Elsa nodded. "Then you go to hell." But before he could move, she offered another opinion. "You know, Carlyle, I used to look at you and think you were quite a nice guy, someone I would like to get to know. But that was before I knew you. Right now I see you as someone who's brash and conceited and prejudiced, and pitiful. And right now I'd rather be seen with a German gentleman than with someone so damned narrow-minded he can't even understand the truth. Good-bye, Carlyle."

Carlyle blinked as his jaw sagged open. A look of disbelief clouded his eyes. Then, with a huff, he stood up, and without saying another word he walked away. So, she thought, now she would have to brace herself for criticism, and, judging from the way rumors circulated, it would only be a matter of time before her parents caught wind of the episode down by the Cottonwood. It would probably be better if she told them first, rather than hide it like some guilty secret. At least she felt better now. The episode was out in the open. If there were any disrespect toward her, she would have to shoulder it. Her father had always told her: for every action there is a reaction. Well, she certainly had a reaction this time. She would tell her parents, and her family, about the incident at supper. She was sure their response would be much less fiery than Carlyle's.

D INNER THAT NIGHT WAS YAMS, FRIED POTATOES and chicken, with canned strawberries as desert, those Elsa had picked from the garden six moths before. Papa pulled out his pipe and lit up while Corina and mother cleared the table. David was drawing pictures with the stub of a pencil on a ragged sheet of paper. The sketch resembled an airplane. Elsa sat still, while trying to put together a suitable opening for the conversation about to take place. Apparently she looked nervous because Papa's eyes were on her. His gaze was tightly fixed, like it always was when he was about to say something. He took a puff of his pipe and blew a slender stream of smoke out the corner of his mouth.

"You look uneasy tonight, Elsa. You've been lookin' at your plate like it's the last dish of food you'll ever get. Now what's wrong?"

Mother and Corina took their places at the table. Both looked questioningly at Elsa. David didn't care a lick about anything. He just kept on moving his pencil, drawing airplanes.

She couldn't hold back any longer. Reason told her to come right out with it, and not to hold anything back. "Remember last Saturday when Erica and I went to the movie, well, we took a slight detour on the way back."

Papa's eyebrows rose. The pipe stem clicked between his teeth. "Go on."

"She drove the car down by the river where the POW camp is located. She wanted to see if there were any prisoners skating on the pond."

Papa's eyes traveled across the table to meet his wife's gaze head on. "And did you see any?" he asked.

"We did, four. Two were skating, and when we stopped one of them skated over toward our car. We weren't close, but a ways back, so he had to shout a little."

"And?"

"He asked if we wanted to go skating with him."

Papa let out a burst of laughter, enough to bring smiles to the faces of the others. "So your curiosity finally got the best of you. Well, dang if that ain't something."

"We didn't stay. As soon as he spoke, Erica drove away."

"And left 'em standing there?"

"Yes."

"So now you had to confess it. Why did you wait until now to tell us?"

"Because some of the kids at school were talking about it. I didn't want you to hear about it second hand."

"You could have told us on Saturday."

"I didn't think it was that important."

"Until someone else mentioned it."

"Yes."

Papa leaned back in his chair and gazed at the ceiling where he found answers to almost everything. He chewed a moment on the mouthpiece of his pipe. The room was locked in total silence. All Elsa heard was the scratching of David's pencil.

Papa's voice was low and distinct. "Well, I talked with some of them boys already, as you know, and what I got from them was nothing but politeness and a strong feeling of thankfulness for us being so kind to them. They're just kids, like most of our own soldiers are, young men caught up in a terrible thing. I expect they just wanted company. And seeing you were a pretty girl probably got their courage up."

"We didn't intend to talk to them. We just wanted to see what they were like."

Papa placed his elbows on the table, and leaned forward, pipe in hand. She knew he was about to say something important because he glanced at her mother and saw her nod.

"I think from now on you should be telling us first, unless, of course, we don't mean that much to you."

"Papa, I—"

"Let me finish. Now there's nothing wrong with talking to boys. Every warm-blooded woman in the world does that. But you have to be careful with these young Germans. You can't forget that they are enemies of our nation, at least in some people's minds, that is. We're fighting them to the death over in Europe, just like we did twenty-five years ago. It seems like they never remember what happens when they overstep their boundaries. So I have to caution you about even thinking about going to see them. No more, Elsa. You'll get a bad name, and I don't want my daughter being the talk of the town. Are you listening to what I'm saying?"

"Yes, Papa."

"I just heard on the news today that we dropped three thousand tons of bombs on Berlin, setting it ablaze. I expect those German boys might be a little riled up about that when they get the word. And I know what getting all riled up can do to a man."

No one at the table moved. Even the pencil ceased its scratching.

"Now let this be the end of it," Papa went on. "I expect we'll be seeing those prisoners from time to time, probably even in our own fields come spring. They're here to help with planting and harvesting, to take the place of our own boys, and if things go right, I might even hire a few myself. I figure if they surrendered they probably had their gut full of war, and I expect they're strong workers who'll give us a good day's labor."

The room went quiet, except for the scratching of the pencil. Elsa doubted if David had heard a word of what was said. Corina, however, had been all ears, and there was no doubt that she had digested every word Papa had spoken. Mother cleared her throat, and without a here nor there she stood up and began her work.

"Thank you, Papa," Elsa said.

"Thank you for telling us. Whatever's on your mind, this is a good place to let go of it."

Then he rapped the pipe ashes into a tray, stood up, walked to the back door, slipped into his heavy coat, tugged the bulky knit cap down over his ears, and headed for the barn.

Elsa was relieved. Papa always knew how to settle things, with soft words instead of spite, with suggestions instead of anger. She loved him for that.

FIFTEEN

Algona, Iowa, February 1945

HENRIK AND EMIL STOOD BY THE WIRE. They gazed out over the flat, endless, snow-covered prairie to where the trees grew way out beyond the road. Emil stood with his hands in the pockets of his long coat, his eyes fixed on the horizon that drew a hard line between the blue sky and the level expanse of white. His thoughts were fixed like concrete in the furrows of his forehead. He was as solemn as Henrik had ever seen him. He didn't say a word. He just looked into the distance. He hadn't uttered a word since he had asked Henrik to walk with him, and now, as Henrik turned to face him, a tear trailed down his cheek.

"Tell me about it," Henrik said quietly.

Emil sighed.

Henrik thought he saw his lips tremble. He gazed again out onto the prairie while waiting for a reply. He knew Emil would answer him when he stopped weeping.

Softly he said, "I just heard that the Americans have fire-bombed Dresden. The whole city was afire. The whole city. Everything. First Berlin, and now Dresden."

"Who told you that?"

"It came in with one of the visitors. They had the front page of a newspaper folded up inside their clothes. They showed it to Harold Albrecht. You know who he is."

"I know him."

"Hundreds of airplanes. Thousands of bombs, most of them incendiary."

"I'm sorry."

"My mother and father, and my young brother Hermann are there."

Henrik raised his arm and settled it across Emil's shoulders. "There is nothing any of us can do about it."

"I know. All I can do is pray."

Praying seemed so futile now. They had prayed before, in battle, daily, sometimes hourly, sometimes every minute, whenever explosions had ripped at their ears like the devil's yowling voice, sucking life-giving oxygen away from the sky, when their stomachs vomited up whatever food they had eaten, when the entire world was in the process of being devoured. Where was God, to allow such things to happen, to allow innocent people to be consumed by flames when they had done nothing to initiate the wrath of war?

Emil had opened his soul, and now his voice poured out, and Henrik could only listen.

"I remember the youth camps, when Hitler came to talk to us, to indoctrinate us into the Nazi philosophy. We drilled, and learned to shoot, and how to bayonet an enemy soldier, and how to throw grenades. Great fun, it was, to play at war, to run and get strong, and to learn how to hate." He swallowed, coughed, and then cleared his throat. "We were taught military strategy, and were given our precious daggers engraved with the swastika and the words, Blood and Honor, and we said *Heil, Heil, Heil Hitler*, over and over and over as if they were the only words in our vocabulary. My god, Henrik, we were just kids, dragged away from our homes by a fanatical leader whose only aim in life was to rule the world. Were we blind then?"

Henrik squeezed Emil's shoulder. "Stop now. You don't have to go through this. Forget those days."

"But I do have to say it. I feel it is partly my fault that Dresden is burning."

"We could do nothing then, but obey."

They were silent for a moment, eyes straight ahead. The light February wind breathed softly against their faces. The morning sun was warm on their necks. "We were replacements, Henrik, replacements for those men who died in the blitzkriegs. My father was drafted into the Wehrmacht to man a Sturmgeschutz assault gun in the Russian front. He is dead now, as is my brother Ernst. And now I am the only one left in my family, and here I am, a prisoner."

"We will be sent home when all this is over."

"Home to what? There is nothing left. Our whole country is burning." Emil swallowed again, wiped his mouth, looked down at his feet. "I was only ten when I joined the Jugund. We camped, and were told that Germans were the best race, and that the English were high-lipped and arrogant, the French were tongue-lovers and sissies, and that Americans were all gangsters. And the Jews . . . well. We believed what we were told. We were told, also, that we were going to die for the Fatherland, and for the Führer. At the time dying for him seemed so honorable. Back then we didn't know what dying was all about. It was a game then. You were the smart one, Henrik. You didn't listen to the loud voices, even if you weren't respected by most."

Henrik didn't say anything. He just listened. It was a good time for Emil to empty his soul.

"My sister was in the Bund Deutcher Madel when she was twelve. She spoke of Hitler as if he was a god. I do not know where Marthel is now. The last I heard she was in Berlin. Maybe she is dead now, too."

Emil lifted his hand and wiped away the last of his tears and gazed for a long time at the sky, to where the clouds piled up, coming in from the west, to bring more snow. He shifted on his feet, and Henrik removed his arm, and then the two of them just stood there. Then Emil spoke again, as if to cleanse himself.

"Marthel was such a beautiful young girl when she was eight or nine, always playing loudly, laughing, and full of surprises. After she joined the BDM she changed. She became like the rest of them, so impudent and insensitive. Everyone could see the change in her, especially my mother, who could do nothing about it."

Emil opened his mouth and took a deep breath, and when he closed it again his jaw moved as if it were driven by gears. His skin flexed, tightened and then loosened, like an animal chewing on carrion. "I was with Marthel one day. I will never forget the day. We were walking down our street, paying attention to no one. We were talking about music, Bach, I think. Then, up ahead, she saw the small boy who lived nearby. He was standing by his fence, minding his own business, back a ways from the sidewalk. We knew him to be a Jewish boy named Jacob. At the time, Marthel was in her uniform, and when we approached the boy he shrank back and was about to run into his house when she shouted at him. Jew-boy she said, stop where you are. The boy stopped but did not turn around. Jew-boy, she said, come here. The boy turned and walked slowly back to us, his head down. He stood in front of Marthel like someone who had just been whipped. Jew-pig, she said. Not Jew-boy, but Jew-pig. She called him Jew-pig. The boy started to tremble and tears came to his eyes. And then Marthel laughed, and spit on him. Go into your house, Jew-pig, she said. You don't belong on this street. The little boy turned and ran into his house, crying, and Marthel just stood there and laughed. Then she said, they are no better than animals, those Jews."

Emil hung his head then and his cheeks blubbered. Sorrowful sounds puffed from his lips. "I have never forgotten that day, Henrik. It still comes to me like a bad dream, like a nightmare, even when I am awake. What did the Jews ever do to make us hate them so? It was not like my sister to do anything like that, not before she joined the BDM."

"It is over," Henrik said.

Emil shook his head. "Not for me. I will always remember all of it, from the day Marthel shouted at the boy, to the end, the day I stood in front of the American tank and raised my arms. I thought I would be shot then, but instead they took me away and sent me here. At one time I thought fighting for the Fatherland was a grand and glorious purpose, but now I see... I see that I was fighting only for an immoral madman, to satisfy his lust for power. What have we become, Henrik?"

"We may be prisoners, but we are still Germans."

"And will we be vilified when it is over? Will the world still hate us?"

"I do not think so. We are prisoners here, but we are treated well. There is no animosity, except from some outside the fence who have lost sons in the war. Still, we work for them, and they pay us, and we eat, and learn, and go to church. We are not so bad off."

"I have heard more, Henrik."

"What?"

"I don't know if it is true, but just today, when I heard about Dresden, one of the men said that the Russians had entered a town named Auchwitz, near the western border. They found there a concentration camp filled with Jews. And in the camp were gas chambers where they killed men and women, young and old, and children, every day and every night, and then burned the bodies in cremation ovens. Thousands of them, for no reason at all except that they were Jews. It made me sick, Henrik, to think that we could have butchered innocent people."

Henrik hung his head. "We knew the Jews were being transported to camps, yet we did nothing. I cannot believe what you have just said."

"We thought they were being taken away to work, not to be slaughtered."

"Are you sure, Emil?

"Who knows what is truth and what is lies."

They fell silent again. The terrible, penetrating silence devoured all reason, stripped away all dignity, and shamed them like nothing else could. Propaganda or truth? They would not know until it was over, all over, until the last bullet had been fired.

"I am sick of it here," Emil said. "I am sick of watching the SS men strut around as if they were gods, with their chests stuck out, and their expressions so haughty and insolent. I am sick of their hatred."

Henrik took him by the arm. "Let's go now. There are things to do. Maybe we can watch a movie, or read a book, or play ping-pong. Let us get away from here."

Emil drew his arm away and looked straight at Henrik so he could see the intentness on his face, the impulsive yearning. "There are other camps," he said. "Many of them, in Minnesota and North and South Dakota, camps that were built after the American Depression for unemployed workers. They are opening them up for those of us who are not Nazis, for those who can work on farms and in factories. The authorities are sending some prisoners to these camps, the ones they can trust to work alongside the Americans. I spoke to the Lagersprecher yesterday. I asked him if there was a chance that you and I could be transferred there. He said he would look into it. Perhaps there is an opportunity for us to leave this place, so we can be with men who think like we do."

"Richard can come with us."

"Yes. Yes. He can come too. What do you think, Henrik?"

"It is worth a try. I would go."

Emil straightened his body, and sighed deeply. A brief smile crossed his face as he breathed the scent of winter in the cold wind. "Now you have heard my story. I had to tell someone. You are the only one I could trust to listen."

Henrik took him by the shoulders and shook him gently. "Now, if you want to get beaten soundly, then let us go to the ping-pong table. I am getting good at the game."

Emil grinned and threw his arms around Henrik's shoulders. "You are a good friend," he muttered.

They walked silently along the wire, toward the game room. Henrik thought about the other camps Emil had spoken about. The winter months would soon be over. In the springtime, the farmers would begin plowing and then planting. It would be enjoyable to work on a farm, like he had in Germany, when the sun was hot and the breeze had the scent of nature in its breath. Yes, he would like that.

SIXTEEN

New Ulm, Minnesota, 1945

THE WINTER DRAGGED ON, with periods of cold and snow and alternating thaws that brought hope of spring. The ice had melted on Bracken Creek for a day or two late that month, until a cold snap swept in from Colorado and froze it up again. The temperature went from forty degrees down to twenty degrees in a single day, and late in the month snow fell heavy on the farm.

It was hard work again to slop the pigs and feed the chickens and provide hay for the livestock, and do the sewing and mending and cooking and cleaning when mother came down with the flu; a week of misery, hot cider, heated blankets, plenty of Va-trol-nol, steamed air, and bowls of hot soup. Papa was at her side most of the night, but she insisted that he not sleep with her, lest he catch the misery. So he slept fully dressed in the big chair beside the bed, waiting for her call in the night, but she never called him.

Papa and Mother worried about polio. An epidemic of serious proportions was sweeping the country and people had been warned to stay out of crowds. Two of Elsa's schoolmates had caught the disease, and one had died. The medical scientists were searching frantically for a cure. The doctor came to see mother on her second day in bed. He said it was just influenza. When her fever broke on the third day, everyone was relieved. David's favorite ewe, a yearling and first-time mother, gave birth to a young lamb in the third week of April. It was a normal presentation, with no problems. He helped the little fellow out and within thirty minutes it was on its feet, seeking milk. Its mother licked it clean. He was determined to raise it to maturity in time for the state fair in the fall. He had entered the ewe the year before but received only a red ribbon for his effort. David had given up drawing airplanes. In his spare time he worked on model airplanes, first a German Messerschmitt, then a Japanese Zero. Every boy in school was building models. The government wanted a half-million of them to use for recognition purposes, for training both soldiers and civilians to identify enemy aircraft. No one thought the enemy planes would ever get close to Minnesota, although air raid drills were common.

As the snow melted, David began getting kite fever. April was near, the best month for flying. He always had a kite, ever since Papa made him his first one. He enjoyed sending it aloft and guiding it with the double-handled cord winder he had made. His kite always had a long tail, one he had fashioned from an old shirt.

Corina began collecting political cartoons from the newspaper, those from the editorial page showing Hitler as a snake, a vampire, a hog, or an ape, caricatures that made her laugh. She said she wanted to be a cartoonist some day. She, like David, had a flare for art. She glued the cartoons into a large book filled with plain paper. It was her way of keeping up with the war.

Elsa struggled at school, especially with mathematics. Despite her determination to succeed, she fell short of her expectations and was often downhearted when she brought her report card home. Papa always looked at the grades with raised eyebrows and a nod. Her mother usually made the statement: I know you tried your best. Elsa always told her mother she would try harder, and she did. She always did well at English and History, two subjects she enjoyed, and for that she was praised. She tackled typewriting with a passion and by April she was rattling off sixty words a minute with few errors. She thought then she might want to work in a newspaper some day, or for a magazine, and so she signed up for Journalism as part of her senior year curriculum.

They all took part in the scrap drives. They brought mother's fat drippings into town, saved and flattened their empty tin cans, stacked their newspapers and cardboard for the drives. Mother and Elsa tore up old sheets once a week at the town hall to be used as bandages for the troops, or so they said. Word came that another New Ulm boy had been killed in action. The news only made them work harder.

The war news that came in over WCCO and KSTP radio brought more encouragement every day. By the end of February the flag had been raised on Iwo Jima, despite staggering losses, and it seemed almost disrespectful of hard-working Americans who kept the war machine going to have a midnight curfew placed on all bars throughout the country, just when celebration was in order. Many said it was just another sacrifice to endure. The populace took it all in stride. On February 28th American forces crossed the Erft River in Germany, preceding the first broadcast of Batman and Robin on the radio.

On March 6 Cologne fell, followed two days later with the bridge crossing at Remagen. American forces were finally across the Rhine River.

Elsa bought a new recording. "Rum and Coca Cola" was on the top of the charts, and in Hollywood, Bing Crosby and Ingmar Bergman received an academy award for "Going My Way." Things in America were looking up.

Elsa was brought up with a needle and thread. She had sewn many articles of clothing over the years, a lot of them from printed flour sacks as assignments for her Home Economics class. And there were, of course, along with rips and tears and darning and mending, those every-day tasks required by hard-working people. Her mother's dream was to someday have a sewing machine, an item right near the top of Papa's provider list.

It was Saturday afternoon when Elsa sat down at the kitchen table with her mother to begin work on a costume she was making for a her part in the school play, a small role that consisted of only seventeen lines, including a quick move forward, a gasp and a startled expression, culminating with a hard shove at Kevin Basquin's back that would send him tumbling to the floor. She was crafting a stunning little jacket and skirt, made from one of Grandfather's old tweed suits that had hung in the closet for almost twelve years. She was thin. The amount of material would be adequate. The skirt didn't have to be full. She had just begun sewing when David came bolting through the room, darting headlong toward the back door.

"I just saw those gray squirrels running on top of the snow. I gotta get my .22 before they head back up the tree."

Mother raised her head. "Slow down a bit. You don't have to rush."

He pulled on his jacket, reached for his hat, and said excitedly. "Do you want squirrel for dinner tonight?"

"You shoot 'em and I'll fix 'em." Mother said.

There was no doubt that David would bring in the squirrels if they were still running. Father had already taught him the four firing positions, prone, sitting, standing and kneeling, and whenever David had a few moments to spare, more often than not he was out near the grove shooting. He was allowed twelve bullets a week, and he used them all.

David could do two things with the squirrels. He could skin them and sell the pelts for a dollar-fifty-cents each, or he could donate them to the war effort to make fur-lined hats and jackets for fighter pilots. He preferred giving them to the troops. He already had fourteen squirrels to his credit. He rushed out, boot laces flapping, his jacket half buttoned, speeding toward the barn where his rifle was kept. Mother didn't like firearms in the house, although she knew Papa always kept a loaded pistol in the bed-table drawer, just in case.

As David rushed toward the barn, Clara watched him through the window, her face garnished with an expression of pure tenderness. She loved David for the boy he was; always obedient, always polite, just like his father. It was only natural that the boy had acquired Papa's habits and personality, having worked at his side since the day he had first learned to walk.

Elsa paused. She put her needle to rest for a moment as she watched her mother's expression transform to one more commonplace. Then, as she continued her work, Elsa said. "You should have had more boys."

"Oh, You were watching me."

"Of course. David brings out the emotion in you. Wherever he goes, your eyes go with him."

Clara nodded. "I guess I'm guilty of being overly protective of him. He's so much like his father, so helpful, and obedient, and polite. He'll grow up to be a good farmer someday."

"I don't think so. He wants to be a fighter pilot."

Clara shrugged. "That's just war talk. Every boy wants to be a soldier, or a sailor, or an airman. He'll change his mind as soon as the war is over. He'll become a farmer, just like his father, you mark my words. The land is in his blood, much more than flying."

"I don't know. He's pretty much set on it."

"So was your father. The day Pearl Harbor was bombed he was ready to rush into town to sign up with all the other men who were lined up at the draft board. But then he realized he could help the war effort more by staying right here at home, providing food for the army, and for us. Besides, what would we have done without him? His initial hatred toward the Japanese ended in the spring when he planted the first seeds. He knew where he belonged, and it wasn't overseas."

"Like I said, another boy or two would have lightened his load. He and David work terribly hard."

"Maybe I would have had another if Corina's birth hadn't been so difficult. Now the doctor says it will be nearly impossible for me to have another. That birth took something out of me that I'll never get back."

"You don't blame her, do you?"

"Certainly not. Maybe it was God's way of allowing me to give all my love to those I already had. No, I would never blame her, not in a million years."

"I guess if David's a lot like Papa, then I must be a lot like you."

Clara nodded. "You certainly are. You're just like me when I was sixteen, which isn't all bad, I might add. You've got my same drive and ambition. You'll be valuable to someone when you leave this farm."

"You mean, when I go to college?"

"College or otherwise. You're not gonna stay here forever, that's for sure."

"Is it for sure that I'm going to college?"

"We're planning on it. We have money saved. Education for you, and your brother and sister, is more important that electric irons or sewing machines. You three are the most important people in our lives. Oh, you'll go to college alright, unless some handsome young dude comes along and sweeps you off your feet."

Elsa shrugged forlornly. "That's not likely to happen."

"And why not?"

"Because there isn't anyone I know of who's even the least bit interested in me. That boy, Carlyle, why he's about as unprincipled as they come. He might be good looking but he doesn't know the first thing about being nice to a girl."

"Being nice takes a certain type of fellow."

Elsa stitched for a while and then drew the thread up tight. She relaxed and looked at Clara with a wistful expression. "How did you and Papa meet?"

Clara laughed. "Well, now, I thought you knew that."

"No, I don't."

Clara shifted, as if settling in for a long talk. Her eyes traveled across the room, selecting certain objects to dwell on. Then she moistened her lips. "Well, I was just a young girl when your father came along. It was just like he dropped out of the sky. I was living in Saint Paul at the time, working at the Montgomery Ward's department store on University Avenue. I was running for the streetcar one day while trying to keep my hat from flying off, when I stumbled and fell, striking my knee on the curbing. Well, there I was, lying in the rain, my knee all scuffed up, my hat blowing away down the street. Then I felt a hand at my elbow. A voice above me said, please, let me help you, miss." Clara snickered. "Well, he helped me up, and the minute I gazed into his eyes I knew he was the man I wanted to marry."

"You just looked into his eyes?"

"That's all it took. Fortunately, he was single, just stopping to buy some overalls. He was running for his truck when I fell. I was sixteen at the time, the same age you are now."

"Just like that you knew?"

"Just like that."

"Why. How could you?

Clara placed her work on the table, realizing that a serious discussion was about to occur. "Funny," she said. "My mother once told me that a woman could tell exactly what kind of person a man was by looking at two things, first his smile, and then his eyes. She said a smile would attract me, and his eyes would offer a look into his soul. After your father picked me up, it took me only a minute to look into his eyes, and what I saw there will stay with me forever."

"What did you see?"

"The same thing I see every day in him. Kindness, generosity, respect, and, of course, love for just about everything."

Elsa sighed. "I'll probably never find someone like that. Half the boys in school are so busy with sports they hardly look at girls. The other half blush when they come close, and those in between are already going steady with the cheerleaders or the pretty ones who strut around like movie stars."

"You'll find someone. I found your father on a rainy day. He didn't even live in the city. He was living here, in this house, with his father and mother. He had stopped at Montgomery Ward's on the spur of the moment, after delivering some stock to South Saint Paul. He was twenty."

"I won't be as lucky."

"It will happen when the time is right. When you least expect it."

"Easy for you to say."

"It is easy for me to say. I lived the miracle."

"If I want a really good man I'll probably have to marry a minister, or a farmer like Papa, or a wealthy businessman."

"There's nothing wrong with a farmer. Ups and downs occur no matter whom you'll marry. You just have to find someone who'll weather the storms, and not feel sorry for himself when the storm is over, someone who can dig in and stand up again. I know for a fact that there's one minister in town who's married to the bottle, and another who can't stop romancing the women. And there are many successful men are who are married to their money, men who don't give a hoot about their wives. So, don't judge a man by what he does, judge him for who he is, for his tenacity and his will to overcome hardships."

Elsa nodded. She continued her sewing, pondering what her mother had said. It wasn't often the two of them talked about personal relationships, but on this particular day she had lifted the lid from her sheltered jar of thought.

Clara looked at Elsa with the same obvious pride she offered to David. "I know you're struggling right now, dead center of a time when a girl's got movements inside her she can't quite control."

"Oh, mama, don't get personal now. I do know something about life."

"I'm sure you do. I'm quite positive you girls don't talk about farming or the weather during those overnight pajama parties. I'm sure the topic of boys comes up more than often than not."

Elsa laughed. "Well, perhaps more than just a little."

"I know. All of us married ladies have been through the same thing at one time or another. I know you've got desires. I only hope you know how to keep them in check."

"Please, Mama, no lecturing. I'm old enough to know what happens when a boy and a girl come together."

"Find the right man before you start experimenting. It's kind of like driving. First you get behind the wheel, and then you proceed with caution."

"I know. I know. Don't worry about me. I grew up on a foundation of moral bedrock, and I intend to stay there."

"Good. Just make sure, that when you do find the man of your life, you look deeply into his eyes first."

Elsa tossed her head. "Sometimes you make me laugh. I don't know if you're a mother, a preacher, or a teacher, or all three rolled into one."

"I'm all three. A mother has to be."

They heard the crack of David's rifle, shooting back in the grove. Elsa sat back and gazed outside. The blue sky framed the barn. The silent spread of winter blanketed the ground. Their short period of dialogue was over.

Mother and daughter attended their sewing with full concentration until David came through the door, his grin broad and boastful. "I got two of 'em," he declared. "The other one made it up the tree before I could get a bead on it." He held the squirrels up by their tails. Their bodies hung down, dead eyes still open. "I'm going out to clean 'em now. Squirrel for supper."

"Don't get any blood on the floor."

"They ain't dripping, Mama. I shot 'em clean."

"When you're finished, go and help your father."

"I know. He told me the same."

David was gone as fast as he had appeared. He dashed toward the barn with the squirrels in one hand, his rifle in the other, eager to display the bounty to his father. Mother smiled again, that sweet, sensitive expression of pure pleasure. She was defined by contentment.

THE WAR WENT ON, AND PEOPLE MADE ADJUSTMENTS. Elsa became infatuated with the music of Frank Sinatra, as did every girl in America, despite the fact that he was 4-F in the draft. She bought his records and played them whenever she could. Music became her passion. She couldn't buy records fast enough.

Overseas, the lights went on again in Paris while Berlin, Hamburg, Dresden, Essen, Dusseldorf, Nuremberg and Frankfurt were reduced to rubble.

SEVENTEEN

Algona, Iowa, April 1945

NEWS OF GERMANY'S RAPID RETREAT leaked into Algona despite all efforts to keep it out. Defeat always had a demoralizing effect on the prisoners. Whenever they were assigned to work in the factory, side by side with American personnel, they were often deliberately exposed to headlines in the newspapers, which some of the prisoners could interpret. For the Americans, it was payback time for the many GIs who had lost their lives on German soil. For the POWs, it was a tragic, crystal-clear indication that Germany was on the verge of total collapse.

So it was on Easter Sunday, that first day of April 1945, when Henrik Arndt emerged from a brief but penetrating church service in which the German pastor had spoken of a courage strong enough to overcome the great sorrows of life. With Germany in ruins, the prayers were lengthy. Some of the prayers brought tears, not only to the younger men, but to those who had seen the worst of war. After the service the sun crept behind the clouds to make the day even less cheerful.

Henrik walked alone alongside the wire, with little else in his mind but the disintegration of his country. He felt forlorn, and farther apart from the Fatherland than he had ever been, as did many of the others who had bowed their heads in prayer that day. He walked slowly, his hands clasped behind his long coat. His boots scuffed through the snow, now almost melted, leaving only traces behind to dampen the ground. Grass had already greened on soil warmed by the sun. The last letter from his parents had arrived three weeks before, telling him that the Americans were poised to cross the Erft River, a short distance from their home, not in so many words, but in a way he could understand, so the censors would not cross it out with their thick, black pens. They had written: soon the horses will come from the western pastures to cross our river, ice filled or not, to head toward the higher ground. He knew the horses were the Americans, and the river the Erft. He had received no letter since, and he was worried about them. By the time he received the letters they were weeks old. He was sure the American army had passed through Bergheim by now. What had they left in their wake?

Henrik felt a yearning, not unlike the hunger for food, a craving for home, a longing for that which he could not have. The air around him was still and cool, much like it was in Germany this same time of year. He could smell spring, the dampness of wet earth, the purity of the sky that rose in front of him like a great, blue god promising deliverance from winter.

He caught the scent of food in the air, drifting through the camp from the direction of the kitchens. He thought it smelled like beef gravy. In the distance he heard the mumbled voices of others who were walking the same path he was on, going nowhere, the same paths he had walked yesterday and the hundred days before that.

Then, for a moment, sound seemed to cease, and he closed his eyes. He pretended to be in the yard behind his house, where his dog was sleeping, where the flowers were just beginning to push up from soil left moist by winter. It was all so vivid to him, so realistic that he almost gasped. But then he heard laughter coming from a barrack to his left, from two men just inside its open window, and the vision vanished like smoke in a wind.

Turning, Henrik looked out over the broad land as he had for the past four months. It had not changed, except for its color. The land made him feel small because of its immensity, stretching from horizon to horizon in every direction as if it were the entire length and breadth of the world. Strangely enough, he had taken a liking to the land for its simplicity, and for its ability to make him feel unfettered at times, for there were days, if the sunlight was just right, and if he was standing in just the right place, that the compound appeared to have no wire fences around it, and that he would be able to walk straight on to the horizon and beyond, if just given a push

Then, suddenly, for no apparent reason, he felt the need for companionship, and so he turned and headed toward his building where Emil was certain to be, unaware that on this same day American forces were landing on the shores of an island in the Pacific ocean named Okinawa, an island that was devouring lives as if it were a ravenous dragon.

When he reached the barrack he found Emil at the table, writing a letter. He did not bother him. Instead, he rested on his bed, the pillow wedged beneath his head, and read a chapter in his book until Emil was finished. Then Emil came over to him, pushed his legs aside, and sat down beside him. "Come with me," he said. "I am going to the canteen to mail my letter and buy some tobacco and cigarette papers, some shaving cream and razor blades. It is time that I shave, don't you think?"

"You remind me of a dog I once had. He was all hair and no bark."

Emil slapped his leg. "Handsome men do not always need to shave. The girls like them no matter what their appearance. Whiskers give them charm, Henrik, and charm will capture the women every time."

"You have no charm."

"No, my friend. But I am handsome, don't you think?"

"No, you are just opinionated."

Emil pulled him off the bed and they scuffled for a moment, laughing all the while like two children at play, until one of the other men told them to stop it and behave like grown men. Henrik was about to tell him to shut his mouth, but he thought better of it, and so he and Emil stood up and smoothed out their uniforms. Henrik placed his book under the pillow and they walked out together.

"I think all the snow will be gone soon," Emil commented.

"Yes. The days are getting longer."

Emil matched steps with Henrik, as if they were marching. "I have news for you," he remarked.

"What news?"

"Tomorrow morning I have a meeting with the Lagersprecher. I told him we would like to be transferred, and he said he would see what he could do for us. You are coming with me, right after our breakfast."

"Did you tell him I was coming with you?"

"Yes. He told me you were welcome."

"It is worth a try. I would like to get out of here some day."

"We might learn something tomorrow."

"I hope so. I need a change of scenery. This place is beginning to irritate me."

Emil nudged against Henrik and then pointed up ahead toward the fence, where a man stood. "There is Porter Bekins, the American guard. He walks around here just like one of us. Did you know that he has a part in the play we are rehearsing? He will play the part of a woman. You should see him in a dress, with the cotton stuffing in just the right places. He will get many laughs. Are you going to see it with me?"

"Is that an order?"

Emil laughed. "Yes, it is. I insist, or I will see that you are transferred to the kitchen for the rest of your days here."

"I will go then. I am a terrible cook."

After going to the canteen they played checkers for two hours. Henrik had acquired a liking for the game, and more often than not, he won.

That night they listened to the orchestra as they played selections from Faust, and by ten o'clock, they were ready for bed.

AFTER BREAKFAST THE NEXT MORNING THE two walked the short distance to the Lagersprecher's office at one end of a building a short distance from the canteen. They waited on a bench outside his office until he was ready to see them. Henrik was nervous. He toyed with his fingers and picked at his nails while gazing through the single window across the room. He tried to remain composed. He did not like being in an office, nor did he like the idea of talking to superiors. During his life, whenever he had talked to an officer, things had gone bad for him, so he remained silent. Then the door opened and an orderly who seemed to appear from nowhere, told them to enter. They walked inside to two waiting chairs.

The room was small, cramped with filing cabinets. A single half-shaded window was directly behind the desk chair. An American flag hung at ease on a pole alongside the window, offering a stark reminder of where they were. A photograph of President Franklin Roosevelt hung on the opposite wall, his face posed with a slight smile. A single light with a white deflector hung on a long cord above the desk. It moved slightly as they entered the room. The wooden desk was bare in the center, but bracketed by stacked files on one side, a pencil sharpener, a book, a large dish full of paper clips, pencils, an ash tray, and other extraneous items on the other. A half-filled glass of water stood within easy reach. There were no signs of German influence: no swastika, no photo of Hitler, nothing to remind them of the Fatherland.

The Lagersprecher stood as they entered, his hand extended, no salute, no hint of past military training. "I am Friedhelm," he said. "You must call me by my first name. It is what I prefer. There is no military protocol here, so sit down. Sit down."

Friedhelm was younger than Henrik had expected. His hair was a light blonde, almost white. His eyes, distinctly blue, were imbued with a hint of humor. Thin, curved brows bridged his nose. He stood canted slightly to the left, favoring his right leg. He was missing a thumb on his left hand. His uniform was spotless, neatly pressed, but lacking any decorations. He looked directly at Henrik and flashed a broad smile. The insignia on his uniform identified him as an *Oberleutnant*, a First Lieutenant.

"You must be Henrik. Emil told me you were coming with him. So get comfortable. You have questions, and I have answers. So let me begin with the answers. It might save you from asking unnecessary questions."

Henrik sat down in the wooden chair, shifted to a comfortable position, and crossed his hands in his lap. Friedhelm lowered into his own chair, reached into a desk drawer and took out some pre-rolled cigarettes. "Do you want one?" he asked.

"No. No. I do not smoke," Henrik said.

"Not for me," Emil repeated

"American tobacco is, well, better than some I have smoked. It has become a habit, and a rather soothing interruption to an otherwise hectic work day." He lit the cigarette, blew a thin reef of smoke into the air, and then cradled it lightly between his fingers. He continued. "You would think that working in an office would be an easy task, but I have three thousand men here, all wanting something. Papers. Papers. They stack up faster than a man can put them away." He puffed on the cigarette. His eyes darted between the two men, and then paused to scrutinize Henrik.

He is trying to test my reactions, Henrik thought, to see how attentive I am, to judge me quickly, and to see if I am disciplined and focused. Obviously, he had been trained to identify the hidden things within a person.

"So you want to know about the branch camps." He settled back in his chair and assumed a leisurely position. "Well, there are thirty-five of them, scattered through at least five of the states directly to the north and west of us. In Minnesota alone, in towns like Ortonville, Princeton, Bird Island, Owatonna, New Ulm and Faribault, there is a significant need for workers. Many of the companies there need laborers who have left their homes to fight the great German army." He looked keenly at Henrik to see if there was any reaction, any sign of resentment toward his statement. Seeing none, he continued. "There are twenty-one camps in Minnesota alone. There we do manual labor, often ten to twelve hours every day, two shifts, around the clock. Last year, in the north woods, we had over fourteen hundred prisoners working both summer and winter cutting wood. The only time they did not work was when the temperature dropped to forty-five degrees below zero, when the axes were too brittle to use. Do you think you could work in conditions like that?"

Henrik nodded. "If hard work in cold weather is required, yes, I would do it."

Friedhelm puffed again, and then looked around the room while searching for words. "Most everyone here is willing to work, except the proud young lions who served in North Africa with Rommel. They have been away from Germany too long, and they won't admit that the Fatherland is in ruins, and that soon Germany will fall."

Again, the long, questioning stare, searching for anything unreceptive, the tightening of an eye, the contraction of the lips, anything that might reveal a listener's true feelings.

"Sometimes these young lions swallow their pride, and they begin to work hard like most of the others. But there are still some who are dedicated to the Nazi doctrines, those who will never change. Are you one of those, Henrik?"

Henrik had not expected a question. He fumbled momentarily for words. "No, I do not have fanatical ideas. I was in the Jugend for a while, but I could not keep up with the others who were stronger and more dedicated than me. I was jeered at, and sometimes beaten, and eventually they let me go back home. I worked in an ammunition factory until it was bombed, and then I was taken into the Volkstrum and given a weapon, and was told to fight in the streets of Aachen. It was there I was taken prisoner. No. I am not a Nazi, nor have I ever been one."

"I believe you. I was also one who went through the Jugend thinking that the Führer was a god in uniform. I believed anything in those days, when I was young."

"Why do you no longer believe?"

"I was in Berlin's Opera Square when we burned the books. I watched the students strip the library of what they said was immoral literature. Among the books were works from Einstein and Keller, Thomas Mann, Jack London and Heinrich Heine. We threw them all into the fire, and then danced and cheered and sang the great hymn that had been given new words, "Deutchland Uber Allis." Propaganda Minister Goebbels was there, declaring that Jewish intellectualism was at an end, that we were moving forward into a new world. I danced with them that night. I helped throw books into the fire. It was later, in Poland, when I saw us murder innocent people, that I began doubting our ability to rule the world. It was a terrible thing, to doubt one's beliefs, and to learn, in the end, that those beliefs were wrong."

Henrik gaze met his eyes. There was not a movement in the room, not a breath taken, until Emil cleared his throat. Then, and only then, did Friedhelm speak again.

"There is a camp in a town named Howard Lake. It is an anti-Nazi camp where they harvest corn and hoe sugar beets. Have you ever worked on a farm, Henrik?"

"Yes. My parents owned a farm near the Erft River, in the North Rhine."

"Good. Good. Farm workers are needed, but not in the winter. But beginning as early as next month we will send forty men to a town in South Dakota. They will spend the first night in tents, on a farm there. Then they will transform an empty building into a barracks, install a water and sewer system, a wire fence and a guard tower to keep themselves in. What do you think of that, Henrik? They will be building their own prisoner of war compound?"

"That is very trustworthy of the people in Howard Lake, I must say. And the dedication of our men will show the Americans that we are no longer monsters, but peaceful people."

"Well said, Henrik." He drew on his cigarette, blew the smoke out the corner of his mouth, and then glanced to his left, to where the picture of Roosevelt hung. "The American President watches over us now. There he is. His eyes are on me all day long. There are some here in this camp who detest him, much the same as most

Americans detest the picture of Hitler. If they had their way they would march in here and burn him and this flag and think nothing of it. Do you know any of these men, Henrik?'

Henrik turned toward Emil, who nodded.

"I know of one."

"And what is his name?"

"I was in a field hospital with him in France, and I met him again on the ship coming here. His name is Arnold Schmidt. He was an SS Captain. He is still fanatical in his beliefs, but I do not think he would get out of hand."

Friedhelm raised one hand. "I know this man. He and I have spoken, right here in this room. He told me exactly what he believes in. He is as radical as you say, a true Nazi. But I think he can be molded to believe otherwise."

Henrik did not reply. He sat still and held his opinion in check.

"There have been deaths in this camp. We always list them as suicides, but we have our doubts. They always die secretly, in some out-of-the-way place, usually with a knife. There is never time to investigate. We think that some of these deaths, or all of them, are the work of the SS, carried out by others who are still under their power. But neither we, or the Americans, have proved anything. So, you see, another purpose of the branch camps is to separate the good from the bad."

Friedhelm crushed his half-smoked cigarette into the ashtray. His smile had warmed, more so than when Henrik had first entered the room.

"We have put our prisoners up in barns, and even in an onion warehouse. We take whatever shelter they give us. They pay us ten cents for every hour of work. The money is ours to keep, and those who are frugal enough can put it into a small account, to use after the war is over. So, you see, if you work hard, you can make a better future for yourself. The branch camps offer a good opportunity. We work the summer in low-priority jobs such as agriculture and on projects unrelated to their war effort. And, because of the Geneva Convention, we are not assigned to dangerous jobs where we could blow ourselves up. It is fair enough, don't you think?"

"Yes. Of course. It is fair.

Friedhelm placed his hands, palm down on the desk and then stood. He paced in what little room he had. "I will keep you in mind, Henrik Arndt. Emil here tells me that you are a good man, and I believe him. There might be a chance for you this spring when the farms come out from under the snow. There will be work in some of the branch camps until November, when most of the men return here to wait out the cold weather." He laughed. "Unless, of course, they are in northern Minnesota cutting wood. There are bears there, and wolves big enough to eat a man."

Henrik snickered as he prodded Emil with his elbow.

Friedhelm returned to his chair. "Well, what do you think, Henrik?

"I would like a chance to prove myself, sir."

"Then hope for the best, and come to see me from time to time. We will talk, and I will keep you updated. Right now we have selected a full compliment of men to go to the camps up north. But things can change overnight."

"I will keep in touch with you."

"Good. Then we are finished here." He reached into his desk drawer for another cigarette. "Ah, I must tell you. There is a good movie showing in Number Ten this afternoon. It is called "Companion of My Summer." Ah, and what a companion she is. You will like it."

Henrik and Emil stood. They did not salute. "Thank you for your time," Henrik said. "You have given me hope that soon I might travel elsewhere."

"We shall see. Last year we had a hundred-and-fifty men working on vegetable farms in Moorhead. I am quite sure that vegetables will grow again this year. The sun does not rest. Good day, gentlemen."

Outside, the clouds had separated. The sun was directly above them, warm on their heads. The scent of wet earth drifted with the breeze. As they walked, Emil said, "Well, what do you think, my friend?"

"I am encouraged. Perhaps we can get a place in one of the camps when spring comes."

"Can you wait another month?"

"Yes. I am a patient man. You should know that by now."

"And what if there is only one opening available when the time comes?"

"Then we will flip a coin. We must agree on that. Whoever wins will go, even if one must stay behind. Do you agree?"

Emil nodded. "Yes, I agree. I have a coin."

"Do you have it with you?"

"Yes. It is an American quarter."

"Then take it out. Let's see who the luckiest man is today."

Emil removed the quarter from his pocket. He flashed Henrik a broad smile and then flipped it. He caught it in his palm, and then slapped it onto the back of his hand. "You must call it," he said.

"It is heads," Henrik replied.

Emil removed his hand. "It is tails. I win. You must stay behind."

Henrik slapped him on the back. "It was practice. It is not yet time to make the decision. When the time is right, we will flip again. And if I lose again, I will wave good-bye to you as you get on the bus."

"Fair enough."

"And then I will hope that they will bring you up north to cut wood, and put you in a place where there are wolves, and bears big enough to eat you."

Their laughter flowed on the breeze. They felt loose and at ease. They walked slowly with the sun on their faces.

EIGHTEEN

New Ulm, Minnesota, April 12, 1945

MOMENTS BEFORE THE SCHOOL BUS stopped in front of the mailbox, Carlyle, who was seated opposite the center aisle from Elsa, raised his hands and stroked one index finger over the other as if say, shame on you. Then, in an immature burst of bad manners, he stared her and said quietly, "Nazi lover."

Elsa glared at him for a second, with fire in her eyes, but self-discipline compelled her to remain quiet despite her anger, until the bus stopped. Then, calmly and in control of her emotions, she walked to the front of the bus. Just before stepping out, she turned, and in full view of her classmates, she called out. "Carlyle." At the sound of her voice, the bus fell silent. Every eye turned her way. When she had their full attention, she shouted, back at him. "Carlyle, you are one big-mouthed, conceited, impudent, rude son-of-a-bitch." Then, as the bus erupted with laughter, she stepped out.

As the bus rolled away she shifted the two books she was carrying from one side to the other, and then began her short walk down the road leading to the farmyard. Most of the snow had melted, except where it was piled up from plowing, and beneath the trees in the grove. On each side of the road the field soil was a deep black, dark and wet from the fresh rain that had fallen just an hour before. Soon father would begin harrowing, then planting. Then would come his constant entreaty for more rain. A new season was upon them with much work to be done.

Elsa was finished with Carlyle. Although she intentionally ignored him, and kept her distance, he continued to chide her about the German prisoners, calling her a traitor and an enemy lover, payback for her refusal to go out with him. The silent war between them reached its peak one day in the school hallway when he slapped her on the back, transferring a small swastika to her sweater. She didn't discover it until third period. Angered, she dashed to the school office and told her story to the principal. Carlyle was brought in. He confessed. He was told that if he ever humiliated her again he would be expelled from school. It was the end of his childish retribution, until he made the sign of shame on the bus. All she could think of on her way to the house were the words: go to hell, Carlyle, go to hell.

As she walked through the farmyard she saw no sign of activity. The hour was late, almost five-thirty. She had remained after school for the final dress rehearsal of the school play. Her spirits were low because of the incident on the bus, but she was determined not to let it spoil the remainder of the day. She knew if she displayed any sign of anger, her mother would begin preaching about stoutness and character and one's ability to overcome obstacles. She was in no mood for motherly advice, although it was, for the most part, usually correct.

Clara was in the kitchen, preparing stew for dinner. They went through the usual banter for a few minutes: how was school, fine, how did rehearsals go, fine, hurry up now I've got things for you to do, fine, you're short on words today, yea, I guess so.

David was in the living room, perched on the couch, his ear to the radio. It was children's hour on ABC and Captain Midnight was in the midst of an ongoing adventure.

They waved at one another in passing. She was just about to climb the stairs when the radio crackled. David moaned, "Oh, shucks, not now!" The radio went silent. Elsa was on the third step when the announcement began.

"We interrupt this programming to bring you a special bulletin. Flash, Washington. President Roosevelt died suddenly this afternoon at Warm Springs, Georgia . . ."

Elsa froze. Instantly, her body went stiff with shock. She realized at once that something world shaking had happened, something that would affect everyone in the country to some degree. Stunned by the announcement, she didn't move for several seconds. Her voice locked in her throat. She was unable to speak, or to utter a sound. Then, as David leaped from his chair, she turned and descended the steps at a run. She sped toward the kitchen. "Mother. Mother. The President is dead," she shouted.

When she entered the kitchen, Clara was already frozen in a standing position. Her hands were trembling. Her face was ashen. The knife she held clattered to the table. The expression on her face was one of absolute disbelief. "Oh, my God," she muttered.

Then, propelled by a moment of absolute dread, Elsa dashed toward the back door, nearly stumbling over the dog. Flinging it open she scurried onto the porch. Her voice screamed across the farmyard. "Papa! Papa! Come quickly. Papa! Hurry!"

Elsa had never heard her mother scream so loud, not since the day Corina had fallen down the steps, breaking her arm. A moment later Papa emerged from the barn, running full out, fear of the unknown driving him forward.

"What is it?" he shouted.

"Hurry! Hurry! The President has died."

He slowed then, stunned, his run reduced to a fast walk, then to a stop.

"It is on the radio," Clara said loudly. "Come. Listen for yourself."

Papa mounted the back steps, his face contorted. He took Clara by the arms and held her tight. "Is it true?" he asked.

"Yes. Come. The children are in the living room. It is on the news."

They gathered around the radio, some seated, some standing, Mother with her fingers curled tight against her lips, Papa with his hands hooked into the sides of his overalls. Corina and David listened intently on the couch while not fully understanding the scope of the message. The announcer's voice was firm, stable, and unemotional. Yes, the President had died. Their eyes shifted to one another. A tear trailed down Mother's cheek. David sat silently, his mouth open. He glanced now and then at his father, whose teeth were tightly clenched.

"I am afraid," Corina said, her eyes squinting.

"There is no need to be afraid," Papa replied.

"But, the war. What will happen now?"

"There are others who will take over. The war will go on, uninterrupted. Men like Eisenhower, Patton and Marshall will continue the fight. We will all cry a bit and then get back to work, just as we always have."

"You make it sound so easy," Mother said.

"It's easy enough. We'll bury him, and Truman will run the country, even though he's a man we don't know much about."

The news kept coming, detailing, and within five minutes the initial shock had ebbed and Papa took a place alongside Corina. Immediately, she sought the comfort of his arms.

Clara wiped the last of her tears away. "Is Truman ready for the job?" she asked.

"He'll be ready. It'll be like cleaning up after a tornado. First comes the fear, and then the storm, and then the ones who survive take over. Things might even get better."

"How can they?"

"They will. Truman is only one man with a difficult job, but he'll have help. Others will rise to the occasion."

"But Roosevelt was almost like a god to us."

Papa nodded. "Almost. I say he worked himself to death. Three terms, plus. No other man has had such a tough job, for such a long time. He is a hero."

David spoke up. "But you said sometimes that he wasn't a good President."

Papa appeared sullen for a moment. Then he pulled David tight against his body. "Everyone has their faults, but he made a way for folks to follow. When you're older, and you get to working for a living in the city, you'll be glad old Franklin came along. It was his New Deal that put this country on a forty-hour work week, and paid us a forty-cent-an-hour minimum wage, and no labor for kids under sixteen. I may have spoken against him from time to time, but he was a visionary, a good man"

"I ain't working in the city. I'm gonna be a farmer, just like you."

"I know that. I was just makin' a point."

Elsa couldn't remember when she'd been so interested in the news. Perhaps when Amelia Earhart disappeared over the Pacific, or that horrendous day when Pearl Harbor was bombed. Oh, she kept up with the war, as did everyone else in school, but this was something of gigantic proportions, something that might ultimately change the world.

"Papa," she asked. "What's Truman like?"

"I don't know. He's a little fella, with a sharp mouth. He's smart, they say, someone who'll stand up to anyone like a bantam rooster. I think he's going to be okay. He's got the guts to lead."

"You always made cracks about Roosevelt."

"Yea, I guess I did. Many others did too. Every President, no matter who he is, has got folks cussin' him, and praisin' him at the same time. It'll be the same with Truman. Once he's up on the pedestal, he'll be fair game. Everyone'll take a shot at him."

"You put it so crudely."

"Well, that's the way it is. It's the natural flow of things."

"Now you sound like my schoolteacher."

Papa shrugged. "Well, honey. Life is a school. The sun will come up tomorrow, the same as it did today. Things will happen that we can control, and things will happen that we can't control. All we can do then is toughen up and see it through. Right now, it's time to get back to work. Old Harry Truman isn't gonna do our work for us."

Papa glanced down at David. "You can stay and listen if you want."

The boy scrambled to his feet. "Naw, I'm comin' with you."

Papa lifted Clara from the couch and pulled her into his arms. He gave her a quick kiss on the cheek. "Now this isn't gonna change anything around here. We go on just like we always have, and we pay our respects to him on Sunday, and pray for the right leadership to come along. God knows, Roosevelt was a father to us all, but by tomorrow the shock will have worn off and the five of us will go right on surviving. Have you all got that?"

The response was almost in unison. "Yes, Papa."

"Then let's scramble. I'll be hungry soon, and so will the rest of you." Then he looked directly at Elsa and smiled. "I guess those German boys down by the Cottonwood will be celebratin' for a day or two."

Elsa frowned. "Do you really think so?"

He hugged her tight in his big arms. "Can't say for sure. What it might mean to them is that the war will go on a little longer, and lengthen the time it'll take to get 'em back home. I think maybe they'll meet the news both ways. Now go help your mother."

Papa and David went to the barn. The girls followed Clara into the kitchen.

Later that day, when the sun was almost down, the western sky glowed red as if to bleed for the dead president.

The mood in the house was somber, and there wasn't much conversation at the table that night.

NINETEEN

Algona, Iowa, April12, 1945

THE PRISONERS AT ALGONA SENSED something was wrong when the guards started running. Up in the towers the searchlights went on early, just as the sun glared like a huge red eye on the rim of the horizon. They milled about and questioned one another, but no one had an answer to the sudden commotion. Then, just after six o'clock Porter Bekins made his way slowly through the compound, his eyes heavy, his movement slow. He talked to questioning prisoners who had just finished their meal, then sent them back to their barracks. Eventually he came to Barrack 27, where Henrik was billeted. He stepped inside and stood by the door. He appeared intense, with something important to say. The prisoners grouped around him. He had a way of scanning men that demanded their immediate attention. His voice was firm. He spoke in German.

"Our president, Franklin Roosevelt, died today."

The room hushed to total silence. Men looked at one another in a calm manner. Some gasped. Others smiled meekly. One nodded as if Roosevelt's death had been foretold.

Porter continued. "Now things aren't going to change much around here. We still have rules that have to be followed, and there'll be no demonstrations of any kind. If any of you want to toot your horn you might find some of your privileges taken away for a while. All services will remain in effect, but for a day or two things might slow down a bit."

"What killed him?" someone asked.

"A cerebral hemorrhage."

Another man near the rear said, "Accept out condolences, Mr. Bekins."

"Thank you," he said. "Now you men just go about your business. Lights will go out at the usual time. Tomorrow when you get up, things will be the same as they were today. We'll have a new man in charge. His name is Harry Truman. He'll continue on with the work of the country."

They all knew what he meant. The war would go on tomorrow the same as it had today. Bombs would continue to drop on Berlin. Germans would continue to die.

As Porter Bekins left the barrack, the men began milling around, discussing the obvious, voices low, expressions mixed.

Henrik pulled Emil aside for a moment and looked at him straight on "I hope this will not change things regarding the branch camps," he stated.

"I don't think it will."

"I hope not. I don't want to lose our chance."

"Nothing will change It will only slow down for a day or two."

Henrik nodded, and then whispered. "Soon Hitler will die as well. If he is in Berlin they will find him, and then they will try him, and when he is found guilty of crimes to humanity, they will hang him, and the whole world will watch him die."

"Shhh. Do not even think about that. Someone might hear you."

"Let them hear. I do not care any more."

"No. You must be quiet about this. Trust me, I know."

"For you I will be quiet."

"Good. Then let's get out of here before everyone begins expressing their opinions. You know, as well as I, that some here still hate the Americans."

They walked outside into the deep twilight to where the scanning searchlights roamed across the compound. A chill had worked its way into the camp, and above them clouds began sealing off the early stars.

"It was good of them to tell us," Henrik said quietly.

"Yes."

"So, I wonder how the people in Germany will react."

They walked on, slowly, hands in their coat pockets, their faces cool with the night breeze. Silently, they wondered what would happen next. For them, the world was a small place surrounded by wire, where thought bred more thought, and where they found refuge in memories.

TWENTY

Algona, Iowa, May 2, 1945

FRIEDHELM, THE CAMP LAGERSPRECHER, was summoned to the provost marshall's office just as he as he was about to begin his morning work. He was reaching for a hot cup of coffee when the door opened and a guard appeared.

"Yes, what is it?" he asked.

The orderly responded curtly. "I have been ordered to accompany you to the Provost Marshall, sir."

"Of course." He knew by experience that any question he asked would remain unanswered, so he lit the cigarette, and then hesitated briefly while a half dozen scenarios ran through his brain. Then he grinned, and walked through the door, following the orderly. They said nothing as they crossed the compound. They exited through two large gates, and approached the provost marshall's office, a shuttered building just beyond the fence. This has to be something important, Friedhelm thought; otherwise they would not have summoned me. Certainly, it is about the war. If it were about camp personnel they would have come to him. No, this was something of a serious nature. He flipped his cigarette away. Before entering, he squared his shoulders, and primed himself for the worst.

The Provost Marshall, whose name was Wallace, greeted him with his hand extended. His brow held furrows that were seldom evident. "Thank you for coming over."

He motioned to a chair. "Please be seated, this will take only a few minutes."

Two other men were in the room, a captain, and a lieutenant. Both stood near the wall on one side of the room in front of a small blackboard, their arms tight to their sides. The provost marshall introduced them briefly. They nodded, as did he. No handshakes. Then he sat down. Wallace took his place behind a desk, stroked his mustache briefly, and then cleared his throat. His fingers tapped on a white sheet of paper, a communiqué of sorts, a brief typewritten note not more than eight lines in length. Sighing, he glanced briefly at the officers. He was direct.

"We learned two days ago that Benito Mussolini was captured by resistance fighters, then executed, and hung from a lamp post in Italy. Did news of this reach anyone in the compound?"

"No, it did not."

"I guess we were perhaps some of the last people in the world to learn of this."

"It does not matter."

"No, I guess it doesn't. But there is something else I must tell you, something of more importance to this facility."

Friedhelm's brows raised. "Go on."

Wallace picked up the piece of paper and handed it across the desk as he spoke. "We just received word that Adolph Hitler has committed suicide in his underground bunker in Berlin."

Friedhelm glanced at the paper in his hands. He was silent for a moment. His back quivered. However, the news of Hitler's death did not surprise him. He knew the Führer would never have allowed himself be taken prisoner. Rather, he would have chosen the coward's way out. His capture would have subjected him to the scorn of the world. Just as he thought of the ramifications the news would create inside the camp, he heard Wallace speak.

"What does this mean to you?"

Friedhelm looked up, his eyes locked. He tried to appear unaffected by the news. "It does not surprise me. This was inevitable."

Wallace leaned back in his chair. "So, how do you think this will affect the prisoners?"

Friedhelm was direct. "In two ways. Some will perhaps be silently thankful that he is dead. Now the war will end, and they will be sent home. Others, well, they will be furious. You know, as well as I, that there are loyalists in the camp who still believe they are citizens of a master race. Some will shout, others will cry. Some may, well, want to join him."

"Suicides?"

"It is possible. The man they revered is gone. The land they love is wasted. They have nothing left."

"What will you do?"

"I would like one copy of this communiqué for each of my barracks. I will select enough men so they are posted all at the same time. I will instruct each of the barrack leaders to come immediately to the church where there is enough room to seat them all, and then I will ask each of them how the posting was received, and tell them what must be done to assure order."

"And how will you assure order?"

"The same as always. The men are obedient to orders. We are all soldiers who know how to follow commands."

Wallace sighed, then leaned back and rubbed his face. "We will have troops stationed just outside the compound in case you need help."

"I will not need troops. Keep them out of sight. They will only worsen the situation. We can handle this ourselves."

"Yes. Yes. I fully understand. You have a direct line to us. Use it if you must."

"I know what I have to do."

Wallace breathed deeply. "You are a good man, Friedhelm. I wish all the prisoners were like you. Perhaps soon we can put this war behind us and seek a new friendship with Germany."

"It is possible. I will look forward to extending that new relationship."

Wallace stood up and scanned Friedhelm's uniform, knowing that soon it would become an item for a trunk smelling of mothballs and age, hopefully to be stored there forever, or at least until some other dictator found reason enough to start another war. "You have work to do, my friend, so I will leave you to it. You know what to do."

"Yes."

"Sorry to have been the bearer of bad news."

Friedhelm stood straight as a rod. "It is not bad news. For most of us it is deliverance. We will restore Germany to its former splendor, and make the world proud of us once again."

Wallace took his hand and shook it. "Then begin here," he said.

Friedhelm smiled. "If Hitler taught us anything, it was determination. When we put our minds to something we always succeed . . . except when it comes to war."

The three Americans laughed as Friedhelm left the room. Outside, he paused to look at the camp, seemingly endless in scope, its guard towers menacing, its fence blazing in the new morning sun. So now the work begins, he told himself, now the mending starts.

Shouldering his responsibility, he walked alone toward the double gate

---

THE NEWS OF HITLER'S SUICIDE WAS POSTED inside Henrik's barrack about ten in the morning, and as the men gathered around it, several things happened. One man screamed, threw his clenched fists into the air, and tore through the crowd like a madman. He charged to the end of the room where he slammed his hands repeatedly against the wall. Several others went quietly to their beds and laid face down. Another cried openly. Most were stunned. It took them a while to speak their minds.

The first words out were, "Now we can go home."

"He is better off dead."

"It was a coward's ending. At last there is retribution."

"It would have been terrible for him, had he been captured."

The man at the end of the room began throwing things, pillows, mattresses, books, anything he could get his hands on. He lifted up one of the footlockers and flung it through the window, screaming, "No! No! No!" He was out of his head. Several of the other men charged him and pinned him to the floor. His thrashing did not cease. He fought like a madman.

"Get some rope," one of them shouted. "We must tie him up."

The man, whose name was Hans, kicked one of the men holding him in the face. Blood began flowing. Others rushed to the scene. They locked his legs and arms to the floor while another tore a bath towel into strips long enough to tie the man.

"Death to the Americans!" Hans shouted. "I am sick of them. They have killed my Führer." His cries were muffled, his hands tied. They pulled him to his feet, tied his ankles together and lashed him to a bed. Someone rushed outside to get the guards.

Henrik pulled Emil over to a window. "What do you think of this, my friend?"

"For some it is the end of the world."

"For us?"

Emil whispered. "Nothing will change. We will go on as before. In a day or two we will forget what has happened here. We will go to work, and dream about repatriation. This is a good day, Henrik."

Henrik looked around to see if any of the other men were standing close to them. "Do not let the others hear you," he said.

"Some are taking the news badly. Most do not care."

"Hans has gone mad."

"They will take him away. We will probably never see him again."

"What about the other fanatics?"

"I think they will be silent for the most part."

"I hope so."

"Look," Emil said, taking hold of Henrik's arm. "You have always asked me for advice. Now I will give you some more. Be silent. Do not display your true feelings about this. Hitler is dead, and we are alive. We must keep it that way. There are still those who will cut our throats if we speak against him. They will call us traitors to soothe their own tangled minds. So be careful, Henrik. I know you can be outspoken at times."

Henrik smiled. "Don't we have freedom of speech here in America?"

"That privilege is for Americans, not for captured Germans."

"Then someday I will become an American."

"We will not have a choice. We will all be sent back home. Your chance of becoming an American is as slim as Germany winning the war."

Henrik punched him gently on the arm "You always have wisdom for me."

"I am older than you."

"Only two years older, yet you have become like my father."

They laughed as some of the others dragged the madman, Hans, outside and turned him over to the guards.

Before the day was over, three would commit suicide by slashing their wrists. Two would bleed to death outside, the third in his bed.

The sun went down that day on a silent camp.

Henrik wrote a letter home that night, on the same day Berlin fell, on the same day the German army in Italy laid down their arms.

TWENTY-ONE

New Ulm, Minnesota, May 2, 1945

IN NEW ULM THE PEOPLE CELEBRATED silently. Germany was finally free of its dictator, and things would be better now. The war would end soon, and their boys would come home. The old country would shudder in its demise, but it would be reborn again as time healed its wounds.

The end was near. In America the citizens could feel it in the air, and in their hearts. On the Sommer farm, as the black soil was turned to accept new seeds, the family prayed for peace.

New Ulm, Minnesota, May 7, 1945

ON MAY 7, AT 02:41 IN THE MORNING, at the Supreme Allied Headquarters in Reims, France, General Alfred Jodl signed the unconditional surrender documents under the watchful eye of General Dwight Eisenhower, declaring that all forces under German control would cease active operations at 2301 hours, CET. On the following day a similar ceremony occurred in a German Army Engineering School in the Berlin district of Karlshorst under the critical eye of Soviet Marshal Georgi Zhukov.

The war in Europe was over.

President Harry Truman was on the radio at nine o'clock that Thursday morning, at the same time Clara Sommer was cleaning up the breakfast dishes. In the next room, the coo-coo clock chimed the hour. At the moment she heard the President's voice she ceased working, knowing that the message he was about to relay could go either way, good or bad. She stood riveted to his words, listening to his opening statement, "The Allied armies, through sacrifice and devotion . . ." She didn't remember hearing the rest of his message. Moments later she flung her apron aside and danced wildly around the table, screaming as loud as she could. She dashed outside, her arms waving exuberantly. As a shout poured from her throat, she rushed down the steps toward the barn, with the dog at her heels. The children were in school. She was alone with Harold who was somewhere out near the machine shed. "Papa!" she shouted wildly.

"Papa! The war in Europe is over. It's over."

Harold came out of the shed the moment he heard her shouts. He was wiping his hands on a rag when she flung herself into his arms. Her voice was wild and out of control. "Over! It's over. Oh, God, hold me. It's over."

Harold drew her close enough to almost squeeze the breath out of her. The excitement of the moment moved unchecked through his body. He laughed and cried at the same time and whirled her about in a circle, their cheeks pressed together. She cried. He laughed. He put her down and stood still and looked into her eyes. He saw tears of joy. "God bless America," he said, his voice quivering. "It is half over, half over."

The war in the Pacific still raged on, but the good news from Europe was almost overwhelming.

Clara wiped her tears away. Her voice danced on waves of delight. "The children will be home early. They'll let the schools out," Her breath came rapidly. Her eyes were afire with an ardor he had seen only a few times before, on those rare moments when she was overly aroused.

"Yes, I suppose so," he said. "They'll be as excited as we are. And the town will explode in celebration."

Her eyes blazed. "I'm so energized I can't stand still. Come with me. Now! To the bedroom. Harold. I need you. God I need you now." Her eyes were wild, intense. Her body moved as if it were fluid. Passion uncontrolled.

"My hands are greasy."

"Wipe them on the way. They'll not be greasy in bed. Come. Now, before the children arrive."

She grasped his hand and pulled him across the yard, up the steps of the porch, then inside, through the kitchen, up the second floor stairs and into the bedroom. There, in the heat of the moment, and with their hearts churning, they stripped off their clothes. Clara fell into bed, her heart racing, her breath as hot as a cinder.

"Hurry! Hurry!" she breathed. She reached out with trembling fingers, pulled him onto the bed, and opened her legs.

He entered her as her eyes went wild. Her movements were frantic, almost uncontrollable.

As he lunged into her, she laughed huskily, "If it's a boy, I'll name him Victory."

THE SECOND PERIOD HAD JUST BEGUN. Elsa was at her desk studying when the teacher was called out of the room. After she had left, there were a few moments of mayhem. Spitballs were launched. Laughter erupted in the back row where Carlyle sat. Someone yelled, "Hey, let's have a party." The students began milling around from desk to desk, talking, clowning.

Erica, who sat up front, worked her way down the aisle and leaned over Elsa's desk. "What's going on?" she asked.

"Don't know. Something good, I hope."

"Maybe the war's over."

"Gosh, I hope so. Hitler's been dead for over a week. Oh, by the way, I got a letter from Kenny yesterday."

"Where is he?"

"He couldn't say. But he's fine. He wants me to say hi to everybody. He misses us all. He didn't say anything sweet to me, just ordinary things. He's overseas now, in the Pacific."

"Tell him hi from me the next time you write."

"I will."

Just then the door opened and the teacher walked in. The kids scrambled to their desks. Silence returned instantly. She went to her chair but did not sit down. She stood silently with her hands crossed in front of her. It was quite unlike Miss Hecht to hesitate, but she did, as if words were hard to come by. Then she smiled and said, "All students will be dismissed early today. The buses will arrive within a half hour to take you home. The President has just announced on the radio that the German army has surrendered to General Eisenhower. The war in Europe is over."

After a second of silence thick enough to cut, someone tossed a bunch of papers into the air. As they fluttered down, the room exploded in cheers. The students jumped up and down, pounding their feet on the floor. Shouts rang out. Some of the students immediately burst into the hallway. Boys grasped the nearest girls and hugged them. Elsa joined in, shouting, and screaming as she worked her way forward to Erica. "You were right," she shouted. "The war is over. Ahooooo!"

The kids poured into the hallway where they met the other classes. Before Elsa got to the door, Carlyle tugged her arm. "Now your German boyfriends can pack up and go back where they belong. Happy days are here again."

Elsa ignored the slur. She crowded into the hallway with the others, with Erica at her side.

Erica was trembling. "Hey, I want to go into town tonight. There's going to be a big party. Come with me. I'll pick you up at about four o'clock. How about it?"

"I think I'll be able to go."

"It's a once-in-a-lifetime experience. How often do we get to celebrate the end of a war? Your mother will understand."

Elsa nodded. "Four o'clock. Yes, I'll go."

The hallway was jammed with students, pushing, hugging, shouting, and crying. Elsa joined in. She was kissed twice before leaving the school.

The ride home was just as exhilarating, hugging, kissing, shouting; a total release of energy and emotion and hope for a future without war.

When she arrived at the house, David and Corina were already there. Papa joined them later. They sat at the kitchen table and talked for a while, and then Papa left to attend his work. Elsa was given permission to go into New Ulm later that day. The favor was not extended to Corina. She was too young to carouse, and Clara thought Elsa was trustworthy enough not to get drunk in the streets.

Erica was a bit late picking Elsa up. When Elsa got into the car she saw that Erica was all gussied up in a skirt and a sweater that emphasized her breasts, her hair done up, and lipstick on. Elsa felt a bit inadequate alongside her.

"Don't you look keen," Elsa said.

"It's party night."

Elsa caught the faint scent of whiskey. "Have you been drinking?"

"I've got a bottle in my purse. Only a pint, but at it's enough to get us going."

"Where did you get that?"

"From my brother."

As the car turned and headed for the road, Elsa remarked. "Well, I'm not drinking."

"Why not?"

"Because my mother insisted."

Erica waved the comment off as if it were unimportant. "You're too old fashioned. C'mon. Whoop it up a little. Break loose."

"No."

"Well, don't think that I'm going to just sit back and be sober. This is a night to swing. How often do we win a damn war?"

"You go ahead and swing. I won't hold you back. Just don't end up in bed with a stranger."

Erica blushed slightly. "It wouldn't be so bad if I did. God…wouldn't that be just too much."

Because of the cars pouring into town, they had to park about four blocks off Broadway, down by Mueller Park. It appeared as if the entire population of Brown

County was there. Even as they walked into toward the main street they heard the revelry. It was enough to make Erica quicken her steps. "If I lose you in the crowd, I'll meet you in front of Eibner's at ten o'clock.

Elsa didn't like the sound of it. "Are you meeting someone else?"

"I might. Who knows who'll come to town tonight."

"But you came with me."

"And I'll go home with you, too. But if you don't want to shake a little dust off your ideals, then I'll be off on my own. My God, Elsa, this is an once-in-a-lifetime event. Take advantage of it."

Elsa wasn't about to stand there and argue. She waved Erica on. "I'll see you at ten. Have a good time." As Erica waved good-bye, Elsa added. "Don't get too drunk. You're driving."

As Elsa approached Broadway she moved forward with the many others headed in the same direction. Then, with a wave and a wink, Erica broke off to go her own way. There weren't as many people in town as Elsa imagined there would be. Small groups of people were assembled here and there, waving American flags, their voices blaring. Some had noisemakers. Others had beer bottles in their hands. Shouts of joy gusted through the air like notes from a base horn, melodies from a flute. The people that walked ahead of her were of all ages, scarf-wrapped, gray, black, brown, blonde or white-haired.

Across the street, a red, white and blue banner tilted and jerked on its poles, raised high by revelers. The banner moved slowly down Broadway toward the Glockenspiel–the clock in the town square–and soon it was lost from sight. The people milled aimlessly, back and forth, going nowhere, crossing and re-crossing the streets, hugging one another at random.

Embraces and kisses flowed freely. More than a few were drinking. Elsa walked along the street, pressing past the people. Smiles and laughter. The younger ones were shouting, whooping it up. She dodged her way along the sidewalk while muttering apologies, getting hugs in return, and occasional kisses from men eager enough to embrace a stranger. The faces slid past her, a blur of young and old, men and women, boys and girls only in their teens, whiskered men in overalls, store clerks, youngsters, those work-lined and toughened. All were rapt and joyous in their unabashed freedom.

Making her way through the crowd, Elsa leaned against a lamppost. She was warm, both inside and out. Her head was full of noise. The sounds got louder, without letup. The shuffle of feet and the blaring noise were discomforting and rasping, and discordant at the same time. The celebration was milder than she had expected, subdued in a way, a small town expression of victory, more thankful than riotous.

A blonde woman with bare arms appeared in front of her. She was carrying a bottle of beer in her hand. She raised it, hollered something about freedom, then leaned forward and grasped Elsa with both arms. "My boy is coming home," she yelled. "My boy is coming home." Elsa danced with her, around and around, before the woman was pulled away to dance with someone else. Then another man about the age of forty came by. He swept her up and kissed her hard on the cheek, his eyes ablaze, his voice hoarse from shouting. "You are beautiful," he said. His breath smelled of whiskey. Then he went on, looking for another mouth to kiss.

Elsa stood alone in a doorway for a while, watching, listening. Then she heard band music playing. Or was it a recording? She didn't know. The song intensified, urgent and heart-pulsing, and everyone began singing the words—"Oh, say can you see, by the dawn's early light. How proudly we hailed, at the twilight's last gleaming". She stepped back into the store entrance as the song reverberated down the street. The melody struck a chord inside her. She felt a sudden weak panic, a climax in her soul. The bleating words lifted her in hard-voiced harmony and she sang out until her voice weakened.

A serviceman passed her, his face smeared with lipstick, his eyes impassioned, his smile curved to its maximum. He paused beside her, then leaned over and kissed her. Surprisingly, she went into his arms. When he backed away and looked longingly at her, she saw hope in his eyes.

"Do I know you?" he asked.

"I don't think so," she said. "My name is Elsa."

"Elsa. Yes, Elsa."

He held her hand tightly. "Are you alone?" he asked.

"For the moment. I am meeting my girlfriend later."

"Come with me," he pleaded. "I know a place where we can go."

His face was aglow with whiskey. She could smell it on his breath, could feel it in the press of his hand. His eyes pleaded silently, drawing her like a magnet.

"No," she said, pulling her hand away. "I cannot."

"Why."

"I just can't."

"For only an hour."

She backed away from him, then turned and rushed down the street with a crowd of people. When she looked back, the serviceman was already talking to another girl. Then another woman grabbed his arm and whisked him away. He fell easily into her embrace; a comforting expression of freedom.

The celebration was so much like a dream, surreal, illusory, unlike anything she had ever imagined, or witnessed, or lived. As the celebration went on she met several of her schoolmates. They stayed together for two hours, walking the streets until the crowd decreased, and soon the town appeared as normal as usual.

She couldn't find Erica anywhere, and so she walked to Eibner's and sat at the counter and drank a coke. Some of her classmates came in, shouting loudly. They hugged her. Together they sang victory songs in the booth. She joined them for a while. At nine-thirty, Erica came in, her face flushed, her hair awry. She did not tell Elsa where she had been.

By ten o'clock the celebration had diminished. Most of the people had gone home. New Ulm appeared near normal again. The grand and glorious celebration that was to have been a monstrous party, had been nothing more than a squeak when compared with the night-long rapture in both Minneapolis and Saint Paul.

Victory, for most of the New Ulm citizens, had been celebrated in church.

THE MEXICANS HAD LEFT THE POW CAMP a month before the first snow fell in mid November of 1944. Only a small group of fifteen Germans remained, enough to fill the needs of the factory to which they were assigned.

On the night of the surrender, several of them wandered away from their barracks to sit on the bank of the Cottonwood, within sight of Schell's Brewery. The sun had just settled down behind the trees. The lights had gone on in the City of Charm and Tradition, as the residents called it, a city that was as reserved and idyllic as its namesake in Germany. New Ulm had withstood Indian attacks, a grasshopper infestation that had nearly starved its people out, and a tornado that had all but wiped it off the map. But on this night it was alive with music and shouting. A party was being held in its streets.

One of the prisoners who sat on the riverbank that night could not help hearing the sound. It came through the silence with a tone muted only by distance, but clear enough to be interpreted.

The German leaned forward and grasped his knees. "Do you hear that?" he asked, emphasizing the obvious. "I have not heard a sound like that for a long time. They are celebrating in the city,"

"It must be something big, for them to make a noise like that."

A young man who had lived near Munich before the war, nodded. "I think the war is over," he said without displaying any emotion.

"Our war?"

"Yes. I think Germany has surrendered."

Neither of the men spoke for a while. They sat and stared and listened and absorbed the far-off gaiety, a sound they had almost forgotten amid the thunder of war. Then they heard an unmistakable melody resonating above the dark hooded trees.

"It is their national anthem," one of them said.

"Ya. Then what you said must be true."

"If the war is over, then we are at peace." The one who spoke puffed on his cigarette and flicked the ash away. Then he moistened his lips and gazed longingly into the sky, over his right shoulder, in the direction of his homeland.

Silence again, a forging of thought, back to a time when contentment was not a thing of memory. Then one of them said. "I have not been at peace since I was a little boy. What do I know about peace?"

"It is something I have dreamed about lately."

"I, too. But then I also dreamed about peace in Sicily on the day I thought I would die, during the bombardment. I was sure I was in Hell that day."

The reply was wistful. "Maybe we can go home now."

"Whatever home may be. If there is a home left."

"We will build a new home, Fritz."

"And live to be old men."

"Ya. And smoke our pipes and love our woman for all time, and make children who can live and laugh and make children of their own."

One of the other men slapped him on the back as the music in New Ulm drifted away on the wind. "It is a good dream. Perhaps some day we will forget what happened to our youth." Another yawned and stretched his arms and lay down on his back, his eyes open to stars that were just beginning to appear in the night sky.

"I think I will sleep here tonight," he said. "And listen to the sound of freedom."

TWENTY-TWO

Algona, Iowa, May 1945

THE GRAY-COLORED BUS WITH THE LARGE POW painted on its side, was only partially filled. Twelve men, attired in their work clothes, caps and jackets, were on their way to a farm south of Algona where they would lay a new roof atop an old shed. As they pulled away from the compound the blinding, white sun lanced straight into their eyes. Clear skies and warm winds were a welcome relief from the preceding two days of rain. It was the second week in May, a week after Germany's surrender, and the moods of the men in the bus were mixed.

The work force consisted of nine men from Henrik's barrack and three from another, Arnold Schmidt among them. Schmidt had refused several work details following Hitler's death, but after five days on bread and water, his self-imposed sacrifice for the death of his Führer had ended. He had chosen to replace his stubborn loyalty in favor of a less punishing detail. The three SS officers wouldn't ordinarily have been assigned to this particular work force, but Lagersprecher Friedhelm was down with the flu, and his assistant had made the decision simply because it had been convenient to do so.

The three SS sat in the front of the bus, just behind the driver. As always, they retained their aloofness and their rigid demeanor. In true form, Schmidt sucked on a cigarette that he held firmly between his thumb and middle finger. The captain was still embittered by Hitler's self-imposed death, a mood that was clearly defined by his haughty, rigid posture, and in the hard-set furrow of his lips. He was humiliated in wearing the work shirt stenciled with a large PW on its back. Most everyone expected that he would be the one shouting orders on top of the roof, to those who would be doing the bulk of the labor. A guard from the compound, armed with a shotgun, sat in the rear of the bus.

Henrik and Emil had taken a seat in the center of the bus, in company with several other men. Henrik was still tired from a fitful night's sleep, and so he sat upright in his seat, his head bent forward, his hands in his lap, his eyes closed. Lolled by the motion of the vehicle, he drifted into a half sleep and remained that way through the five-mile ride, up to the time they pulled into the farm yard. When he opened his eyes he saw the farmer waiting for them, his hand clipped into the sides of his bib overalls, his face tense. A woman stood close to him. A young child with a thumb in its mouth seemed attached to her side

The men filed out of the bus and stood in a tight group just beyond the door while the driver went to receive instructions from the farmer. The farmer pointed to a shed adjacent to some pigpens. Henrik could smell the pigs from where he stood. The shed's roof was bare, having been stripped of its shingles. Only two lengths of tarpaper ran the length of it. The rest of the materials were stacked at the shed's base. Evidently, the farmer had more important things to do than shingle a roof.

The guard stood to the side of the bus where the prisoners had gathered. When the driver returned, he told them to assemble and then stood leisurely, cradling the shotgun in the crook of his arm. His face was expressionless, his patience endless.

The farmer came over and stood casually at the driver's side. The farmer was a short man, very stout, with a clean-shaven face, hair as black as field dirt. A ragged scar, recently formed, trailed down from the corner of his mouth to his chin. His eyes were hard and piercing, his hands tough-skinned and calloused. He scanned the prisoners with obvious disdain. He spoke as the driver translated.

"Mister Lasken, here, says he had a group from the compound yesterday who weren't worth dust. He sent 'em all back early and asked for a new bunch today. He hopes you'll do a better job than the others."

Most of the prisoners nodded.

"The materials are just inside the shed, tarpaper and shingles, plenty of nails and hammers. He wants to make sure that the tarpaper is overlapped so the rain won't run in. The shingles, too, have got to be lapped. Now who's in charge of this work party?"

Arnold Schmidt didn't hesitate. He stepped forward. "I am in charge," he said.

The driver nodded. "Good enough for me. Now you take these men and get started. He'd like to have the job finished by noon, before more rain comes. Should be an easy task with all you men here, double the amount he had yesterday. So get going. The ladders are on the far side of the shed. Hustle now."

Schmidt stepped out in front of the others and stood rigid for a moment while he scanned the ones he would be directing. "You four," he pointed them out. "You will transport materials to the roof. You others," his eye settled on Henrik as he spoke. "You will begin the nailing. I will make sure you do the job correctly."

Spoken like a true officer, Henrik thought, direct and commanding, and authoritative. His chin-out stature and piercing eyes were all the authority he needed. Then he singled out the two other SS men. "You two take the lead here. Erich, you on the roof, and you, Helmut, on the ground. You know what to do. This must be done quickly and correctly. Now go and get to work."

Six men to do the work. Three to command. Henrik had imagined it would be that way. As they started to move as a group, he muttered to Emil, "This is not the army."

Schmidt stiffened. "Halt!" he ordered.

The small procession stopped.

"Who said that?" he demanded.

One of the men looked directly at Henrik. There was no concealing his identify. "It was me," he confessed.

"Ah, you, Henrik. I thought it would be you. I remember you as being resentful of your military service. But I must remind you that you are still a soldier of the Third Reich, and orders must be obeyed without question."

"And I must remind you, Herr Schmidt, that I am no longer a soldier of the Third Reich. I am a prisoner of war in the United States, and I am here to repair a roof. It is quite different, I think."

Emil jammed him in the side, and whispered. "For God's sake, Henrik, stop it, or you'll get yourself in trouble."

"I am already in trouble. I have been in trouble with him since the night we met in France."

Schmidt's face had reddened. He stood lock-still, his eyes bearing hotly on Henrik. His hand tapped the side of his leg as if he were holding a swagger stick. "You have profaned everything we stand for," he said, looking directly at Henrik. Then, in the same breath, he smiled at the others. "But we have work to do here today. So we must forget the words of a fool and put our minds to laying a fine roof on this farmer's building. I will deal with insubordination later."

Henrik didn't reply. He followed the group as if nothing had been said. Then Emil whispered again. "Now you have done it."

Henrik shrugged, bolstered in part by his own youthful tenacity. He did not feel inferior to Herr Schmidt, as he chose to call him. Now that he was out of uniform he was nothing more than a prisoner. Herr Schmidt could kiss his ass as far as he was concerned. Henrik's youthful ardor had been strained, and now he felt an intense determination to oppose the Nazi sympathizer, despite the apparent danger. He was young, impetuously cocky, and confident of his ability, and no damn threat was going to prevent him from standing up to a has-been captain who was blinded by his own vanquished power. If he could just get through the remainder of the day without any further contact with Schmidt, he thought the present situation would be forgotten.

Herr Schmidt would go back to his own barracks, and Henrik would return to his, and, like before, each of them would smolder for a while and then go their own way. Schmidt's SS powers were gone, finished, destroyed along with all the other Nazi doctrines that had died with Hitler. Besides, it felt good to stand up to authority. It was something he had not done during his entire seventeen years in Germany.

Emil pulled him aside as they approached the shed. "Didn't you hear what the Lagersprecher said? Schmidt is a Nazi. He still has power here. Don't put your life on the line just because you oppose him."

"He is a has-been."

"He might be, but he still has power. Stay clear of him, Henrik."

Henrik nodded. "Yes, I will be a good boy and show him my back. And if he talks to me again I will swallow his words like good medicine."

"Good. Good. You must stay out of his way. Remember, we still want to go to a branch camp. If you get in trouble with Schmidt, it may ruin our chances."

"He is a Nazi. We are not. That will be enough to get us transferred."

"You are a stubborn optimist."

"That I might be. But I feel the same way an ox must feel when it is free of its yoke."

Emil gave him a shove, breaking his stride. "Henrik, poor Henrik," he said. "You are nothing more than a fantasist."

As they gathered below the roof Henrik could smell the combined odor of manure and mud and age. The farm was not well kept, perhaps because it was too much work for the farmer who now relied on German manpower to repair his buildings. Nearby the hogs grunted behind their fence, and beyond that some black and white cows milled in a field. The wind was dry, despite the moisture, scented with pasture and hay and urine. A single ladder was propped against the roof at a steep angle..

Schmidt began giving orders, pointing, "You, you, you and you. Go inside and bring out the supplies." Then he turned on Henrik. "As for you, Henrik Arndt, you will carry the tarpaper up the ladder and place the rolls on the roof so the men can begin their work. One roll at a time. It will be good exercise for you."

Henrik did not question the order. He merely looked Schmidt directly in the eye to register his silent disgust, and then he went quietly to the inside of the shed and shouldered the first roll. Some of the men snickered. He ignored them. As he placed his foot on the bottom rung of the ladder he heard Schmidt say to Emil,

"Now you wait until he has all the rolls on the roof. Then you can go and help the others carry out the shingles."

By the time Henrik had gone up the ladder for the sixth time, his legs were beginning to ache in the calves, and the pain in his shoulder was more acute. Still, he did not complain. He shouldered the rolls with dignity and scurried up the ladder with a haste that surprised even Emil. He and Emil made eye contact several times, and in doing so Henrik recognized the admiration Emil had for him. It made him hurry faster.

When the last roll was on the roof Schmidt said to his men. "You can go up now. Be sure to overlap the tarpaper. Nail it down firmly. I will be watching to make sure you do it correctly. Henrik," he shouted. "You can come down now. You have earned a rest." To one of the SS men, he said. "Erich, you go to the roof. Helmut, you stay down here with me and Emil here."

As soon as Henrik's feet touched the ground the five others climbed up the ladder. When they were all on top of the roof, Schmidt turned to Henrik and Emil. "Now you two, just step back against the building here. I have something to say to you."

They did as they were told, as if standing before a firing squad, their eyes straight ahead, wondering what would be said to them. Schmidt and the other SS man stood in front of them in a commanding position, their shoulders squared, their feet together as if they were uniformed. Schmidt began.

"It seems that you have a definite dislike for authority, Henrik Arndt, and it appears that you no longer consider yourself a part of the German army. Am I right?"

"I am a prisoner of war."

"Ah, so you are. So are we all. But it does not mean that you can disregard your allegiance to the Fatherland. As of now, right now, I expect you will both consider the consequences of disobedience." He scrubbed a finger across his lips. "We are not done fighting. The war may have ended, but the doctrines the Führer established for us still remain." His eyes tightened with a sneer. "You are German soldiers, and you will conduct yourselves accordingly. If I find either of you talking against the Fatherland again, I will not hesitate to punish you. Am I clear on this?"

"Yes, you are clear," Emil said quickly.

Henrik did not speak.

"And you, Herr Arndt. Your reply."

Henrik felt the need to spit in his face, to tell him he was a fallen eagle, never to fly again, to tell him he was nothing more than a failure as a human being. But he held his temper, felt it drain away like hot water from a spout. He relaxed in a noticeable way that clearly demonstrated his submission. He hated himself for the short statement he was about to say. "I hear what you say. You will never again hear me speak against the Fatherland."

Schmidt took one step forward. His eyes pierced Henrik like a dagger. "Ah, that is good, Henrik, but I sense that your words were spoken merely to appease me. Well, I have listened, and I have heard you, and now I will decide what to do with you. Go now, and help repair this roof. We will finish before noon, before the next rain."

They worked on the roof for three hours, laying the tarpaper, then nailing down the shingles. By then the sun was high, and they were beginning to feel the heat. Patches of sweat dampened their shirts. Their brows dripped. The palms of their hands began blistering. An acute soreness settled in their limbs from the bending and lifting and straining. When they had to relieve themselves they went to the back of the shed and peed over the edge, to where rusted parts of farm equipment lay among weeds already two feet high.

It was mid-morning when the woman of the house came out with a bucket of water and a dipper. She stood well aside as they drank, gazing at them with a blank expression, standing like a rag doll against the fence, her arms thin and white, her face like chalk from the winter months indoors. Out in the farmyard the bus driver and the guard with the shotgun leaned listlessly against the vehicle. Later, when the prisoners were on the roof again, they were invited to sit on the porch in the shade, where they ate a sandwich and petted the dog, and dozed a bit while the hot, morning sun poured down on the shed where the men worked.

The SS man, Erich, had been on the roof for most of the morning. At times he would help carry shingles. Most of the time he just stood erect, observing. Occasionally he would help move shingles. Then, as if exhausted by watching, he would retire to one side of the roof to smoke a cigarette, or to gaze into the distance where a line of trees scalloped the horizon. On the ground, Schmidt and the other SS officer stood in the shade. They smoked and told jokes. The workers on the roof heard their laughter from time to time.

When they were finished, Schmidt and Helmut climbed the ladder to inspect the work. Schmidt walked across one side of the roof while the men stood on the other. Then he moved them and inspected the opposite side. At one point he stood still for a moment, stroked his chin, and then he called over to the men. "Henrik, come here."

Henrik crossed to where Schmidt was standing.

"That shingle there," Schmidt pointed. "That one. See, it is crooked. I want you to fix it. Remove the crooked one and replace it. This roof is incomplete if just one shingle is out of place. We must set a good example for this American farmer. We must show him that German work is of superior quality."

Henrik did as he was told, without a word of objection, while the others watched.

When he was finished he stood up and wiped a bead of sweat from his nose.

"Good work, Henrik," Schmidt said. "Now we will go." Schmidt left the roof first, followed by Erich and Helmut. Then, as the others began their descent, Emil tugged Henrik aside. He spoke in a low whisper.

"When you were repairing the shingle I heard the two SS speaking in a low voice. I was right next to them. The one named Helmut said: He is finished, that one, meaning you. Then he said, he will be gone before the weekend is over. Do you know what that means, Henrik?"

They were the last to leave the roof. When it was their time to descend the ladder, Henrik gave Emil a gentle shove. "Go down now. We will talk on the bus. Sit near the back, away from the others. Go now."

The farmwoman came out and thanked them, and then offered them some water. She stood well back, and looked at them without altering her expression. She kept her arms crossed over her chest. The breeze ruffled her dress, and a hank of hair drifted across her brow that she brushed away. She moved back toward the house as Henrik boarded the bus. He and Emil sat as far back from the others as possible, two rows in front of the guard with the shotgun. The bus pulled out of the farmyard and onto the gravel road. The gravel pinged beneath the floor of the bus like shots from a machine pistol. Emil whispered. "They are going to kill you, Henrik. You have angered Schmidt once to often."

"Would he dare to do that?"

"Not him. Others. Someone you would not suspect. Other Nazi's."

Henrik breathed deeply. His thoughts shifted in waves of anger, waves of fear, "Then what am I to do?"

"I think we should see the Lagersprecher as soon as we get back. He will help you."

"He is sick."

Emil persisted, his voice low but firm. "He will see us. I know he will.

Henrik's jaw tightened. "This is what I get for speaking out."

"Yes. But now you must think clearly, and remember that it will take only a second for someone to put a knife into your heart. A second, Henrik."

Henrik thought: There is such a thing as loyalty, such a thing as duty to a friend, but there is also self-preservation. This was no time for Emil to put himself in harm's way "You should not be part of this," he said.

"I am your friend."

"I can fight my own battles."

"There you go, acting like a hero. No, you will not do this alone. I have built up a friendship with Friedhelm. He will listen to me, perhaps more clearly than he will listen to you."

"And what could he do?"

"I don't know. Maybe if he cannot send us to a branch camp, he might be able to send Schmidt away. He knows what a troublemaker he is."

Henrik nodded. "One time. I will see him one time only. If he cannot help us, then I will fight this battle in my own way, and you will stay clear of me."

"All right, I promise you that."

Henrik shifted in his seat, and said to Emil. "Now sit back and relax."

Just then Schmidt turned and looked back at them. A slight smile, or was it a sneer, worked its way across his lips, and for just a second Henrik thought he hissed at him. He will not let up on me, Henrik thought. Until the day I am out of here, he will be my nemesis, unless I am lucky again. So, the Lagersprecher will either move me to another camp, or I will have to defend myself day and night, against someone who will strike at me when I least expect it. So now I will pray. Perhaps God has one last good miracle to perform. Perhaps, if God has his way, Henrik Arndt will live to see his way out of this mess.

The morning work had tired him. His head lolled forward as he listened to the drone of the engine and the clatter of the road stones beneath the bus. Voices murmured ahead of him. He peered out the window and saw the long, flat land, and at that moment a familiar voice within him told him not to worry: his mother's voice, coming to him again across all those empty miles, distinctly clear, just the way she had spoken to him when he was a child. Then he closed his eyes, and he thought he saw her there, her long hair gathered into a bun, her face lined with premature wrinkles, her smile but a reflection of who she really was.

Then the bus hit a bump, and he jerked awake, and for just a moment he forgot where he was. He expected to see her again, but all he saw were the dark fields, a sky piled with clouds, and the road that curved away to his left, as if it were meant to carry him a long way to freedom.

So, THOSE WERE HIS EXACT WORDS?" Friedhelm asked.

"Yes."

The Lagersprecher sat back in his chair, took a deep breath, a coughed into a handkerchief. His eyes watered. He dabbed them with the cloth and then cleared his throat. He tugged a woolen blanket tight around his shoulders, shivered a bit, and then winced. "I think you were wise to come to me. This man Schmidt is no doubt dangerous. He has given me enough trouble already, refusing to work, bread and water, inciting others to follow his dead cause. He is stiff and inflexible, and my assistant was wrong in sending him to the farm with you. That is what happens when the top man gets sick." He laughed as if to make fun of himself, and then coughed again. His voice rasped. "I will do two things for you."

Henrik and Emil sat patiently as Friedhelm wiped his nose, took a drink of water, and gasped for air. "Goddam cold," he muttered. "It is enough to make a man wish he were dead."

"Don't die on us now," Henrik said.

"No, I will not die just yet." He wiped his mouth. "I will have a car waiting at the front gate tomorrow morning at exactly seven o'clock. It is a staff car, one given to me for my use. It will take you to Minnesota, to a town named New Ulm, to our Base Camp Number Seven. Yes, it is a town named after Ulm, which is in the province of Wurttemberg. It is a German town with a rich history. You will like it there. They have asked me to send more men up there to work in the fields this summer, to help plant and hoe and harvest their crops. You will have four months there, maybe five. Then you will return. Soon the reprocessing will begin, to send us all back to the Fatherland where we will have much more work to do."

Henrik breath came faster, excitedly. "You would do that for us?"

"Of course. I will do what I can to save men like you."

"How can we thank you?"

"By being good Germans. By showing the Americans that we are honorable men."

"Yes, yes. We will do that."

Friedhelm took a deep breath, coughed up some phlegm, and wiped his hand across the towel. "As for Captain Schmidt. There is a camp in Kentucky that is looking for men to clear a forest. I think he will be sent there within a week, along with his two friends who were with you at the farm this morning. They will like Kentucky. It is hot there. And in the mountains, they will work very hard. What do you think of that?"

Henrik and Emil looked at one another. Then Henrik said, "I think they will not like Kentucky."

Friedhelm laughed, then coughed, holding his chest. "We will do it then. To-morrow you will leave here, and I will not see you again until we send you back to Germany. Be at the gate with your belongings no later than seven. The man who will drive is an American soldier. He will not be armed. We will trust you to be obedient to his needs." He looked at them through tired, reddened eyes. "Now you can go. Have a good journey. Write to me, and tell me how you like your new home."

"I will write," Henrik said.

"Good. Now go and pack your things. Tomorrow you will get a chance to see what this country is made of. I promise, you will not be disappointed."

TWENTY-THREE

New Ulm, Minnesota, May 1945

AT THE HAROLD SOMMER'S FARM, spring was in full bloom. The lilac's had blossomed almost overnight, as had the apple trees, now a profusion of white, a line of them along the garden fence where the morning glories had burst open, their flowers wide to the sun, the scent of them so powerful in the early hours so as to freshen the kitchen if the window was open. Back in the woods the moccasin flowers had bloomed; beautifully pink, like small slippers, delicate and fragile.

It was time to clean and scrub, to brighten and lighten. After the clothes were washed they were pinned up outside on long lines to dry in the sun, to smell clean and fragrant again from sunshine and wind. Papa took down the storm windows. Elsa and Corina were in charge of removing the rugs, hanging them on the lines and beating them with a wire switch to purge the winter dirt.

David carried garbage to the pigs, left-over food, potato peelings, apple cores, whatever remained from cooking. The pigs had voracious appetites in the spring. The cows were free to roam in the pasture again.

The girls watered the asparagus with salt water to keep the weeds in check, and to protect the roots. The garden had been planted: corn over there, potatoes in three rows, beets, carrots, cabbage, a pumpkin patch, beans and peas. It was a daily task, tending the garden, weeding, watering, waiting for rain, and fertilizing with manure trekked over from the barn in a wheelbarrow that always wanted to tip over.

Elsa cleaned the chicken coop. Armed with a shovel, she scraped, and piled, and pitched, and covered her face with a neckerchief when the dust rose to emit its horrible odor, enough to water her eyes, and to stuff up her nose. It was the worst job; something a man should do. But Papa insisted. David laughed. Corina always hid whenever chicken duty was mentioned.

The school was preparing for graduation. Studies were winding down, and there was an air of relief in the classrooms and hallways. Summer would bring lazy days and long nights, swimming, and rest while the crops were growing. Spring was a good time of year.

Elsa had received three more letters from Kenny. He told her of a buildup of troops and materials, but didn't mention where. Some of the sentences were blacked out, censored by the military. He was in a battle zone for sure, unable to speak his mind. He rambled sometimes, about life back home, about school, about his inability to capture her heart. There was always a bit of sadness in the letters, unwritten emotions between the lines, hope unrealized, and a sense of fear hidden within the words. She sensed that he wanted to be home, although he didn't come right out and say it. She kept the letters, only because she thought she should.

Elsa was happy and excited about the coming summer months, the last of them before her senior year. Romance was the farthest thing from her mind. Boys were just something to be spoken of offhandedly, which she and Erica always did whenever they were together, usually on Sunday afternoons. And although she felt stirrings in her body that often left her weak, she had no desire to satisfy them.

So she played her music on the Victrola. Ella Fitzgerald was singing a new song then, one that seemed appropriate to her mood. Its title was, "It's Only a Paper Moon." She read Hollywood magazines, and thought she might be fortunate enough to meet someone in college, or at a place beyond the farm, far removed from the fields, in an unknown location that existed only in her imagination.

Twenty-Four

Going to Minnesota, May 1945

THE STAFF CAR CARRYING HENRIK AND EMIL crossed the Minnesota border into green hills and meadows and massive plots of trees that filled the countryside with freshness, giving Henrik a feeling of new life. The terrain was beautiful, unlike the stark dreary expanse of Iowa that had often drained him of emotion. Almost at once he began anticipating his new home.

The driver, a sergeant who hadn't spoken a word since Henrik and Emil had entered the car, drove with his eyes straight ahead, intent on the road, and just when Henrik thought he had been born speechless, he said, "Where are you boys from?"

"Germany," Henrik said.

"Well, hell, I know that. Where in Germany?"

"You wouldn't know, even if I told you."

The driver snickered. "Guess not. As for me, I'm from Benson."

"Where's Benson?"

"You wouldn't know if I told you."

All three of them laughed. The laughter took the edge off of their nervousness.

"I was raised there," the driver continued. "When the Japanese bombed Pearl Harbor a bunch of my friends and me joined up. None of us liked the Nips. We wanted to fight in the Pacific, but the Army sent us to England instead."

"What did you do in England?"

"Supply Corps. Never saw any action. Got wounded in an air raid."

"By one of our bombers, yes?"

"Huh. They blew the hell out of London. Back and forth we went. Back and forth. Helluva way to pay back one another."

They fell silent then. Henrik told Emil what he had said. Emil shrugged. The driver continued on as if neither of them had spoken. Then, after looking at the trees again, Henrik continued the conversation.

"What is it like in the camp we are going to?" Henrik said.

The driver lifted the cigarette from his lips. The ash fell into his lap. He brushed it away, and then glanced at them through the rear view mirror. "You'll like it there, I think. Not much of a camp though. Small place next to a lake, down at the bottom of a gully."

"Is it far from the town?"

"Naw. Right up next to it. There's a brewery across from the Cottonwood. That's the name of the river. The town's just beyond it. Nice place, full of German descendants and battle monuments and old churches and stuff. It's got an 'old world' flavor to it. The barracks are left over from a Roosevelt conservation camp. A bunch of old buildings all redone. The prisoners who were there first fixed it up decent and comfortable."

"Sounds like a nice place."

"Better than where you came from. And, oh yeah, if you feel like walking away, you can just hike around the fence and pound shoe leather all the way to California if you want. No one ever finished the fence. It's got a sign on it saying No Tres-passing, but that's not enough to keep anyone in or out. You wanna go fishing, then go fishing. You wanna swim, then go swimming. The boys even go ice skating in the winter. Hell, the town folks don't mind you guys being there as long as you don't offend them. Nice place. Yea, you'll like it there."

"Are we going to help the farmers?"

"Nice bunch of folks, most of them. Some' of 'em are a bit pissed off at the Germans for taking their boys away, but for the most part, working the farms is pleasant enough. You guys won't have any problem there."

"Now you make is sound like a better place."

"It is. By the way, my name is George Putnam. I drive up here a couple times a month to deliver stuff. I might see you once in a while."

They talked on, getting to know one another. By the time the town came into sight they turned onto Cottonwood Road and drove down through the ravine to Lake Flandreau.

The car pulled to a stop, and the three got out. Henrik and Emil stood silently for a while, breathing the air, a blossoms and spring leaves and river water scent, just as pure and refreshing as nature's perfume could be.

The camp consisted of eight brown, one-story wood-sided buildings, set in two groupings of four, beneath a bower of trees. Each of the barracks housed thirty men. There was a recreation hall, a mess hall, and near the lake, a soccer field. Behind them the wooded bluffs separated it from the rest of the world. An aura of silence covered the neatly mowed grass on which the buildings stood. Above them the blue sky whitened with sunlight. From a distance they heard the trickle of water.

Henrik stood silently, looking at his new prison camp. He could not believe what he saw. It was as different from Algona as night was from day. No guard towers, no visible fences, no barbed wire, and no guards in sight.

And for a moment, just for a moment, he thought he was in nirvana.

TWENTY-FIVE

New Ulm, Minnesota, May 1945

THE ALFALFA HAD POLLINATED, and bees were in the fields. Papa had put in his corn when the soil was warm, at close to a two-inch depth as he could get; perfect planting he said. He expected a yield of fifty-three bushels an acre provided the conditions were favorable, rain and sun combined. He planted the spring wheat in mid May so he could harvest it by mid September after the searing hot dog days were over. He came in when the sun went down, and was already in the fields when the rooster crowed at the rising sun. He worked all day, took time out only to eat, saw little of the family during those long hours. Elsa and her siblings finished up with school. Elsa sang alto in the choir that would perform at the graduation.

In town, the two root beer stands opened for the season, the A&W on the north side, and the Mug on the south side. The Mug served snacks in the summer months. It was a favorite hangout for teenagers during the twilight hours when slapping mosquitoes was usually followed by curses, silently or otherwise.

Every night, as the sun settled down behind the fields, and if the wind was just right, one could hear the mournful three-noted cry of Whip-poor-wills as they began their nightly foraging.

In that last week of May, when the flowers were blooming along the base of the New Ulm Public High School, Elsa and Erica often ate their lunch outside in the sunlight. They sat far enough away from some of the others kids, on the grass lawn near the front steps, so as not to be bothered. Both had a bottle of warm Coca-Cola to drink. Elsa carried a bottle opener in her small purse.

Erica, or Little-Miss-Plan-Ahead, as Elsa liked to call her, nestled down next to Elsa, and, true to form, she started making plans. "Right after school's out, let's you and I celebrate."

"How?"

"I just bought a new two-piece bathing suit. How's that for keeping up with the times? We'll take a picnic lunch down to the lake and lay in the sun, and if the water's warm enough we can go for a swim."

Elsa shivered at the thought. "The water won't be warm. It's not even June yet."

"Well, maybe we'll limit ourselves to wading. We can just lie around and plan our summer." She giggled at the thought.

Elsa shrugged, aware of the responsibilities she would have to shoulder during the warm season. "I'll be working most of the summer, haying, tending the animals, doing all the farm stuff. I won't have much time to just lay around."

Erica giggled again, revealing her true intention. "I thought if we went down by the lake we might see some German boys again."

Elsa's expression widened with surprise. "You're crazy."

"No, I'm not. I know they go there."

"How do you know?"

"Because they're practically free-roaming, and they don't work on Sunday's."

"How do you know that?"

"Because they've been seen down by the lake on Sundays. You know Howie Cordel? Well, he and his family were there last Sunday. They were building a campfire when two of the prisoners returned from a walk along the river, over where they built those footbridges on the trail that runs up to Alwin's Bridge, at the upper end of the park. His father spoke some German, and so he began talking to them. It turned out that both of them had been captured in North Africa. They said they were Austrians."

Elsa's reply was direct. "Papa would never allow it. He cautioned me to stay away from them. Besides, I've already been branded as a Nazi lover by Carlyle."

"That will pass."

"Not soon enough to suit me."

"Carlyle is just a blabber. Most of the kids don't even listen to him."

"Even so, I don't want to give him reason to expand his crusade."

"What? And smother your curiosity? My God, there's no harm in talking."

Elsa casually examined her fingernails. "Even so, my father would have a fit if he found out I'd done something like that on purpose."

"If he ever did find out, which I doubt he ever would, just tell him it was an accidental meeting, like what happened to the Cordels."

Elsa began eating her sandwich. "You're just trying to get me in trouble. Besides, lying to my parents would be inexcusable."

"I wouldn't think of getting you in trouble. Talking to someone is not getting into trouble."

"With German prisoners it is."

"They're just people. My gosh, they walk into town whenever they want. All they need is a shirt without the big PW printed on the back. Every one of them has one. Some have gone to the movie in town. They've even ordered beer at the local bars. They're always walking along the river. It's not like they're real prisoners. People trust them. Have you seen the fence around their compound, on the downriver side of the camp, near the dam? It's made of chain link with metal poles about eight feet high. A person can walk right around it. There's no security anywhere. You know yourself that some of the kids from school have met the prisoners and traded for insignias. C'mon, Elsa. I want to meet them. I want to see what they're really like."

Peer pressure. It stabbed at her with a knife-sharp tip, and she felt herself weakening even as Erica spoke. Secretly, she had wanted to see them again ever since the incident at the lake, the day the blonde-haired boy had asked her to go skating. Papa had been wise enough to recognize her hidden desire the day she told him about meeting them. What was it he had said? Nothing wrong with talking to boys–but. He had cautioned her about going to see them. After all, they were former enemies. Still, one little accidental meeting wouldn't exactly brand her as a tramp. Peer pressure. It was a terribly strong enticement sometimes, especially when one had a nagging curiosity.

"I don't know. I'll see," Elsa said.

Erica wriggled. "I knew you'd weaken. Just one little peek, a few exchanged words. Who's going to know?"

"The people that are there at the lake, that's who."

"We'll sit off to the side, away from the picnic area. I know a place."

"You've always got an answer."

"Well, I've been thinking about it."

Elsa shook her head. "Well, no thank you. I will not meet any stranger in my bathing suit. It's not only improper, it's, well, it's suggestive."

"Oh, Elsa, you're such a prude."

"I'm not going to flaunt my body in front of anyone, much less German prisoners."

Silence came just then, a long minute of it, as if the breeze had brought it to them. They ate, and thought, and when their eyes met, they giggled.

Then Erica said, "Would you be opposed to just walking along the river on the footpath. It would be accidental as hell if one or two of them just happened to be walking the same path at the same time. Coincidence. Who could point a finger at coincidence?"

Elsa slapped at her, playfully. "You are a little devil, and I think you're trying to drag me right down into the fire."

"No. I'm just curious, that's all."

"You know what happened to the curious cat, don't you?"

"It's just a story. Nothing bad happened to the cat."

"Curiosity killed it."

"Like I said, it's just a story."

Elsa finished her sandwich, took a long drink of Coca-Cola, and then leaned back on her hands to catch the sun on her face. Lord Almighty, she thought, pressure again. Which was worse, taking a chance on a thousand-to-one shot that she'd meet a German boy on the river path, or having a reputation of being a goody-goody girl without a mind of her own? Just once she'd like to throw caution to the wind and reach out for a little adventure. The thought of it made her thighs tremble.

"I'll let you know," Elsa said, realizing at once that she should have kept her mouth shut.

"Okay, first Sunday after school's out. We'll set the time later. Thanks for being a friend. Oooohh! I can't wait."

SUNDAY AFTERNOON. THE SKY WAS CLEAR BLUE. Boaters had arrived down by the lake adjacent to the camp, and on its shore a few families were enjoying the day. The shouts of children came clearly across the road to where three of the prisoners lay, their bare torsos warming in the sun. The three were Henrik and Eric, and a young fellow who had been at the camp through the winter months, a rusty-haired lad named Niklas who had been raised in Durbach, Germany, in the *Schwarzwald*, the Black Forest. He was in his early twenties, and he carried scars from combat in Sicily.

The three had worked together at the Ochs Brick and Tile Company in Springfield, loading trucks for the past three days, hard work, but satisfying. As muted shouts from the lake reached them, Niklas turned and glanced over his shoulder toward the water. "The children are noisy today," he said. "I wish we could be there now, in the cold water. How much better the sun would feel then."

"Maybe tomorrow, when the people are gone, we can go there."

"No. We work tomorrow. I think we will be going back to the brick factory."

"Ya, there is always work."

"Besides," Niklas said. "The guards said we must keep our distance from the boaters and bathers. If we are not careful the camp authorities will add more guards, and we will lose some of our privileges."

Henrik replied. "They should set times for the civilians, and different times for us. Then we could all enjoy the water."

"It is their lake, not ours. We have to be content with that."

"Did you hear the radio today?" Niklas asked. There were four radios in the camp. One was always playing. And they had access to two newspapers that were delivered each morning.

"No, I did not."

"Then you did not hear the news. ReichFührer Himmler has killed himself."

Henrik was unmoved. If anything, he felt a pang of relief. "Then the last of them is gone."

"He swallowed cyanide," Niklas said.

"A coward's way out."

"The world is better off without him and his kind. He was a little mouse."

Himmler had been a poultry farmer after the first war, until he became the leader of Hitler's personal bodyguard, the *Schutzstaffel*, the ones who strutted around behind their death's-head badges and black ties, enlisting young Germans into their suicidal ranks.

"He was responsible for the Night of the Long Knives, I think."

"Ya," Emil said. "Himmler believed Hitler was the Messiah, and in his eyes he was. The Führer was judge and jury in Germany, with the power to decide who lived and who died. How could one man become so powerful?

"Because we all stood back and watched him bewitch us. We did nothing. He became a god to more than Himmler. Don't you remember how many of the children in the Jugend adored him? Fortunately, I was not one of them."

"Well," Henrik said. "We won't have to worry about him any more. Thank God he is dead. Maybe now Germany can rise from her ashes."

The breeze came and brushed their bodies. Henrik could smell the river, and the fragrance of flowers from up near the brewery. Then he heard the sound of music, muted and low, but lively. He nudged Niklas.

"What is that music?"

"It is the band. Schell's Hobo Band. They play music from the circus, and they act like clowns. They are popular here."

"Music sounds good on a Sunday."

Niklas yawned and then cupped his hands behind his head. "Ah, soon we will be working in the fields. The flax crop will need cutting soon. There will be long days in the sun, and farm girls to bring us water."

"Farm girls?"

"Ah, yes, they are lovely, most of them. In the fall, when the farmers harvest their crops, we call it skirt-chasing season." He laughed. "It is said that American girls are fine lovers."

"So were the German girls."

"Ya, if you could find one that was not in love with Hitler."

They laughed and punched one another, and felt the sun on their faces. The trees, content with their new foliage and the sun's warmth, rustled nearby. The music came like whispers at times, louder at others when caught by the breeze. They were prisoners, yet free, content in this new place.

"I am going into town tonight," Niklas said.

"Why?"

"Just to walk the streets before curfew. Some nights it is almost the same as being back home in Durbach. For me, the memories come easily."

"Some night I will go with you."

"Yes, you must. We must tell Carl, the guard. He trusts us. He is a friend to us. As long as we obey we will not be confined. I will get you a shirt without the PW on the back. No one in town will know who you are. You will be just like a visitor from Sleepy Eye,"

"What is Sleepy Eye?"

"A town just west of here. We drive through it on our way to Springfield. There is a cannery there, where we work sometimes."

"It is a funny name."

"It was named after a Dakota Indian. You see, I am already an historian. Many of the towns here are named after Indians."

Henrik lulled in the sunlight. His thoughts drifted, first to home, then into a wonderland of imagination. He was content for the first time since coming to America, and he thought of what it must be like to live in a free country, without storm troopers and forced youth camps and political strife, or war. It must be a paradise, he thought, where you are free to do what you wish, to raise your families without fear, to love whomever you chose, and to have children who will not be forced to sell their souls to a fanatical leader. It is what he would want, if only he had a choice. But for now he would be content with 3,400 calories a day, a warm breakfast every morning, sandwiches and coffee for lunch, and another warm meal when he returned from work.

Henrik's only concern was the lack of mail from home.

MEMORIAL DAY CAME ON A WEDNESDAY, the 30th, long before Congress changed the holiday to the last Monday in May. On that day the Sommer family took flowers into town and placed them on the graves of their grandparents, and said prayers at their graveside. It was a solemn time. There was a parade in town later in the day, soldiers and flags and bands, along with the New Ulm Battery in uniforms of the Civil War, always the highlight of the parade. The officers rode on sixteen grand and prancing horses. The enlisted men sat on the cannon and caissons, their eyes straight ahead, their gold buttons flashing in the sun.

Overseas, in the battered city of Munich, elements of the American army gathered on the *Konigsplatz* town square to pay silent tribute to their fallen comrades, their ranks backed by tanks and armored vehicles. "Volleys" and "Taps," where once there had been war.

Gasoline was still rationed. Car owners were entitled to three gallons a week. The farmers fared much better.

In the Pacific, American forces girded for an attack on the Japanese mainland, a cataclysmic event that was sure to take countless thousands of lives, if not millions. The battle, yet to be fought, was on everyone's mind

TWENTY SIX

New Ulm, Minnesota, June 1945

SCHOOL HAD ENDED, AND NOW THE summer months stretched ahead of Elsa as they always had, work upon work, in the garden, in the fields, in the barn, anywhere she was needed. Still, it was a glorious time of the year, a time of long days and soft nights and warmth aplenty. Elsa was in a happy mood during those months.

Papa sprained his ankle badly that first week in June. He came hobbling back from the barn late one afternoon, puffing, grimacing with pain, his face flushed with agony. He sat down in the kitchen and gingerly unlaced his boot. He eased it off his foot while mother boiled some water. He soaked the foot for hours while worrying about the work that had to be done. Later, Clara wrapped his foot up tight in cloth and fed him some aspirin. He grumbled all the while, puffing on his pipe until the room was blue with smoke, complaining about the unfortunate situation that had caused him so much concern. A portion of fence had fallen in the south pasture and two of the cows had worked their way into the ditch where the grass was higher. It had taken him almost an hour to get them back inside the fence line before his foot dropped into a hole, twisting his ankle. Then it took him the better part of another hour to herd the cows back into the barn. Now the fence needed repair and he thought David was not physical enough to dig and set posts and rewire the thirty feet that had fallen, even though the boy was willing to give it a try. He stewed that entire night, went to bed early with his foot still throbbing. By morning, he said, he would know what to do. And he did. He laid it all out at the breakfast table.

His conversation was with Clara. The kids just listened.

"I called up George Jenks before you all got up this morning. He's the new POW farm dispatcher in New Ulm. I asked him if he had any workers available to help a man with a bum foot. He said he did."

There was silence at the table. Elsa continued eating, afraid to even look in Papa's direction lest he noticed that she was interested in what he was saying. Corina stopped eating her oatmeal long enough to glance at Elsa. David just kept on eating.

"What did he say?" Clara asked.

"He's got a boy or two, strong ones, he says. All I have to do is drive in and pick one of 'em up, bring him out here, have him do the work, and return him in the afternoon."

"Are you going to get one?"

"I haven't made up my mind yet. I want to walk a bit on this foot to see if it's healed any. I doubt it though. It's still damned sore." He glanced at the children, and then added. "Sorry for the cussing. This foot's got me in a terrible fix."

Elsa listened with rapt attention. Her curiosity had been heightened, but during the long moment of silence that ensued she didn't say a word. Papa kept on eating, not saying anything. David strained to say something but he kept his mouth tight while chewing on his food.

"George says I gotta pay forty cents an hour for the use of a prisoner. The prisoners get ten cents, and the rest goes toward housing and feeding them. I guess the government makes a little profit on the deal as well. But forty cents is forty cents. Seems like quite a bit to me."

Clara laid her fork down. Her glance went right past Elsa. "Not if you can't do the work. Besides, they'll probably do it twice as fast. I think you should go and get one."

Papa nodded. It would be all right with him as long as Clara agreed. Then he glanced at the children. His eyes had that intense look to them, the way they always did whenever he had something important to say.

"Now you have to know something," he said. "I'll be bringing a prisoner of war into our yard. He'll be helping me with the fence. He will not come into the house, nor do I want any of you to go prancing around to see him. Do you understand?"

Each of them nodded. Then his eyes turned toward Elsa. "Now you, young lady. You seem to have a fancy to talk to one of these men, and now you might have your chance, but it'll be slight, so don't go on expecting the opportunity. First, we'll come here to get the posts and wire. Then I'll bring him to the fence. He'll dig while I observe. Then he'll set the posts and run the wire. That's all. David, you can come along and help. When we're finished, I'll return him to his camp. He'll be here for three, maybe four hours. During that time you'll help your mother. You'll probably get a glance at him, but that's all."

"I understand, Papa."

"Good, then." He pushed his plate away, stood up on his good foot, and limped toward the door. "I'll be back as soon as I can."

He grimaced, then hobbled out the door and went directly to the truck. David was right at his heels. Within two minutes they were gone.

W HEN HAROLD ARRIVED AT THE CAMP, the prisoner was already waiting for him just outside the camp office. He was an average looking boy with blonde hair, slightly built, curious with his glance. He simply nodded as Harold went inside and signed the papers.

When Harold left the office he descended the three steps and walked directly to the prisoner. He held out his hand. *"Guten Morgen,"* he said.

The prisoner shook Harold's hand, smiled, and replied. "I speak English, sir. My name is Henrik Arndt."

Harold nodded. "Well, that is a surprise." He looked down at David who was staring wide-eyed at Henrik.

Harold had always put a lot of emphasis on first impressions. His meeting with this prisoner was no different. The boy was firm with his handshake, bright eyed and eager, with a sense of determination about him. He had a limited military presence, and he seemed immediately at ease with the both of them.

Harold was direct. "I've got a fence to repair. Three or four hours of work, with this lad, my son David, to help."

"I will do anything you want me to do, and without complaint, sir." He reached over and shook David's hand as well.

"My foot went bad on me."

"I am sorry to hear that, sir."

Harold chuckled. "No need to call me sir. My name is Harold."

"Harold, yes."

Harold gestured toward the car. "Well, come along then. Can you drive a car?"

"Yes, of course. But I have not driven for near two years."

"My foot is paining me, so get behind the wheel."

"I have no authority to drive here. I am not even a citizen."

"We got about five miles to go, most of it straight, with only a couple of turns. I just want to rest my foot. Just go. I'll tell you where to turn. David, you just squeeze in alongside me while Henrik takes us back home."

Henrik got behind the wheel. Harold explained how the pickup truck shifted. Henrik nodded. Within minutes they were on the highway. On the way back Henrik did most of the talking. By the time they arrived, both Harold and David felt as though they had known him for years instead of minutes.

CLARA AND ELSA WERE WORKING IN THE GARDEN, watering and weeding, when the truck pulled into the yard. Elsa had only a moment to glance toward the shed where the pickup came to a stop. Curiously excited, she strained to see beyond the wire fence festooned with morning glories, but from her position she could see only the vague shape of a man with a PW stenciled on his back, not enough to make a connection. Still, the sight of a honest-to-goodness German war prisoner sent a ripple through her body.

Mother paid little attention to the arrival. Elsa, however, continued to watch while mindful of her task, curious enough to steal a look now and then. In doing so, she felt a surge of curiosity almost too intense to ignore. She flushed as the POW entered and exited the shed, loading posts and wire into the back of the pickup. Then the three of them were off, driving out the back road toward the pasture.

As her body relaxed, a warm glow flowed through her, but this warmth was not from the sun. With her curiosity peaked, she continued her work, and thought: You are a silly girl, to have emotions like that. Your interest was simply nosiness, and nothing more. Forget that you have seen the German boy, and get back to work. Silly girl.

Fifteen minutes passed before her mother stopped working and wandered over near the fence, into the shade of an apple tree. She stood there for a moment, cooling herself. She wiped her brow and then said to Elsa. "Go to the house and bring back a jar of water. I'm thirsty. You must be thirsty too. We'll work a while longer, and then there's laundry to do."

"I am a bit thirsty also," Elsa replied, laying her hoe aside. She walked hurriedly to the house so as not to keep her mother waiting. In the kitchen, she filled a fruit jar with cold water. She was about to leave when the pickup truck swung into the yard, close to the house. She looked out through the window and gasped. The man getting out of the pickup was the German POW. Startled to the point of nervousness, her legs began trembling. He was headed toward the porch.

His knock came at the same moment she approached the screen door. Nervous or somewhat fearful, she pressed the water jar tight to her chest. Her legs didn't want to move. Her body stiffened. Slowly, she advanced one step, then another. Then she turned and gazed into his face. Instantly, she felt a tightening within her body. Her mouth went dry.

The boy looking at her was tall and blond. His expression was one of surprise. If she saw anything at all, it was the intense blueness of his eyes, and the calmness of his face. She remembered instantly what her mother had told her, that eyes were the door to the soul. He smiled then and took a step back, and for a moment neither of them spoke. His hands folded slowly in front of him as if to imply that he was no threat to her. The jar in her hands trembled. Then she realized that her mouth was open. She drew her lips together at the moment he spoke.

"I was told to come for water. The man of the house said his wife would know what to do."

Elsa raised the jar of water in her hands, as if it had miraculously appeared from nowhere. "I have some," she said.

Henrik opened the screen door slowly. She walked out onto the porch as if swept there by a breeze. They stood eye to eye; she slightly shorted than he, but tall enough to look at him straight on. She was surprised, almost overjoyed, that he spoke English.

He smiled. "I think you are not Mr. Sommer's wife."

She handed him the jar. He took it from her. "No, I am his daughter, Elsa."

He nodded. "Elsa, yes. A good German name. My name is Henrik."

She stepped back, simply because the narrow space between them seemed to imply intimacy. Her cheeks flushed a bit. She fumbled for someplace to rest her hands. She had to say something, quickly, before he turned to leave.

"I am surprised you speak English," she said.

"My Uncle Herman came from America. He taught me when I was younger."

For some reason she could not reply. Words were tangled in her mouth. She was entranced by his eyes upon her, those blue eyes so radiantly pure.

He did not let the moment pass. Almost apologetically, he said. "Do not be afraid of me. I am not a threat to you."

His words broke her concentration. She felt suddenly at ease, not because of what he had said, but because of the way he had said it, calmly and with perfect intent. "No, I am not afraid," she replied. "Do not think I am."

He breathed deeply, relieved by her answer. Then he smiled again. "I must go quickly. Your father said I should not delay. I have driven his truck because his foot was sore." He nodded graciously. "It has been a pleasure meeting you, Elsa."

He bowed graciously, only a nod, but the manner in which he did it sent another shiver through her body. Then, without pause, he descended the steps and entered the pickup. As he settled behind the wheel, he turned and flashed another smile, then drove away.

She stood stark still, and for a moment her feet did not want to move. She was frozen in an instant of wonderment. They had spoken only a few words, and yet it felt as if she had known him for years. Then she heard a voice.

"I have been waiting for the water."

Elsa turned and saw her mother standing near the end of the porch. As the shock of Henrik's presence faded, she smiled. "I was about to bring it, when…"

"I see you have met your German boy," her mother said.

Elsa nodded.

Her mother laughed. "And I see by your expression that he has made a favorable impression on you. Was he all you expected from an enemy soldier?"

"Papa sent him to get some water. I gave him the jar I was bringing to you."

"You didn't answer my question."

Elsa shrugged, freed from her moment of exhilaration. "He was kind."

"You look a bit flushed."

Elsa tapped her cheeks. "It's warm today."

Clara approached the porch. "He was a handsome gentleman, don't you think?"

"I didn't notice."

Clara came up the steps and stood directly in front of her. The slight smile on her face said everything. "I beg to differ with you. I think you did notice. You are unnerved."

Elsa had regained her composure. She struck a rather defiant pose. "Honest, mother, I am not unnerved. He was kind, and he spoke English. I was curious about him."

"And now he's gone."

"Yup!" She broke her concentration and turned to enter the house. "I'll get another jar of water. I'll just be a minute."

"No need to hurry now. I think we're done in the garden. Do you want to just sit and talk a bit?"

"Elsa swung her head around. "No. I think I'll go and feed the chickens now."

"Suit yourself. Bring in some eggs."

Elsa stepped off the porch and headed toward the chicken coop. She walked at a moderate pace, trying to recall every bit of the short conversation between her and the boy named Henrik, but all she could remember was the set of his eyes, those sparking blue eyes that had peered right into her soul. Then the questions came. Who was he? What was he really like? Where did he come from? Had he been a fierce warrior? Had he killed Americans? Was he, in fact, a Nazi?

Then she was at the door. She paused and looked at the small, round knob as if seeing it for the first time, and when the questions came to an end she reached out, turned it, pushed the door open, and stepped inside. Immediately the clucking began, the flapping of wings, the rustling of feathers, all the commotion of unsettled birds. She went about her work at once, wondering if there was any possibility that she would ever see him again. Certainly she couldn't ask her father to bring him back another day. If she did, Papa would refuse her. If he thought there was even a hint of interest, he would never go back to the camp to get him. If she did see Henrik again, it would have to be through the working of fate, chance or luck. Impossible, she thought. He is a prisoner of war, and she a farm girl. They were miles apart from one another. It was impossible to think that she would ever see him again. Besides, he might be different than he appeared to be. Maybe he would just as soon strangle her as look at her. Maybe his blue eyes were just a shield, to hide his real persona. She recalled how she had once admired Carlyle, only to have him reveal his true self. Maybe this boy, Henrik, was also different, a predator in disguise, or a war-hardened killer. So, she might as well forget the incident. He was gone, and he would probably never return. It was stupid of her to think otherwise. One thing was certain, however. She would never tell Erica about the meeting. Erica would only call her a liar,

She scattered the seed and watched the chickens pick at it, their heads bobbing, their steady clucking creating a riot of sound inside the warm enclosure. Then she gathered four eggs and put them in one hand, and headed back toward the house.

When she entered the house, her mother was in the kitchen. She turned and smiled, removed the eggs from Elsa's hand, said thank you, and resumed her work. She said nothing about the accidental meeting with Henrik, unless one could place words to the lift of her eyebrows.

Papa came home after returning Henrik to the compound. He apologized for having sent the boy to get water, explaining that his foot had hurt so bad he didn't want to walk on it. Then, to satisfy everyone's curiosity he said, "The German boy was a fine lad. He worked hard without complaining and he did a good job, more than I expected of him. He was a farm boy all right. You could tell by his determination to get the job done. He said he came from a town named Bergheim. That's all I know about him. He just worked until he was done, and then I took him back. He thanked me for allowing him to work. I must admit, I was surprised by him. He was different than I expected."

Elsa just had to speak up. "I met him on the porch when mother was in the garden."

Papa's eyebrows rose. "And what did you think of him?"

Elsa shrugged. "Well, he seemed nice enough. We didn't talk much. He just took the water and left."

Papa nodded. "So there. I told him to hurry. I wasn't paying him to talk, you know."

"Maybe he was nervous." David said.

Papa scratched his face, concentrating on his chin whiskers. "No. I don't think so. I think he just wanted to make a good impression, hoping maybe I'd ask him back some day."

Elsa's question was indifferent. "Will you?"

Papa removed his pipe and tapped it on the ashtray, releasing some imbedded ashes. His reply was slow in coming. "Well, that all depends on what work needs to be done. Forty cents an hour, well now, that's somewhat prohibitive. But if this foot is slow healing, and there's some heavy work to be done that David here can't handle. Well, you never know. I can't say right now." Then he looked directly at Elsa.

"Why do you ask? Do you want him to come back?"

She was startled at the question, but she held her emotions in check. "It doesn't matter to me. Any one of them would do, I guess."

Papa winked coyly at Clara as he replied. "He was a handsome lad, don't you think?"

Clara answered immediately. "Oh, Harold, stop it now. You're being uncouth."

His eyebrows lifted teasingly. "I just wanted to know if he tickled her fancy."

Elsa face reddened slightly. "Oh, Papa, don't be silly."

Clara knew what was coming. He would keep it up until Elsa marched away from the table with a bug in her bonnet. Papa could be a real tease sometimes. So she spoke up. "Now you just smoke your pipe and leave Elsa alone. She saw the boy, and he left, and that's the end of it. There's nothin' in it to stir your curiosity."

Papa appeared surprised, but he wasn't. "No need to get flustered. I was just talking."

"I know your talk sometimes. You like to push some people to the end of their patience."

Papa packed more tobacco into his pipe. "I guess you know me all right. I got a teasing streak in me that's just gotta be satisfied sometimes."

"Well, now is not the time."

"That's okay, mother," Elsa said. "I know how Papa is. I can take it."

"That's my girl," Papa said, lighting his pipe. "Now why don't you go out and bring down some hay, and clean up the separator room, while Ma doctors my foot. And I'm sorry, honey, if I teased you too much."

"It's okay, Papa, I know you."

"Yea, I guess you do."

Elsa went outside and worked the afternoon away, helping David and Corina at various tasks. When it was suppertime they washed up and went inside and ate, and later that night, after they had listened to the Edgar Bergen, Charlie McCarthy show, Elsa and Corina went out onto the back porch and sat in the rockers. Out behind the barn, ghostly flashes of heat lightening lit up the darkness as if the storm god was waving its wand, while nearby the windmill creaked in answer to the wind.

It was cool on the porch. The air had a rain scent to it. From deep in the distance Elsa could hear the low rumble of thunder as a storm paraded across the horizon. The sound was resonant enough to disturb the stillness of the farmyard. She lay back in the chair, cushioned with an old blanket, and allowed the evening solitude to cloak her in tranquility. Then she closed her eyes and thought back to where the boy had stood, just a few feet away. She came so close to reliving the moment that she failed to hear Corina's voice.

"What was he really like?" Corina asked quietly.

Elsa smiled while forming her reply. "He was...different."

"What do you mean, different?"

"I don't know. The way he stood, the way he smiled, the way he looked at me."

Corina giggled. "I think you liked him."

Elsa closed her eyes again. She tried to envision the way he had looked at her, with a tenderness just beneath his gaze. "He was so unlike the boys at school. He was a gentleman."

"He was only a boy."

"Not really. He's my age or there about. I would say he was seventeen, or eighteen."

"Was he fierce, like we always thought German soldiers were?"

"No, he wasn't at all fierce. He was kind . . . and handsome."

"I wish I could have seen him."

"Well, maybe some day you will."

"Do you really think Papa will bring him here again?"

"There's always a chance."

"David wants him to come back. He said it didn't matter to him if there was a German soldier hanging around the farm."

"David's a boy. He's too much into the war."

"I don't think it'll matter. Papa will make up his own mind."

"Yes, he will."

Elsa remembered the blue eyes most of all, and what her mother had once said about judging a man. Elsa was already convinced that Henrik was not a dedicated warrior like the goose-stepping, hard-faced soldiers she had seen in the newsreels, those who had poured through Poland and the lowlands and into France. This one was different. This one was someone she could . . .

The thought was interrupted by the invigorating scent of rain and the soft patter of drops on the porch roof. The lightening was closer now, flashing, darting, shifting across the leading edge of the storm. Soon the rain intensified and the wind carried it onto the porch. Elsa and Corina went inside.

In bed that night, as the room pulsed with the last brief flashes of lightening, Elsa confessed her secret longing. "Erica and I are going to the lake this Sunday if the weather is nice. We're going to walk along the path next to the POW camp."

"You wouldn't."

"We are. Please, don't tell Mother or Papa. They might not like it. The only reason I'm telling you is because I've got to tell someone."

"I'll keep your secret."

"Promise?"

"Sure. I know how important secrets are. You can trust me."

They went to bed, and in the darkness, as the storm receded, Elsa thought about Sunday, and the possibility of maybe meeting Henrik again.

And as the thought intensified, she felt stirrings she had never felt before.

W HEN HENRIK RETURNED TO THE CAMP after his morning of work at the Som-mer farm, he went directly to his cabin, only to find Emil gone, assigned to work at the brick factory. It wasn't until six o'clock that evening that they met again for dinner. It was then Henrik told him about meeting the young girl at the farm.

"You have all the luck," Emil remarked. "I saw nothing but bricks today."

"She was lovely, sixteen or seventeen, I think."

"And how long did you talk with her?"

"No more than a minute."

"So little time. And what did you talk about?"

"Nothing. I told her I came to get water for her father, and she told me her name, and I told her mine, and we said good-bye. It was nothing to get excited about."

"But you were excited."

"As I said, she was lovely, and I thought how nice it would have been to have stayed and talked longer, to get acquainted."

"What was your impression of an American girl?"

"She was, well . . . she was . . . what you would say . . . very pretty and . . . with a voice that was soft and . . . alluring."

"Alluring?"

"Yes. She captivated me."

Emil punched him on the shoulder. "Don't tell me. Three or four words spoken, and you are already in love with her."

Henrik laughed. "Love. No! It is the farthest thing from my mind. I will perhaps never see her again. I will probably haul bricks for the remainder of the summer, and then in the fall we will return to Algona."

He hesitated as his smile faded. "Besides, what would an American girl want with a prisoner of war? Nothing. Still, it was a moment in time I will not soon forget. Now eat and get fat so you can work tomorrow."

THE WEEK ENDED, AND SUNDAY CAME. Rain fell throughout the day. The prisoners stayed inside and played cards, and some of them napped in the afternoon while others read and wrote letters. Then, later in the day, several of them walked outside to view a rainbow that crowned the hills on the other side of the Cottonwood, up near the Nightingale Club by Camelback Hill. Later that night they watched a movie.

The following week most of them worked at the brick factory. Some were sent to Sleepy Eye. They fell into a routine; every day the same, up at five-thirty, to bed at ten, nothing changed except the weather.

Every inch of the land was green again. The sun was warm. Rain came and refreshed the trees and the grass, and the river ran clear. The nights were balmy and peaceful, and some of them walked at twilight when the day was at its best, when the birds chirped and when the sun was golden-red on the horizon. And at the end of each day some of the local kids came to haul scraps away from the mess hall, to feed their pigs.

Sunday came again. Those who chose to worship went to church, to kneel in front of the altar they had made for themselves, in front of the cross they had fashioned from old lumber. The sun was high by noon. Across the lake some of the town folks had gathered to fish and to swim, or to picnic at one of the fire pits. It was an idyllic day, one of warmth and bright sky, when the leaves were unruffled and sounds carried a long way. It was the sort of day that came infrequently, the sort of day that fashioned memories.

After lunch that day Henrik and Emil listened as a young man from Munich played music he had composed himself, on the donated, self-tuned piano. Then Eric went and laid on his bed and fell asleep while Henrik walked outside through the trees, to where the path was, and there he looked out over the Cottonwood at the verdant hillsides opposite the river. He had little on his mind. When a family came along the footpath he stepped back behind the trees so they would not see him, and there he sat down on the ground. Soon his head nodded. He was about to lie down on the grass when he heard the sound of female voices, two of them, coming from the direction of the lake. He sat up, curious as to who they were. As he peered out from behind the tree, he was momentarily stunned. He was on his feet immediately. He was sure one of them was Elsa Sommer, the girl he had met at the farm. As they came closer he walked forward. They hadn't seen him behind the trees. They were talking head to head. When they were close to him, he spoke.

"Elsa," he said. "It is good to see you again."

The girls stopped immediately. Their faces blanked. The girl with Elsa said, "Who is that?"

Elsa swallowed hard. "He was at our farm, helping my father."

"Why didn't you tell me?"

"I thought it was unimportant."

The girl with Elsa flushed. "Oh, my God," she said.

Elsa moved slightly ahead of the other girl, her head high, her eyes straight ahead, as if she had anticipated his being there. "Hello, Henrik. I didn't expect to see you here today."

He approached her, smiling. His blue eyes flashed. "Well, here I am. I am always here. This place is my home away from home. And who is this with you?"

Elsa turned to Erica, whose expression was one of shock. "This is my friend, Erica Pauls."

Henrik bowed courteously. "And how are you today, Miss Pauls."

For a moment Erica was spellbound. She appeared to be nervous. She fumbled with the buttons on her sweater. Then she said. "I am fine."

Henrik's realized that his first task was to relax the moment, to take the sudden surprise away, to put them both at ease. He did this the only way he knew how, with words. "And how is your father's foot, Elsa. I hope he has recovered."

"His foot is fine. He is up and about now."

"Good. Good. I am happy to hear that. I was worried about him. He is the type of man who likes to do everything himself. I had a hard time convincing him to just sit and watch me while I worked." He paused to study their expressions, and found both of them still hesitant to speak. He continued talking in his own way.

"And now we have a problem. I am here and you are uneasy with me. It is not right that we have this barrier between us." He motioned to his right. "Perhaps if we walk a ways, this barrier will disappear."

The girls looked blankly at one another. He thought he saw Erica shake her head from side to side. He knew he had to convince them quickly.

"It is not a serious problem," Henrik continued. "Up ahead there is a grassy area, behind some bushes. If we go there we can talk without being seen. I think you might prefer that to standing here. It might be conspicuous if others come by. Or I can just wish you a good afternoon and go back to my cabin and try very hard to forget that we have met today."

The two girls huddled. He could hear some of their words, hushed though they were.

"I'll go back to the car," Erica said. "You can meet me there later."

"No, come with me."

"Why?"

"Because I want you to."

"Oh, my God, Elsa, this is weird."

Henrik thought it best not to remain where he was, so he began walking toward the bushes he had mentioned "I will be over there," he said. "If you come I will meet you there. Otherwise, I hope to see you again some day, Elsa, if your father needs a good strong German boy to help him with his work."

He began walking, now out of earshot. He looked back once, only to see the girls huddled together, talking rapidly. He wanted desperately to meet with Elsa again, to talk to her, to learn more about her. He didn't care if her friend came along because he knew Elsa would feel more secure in the presence of her company. She might be more talkative then, and not so nervous. Experience had told him so.

Reaching the bushes, Henrik stood in the shade, wondering what they would do. He looked back and saw them headed in his direction. Now he had to be very careful about what he said, or they would leave. He felt suddenly unsure of himself. He was as nervous as he had been behind the brick pile in Aachen. Only this time he was not facing an enemy. He was facing two women who didn't know the first thing about a German prisoner of war. He would have to convince them that he was not threatening.

As they approached him, Elsa smiled and then said. "We will talk with you for a while."

"Good. Then we will go to the place I suggested, if that is alright with you."

"Yes. Away from prying eyes."

He nodded. "I see. A good choice. It is right over there." He pointed to a large lilac hedge that curved up and away from the walkway.

"It goes on to where the fence should be," he said. "It is nature's way of keeping us inside the compound, only it does not do a very good job of it."

The girls looked both ways. Seeing no one, they nodded.

"It is sunny and bright there," he said. "We can sit down on the grass, you and Erica together, and I close by. Come, I will show you the way."

They left the path and walked up behind the hedge, to where it curved down toward the river, then back again and up an embankment. The open space he referred to was situated beneath a huge cottonwood tree, unseen from the pathway.

"I assure you, we will be quite comfortable there," he said. "We can exchange questions and answers, and whenever you wish to leave, all you have to do is go. Ah, here we are."

He stopped at the place where privacy was assured, unless a nosey guard came by. He motioned them forward. They settled down and gathered their skirts around their knees in a modest fashion while he took a place a good three feet from them. Then he smiled as broadly as he could. He kept his voice low. "Well, here we are, and I will start, for then you will know something about who I am. It might put you at ease with me."

Henrik began, telling them about his boyhood in Bergheim, about his farm, and his mother and father. He told them also about his brief period in the Jugend and about his capture in Aachen. He went on to tell them about Algona and his run-in with Schmidt, and how he obtained a transfer to New Ulm. Then he spoke directly to Elsa.

"When I first saw you on the porch I was speechless. I did not expect to see a girl, especially one so pretty. I knew right away you were not the woman I was sent to see. It was so unbelievable. But, much to my sorrow, you had the jar of water ready for me, so I could not delay my departure. I wanted so much to stay a while, to talk to you. You were the first American girl I had seen up close and I wanted to know you better. But then I saw your mother coming from the garden, and I did not think she would want to see us together. I didn't know at the time how any of you felt about us German prisoners. As far as I knew we were looked upon as being the enemy, but I want to assure you, I am not your enemy. I wanted to tell you that I was just a boy who was pulled into the war to shoot the same kind of people I admired as a child, when my Uncle Herman was with us, when he taught me English."

"Then you are not a Nazi," Elsa said.

"Of course I am not a Nazi. But I was there at the time when Hitler would come to the camps and shake hands with the boys, and we would all shout, 'Youth, Youth. We are the soldiers of the future.' And we learned that self-sacrifice was the highest honor a boy could give to his Führer. The uniform was an obsession to many, but not to me. Perhaps it was not the honorable thing to do, but I did not conform as others did, and soon I was sent home."

"Were your parents also objectors?"

"Yes. It was they who told me what to do in camp. I was to fail. If I failed I would be sent home. I did exactly as I was told by my parents. And it worked."

"What subjects did you study in school?"

"Oh, I was good in mathematics. I wanted someday to be an engineer, to build things, not destroy them. I wanted to build bridges, but why I don't know. Perhaps because I traveled over them when I was a boy. I marveled at how something without much support could span a canyon or a river."

While he spoke he studied Elsa's face. He saw in her expression a genuine interest in what he was saying. She was intent on him, not looking elsewhere, but directly at him, with eyes as clear as gemstones. And he felt an emotion that was unfamiliar to him, a warming inside, a glowing of his spirit, comfortably aroused. He didn't look at Erica, but for a few glances, because his eyes were on Elsa, traveling at ease over her smooth face, her hair, the lines of her cheeks, the depth of her eyes, the softness of her lips, her sensitive expression as he spoke. Something about her made him feel at ease, and he could have talked forever.

"When you were on the farm, did you have a dog?" she asked.

"Yes, I had a dog."

"A girl dog, or a boy dog?"

"Of course, it was a male. It was a German shepherd, full of hair, and rough around the edges. It used to nip at my heels when I ran."

"What was his name?"

"Herman. And your dog is what?"

"He is a black Labrador."

"A big one."

"Yes, very big. Its name is, well, Blackie, and it is always underfoot."

"Dogs are all the same. And your family? Do you have brothers or sisters?"

"I have both, a brother named David, who you met, and a sister named Corina. I had an Aunt named Clara. I met her only once, at a funeral, when I was just a little girl."

They talked on, about themselves. Erica joined in on the conversation, but left most of it to Henrik and Elsa.

They spoke for nearly a half hour before Henrik said, "You know, if they catch me here they will put me on bread and water for a week."

"Really!" Elsa responded, her face wreathed in surprise.

"No. I was only joking. But they could make it hard on you. And maybe they would clamp down on me just a little."

"Then we must go."

"I think, yes, soon now. Sometimes the guard patrols the perimeter of the camp. He may take your names and notify your parents, and I do not think you would want that."

"You're right, we wouldn't want that."

He nodded. "All right then. To be safe I think we should put an end to this day."

The two girls looked at one another and nodded. Henrik could see the sadness in Elsa's eyes, and he felt good about her not wanting to go.

"I want you to know something," he said, as Elsa turned to look at him, her eyes full of disappointment. "It has been a wonderful day for me. Meeting the two of you will brighten my entire week. I will use this day as a means to chase away my sorrow."

Elsa reached out toward him, but retracted her hand as if compelled to do so. "I want you to return to the farm."

He nodded. "I will if I am asked. I hope your father comes for me soon."

"I cannot ask him to do so."

"I know. I will wait and hope. In the meantime, I will think of you."

Erica nearly swooned.

"Miss Pauls," he said then. "I have a good friend whose name is Emil. He is here with me. I am sure he would like to meet you."

Ericka's eyes widened. "Why I ..."

"You needn't say anything. But he is a handsome boy, and lonely. I think you could cheer him up. Now go, you two. I have taken up enough of your time. But remember this." He hesitated, unsure if he should utter the words his heart had prepared. But then he looked into Elsa's eyes and saw an expectation that needed to be fulfilled, and he said. "For every star you see tonight, each one will be filled with a thought of you."

He saw Elsa's lips tremble, and watched her eyes close. Erica cupped her mouth to catch a sigh. Then they stood, and he did the same, and for just a moment he gazed into Elsa's eyes, and felt a need for her, greater than any emotion he had ever experienced. But he was sensible enough to know that this might be the last time he would see Elsa Sommer. If chances were to be played out, it would be a thousand to one that he would ever come in contact with her again. But still, this place remained, this ground on which they stood, and there were still Sundays ahead of them.

"I will be here next Sunday," he said. "It has already become my favorite place."

"I cannot be sure," Elsa said.

"I know."

The two girls joined hands, and Elsa looked at him with misted eyes. "Goodbye," she said. "I will look forward to next Sunday."

"Take care of yourself."

"I will."

"Good-bye, Henrik," Erica said, taking Elsa's hand.

Together the two girls walked past the hedge and turned the corner, and with one last turn of her head, Elsa disappeared.

Henrik stood there for a while, breathing the scented air, his eyes closed, his thoughts aroused.

What had been a chance meeting on the porch of her farm had now become a clandestine meeting at the edge of his camp, in a place secluded from other eyes. His thighs trembled. A warm chill snaked up the center of his back. Something far more powerful than mere emotion was wielding its influence in him. He wanted to see her again, already, even though her absence was no more than a minute past. He wanted to run after her and draw her back, but he knew he could not. Forces in command of his life would not allow it. Elements beyond their control would keep them apart. It was folly to think that anything would bring them together again, foolish to think that even fate would intervene on their behalf. He was also sensible enough to know that even though he was eager to see her again, she might not wish to see him.

Their time together had consisted of nothing more than conversation. What dreams could be built on that? No, he would go his way and think back on this moment as something marvelous, knowing that when he was back in Germany, he might even forget this warm day in June, in New Ulm, Minnesota, when he met a most beautiful girl.

He turned and walked back to the fence. The girls were already out of sight, and he felt like a prisoner again.

W HY, YOU LITTLE SNIT, ELSA SOMMER. You met this boy, this prisoner of war, and you didn't even tell me. I'm your best friend. My God, he nearly scared me to death when he called your name."

They were walking quickly toward the car, almost skipping with delight. Elsa looked back over her shoulder to get one last glimpse of him, but he wasn't there. "Isn't he delicious?" she said.

"Delicious? Oh, my God, he's more than delicious. He's scrumptious. Why didn't you tell me about him?"

"He came to the farm to set some fence posts. I never thought I'd see him again, ever. I was as surprised as you when he called my name."

"No. You came here today hoping you'd see him again, didn't you?"

Elsa slowed down and took a deep breath. "Well, I was hoping."

"You were more than hoping. No wonder you were so fidgety today."

"Well, he's been on my mind."

"On your mind. Oh, my God. It's a wonder you can sleep at night."

"Who said I sleep?"

Erica shook her hands like bell ringer. "You are so . . . so . . . unpredictable. I don't know what to make of you. " "

Elsa pulled up sharply and faced Erica head on. Her voice took on a different tone. "Now that you've seen him, you've got to promise me something."

"What?"

"That you'll never speak a word of this to anyone, not to anyone."

Erica crossed both her fingers as a sign of trust. "I won't. I promise."

"If my parents find out about this I won't be able to leave the farm all summer. Papa would be furious. He told me to stay away from this camp. He knows I came to the lake today, with you, but this road is the boundary. If he thought I was . . ."

Erica took Elsa's hand. "Don't worry. I won't say a word to anyone, nobody, no how. You can trust me."

Elsa stood quietly for a moment. "I'm trembling all over."

"Let's go and sit down."

"Yes, I think we better."

They walked to the car and got inside. The heat wrapped them silently and in just seconds Elsa felt her anxiety ease away, leaving questions she couldn't answer.

"I don't know why I came here today," she said. "In the back of my mind I knew it was wrong, but I wanted to see him again. Something almost forced me to come, and now I'm afraid of what might happen."

"Nothing's going to happen. Everything will be just fine. Just stay away from him. Put him out of your mind, if that's at all possible."

Elsa pressed her fingers to her forehead. "I don't know if I can."

"Why not?"

"Because he's all I think about, day and night. Ever since I met him on our porch he's been in my mind, like a song I can't dismiss."

"Then he's become an obsession."

"Yes, I think he has. Something happened that day on the back porch and now I can't get rid of it."

"Simple answer. I think you're falling in love."

Elsa swung her hand and struck Erica lightly on the arm. "Stop it. I'm not in love. I just can't get rid of this feeling. Why would I want to be in love with someone I can't be with? What kind of future would I have with a man who fought against us? Why would I love someone who doesn't even live in our country, someone who'll be returning to Germany for the rest of his life? It's so . . . damn confusing I could scream."

They both fell silent for a while. Their eyes scanned through the window at the people on the shoreline; the kids playing, the parents resting in their chairs, a boat, bow up on the sand, fishing rods leaning at an angle. Elsa looked to the right, where the camp was located, behind the sheltering cottonwoods. Her emotions welled up again, and within moments she was crying.

"What am I to do, Erica?" she cried.

Erica took her hand. "Oh, my God, I've never seen you like this. He has taken you by the heart, hasn't he? Come on now, confess. There's more to this than just a friendship."

"How can it even be friendship? I've seen him only twice, once for a couple of minutes, again today for, what, a half hour, if that. I guess I just want someone new in my life after that mess I had with Carlyle. All I know is, I've got to get over this."

"You will."

Elsa took a deep breath. "I know I will. But today, just talking to him, just looking at him, just being with him...I can't imagine that I will."

"Maybe I can help." Erica turned in the seat and took Elsa's left hand in her own. "Look, he's a prisoner, right?"

Elsa nodded.

"And he's all but locked up, right?"

Again, the nod.

"And you'll probably never see him again, right?"

"You're right."

"So why the fret? Forget Henrik, whatever his name is. He won't be coming around again. And try to remember that he's a German soldier who'll be going back home, probably by the end of this year. That's only months away. And you'll never see him again. Never! End of story."

Elsa smiled weakly. She wiped a tear away. "Yea, I guess that's all there is to it. Just wipe him away like a...tear. So easy to do . . . so easy."

"So there we are, all settled. And if you send him away to memory lane, I won't ever have to concern myself with meeting his friend, what was his name, Emil."

Elsa laughed. "Imagine the two of us, head over heels with two German prisoners. Why we might just make the front page of the paper."

"Or land in jail."

"Or be banished from New Ulm."

"Or maybe we'd never be allowed in school again."

"Hooray!"

"Or maybe we'd go back to Germany with them and dig in the debris, and drink warm beer because there isn't any ice, and eat weinersneitzel for the rest of our lives."

Laughter again, belly-rolling laughter. Then silence as they gathered their breath. Erica started the car and backed out of the parking space. Elsa turned and looked once more at the thicket concealing the POW camp, and as she did, that often-tortuous urge swept her again, and she couldn't imagine dismissing it with humor.

Elsa sighed. "The end of a perfect day."

"The last of its kind," Erica added.

"Good-bye Henrik, whoever you are."

Erica sat back and gazed through the windshield as they drove up the road through the ravine. "It's a good thing we got that settled," she said. "If you remember, Mae West once said: Too much of a good thing can be wonderful."

They glanced at one another and laughed some more, but as they turned out toward the farm land, where everything was green and fresh and as perfect as nature could make it, Elsa closed her eyes and tried to envision Henrik's face, and his bright, blue eyes, the windows to his soul.

And she felt the longing again.

Henrik walked slowly through the trees after the girls had left. He caught sight of them occasionally, until they disappeared from sight. Then he roved through the campsite, reviewing what he had done. It had been foolish, drawing them into his world, and he felt guilty for having interfered in their lives for the sake of enlightening his own. If they had been found together behind the bushes it would have been hard on them. Algona was only a half-day's distant. The authorities might have sent him back. The girls would have been chastised, a letter written to their parents, with parental punishment close behind, if his judgment was correct. He would not do it again, not here, not in this place. Nor would he tell Emil. This sojourn would become a secret, never to be revealed.

But despite his resolve, something nagged at him. He could not shake away the vision of how she held her hands together, of how warm and bright her smile was, and how her eyes roved over him as if seeking something more gratifying than his mere presence. He had wanted so much to touch her, but had rejected the impulse as improper and reckless. She was beautiful, he thought, soft-skinned and appealing, and he wanted so much to see her again, alone, in a place where they could exchange feelings, touches, and perhaps an embrace. But that was impossible. He could wish a thousand years, and they would never have such an opportunity. Their lives were as far apart as any could be, and nothing would change their positions.

Henrik walked sadly through the trees, then back down to where they had sat together, and there he listened to the whisper of the river and the wind through the leaves, and when his eyes closed he could see her there just beyond his reach. Strange, he thought, to have such emotions, when she was little more than a name to him. Strange, to have seen her only a half hour before, in this place, where now only emptiness remained. Strange, to think that this could happen to him, in a land where he was a prisoner, in a place surrounded by his captors.

He went back to the cabin and picked up a book, and sat down in a chair where he pretended to read, but his eyes did not see the words. He saw only Elsa, sitting on the grass in her bright flowered skirt and her spring-green sweater, with her golden hair flowing across her neck, and her eyes so brightly fixed on him.

Within minutes, the book had fallen to the table, its pages tight together. He closed his eyes. He slept in a dream, then, his head cradled in his arms, and there, in his fantasy world, he walked hand in hand with her along the river path, and spoke to her the words he could never say in person.

TWENTY-SEVEN

New Ulm, Minnesota, July 1945

THE FOURTH OF JULY CAME QUICKLY. The flag was flown on the porch, as it was on Flag Day, Labor Day and Armistice Day. It was a day of celebration and noise. David had his fireworks. He made good use of them by blowing empty tin cans into the air, by devastating sand castles, by blasting bark off the trees, and destroying all the anthills he could find. As on Memorial Day, the parade in New Ulm was festooned with flags and filled with marching veterans. Beer flowed like water.

Dinner was magnificent. Sliced ham on a red, white and blue platter. Heaps of potatoes, with yams and lettuce salad and two types of pie, apple and pumpkin. They all ate their fill. Papa collapsed on the sofa while the girls cleaned up. Outside David and his friend from the neighboring farm waged make-believe war in the grove with their cherry bombs and M-16s. Later, photos were taken on the porch. In the evening they all lit sparklers and pinwheels and roman candles. And that night, when the fireworks were all gone, and peace had settled on the farm, Elsa sat on the porch and looked into the sky where the stars were massed like a sequined blanket.

And in the darkness she imagined that Henrik was looking at them also.

BY THE TIME THE CORN WAS KNEE HIGH, it was time to harvest the oats, and Harold Sommer knew he would need help, help he could not expect from the girls. Two of the young men he had used the year before had gone to war, both to the Pacific to battle the Nips. He thought hard about using the German POWs. He decided he had no other choice, and so he made up his mind to hire two of them for the length of time it took to cut, bundle and shock the crop, two days at best.

As usual, he and the family were awake at five o'clock, at the same time the sun labored up from the fields. The four of them dressed, and together they marched out to the barn with sleep still tight in their eyes. Papa let the cows in. Belle, the largest of the herd, always led the way. They all knew their own stanchions and marched obediently into them, mooing in pain from their engorged udders. David had the job of throwing hay down from the haymow. Corina forked hay to each of the cows while Elsa fed them their supplements. Both the girls finished the morning by washing the cows' udders. Papa and David did the milking, taking the same cows in hand everyday. It was a quiet time. The only sounds came from the cows as they chewed their cuds, from their contented mooing, from the staccato rapping of the milk streams against the metal pails, and from an occasional spurt of urine or the plop of manure into the concrete trench.

The milk was carried to the separating room where the cream was spun off. The hogs always got the skim. The cream was usually kept in the water tank until the creamery picked it up by truck. With their work finished, the four washed up, and then went in for their waiting breakfast.

Papa was the first to lift four pancakes from the stack and pile them on his plate. Elsa did the same. She loved maple syrup. David ate his Wheaties. Corina spooned her Malt-O-Meal. Toast all around.

"I'm going in to town this morning to pick up two more of those prisoners," Papa said between mouthfuls. I need help with the shocking."

"I can do it, Papa," David said.

"Not alone, you can't. I'm going to get you a couple of strong German boys to give you a hand."

"They probably don't know the first thing about shocking."

"There's farm boys among them who'll know what to do."

David squared his shoulders. "Yea, but the ones you get today won't be as good as the last one was. I heard my friend, Brian say that some of 'em ain't worth sh— they ain't worth nothing."

Papa stared him down. "That was a close one, son. You better mind your mouth or you'll get it soaped."

"Sorry, Pa."

Elsa didn't say a word, but her thoughts raced. She wanted to mention Henrik's name, but she dared not. Whoever came would be of Papa's choosing, not hers. She ate slowly, while trying to appear disinterested, imagining what would happen if he did choose Henrik. Would she see him again? Would they be able to converse? Or would the men be confined to the fields all day? She ate slowly, her mind awhirl. She remembered what she had said to Erica that day they drove up and out of the park.

Elsa was in the kitchen when Papa drove into the yard. She was helping her mother with mending again. Immediately her curiosity got the best of her, and she walked quickly to the window. Papa's car went right past the house and stopped in front of the machine shed that lay to the far left of the yard. Even when pressing her face tight against the pane, she could not get a very good view of them. She did see Papa when he got out of the car, then two other men. They were far enough away so she couldn't distinguish their features.

"They're here," she said.

"Why are you so interested in them today?"

"I want to see if one of them is the same one who was here last time."

"Is he?"

"I don't know. One has dark hair and the other light. Henrik had light hair."

Clara's eyebrows rose. "Oh, so you remember his name."

Elsa turned away from the window. "Why, yes. He was kind enough to give it to me. I remember it because it was almost the same as Henry Porter's name."

"That is a coincidence."

Elsa peered out the window again. "There. I see them now. Yes, one of them is Henrik."

Clara had finished her sewing. She tied off the knot and bit the thread. "So now what are you going to do?"

"Nothing. They're helping Papa bring out the binder."

They had pulled the binder out of the shed and had moved it to a position behind the tractor. It would take only minutes to hook the two together, and then they would be gone. She felt an urgency she could not contain. "Can I go out and see them?"

"Not now. They're busy, and besides, Papa wouldn't like the distraction. Maybe later. I'll fix them some sandwiches for lunch. You can bring them out into the field."

"Really?"

"Why, yes. Unless, of course, you don't want to."

"I do. I'm curious about them. I always have been. I want to see what they're really like up close. The other day I hardly had a chance to say hello before he was gone."

"What a shame."

Elsa left the window and sat down at the table. She sat quietly with her hands in her lap. She knew she had to say something to justify her curiosity.

"You sound patronizing," she said straight out. "How often do we get an honest to goodness prisoner on our property? This might be the last time. I want to satisfy my curiosity. All I've seen of them is in the newsreels, goose-stepping and saluting and all smart in their uniforms. I think they might be much different now that the war is over."

Clara sat back and snickered. "You have the curiosity of youth."

"I guess I do."

"But I think it also has something to do with the fact that you are a young girl and they are handsome young men."

Elsa appeared shocked. "Mother, how can you think that way?"

"Easily. I was once young myself. I know how girl's emotions can sometimes run away with her."

"Mother, don't be absurd."

She patted Elsa on the hand. "Forget what I said. I was just joking. Perhaps it's better if you do see them. Then you'll forget about them and concentrate on other, more meaningful, tasks, like finishing your mending."

Outside, the men hooked the binder up to the Farmall tractor just as David rushed out of the barn to join them. He stood aside, assessing the Germans with a curious eye, until Papa made the appropriate introductions. There was a shaking of hands, and some words spoken, and then Papa ordered him up onto the tractor seat where he started the motor. Then, with his eyes straight ahead, he drove the joined units out onto the road. Papa and the two prisoners trailed behind at a casual pace.

WHEN THEY WERE IN THE FIELD PAPA TOOK over the tractor. David was given the job of explaining to the prisoners how the work was done, and to set the pace. As they stood in a small group waiting for Papa to begin cutting, David stepped out in front of the others and stood as erect as he ever had, his jaw firm, his eyes hard set. This was the first time he had ever spoken to a prisoner of war, and inside he was a bit nervous, but he didn't want it to show. He turned his attention to Henrik, because he knew he spoke English.

"Have you ever shocked oats before?" he asked, his voice firm.

Henrik nodded. "I have. I was raised on a farm in Germany. Only we did not have a tractor. We used a team of horses to pull the shear."

David was surprised. If they could build airplanes and tanks and ships, why didn't the farmers have tractors?

"Well I guess the results are the same whether you use tractors or horses, but I'll tell you anyway. The sickle bar will cut the grain and drop it onto a canvas belt. From there it'll be conveyed to the binding mechanism where a portion of it will be tied with a piece of twine, making a small bundle we call a sheave. Then they'll be kicked out about every sixty feet."

Henrik nodded, and then conveyed the information to the other POW. When he was finished translating, he turned back to David, who continued the instructions. "We're going to follow the binder and gather up the sheaves, butt side down, grain side up. Then we're gonna pile 'em in groups of eight or twelve, depending on their size. Then we'll shock 'em into stooks that look like small teepees. Do you know what a teepee is?"

"Yes, or course. It is like an Indian tent."

"Yeah."

Impressed with the boy, Henrik asked, "How old are you, David?"

David stood proudly. "I am thirteen, why?"

"Because you act so much older. You are more like a man."

David grinned. His body shifted nervously. "Thanks," he said, continuing on. "Now sometimes the twine's gonna break, and when it does you gotta pull some off another twine ball and retie the bundle. Now, here, each one of you gets a small jack knife to cut the twine with." One thing he didn't like was the thought that each of them now had a weapon.

David continued talking. "Sometimes you can take the oats and run 'em through the binder again, but that'll slow the operation, so use the knife."

Once again, Henrik related the information to the other prisoner, who nodded in return. Message received.

"Now we get two breaks, one in the morning, and another in the afternoon. I think maybe my sister will bring out some sandwiches for lunch. If you want water there's a ten-gallon cream can on the binder, and a dipper. Drink all you want. We'll probably empty the whole thing before the day's over. We're getting a late start so I think there'll be more work tomorrow. Have you got all that?"

Again, the translation, the nodding of heads.

Then David smiled. "Well, I think you got it all, but there's one more thing left. If you're gonna be a real farmer, then you gotta be chewin' a weed while you work." He reached down near his shoe, snatched the stem of a weed from its stalk and placed it in his mouth. "It'll bring up the saliva," he said.

The prisoners laughed and did the same. When they were all chewing their weeds, Henrik looked back toward his father who was mounted on the tractor seat. "I guess we're ready to go," he shouted.

As the binder moved into the field, the three fell in behind it. The engine revved, startling a group of crows that took off squawking, their wings fluttering like black fans. David walked out ahead of the Germans, proud that he had done his job to the best of his ability. He was satisfied with Papa's choice of men, especially the one who spoke English. His opinion of a German soldier had taken a turn for the better. As they walked onto the field the sun seemed as hot as it would ever get, but even that was misleading. Before noon arrived, the temperature would climb into the high eighties and all of them would be bathed in sweat.

The binder rattled and shook. Its blades gnashed, and it began kicking out sheaves. Henrik shouted at the top of his voice. "Good thing we're not cutting barley. That stuff's got nasty beards that are prickly as hell. It'll cut you up if you're not careful, and if it gets inside your clothes you'd think the devil himself is in there trying to itch you to death."

David laughed, and then charged into the work. He was happiest when working, when his body was being tested, when his arms were doing what they were meant to do. He'd work all day at full speed if he had to, to toughen him up for the real work yet to come, when he was older and in need of strong arms and legs, and to teach his own children what farming was all about.

Henrik dove into the job with all the drive and energy he could muster, his thoughts centering on only one thing. So the boy's sister was going to being out sandwiches for lunch. The thought almost made him skip. He hoped it would be Elsa. As he began bending and lifting and rising and setting, and sweating, he forgot the pledge he had made to himself that Sunday in the woods. The thought of her coming out to the field raced his heart, and he worked to a fever pitch. He would not ignore her. He would do all he could to get near to her, and talk to her.

He was hard-pressed not to let out a hoot when David looked at him once and said. "You're doing a great job there, Henrik. You're gonna wake up your appetite for sure."

IT WAS CLOSE TO ELEVEN O'CLOCK WHEN mother called Elsa into the kitchen to make sandwiches for the crew. There were four men in the field, two sandwiches for each, a total of eight to be made with beef slices, lettuce, mayonnaise, and pickles. She packed four apples as well, and a large jar of lemonade sealed with a tight cap. As she handed them off to Elsa, she said. "Take the bicycle. They'll be hungry by now."

The Western Flyer always stood alongside the fence. They had bought the bicycle about seven years earlier, for Elsa's tenth birthday. Since then everyone had ridden it, to all the fields and beyond, into town, even out to Swan Lake once for a class picnic when the car was being repaired, a near sixteen-mile ride. She lifted it off the fence.

It was a sorry sight. No one took care of it any more. She placed the package of sandwiches and the bottle of lemonade into the carrier, and then pushed off toward the field. The oat field was a short ride across the main road, about half mile distant.

So Henrik would be there. She didn't let it complicate her thoughts until the field came into sight. When she heard the tractor running and the chatter of the binder, she knew she would have to say something to him. Obviously neither of them would mention the meeting at the river. Both were sensible enough to keep that secret to themselves. So what would she say, how would she act?

The questions became perplexing when she pulled off onto the dirt path and rode down alongside the cornfield. There they were, working in the distance, out where the small chaff cloud appeared, just a smudge against the clear blue sky. Papa must have seen her ride up the road, because he waved and cut the motor, and as the tractor stopped he jumped off and began walking toward her, followed by the other three.

Elsa was dressed in overalls, the same as David, only hers were unsightly and worn thin around the knees, and one of the pockets was ripped and hanging like a flap. She wore a light blouse beneath it, and underclothing. David wore only his under-shorts, no shirt beneath his overalls. His skin would be sweating chaff. Her hair was undone, spreading across her forehead at times, as if it didn't know its own place. She brushed it back. She felt ragged and boyish, and she imagined that she'd be unattractive to Henrik, given the way she looked. Oh well, what the hell, she thought, nothing was going to come of the meeting anyway. She'd give them the sandwiches and then ride off, simple as that. Henrik wouldn't want anything to do with her with Papa close by. Even if he did talk to her it would be quick. The men were there, and he'd want to be with them. Men were all alike that way.

As they came closer, Henrik eased his pace and waved to her. She had her hands full and couldn't return the greeting, but she did see his smile, that wide, beaming grin that filled his entire face with delight.

"We're starving," Papa shouted. When he came closer he wiped the sweat from his forehead. "These men are as hungry as bears. They were about ready to run into town when you came peddling down the road. Now what have you got for us?"

"Beef on bread, two sandwiches for each, and lemonade."

"Good enough." He motioned to the others. "Come on now, get your own."

Papa took his first, then David. The prisoner she didn't know came third, then Henrik. When he stepped up to her he said, "Good morning, Elsa. How are you this fine, hot day?"

"I'm well, thank you. You look like you've been working."

He laughed. "Your brother here is a taskmaster. He would not let me slow down. To keep up with him is like trying to keep up with a horse."

David laughed with his mouth full of food. "A horse wouldn't stand a chance against me."

"That I believe," Henrik said.

They ate, and all the while, Elsa stood aside and watched them, trying not to interfere. Occasionally, Henrik's glance swept her way, his eyes bright and magnetic. His hair drifted lazily across his forehead. His face, slick with sweat, glistened in the sunlight. He had not bothered to remove his camp clothes. The large PW stood out boldly on the back of his shirt. Perspiration had dampened it with a dark, crablike pattern. He laughed with the men, and mussed up David's hair with his hand, acting much like one of the family. He did not withhold his words or his humor. He spoke with gusto, matching comments. Occasionally he would look out over the field festooned with shocked stands that marched like a silent army across the flattened field. Then he would look her way and grin. She did not respond, although her heart was beating faster than it should. His smile quickly demolished her self-control.

She could not stay much longer. As the men finished eating, she picked up the empty lemonade jar and placed it in the basket, then raised the bicycle and began walking toward the dirt path. Halfway there, she turned and saw Henrik talking to her father.

"Mr. Sommer, I would like to talk to Elsa. Would you mind very much if I did?" He had pondered the question, and had came to the conclusion that all her father could say was no.

Even so, it was a difficult question for Harold, one he had not expected. He looked quickly at Elsa as she approached the path. "Why would you want to talk to her?"

"Because we met the other day, when I was here fixing the fence. We did not talk then, but I would like very much to introduce myself in a proper way."

"Can I trust you to be a gentleman?"

"Why, yes sir. I will be gentleman. I do not know how to be otherwise."

Against his better judgment, and because Henrik had worked so hard for him the past hours, he nodded his agreement. "Go ahead. A few minutes only. We still have work to do."

"Thank you, sir." Then he shouted. "Elsa, wait. A few words, please."

She hesitated and stopped, then turned and saw him striding toward her. Her heart jumped a beat. Oh, no, she thought, father will be furious. Then she saw Papa looking her way, with his face set in a hard stare, and she knew he had given his permission.

She pulled up short and leaned into the bike. Without trying, a smile came to her face.

"I have only a minute," Henrik said. "You father was kind enough to let me talk to you."

She felt flushed, but not from the sun. As he came closer, she could hardly hold still.

He walked up next to her and stopped two paces away, knowing he had to keep his distance. His face was damp, scattered with chaff. Her first impulse was to brush it away, to touch his warm skin with her fingertips.

Henrik's voice was mellow. "I thank God for my appetite today. It was He who sent you here, to feed us hard workers, and to let me see you again."

"It is good to see you too."

"Ah, so formal. I was hoping you would at least give me a smile."

She glanced over her shoulder to where Papa was standing.

"Ah, I see," Henrik said. "You think he is watching you. Well, in that case you can keep your smile for another time."

"Another time?"

"Well, I have not seen you at the river. I go there whenever I can, hoping you will be there, but all I see are ducks and geese in the water, and strangers on the path. What can we do about that?"

Her lip began trembling. "Nothing, I'm afraid. I probably will not go there again."

"Ah, so you will make me a very lonely boy. How can you do that and feel good about it?"

"My father is watching."

"He will not know what we are talking about. You see, I am keeping my voice low. And now I will laugh, so he does not think I am being forward."

He did laugh, loud enough to be heard, and she laughed with him.

"Come here, Henrik." The shout came clearly from David. "It is time to work again."

Henrik turned and shouted his reply. "I will be there in a moment." He looked at Elsa again, his eyes deeper this time. They were different now, filled with an emotion she had not seen before. "I want to see you again, but I know how difficult that will be for you. So I will only hope that God will give me another chance."

She was drawn into his eyes and for a moment her knees weakened. She didn't know what to say. Words were wedged in her throat. Then, as he was about to turn, she uttered. "I will try."

His grin was broad. "You have made my day worthwhile," he said. Then, turning, he walked quickly back to the others.

Without a moment lost, Elsa walked the bike onto the dirt path, mounted it, and peddled out toward the road that would take her home.

Before they returned to the field, Henrik said to Papa. "It was nice of you to allow me to talk to Elsa. I wanted to thank her personally for bringing our lunches. You have a fine daughter there."

At five o'clock that day they called it quits. They left the tractor and the binder in the field and walked back to the farm There they washed up in the tank and drank their fill and Papa drove them back to the camp with David riding along.

Twilight had set in when Papa and David drove into the yard. At dinner, not a word was said about Henrik, which Elsa found very odd. She went to bed that night with Henrik's name ringing in her head. Henrik! Henrik! Henrik! Henrik! What am I going to do about you? If I don't see you again, I will surely lose my mind.

Henrik turned restlessly in his bed that night although he was exhausted from the day's work. Thoughts of Elsa kept him awake. With every turn of his body he saw her standing in the sun as the breeze ruffled her hair. Then she smiled, and her face gleamed: a reflection in the mirror of his mind. It should not be this way, he told himself. She should not occupy my mind so completely when I have only seen her for a few minutes of my life. Why is this happening? Why am I so filled with her?

Henrik had never had a girlfriend. He had never touched a girl fondly, had never kissed one. He had seen them unclothed only in pictures. He had read about sexual experiences only in the small palm-sized books that were passed along from boy to boy in school, and he had erections and seminal discharges, most often at night when dreams brought the pictures to life.

Ever since his introduction into the Jugend he had met only those girls who were loyal to Hitler. Boys never seemed to interest those girls. The ones who were not part of the movement were either homely or withdrawn or sheltered by their parents. Then the war came, and the bombs, and the fighting, no one thought of love. No one thought of a future. No one thought of anything except survival.

Now there was Elsa, an American girl who lived on a farm miles from where he slept, with a protective father to watch her every move. He had made a silent pledge not to allow her into his life, but there she was, as compelling as the breaths that kept him alive. He knew that he could not ignore the magnetism. He knew that he had to do something that would allow them to communicate, despite the distance, despite the overwhelming odds against them. He could not put her out of his life. Not now. Not when he was so overwhelmed by her.

Tomorrow he would go into the field again. Tomorrow she would bring lunch to them, and he would see her again. Tomorrow he would find a way to communicate with her. By tomorrow he would know what he must do to keep this incredible feeling alive. His only other hope was that, she too, would feel the same longing, the same need, the same affection,

THE DAY WAS BRIGHT AND CLOUDLESS. In the dry warmth of summer, one could smell the fields and the scent of clover. They began cutting and shocking before ten o'clock, and by noon their appetites cried for food. Elsa came on the bicycle again, the same as she had the day before, this time bearing chicken sandwiches, raw carrots, chocolate cake, and apple cider. The crew ate sitting down, with the sun on their shoulders, and again, as Elsa was about to leave, Henrik asked permission to bid her goodbye, knowing they would not return the following day. Again, Papa gave his permission, under a watchful eye. As he approached her, Henrik said, "Walk with me."

They began walking slowly down the dirt path as Papa's voice reached them. "Do not go far. We will be starting again soon."

Elsa turned and shrugged. "Yes, Papa."

Henrik had little time to speak his mind. How could he express himself in only a few minutes? He struggled to put everything in order, but found it difficult to form a single sentence. They had taken only a few steps, and during those short moments time had compressed to seconds. Henrik was quick with his remark. "I will not return tomorrow," he said.

"I know."

"I have so much I want to say to you, some of which you must hear, but I cannot express myself in front of the others. I will say only that I have strong feelings for you, and I would hope that you have the same for me, impossible though it might be. After we met that day by the river, I told myself I would put you out of my mind, but I have been unable to do that. I think of you always."

Her eyes misted slightly as she gazed at him. "I think of you, too," she confessed.

"I am pleased to hear you say that. And now today, when I met you again, I know I want to see you again sometime, without Erica, just you and me together."

"Why?"

He breathed deeply, searching for the right words. "Because of the way fate has brought us together. I feel that our meeting is not just coincidence."

"What are you asking of me?

"Nothing. I ask nothing. I am just a lonely boy who can offer only the feeling I have for you."

She pulled the bicycle to a stop. "Do you know how this sounds to me?"

"Yes, I believe so. I think it sounds like something inappropriate."

"Is it?"

His face flushed. "Oh, no. Do not take me wrong. I have only the greatest respect for you. I would do nothing out of place." He stopped and took a deep breath, and looked out over the cornfield to where the tree line etched a wall of green against the horizon. His passion seized then, and he felt a great loss, as if he had stumbled and fell into a hole from which there was no escape. "I think maybe I have said the wrong thing. Please forgive me."

She stopped, glanced back at Papa, who was still watching them. Then she eased her shoulders back and looked him straight in the eye. "We cannot go farther than this. My father will surely be angry if we do. But let me say one thing. I will see you one more time if I can, at the same place we met before. I will try to be there next Sunday in the afternoon. If you can be there, fine. If not, then we will both go our own way."

Henrik felt relieved. "You have made me very happy."

"It is the least I can do for a lonely boy," she said, to repeat his own words. "Now go back and work. I promise nothing except that I will try. Do you understand me?"

"Yes, yes, I do."

"We will see where this fate of yours takes us."

"Thank you, dear Elsa."

She reached over and touched his arm, briefly. "You are different than I ever imagined you would be. I am amazed by you."

"For whatever that means, thank you. I will pray for Sunday. Go now, and laugh when you do. The laugh will do you good. Pretend you are the wind and you must blow away from me now."

She laughed at the ingenuity of his words and then turned and walked away from him before mounting the bicycle. He waved, and then watched her pedal down the dirt path, past the cornfield and onto the road, and all the while he felt as if a great burden had been lifted from him. Then, with a mood of euphoria wrapped around him, he turned and walked back toward the men who were passing the jar of apple juice from hand to hand.

As he approached them, Papa yanked a weed stalk from the ground and began picking his teeth with it. Henrik was unable to read the silent message in his eyes. "You two have formed a friendship," Papa said simply.

"A brief one," Henrik replied.

"I think you like her," David put in, snickering.

"She is a nice girl," Henrik said, mussing the boy's hair with his hand.

Harold turned his head and glared at his son. "You must mind your words. Think before you talk."

"Forgive him," Henrik said jokingly. "I am a German soldier, and I have only one objective in mind, and that is to return to my homeland."

"That is enough to wish for," Papa said. With that he arose and brushed off his coveralls and walked straight toward the binder, his feet scuffing through the stubble. The others stood up and followed him.

Henrik turned and looked down the dirt road. Elsa was already out of sight.

THEY FINISHED THE FIELD THAT DAY AND RODE back to the farm, perched on the equipment. The air was cooler. The sun had vanished behind a thin haze, but its light still burnished the sky. Back in the yard, they moved the binder back into the shed and then washed up. Elsa was not to be seen. Henrik and the other prisoner were driven back to the camp just in time for their dinner.

That night at the Sommer farm, there was little conversation during the meal. The still mood was broken only when Papa leaned back from his plate and lit up his pipe. "We accomplished a lot these last two days. I had a good crew. Those Germans worked hard. I was impressed by them, especially Henrik. He is a good man."

"He's my friend," David boasted.

"He was the only one you could understand."

"Yea, but he didn't say much to me. He was too busy talking to Elsa."

Elsa threw him a disgruntled look. "He talked to everyone."

"Not in private."

"He just wanted to say good-bye. I'll probably never see him again."

Papa puffed on his pipe. "It all depends on where they send him. He could go anywhere."

"I'll have to say this," Elsa replied. "He wasn't like anything I expected of a German prisoner of war. I never imagined any of them would be polite."

"He was that," Papa agreed. "He ain't like some of them. Old Barney Howlis had a couple of 'em for a day or two. He said they both did as little as possible and were as haughty as they could be, like a couple of stormtroopers. He won't have 'em back."

"Will you have Henrik back?" David asked.

"I can't say. Maybe if I do he can stay for dinner with us one night. Maybe we can sort of adopt the boy 'till its time for him to be shipped back to Germany."

Elsa didn't say a word. But she could feel a stirring of her emotions.

Corina sat upright. "Would you do that, Papa? I haven't even seen what he looks like yet."

"He looks just like everybody else," Elsa explained.

"I still want to meet him."

"Well, maybe you will," Papa answered. "I think the boy deserves a good German New Ulm meal, maybe some sauerkraut and sausage, and some of Mother's good potato salad."

David beamed. "Hey, once he tries that he probably won't want to go back to Germany." He laughed at his own statement.

"Remains to be seen," Papa said. "Now finish up and get to your chores. There'll be time for reflecting later on."

Papa's remark billowed in Elsa's mind throughout the evening, right up the time she crawled into bed. Wouldn't that be something, having him in the house like part of the family? Would it ever happen? Or would he be sent elsewhere for the remainder of the summer? She lay on her back, with her face toward the bottom of Corina's bunk, and all her thoughts that night were centered on him, and what might happen if she was ever to meet him face to face again. Lord, she thought, this might just be too much for my young heart to handle. This is something I cannot comprehend. This is something that only happens in the movies. This is incredible. Negatives did not enter her mind. If she were able to go to the Cottonwood on Sunday, the chances of them being found together were totally outweighed by the positive. She was too far into delight to imagine anything distracting. She felt only euphoria.

Elsa snickered when remembering the words Erica had uttered that day they drove up the ravine away from the camp, the words Mae West had once spoken: Too much of a good thing can be wonderful.

THE FOLLOWING EVENING, WHEN MOTHER was upstairs, and Papa and David were in the barn, and the Corina was drawing at the kitchen table, Elsa telephoned Erica, hoping that the party lines were silent. She did get a connection, and after talking for a while about everyday events, she ended the conversation by asking a favor that had lingered on her tongue far too long. Hesitantly, she said. "Erica, I want you to do something for me this coming Sunday afternoon."

"What?"

"I want you to drive me to the lake."

The brief silence was met with both hope and expected disappointment. "I think I know why. Is it . . ."

"Yes," Elsa said.

Erica's gasp was clearly audible. "Do you know what you're doing?"

"Not entirely, but, yes, I think so. Can you give me a ride?"

"I have nothing else planned."

"Will you do it then?"

"I suppose so, but jeez, are you sure you've thought it over?"

"I have. I need only be there for an hour, no more. It's something I have to do."

"What if it's raining?"

Elsa paused, thinking. "Then we'll take in a movie."

"Oh, I understand. Yeah, a movie."

"Can you pick me up about two o'clock?"

"Sure. But if you change your mind, call me beforehand. If for some reason I can't use the car, I'll let you know. My God, Elsa, you're a brave one."

"Bravery's got nothing to do with it."

"See you on Sunday."

"Good-bye."

She hung the receiver gently back onto its cradle and then sighed. Her hands trembled. She brought them tightly to her lips and for an entire minute she did not move. Now she had done it, she thought. Now the cat was out of the bag, and she was the only one who could put it back in. Crazy, she thought. Crazy! This was more powerful than taking her first taste of whiskey, or her first drag on a cigarette, or receiving her first kiss. This heartfelt association was not something that would end easily, nor was it something to be decided by fate. She would determine the outcome.

Sunday could easily change her future, or put everything back in perspective.

TWENTY-EIGHT

New Ulm, Minnesota, July 1945

THE SKY WAS FILLED WITH PILLOW clouds on Sunday. Elsa was nervous most of the morning and at church as well. She asked God to lead her in the right direction, and to make her decision, His decision. Erica arrived about one o'clock. As Elsa walked out the kitchen door, Clara told her to be home by four.

As they drove out of the yard, Erica turned a stone-cold stare in Elsa's direction. "Do you know what you're doing?"

Elsa sighed. "I don't know if I do."

"I think you're falling for the guy."

"Don't be ridiculous. This might very well be the last time I'll see him."

"You said that before."

"Well, chances are, he won't be coming back to our farm anymore."

"As if that means anything."

"What do you mean by that?

"Well, you are going to see him today. What will stop you from going to see him again? Besides, I won't be an accessory to your foolishness. This bond you seem to have created won't get you anywhere. My God, I wish we hadn't stopped that day last winter when they were skating on the pond. That's when it all started."

"No, that wasn't when it started. It started the day he stepped foot on our porch."

"And charmed your socks off."

"No, it wasn't like that. I can't explain it."

"Of course you can't. Love is hard to explain."

Elsa turned and looked out the window. She didn't want to get into an argument with Erica, not when she was doing a big favor for her. She would rather remain silent than take a chance on wrecking a friendship. She sighed. This was beginning to mushroom into something larger than just she and Henrik. How much more confusing could it get.

The cornfields were green now, the stalks high enough to block out the black soil. Along the ditch line a dog was chasing a cottontail, back and forth, back and forth, until they darted into the corn. The chase? Is that what she was on, a chase? And what was Henrik's reason for extending their friendship? If it was to make love to her, forget it. She would have no part of any sexual bonding, not with a prisoner of war, not with someone who would be out of her life within months. Be careful, she said to herself. Tread cautiously, and don't allow your emotions to get in the way of reason. For all the concern and problems this alliance was causing, she thought she might just wish him luck, tell him good-bye, and then get out of his life.

"I'm sorry," Erica said. "I didn't mean to criticize. I don't want anything to ruin our friendship."

Elsa touched her arm. "It's okay. Nothing will happen. I might just say good-bye to him and leave. If I do we can just go into town and see a movie."

"I'll bet you a double malt with whipped cream and two cherries on top that you won't say good-bye."

"It's a bet."

Erica laughed as the car ate up the last mile of road. "I'm sure gonna like that malted."

Erica parked the car near the lake. Both of them got out and stood silently for a while, saying nothing. Then Elsa asked Erica if she wanted to come along. Erica said no. Following a few moments of nervousness Elsa turned and walked to the footpath, then to the point where it met the dam. She looked both ways. Certain there was no one watching, she backtracked and eased through the gap in the lilac hedge into the compound, and headed toward the tree where they had met before. Her nerves were tight, her teeth hard set. Despite the warmth of the day, a chill ran up her back. She rubbed her hands together to calm herself.

Henrik was there, leaning shoulder-tight against the tree, his smile as broad as the river, his blue eyes tantalizingly bright. He was dressed in a light tan shirt with the sleeves rolled up past his elbows, and khaki pants, neatly pressed. As she approached he stood up straight, and bowed slightly toward her, and said, "Hello, Elsa."

At the sound of his voice, her apprehension faded. She smiled and moved toward him, confident of her ability to handle the moment. The sun slanted across his face. She glanced around, breathed a sigh, and then said. "Hi. I'm glad to see that you're alone."

He took two steps toward her, his hands outstretched. "Oh, you are referring to Emil. He is busy playing checkers. No one will bother us here, I assure you. How did you get here?"

"Erica drove me."

"Ah, yes, Erica. And where is she now?"

"She's waiting for me by the lake."

He grinned again. "I hope she is a patient girl."

She did not take his hands, so he nodded and motioned to the ground. "Sit. Sit. Let me have a look at you. You are handsome today, all dressed up. You see, I wore my other shirt, the one without the markings. I look more like a local boy, don't you think?"

She giggled, "You look better than the local boys." She fluffed her skirt and drifted to the grass. He crossed his legs and descended to a spot two feet away, facing her, his smile unbroken.

"You have given me a compliment, I see." He looked skyward for a moment, then took a deep breath, released it, breathed again, and then fixed his eyes on her. "I am happy that you are here. I was hoping you would be able to come. There is so much I want to say to you. I have been practicing all week, but now that the time had arrived I am hesitant to say what is on my mind. I am like a little boy who is about to give his first speech in front of a large crowd. I am nervous."

She adjusted her skirt to cover her knees. "If it will help any, I'm nervous too."

He nodded, relieved. "Then we are both in the same boat, so to say. It is I then who will start rowing."

Their eyes met and found peace. He cleared his throat. The brightness of his eyes mellowed. "That day when I first saw you on the porch was one of the most memorable times of my life. I expected to see your mother, but then you were there and I could not believe my eyes. I did not expect to see a beautiful girl."

She blushed. "Now you're being patronizing. I am not a beautiful girl."

"Oh, but you are. There is something about you that has made me push caution aside, something that has demanded more of me than ever before. I cannot say what it is, but I know there is an attraction unlike anything I have ever experienced. I say this outright, because I realize that time is not on my side. I realize that I must speak my mind clearly, so you will understand what I feel for you. And I realize that you might laugh in my face because I am so outspoken and crude. But I must take the chance."

Henrick paused, capturing her gaze, and within a second or two he felt confident enough to continue. "Those two days in the field, helping your father, were the best days I have had since being captured in Aachen. The sun, and your brother's companionship, and the feeling of freedom were special to me, and the hard work made me feel as if I were back home again. And then you came and everything was changed by your presence. And when your father gave me permission to talk to you, why, that was more than I could have wished for. Those minutes with you made me want to meet you again." He sat back and placed a hand to his mouth as if to stall his words.

Elsa saw honesty in his eyes, the truthfulness of what he had said, and she felt the need to respond. Her gaze descended, "I didn't know what to expect when I rode the bicycle out to the field that day. I didn't think you would be able to talk to me. My father had told not to associate with anyone in this camp. If he knew I was here today he would be very angry with me."

"But he gave me permission to talk to you in the field."

"With his eyes on us all the time."

"Still… ."

"He trusts me. He knows I would do nothing to shame him."

"Nor would I do anything to shame you?'

She shrugged. "But here we are, together."

"It is not shameful to talk, to express one's views.

"Perhaps not."

"Today you have come here for a reason."

"I did," Elsa said.

"What is it then? I would hope it is because you have the same feelings for me as I have for you."

"Do you want me to be truthful?"

"Truthful, yes, by all means."

She looked away from him while collecting her words. The truth was difficult to speak under the circumstances. "When I saw you in the field I almost couldn't walk close to you, because my legs were shaking so badly. I was all nervous inside. Just seeing you made me blush."

"You are not blushing now."

Her eyes settled on the tree, the grass, the foliage farther off, the sky, then back to him. "I am calm. You have calmed me."

He seemed relieved. "Good. Now we are both the same."

She looked at him again, deeper into his face, into that reservoir of thought. "Your eyes are so vividly blue," she said,

"I have my father's eyes. Looking at him was like looking into the sky. My father is much like yours, strict, but still lenient, hard working, comfortable in his chair at night, loving to us children, but harsh when it came to discipline. We are both from good German stock. That much we have in common.

Her gaze drifted to her lap, to her folded hands. "My father would punish me if he knew I was here today."

Henrik nodded. "Yes, I expect he would, and it would be the last time I would see you. It is brave of you, to be here."

The comment brought silence, a profound break in thought and presentation. Both of them moved and shifted, and glanced at one another. There was an element of nervousness in their uneasiness. Then Henrik spoke again. "Your friend, Erica, what does she think of all this?"

A gentle shrug, a lift of her shoulders. "She is as confused as I am."

"Why are you confused?"

It was time to look straight at him, into his soul. "Because I am doing something I would never have done, before you came into my life."

"Then you are drawn to me?"

"Yes. Even though I know our friendship will end."

Just then, the luster in his eyes faded. He became reserved, in a way that signified sadness. "Yes, it will end. The war is over, and we will be repatriated. Before the snow comes again I will be sent back to Germany."

She felt tense again, unprepared for the truth. "And I will never see you again"

"Perhaps not. I hate to think of that."

He tugged some grass from the turf and threw it to the sky and watched it descend. Immediately, he wanted to extend the time, which he felt was going too fast.

"Where is Erica now?" he asked.

"Over by the lake. I told her I would only be here for a short while."

"A short while is not very much time."

"I know."

He shifted closer to her, close enough to touch her, but he did not, although he wanted to take her hand. His movements were abrupt, nervous again, laced with uncertainty. He looked at her, his eyes moist with emotion. "Last night, when I was lying awake and thinking of today, I was saddened by the thought that you might not come here, and because of that my heart ached. Then I would think of us together and the ache would go away. It was that way over and over and over again, and I thought I would never go to sleep."

"I did not sleep well either," she confessed.

His smile returned, and with it a slight laugh. "Ha, we are both insomniacs. And if this day goes well, I may never sleep again."

Her eyes mellowed. "That would be terrible, never to be able to dream."

"Then we must do something about that."

He reached out to touch her hand, but she jerked it away without thinking, acting on impulse alone. She was merely reacting to her father's sound advice, as she had her entire life, wanting to obey, wanting to please him, wanting to be obedient.

Then she heard Henrik speak again, his voice just above a whisper. "Have you ever been in love, Elsa?"

She knew it was a question that needed answering, but for a moment she was tongue-tied. What was she to say to him? The truth? He would want to know the truth. "Oh, I don't know," she said wistfully. "There was a boy in school. He used to hold my hand, and one time he kissed me. I was only thirteen then, and although we were close, he found someone else the next year. Another tried to take advantage of me, but I was firm with him. Another boy who I admired was not what I expected him to be. No, I have never been in love. Have you?"

"Yes, I have, only one time."

"When was that?"

The expression on his face softened. "Here, on this day. I think I am in love with you, now."

"With me?"

"Yes, with you. Although I have never felt this way before, I think this is the way a man must feel when he is in love. I want you always near me. I want you to know how much you mean to me. I want to be able to express myself openly, without fear of rejection. I know how this must sound to you. I know it must be an unbelievable thought, a man with nothing, telling you he loves you."

"But you hardly know me."

"It does not matter to me. I know only what my heart tells me. So now I ask you, why did you come here today?

"To see you."

"Why?"

"Because you asked me to."

"Is that all, just to satisfy my wish?"

"No."

"Then why are you here?"

"Because I feel the same way you do."

"Even though we must separate soon?"

"Yes."

"Even though our time together will end with memories and nothing else?"

Her reply was a forceful "Yes."

He made an almost futile gesture then. "I have no control over my destiny. My life is in other hands. I must do what I am told to do until I can find my own way in life. Someday, who knows, I may come back here. But I would not expect you to wait for me. I would want you to go on with your life and meet a fine man and get married and have children, and love him forever."

"You make it sound so easy."

The blueness of his eyes seemed to gray a bit. "Life is never easy. It is only what one makes of it."

She stood up then, and he stood with her, afraid she might walk away. But she held her ground. She turned and gazed away into a far place, and she felt turmoil again, as if she were all mixed up inside. Then she said, tearfully. "My heart is telling me to go one way, and my head is telling me to go another. What am I to do?"

He reached out and touched her shoulder. She did not move away. "Choose a path," he said. "Look at the fork in the road clearly, and with open eyes, and select which way to go, back home to forget all about this German boy, or to come here and spend the days that are left to us."

Her voice cracked. "I know which way I want to go. I also know which way I have to go."

"Decisions are never easy."

She turned to look at him, her eyes filled with tears. "If I choose to come here, then we must be friends only."

He nodded. "I understand. I would want it no other way. There is no other way."

"We will just talk."

"Of course. I would ask nothing more of you. I will be the perfect gentleman."

She sighed. "Yes, I am sure you would be."

"I was raised to be proper. Even in Nazi Germany there were proper people."

She breathed deeply. All her objections faded away. Her decision had formed and now it needed to be said. She wiped a tear away from her cheek and smiled at him. "All right, it is settled then. I will see you from time to time, on Sunday after-noons if the weather is cooperative."

He issued a sigh of relief. "Fine. Today is July. I expect we will be leaving here sometime in September. That will give us, at the most, eight Sundays of talking, if we can meet on all of them. By that time you will know everything there is to know about Henrik Arndt."

"I didn't know your last name until now."

"Well, it is Arndt, Miss Sommer."

She smiled again, and walked around the tree and came up behind him. He turned, wanting to take her into his arms, to hold her close. Instead, he just looked at her, to make mental notes of her face, her eyes, the way she dampened her lips, making them shine in the sun. She snickered. "I think our introductions have been proper enough. Now, what shall we talk about for the next eight Sundays?"

Henrik felt the need for humor. "Well, there is the weather, and the farm, and our families, and life in a prison camp, and how deep the water is in the river, and whether or not I shaved before you came to see me. Or we can talk about what might have been, or what might still be, if fate will once again grant us a favor."

"Do you think it will grant us a favor?"

"That is like walking into a dark room and not knowing what is there. We can only hope that fate will be on our side, fickle though she is."

"Is fate a woman?"

"I do not know. Fate may be a man, but then he will favor your wish and not mine, because a man always favors a woman."

"Not always."

"This man would. It is what my father always did."

"My father as well."

"Good. Then we will put our fate in the hands of a man, and we will call him Herman, Herman the German. Is that not a good name?"

"It is. You make me laugh."

"Good. Then I will make a habit of it."

They talked in the shade for another half hour, about casual things, always avoiding the subject of love. They were just two friends together on a Sunday afternoon, enjoying one another's company, away from prying eyes and curious thoughts and those who might think of them as lovers. And when the hour was nearly gone, according to his watch, they arose and looked at one another without saying a word. Then he took her hand and kissed it, and she felt the desire to return the kiss, on his lips this time. But she didn't move forward, nor did he. Then he let go of her hand and stepped back.

"You have made a memory of this day," he said.

"Thank you for being here. Thank you for asking me to come."

He nodded. "Now we both have something to take away with us."

"Yes, a fond memory."

He sighed deeply. "So it is good-bye, for at least a week. I will pray for good weather next Sunday."

"So will I."

"Then good day, Miss Elsa. You have made me very happy."

She kissed her own fingertips then and touched then to his cheek, and for a desperate moment she felt compelled to step into his arms. Every emotion told her to react. Every vivid thought raised her to the tips of her toes. Every impulse strained her forward to be received. But she didn't move. Her steadfast morality held her motionless, and a breath later she stepped backwards.

"Next Sunday," she said.

"Yes, if it is possible."

She turned then, and gave him a slight wave of her hand, and walked away, each step magnified by the desire to return. Then she was through the hedge and onto the walkway. Instantly the tears came, first one, then another, and she stopped to wipe them away. Oh, my God, she thought. What is happening to me?

TWENTY-NINE

New Ulm, Minnesota, August 1945

NOW LATE SUMMER, THE SCENT OF Clara's freshly baked bread overpowered the farm smells at times. In the sweet, aromatic late afternoon calm, the cattle swayed down the dirt road from the outer pasture and headed for the barn in anticipation of their evening milking. During the twilight hours, crickets leaped underfoot, their melodic calls ringing across the fields. Meadowlarks sang in the high grass. Fireflies danced in the darkness.

In her spare time, which was often limited, Elsa would walk out on the dirt road and watch the heat waves quiver above the fields, and sometimes she would stand in wonder as huge, white thunderclouds formed on the horizon, burgeoning in the winds that moved them along. When she walked in line with the ditch, the grasshoppers would whir out in long, suspended glides and skid to a stop in the dirt before taking off again in a buzzing curve, to land on weed stalks. Across the road the corn plants rattled in the wind like a melody being played on one of nature's unseen instruments.

The sun was at its hottest now, baking down on the fields, threatening drought whenever rain failed to come. But then it would rain, on days when least expected, and sometimes she was caught outside and had to run for the barn, her feet sloshing in mud, her wet hair streaming behind her.

She was saddened these days because Erica had been unable, or unwilling, to drive her to the lake the Sunday following their last meeting, and it was doubtful that Papa would need Henrik at the farm until the wheat was harvested. There had been no talk at the table about needing assistance, nor any mention of the POWs for days on end. She was about ready to give up hope, until a strong wind ripped a string of shingles off the barn roof and toppled a tree near the end of the hog pen. It was then Papa made a decision.

"I'm not about to climb up on that roof," he said, his pipe in hand. "With harvest almost here, I don't need a broken arm or leg. I guess I can hire a POW a lot cheaper than I can hire an entire rig. It'll take the better part of a day to cut up that tree and nail down some shingles, so I'm goin' on into the camp and bring back a prisoner. If it's Henrik then we'll make some supper for him as our way of saying thanks. Does everyone agree?"

Everyone did agree. Elsa did not appear overly excited, but deep down inside, her stomach danced.

The following day Papa drove in and selected Henrik from several others, and Elsa and Corina helped their mother began preparing the evening dinner.

It was near dusk when the men finished working. The wood from the downed tree had been cut and stacked, and the barn roof had been repaired. The sun had already lost its brightness and had drifted down into a blanket of clouds when they entered the house, washed and ready for dinner. As they stood together inside the kitchen screen door, Papa in front, Henrik behind, the family gathered, wide eyed and anticipatory. Papa ushered Henrik in and put his arm around his shoulders and said, "This is Henrik Arndt. David, you have already met him, as have you, Elsa. This lovely girl here is my daughter, Corina, and this is my wife, Clara, who will now feed you like a king."

Everyone laughed. Henrik moved forward and offered his hand to each of them. "I am honored," he said. "For me to be here in your home is something I had not expected. To share a meal with you is almost unbelievable. You make me very happy, and I thank you from here."

He tapped his chest, where his heart was. Clara's expression conveyed her sentiment as no other could. Then he turned to Elsa and David and said to them both. "It is good to see you both again. I have fond memories of our time together in the field."

Henrik did not appear to be nervous. He glanced around the kitchen and then said, "This house is very much like my own. Here the stove. There the sink. Yes, much the same."

Clara motioned them toward the dining room. "Come, let's sit down, the food is ready to serve." The table was grandly set, as if for a holiday: a cloth of white, the fine dishes grandmother had once owned, candles and flowers, folded napkins beside the plates. Henrik was given a seat next to David. The two girls sat opposite them, Elsa facing Henrik. Papa and Mother took their usual places, one at each end of the table.

Henrik knew he would have to be cautions in his eye contact with Elsa. Papa would be watching for sure. He would have to pay equal attention to all. He sat and waited to see what the family protocol was. A second later Papa said, "Let us pray."

Everyone, including Henrick, folded their hands as Papa gave the blessing. "Lord, we thank you for this blessed day, for this bounty, and for the country that gave it to us. Be present with us, and with our new friend, Henrik Arndt. Give to him the best that he deserves. In God's name we pray. Amen."

The setting, the room, the people, the atmosphere, and the humbleness of the moment, were almost too much for Henrik to assimilate, and as the prayer ended he choked up, and tears came. He picked up his napkin and brushed it across his eyes

"Forgive me," he said. "I have not been at a table like this since I was fourteen. I had forgotten how grand it was, and how close I had been to my own family."

No sooner were the words spoken than Papa said. "Good. Then we have done you a service, but now we have to eat, so I hope you have worked up an appetite because I think you have not eaten a meal like this in the camp. Clara, bless her heart, is the best cook in Brown County, maybe in the entire state. So let's eat up and put on another pound or more so we can work again tomorrow."

The food came in order, a lettuce salad garnished with carrots, celery, cucumbers, and onion, topped with Clara's own tomato dressing. Chicken, potatoes, corn, and celery sticks came next, with thick gravy and hot white bread the prisoners called cake. For desert they were served candied apples in a rich cinnamon sauce. During the dinner Henrik answered all their questions. He told them about his childhood on the farm, his early education, about his short time in the Jugend, about Hitler's stranglehold on the country, and what little he knew about the war, the bombings, and his forced defense of Aachen. And sometimes, the only sound heard was silence, just the noise of silverware and muted chewing

He thought he saw Elsa eyes misting when he spoke, and he caught her glance several times, and held her gaze until one of them turned away. There were veiled expressions in those short contacts, glimpses that gave strength to their hidden affection; from Elsa, a mellowness and softness that stirred his emotions, from Henrik a gentle fondness that at times seemed to float her away into another realm. For Henrik, it was one of the most delightful days of his life. On that night, when the entire family was gathered around the table, when Elsa sat directly across from him, and when the spirit of love was strong in the room, he felt as though he were home in the presence of his own family, in a house once so dear to him. Moments during the meal he paused to let the emotions invade him, so as to remember them forever.

After the meal, he and Papa and David went out on the porch and sat in the chairs. In the western sky, the clouds had billowed off to the north leaving a field of stars glimmering like scattered diamonds on black silk. The warm, moist scent of the farm was everywhere, a perfume of a different kind, a scent that gave life to darkness.

Papa puffed on his pipe. Ringlets of smoke glazed away into the warm breeze. David sat beside the rocker, near to where Henrik was seated. The night mood brought back thoughts of earlier days, and he could almost imagine his father seated where Papa was, with mother nearby, and his brother spread out on the ground looking up at the stars.

Papa's voice seemed to come from nowhere. "I've got a few things I want to say to you, Henrik, so I'll be direct."

Henrik replied, "Go on. I am listening."

"I'm going to talk to the camp official tonight when I bring you back," Papa said. The statement brought Henrik to full attention. "I'm going to ask him to reserve you for work here, whenever I call. Would you mind if I did that?"

Henrik leaned forward in his chair. The wood gave of a creak as he spoke. "No. I would like that very much."

Papa's voice was low but distinct. "You've been a big help to me. I didn't expect a prisoner of war to be so eager to work. Before you came here, I was told that some of you were disobedient and did as little as possible. Those few gave your compound a bad name. Many of us were hesitant to have you help us. But you've been different. I couldn't have found a more able and helpful worker if I looked all year."

"Thank you, sir," Henrik said.

"Besides, my boy David here said he wants you to come back, and that's a reasonable recommendation, because just a few months ago, when we invaded France, he thought all Germans over there should be killed."

Henrik tousled David's hair. "I can see why he thought that. We are not well liked in the world." Then he cleared his throat loudly. "Over in Germany, the Americans have found the concentration camps where the Jews were sent. I think you know that they were gassed and cremated and buried by the thousands in open pits, men and women and children, just because they were Jews."

"Yes, we have heard that."

"Terrible thing. The world might never forget something like that." Henrik cleared his throat again. "I think the world has every right to condemn us. We were not, what you would call, honorable. But it was the Nazis who did such barbaric things, not everyone. It will be up to us who denounce such things, to build a new and respected Germany."

Papa nodded. He liked the answer. "We've lost some good boys over there, just like we did in the last war."

"Yes, I know. And we have lost some also."

The pipe smoke scattered as Papa rocked. "I just wanted you to know that my feelings about the war run deep. For some, there's reason for hatred."

"Yes."

He glanced over at Henrik; saw him sitting calmly in his chair, his blonde hair highlighted by the moonlight, his face serene. "But I do not measure a man by what others have done. I measure them by the strength of their work and the goodness in their heart. I think you are a good man, Henrik."

"Thank you, sir. I will do my best to live up to your opinion of me."

"There's harvesting ahead, flax later this month, corn in September. I expect when it's finished they'll be sending you back to Algona."

"Yes, sir, they will."

"Then I'll tell you the news that was broadcast today."

"Go ahead."

"We have dropped a bomb on a city in Japan, Hiroshima. One bomb. An atomic bomb. It has destroyed the entire city. One whole city gone with only one bomb."

"Oh, my God," Henrik sighed.

"It is a terrible thing. I cannot imagine it. I find it terrifying."

Henrik did not reply. He thought about the bomb, one device destroying an entire city, and he imagined what might have happened to Germany had America developed such a devastating weapon one year earlier. It all came in on him like a tidal wave and for a minute he was absolutely still, enveloped in a veil of disbelief and sadness. He held his mouth to stem an escaping sob, and then he rocked forward and leaned into the palms of his hands, and found peace in his surroundings. "I will never again wear a uniform," he said.

Harold puffed on his pipe again. "I did not want to tell you about the bomb, or my feelings, but I thought we should clear the air before you came here again. I want you to know what I think. I want you to be sure of me, and I want to be sure of you."

Henrik leaned forward in his chair. Silence crept across the porch to obliterate all other sounds. David turned and looked up at him, waiting for him to speak. Then Henrik said, "You can be sure of me. I am not like the others. The reason I am here in the first place is because I was threatened in Algona for being contradictory of Hitler. They would have killed me had I not been transferred."

"Thank you for telling me."

Henrik looked into the sky again as his emotions surged. "This is like a new home to me. You and your family . . . I have never been treated so well . . . and I will be saddened when I am forced to leave."

Papa nodded. "Then we'll make your stay with us as pleasant as possible."

"You are very kind to me."

"You're just like we are. The only difference is, you were born in Germany and we were born here. We are both German. I think that's enough to make us alike."

"I will never be able to repay you."

"I don't ask for payment. I ask for good work, honesty and friendship. They're the only things that make sense to me."

The screen door squeaked just then, and Elsa stepped out onto the porch, bringing the scent of the kitchen with her. Not a single sound spoiled the serenity. She glanced at Henrik and smiled, then walked past him and down the steps, her heels clicking on the wood. Then she turned, and softly said, "I'm going for a short walk. I'll be back soon."

She moved away, past the bicycle and through the gate, her light-colored skirt capturing the moonlight. She paused to look up at the fleets of stars resting on an ocean of darkness. Her presence brought Henrik to full alert and as she took one step, and then another, away from the house, he turned and said to Harold. "Do you mind, sir, if I accompany Elsa on her walk?"

Papa's teeth clamped down on his pipe stem. His thoughts were almost visible. "Why would you want to walk with her?" he asked.

"Because she is my friend, and the evening it pleasant, and I would like to talk to her."

"Three good reasons, I guess."

Harold watched Elsa turn the corner and disappear into the darkness, and he puffed again, chewing on the stem of his pipe. He thought back on their brief conversation and concluded that Henrik was trustworthy enough to be with Elsa, but at the same time he pledged to see Henrik on the first bus south if that trust was ever violated. For now, he would take Henrik at his word as proof that he did not doubt his sincerity. "Go," he said, "before she walks into the next county. But don't delay. I've got to get you back before ten."

"Thank you, sir."

Henrik rose slowly from the chair so as not to appear hasty. He felt a sudden exhilaration as he descended the steps. As he cleared the gate, he turned and waved.

David snickered and said, "Have fun."

Papa harsh words followed, "Mind your own business, boy."

When Henrik reached the end of the fence, he turned and increased his pace. He saw Elsa ahead of him some thirty paces. She appeared as a specter in the moonlight and in that moment he felt the evening warmth as something exhilarating. He called out, "Elsa, wait for me."

She turned, and as the moonlight burnished her face he closed the distance between them.

"Henrik," she scolded. "You shouldn't be here. My father will be angry. Now go back to the house!"

He stepped up close to her, just a touch away. "No, it was he who gave me permission. I said I wanted to walk with you, and he asked me why, and I told him it was because I was in love with you."

Her expression was one of half anger, half surprise. "You didn't say that."

"Well, not in so many words, but it is what I wanted to say."

"You're kidding with me."

"I am a tease. Guilty, yes. I am guilty."

"No, you're incorrigible."

"Yes, I am that also. Now tell me, where are you going this fine night?"

She motioned. "Out to the end of the road. It is peaceful there. Listen."

He nodded and stood still and looked out over the fields. He heard the chirp-chirp of insects and the almost silent whisper of wind. He smiled. "I hear them," he said.

"Crickets. And we have an owl in the woods. He calls to us sometimes."

They walked, side by side, slowly, toward the mailbox. "And where are you going from here?" he asked

"Back to the house."

"No, I was not clear. Where are you going when you leave the farm?" They moved forward on the well-defined road, corn rows on one side, flax on the other. The moon bathed the road in light. Out ahead of them the stars clustered in exquisite patterns as if woven onto a cloak of ebony cloth. He walked beside her, slowly, step by step, as thoughts came. What is on her mind? Should I be silent, or should I be talkative? What would she like me to say? Should I be forward or cautious?

Looking up at him, she waited. Then, because she felt compelled, she reached out and clasped his hand, and felt his fingers tighten on hers, as if he had been waiting for her touch. "Papa wants me to go to college. I think I will. If the crops keep coming in as good as they have, and if the market survives after the war, I might give it a try. Otherwise, I'll stay on the farm."

"And you will meet a young man, and get married, and have children."

She shrugged, and swung his hand. "I doubt that."

"Why?"

"There are no eligible men here. They are either in the army, or with someone else."

"They will come home."

"No, the kind of man I want is not among them."

"And what kind of man do you want?"

She stopped and looked down at the road. Then her face came up and she peered into his eyes with an expression that almost took his breath away. "Someone like you," she said.

Henrik took a half step toward her, nervous with the movement. The impulse to draw her into his arms was so great he could hardly resist. He wanted her there, inside his embrace, to hold her close, to breathe the fragrance of her hair, to feel her body against him, to touch her skin with his fingertips. But he resisted the impulse. He had to. Any sign of affection would be improper. If her Papa found out, it would be the end for him.

"You honor me," he said.

She moved then, impulsively, and began walking again, his hand still gripped in hers. "It's true," she said. "You're not like any of the boys around here."

"Does that mean I am better, or worse?"

She slapped at him playfully and he flinched. "Better, of course. You'd put them all to shame."

He swung her arm forward and back. "Then I shall stay here, and we will buy a farm somewhere nearby, and I will become a farmer."

She laughed. "Here, we call a statement like that a pipe dream."

"I have heard that phrase before. What does it mean?"

"It means that your dream is nearly impossible."

He drew her around in front of him. Even in the darkness his sincerity was obvious. "Any dream is possible," he said.

"Not that one."

"Time will tell."

She released his hand and walked out ahead of him, then spun around in a full circle, her arms outstretched. He watched her twirl, once, twice, dancing ahead of him like a ballerina, swaying on unheard music, bending and twisting beneath the stars.

"Come here," he said.

"What for?"

"I want to show you something."

She came to where he stood and he put his arm around her shoulders and pointed into the sky. "Do you see those stars there, the ones that look like a W tipped to the right?" He traced them with his hand.

"Yes," she said. "I never noticed them before."

"That is Cassiopeia."

"So?"

"It is a well known constellation."

So?"

"That star on the top, the one above the center star. It will be our star. It is named Epsilon."

She looked up at him. "Where did you learn about stars?"

"Again, my Uncle taught me something besides English. When I was a boy, we used to lie together on the side of the hill and look into the sky, and he used to point out the Constellations. He was a brilliant man."

"Epsilon," she said. "It is a beautiful name."

"As beautiful as you," he said without thinking.

She shrank a bit, as a warm finger of emotion tracked down her spine, and she felt things she had never felt before, closeness, and passion, and a wonderment so ecstatic that she could hardly remain standing. Her knees nearly gave way beneath her, and as she gazed at Epsilon the breath she had held went out of her.

Henrik drew her close, and without a thought of what the consequences would be, he embraced her, and drew his fingers across the soft skin of her forearm. They stood together there, on the road, body to body, as the starlight bathed them, and in the silence of night they formed their first link to something greater than friendship. They did not move for several minutes, but when they did he leaned forward and kissed her on the forehead. As he backed away, her eyes melted before him.

"It is enough," he said. "I can give you nothing more."

"Why not?" she sobbed.

"Because of who I am. I have nothing, nothing to give you."

She sighed, knowing he had spoken truthfully. "You could have me," she said. Then she gasped softly, in disbelief of her own words, those that had drifted from her heart.

"Yes, yes, I would like that. But it is only a pipe dream."

Elsa held him close, not wanting to let him go. She wanted to stay in his arms forever, to feel his body against hers, to melt into his embrace. It was a wonderful moment, so quickly passed, so impossible to relive.

Henrik ended it. He stepped back and peeled her arms away, and pinned them to her side. Then he looked into her eyes and said, "You are everything to me. I did not expect this, but now that you are here I know no one else will do for me."

"I will wait for you," she sobbed.

"No. You must go on. I will be gone. I do not know what awaits me when I am home. For all I know, I have no home. No, Elsa, I am not for you. I am nothing."

Standing back, she felt beaten, unsure, confused. She saw in his eyes an expression of defeat, and it pained her. They both stood where they were, listening to the breeze through the corn and the far-off cricket serenade, and each of them felt their impending separation like a sickness. Then she moved away from him and walked a short distance up the road. She wiped her eyes, then turned around and walked back to him and took his hand. She looked at him with determination in her eyes. "We will see, Henrik Arndt. We will see where the future takes us."

"Yes, we will see."

Firm in her resolve, she stood up straight, and looked up at Epsilon. "We will find our star each night. And we will wish upon it."

"Yes," he said.

Her expression mellowed. "We have to go now. Papa will be waiting to take you back to the camp."

"It is alright. I will come here again, soon."

Her eyes were sorrowful. "I want to share as much time with you as I can, before you have to go."

"It is also my wish."

"I hope my father will be understanding."

"But you cannot tell him about us."

"I won't. But as casual as our time together will be, I want you to know that it will only make me want you more."

He squeezed her hand, "Enough," he said, brushing her hair back from her forehead. "From this time on our thoughts must carry us."

She smiled broadly and stepped away from him. "Come," she said gleefully. "I'll race you back to the porch."

At that instant she dashed away and ran as fast as she could toward the farmyard. He ran to catch her, but she was faster than he was. She stumbled onto the porch just as he was turning the corner of the road. Laughing, she crumpled at Papa's feet.

When Henrik walked up the porch steps he thought Papa would get up and take him to the car. Instead he told him to sit down. Then he called into the house. "Clara, bring Corina out here. You come also. I have something I want to say to all of you."

Moments later the entire family was on the porch, some standing, others sitting casually against the wall. When they were all there Papa tapped the ashes out of his pipe and looked at them, one after the other.

"I have something to say," he said, his voice firm and commanding. "On the first day I met Henrik, when he came to repair our fence, I got to know him quickly.

I found him to be honest and hard working, and trustworthy, and later when he and the other prisoner came to help in the field, I got to know him even better, as did some of you."

Pausing to let the words sink in, he continued. "The reason I have invited him to share our table is because I want all of you to realize that even though a man wears the uniform of an enemy, it does not mean that he is a bad person. So, with that in mind, I am bringing him back here to help with the harvesting, and I would like each of you to treat him as if he was a brother or a sister. I want Henrik to carry back good memories of us. I want him to know that we do not hate a man simply because he wears a different uniform." He settled back in his chair, nodding, satisfied with what he had said.

"I am in favor of it," Clara said.

The children chimed in unanimously. "Yes. Me, too. Alright!"

"Well, Henrik," Papa said. "I guess we have adopted you for a while."

Henrik stood up. His gaze passed over each of them, hesitating, moving on. He shifted humbly. "I do not deserve your kindness, but I thank you for it. I will do my best for you, every day, until my time with you is over."

Papa arose from his chair and clamped his arm across Henrik's shoulder. "It is getting late. Time to go. The rest of you can stay here. It is a good night for talking on the porch."

They left then, and as soon the car drove out of the yard, Elsa looked into the sky. But from where she sat she could not see Epsilon.

THIRTY

O N AUGUST 9, THE UNITED STATES dropped a second atomic bomb on the city of Nagasaki in Japan. The horrendous attack, praised by some, and scorned by others, brought the war closer to an end.

The world-shaking event did not, however, change anything for those working the farms. Harvesting season was upon them, and hard work became the priority. Flax was ready for cutting and shocking. It was an important crop. Its seeds would be crushed for linseed oil, its stalks converted to linen and cigarette paper, and its seed husks pressed into cakes for cattle. When flax was in bloom the entire field could easily be mistaken for an ocean of blue, shifting and weaving with the breeze, expansive in its motion. It was then that Henrik Arndt became a daily visitor to the farm.

This was also a time when the night sky was bejeweled with thousands of glistening stars, and when city lights could be seen from as far away as thirty miles. And on some nights the Aurora Borealis flashed so vividly across the northern horizon that one would stand aghast just to view its splendor. Also, in the softness of night, if the breeze was just right, one could draw in the heady scent of the barnyard or the final aroma of supper from the kitchen, or clover from the fields. One could also glimpse the intermittent flight of lightening bugs and cabbage moths against the dark outline of the grove, or listen to the muted croaking of bullfrogs from out in the slew, or the soft chatter of cicadas, or the hoot of the owl in the grove.

The men worked long and hard in the fields. Papa tended the equipment. David and Henrik did most of the physical labor. Elsa continued to bring food to the field, and each day she lingered longer than she had the day before, conversing, teasing, all in front of Papa's watchful eyes.

Papa was no stranger to physical affection, or the attractions that often grew with repeated involvement. He and Clara had met by accident, and he remembered the pull their attachment had on him, the times when he was determined to see her again despite all odds or complications. He had nothing against the apparent friendship that had arisen between Elsa and Henrik. They were happy with one another, more than a brother or sister would be, and he expected, if Henrik was to remain in America, that their friendship would eventually blossom into something more defined. He would accept Henrik into the family, for he considered him to be a fine lad. But there were reservations. The impending repatriation, the distance, and time itself, could destroy any romance if extended too long. So he watched their antics, and laughed with them, and did whatever he could to keep the distance between them farther than arm's length.

Henrik could not remember another time when he had laughed so much, or when he had looked upon such a cheerful, radiant, friendly girl as Elsa. Each day when he came within sight of her he felt his attraction strengthen, and when they were alone he felt the tug of her like a rope around his neck. When her eyes were upon him, with a softness he wanted desperately to match, he felt a passion he was hard pressed to resist. But he knew his limitations. He kept her at a cautious distance, never bending to desire, taking her hand only when the two of them were alone, and accepting her affection through eyes that gave of it so generously.

Elsa felt it also, that quivering, silent passion that enthralled her day to day and to those beyond. Within a short period of time she was captivated by him, by his smile, his antics, his behavior, his enthusiasm for hard work, and his apparent devotion to the family. She wanted him then, not just as a friend, but as a lover. She could feel his presence like a magnetic pull, and there were times when she wanted to throw caution away and rush into his arms and drag him down onto a field and make love to him until the day went from light to dark and into light again. On each of the days when she was within sight of him, or close enough to touch him, she knew she wanted him, if ever there was another as fine and as handsome.

They were together one day, in the field, at a time when Papa was busy with the tractor. David had gone to the house to bandage a slight cut on his wrist. They were resting beneath a tree at the edge of the field, shielded from the sun by an overhanging branch. A soft breeze, scented with clover, cooled them both. They stood about six feet apart, an appropriate distance that would meet with Papa's approval, and as the sun winked through the leaves, Henrik's eyes settled on her, and he said.

"I am in love with you, Elsa. I know it now, as sure as I know my own name. I want you to know that, in case tomorrow is our last day together."

Surprised, almost instantly her lips quivered. Her eyes misted as they caught a sparkle of sunlight through the branches. She fought the impulse to walk into his arms. "I love you too," she said. "I have, I think, since that first day we met."

"That day of miracles," he replied.

She saw Papa out of the corner of her eye, looking back at them, and so she leaned against the tree and looked away, until he went back to his work.

"What are we to do?" she asked.

"Nothing," he said, picking at a leaf, tearing it gently. "We are trapped in time. I do not think even God can help us, even if we prayed all day."

Her eyes rolled back toward him. "There are days when I actually hurt for you. I don't know how much longer I can go on like this. You have no idea how desperately I want you."

"I, too. Each moment I am with you is so beautiful, yet so torturing."

"And the days go so fast. Morning comes, and you are here, and then it is dark and you have to go. Why do they go so fast?"

"I don't know."

Out in the field, Papa had finished his work. He would soon start the tractor and head for the barn. The sun was already sinking low. The narrow ribbons of clouds that framed the cornfield had taken on a pink hue. Only moments remained before they would have to leave.

"Tonight will be your last night with us for a while," Elsa said.

"The last night of you."

"We'll be harvesting oats soon. The threshing rig will be coming, along with the other farm crews. We're cooperative, part of a four-family unit that travels from farm to farm. Each of us contributes a two-man team. You'll be one of them."

"Yes, your father has already told me."

"David will be working with you."

"Yes, I believe so."

"It'll be a busy time. I won't see much of you. I only hope Papa can obtain permission from the camp to keep you overnight."

Henrik shook his head. "Impossible. I must be back every day by ten. There is no changing that. The rule if firm. I am lucky enough just to have dinner with you once in a while."

Elsa's head came up suddenly. "Here comes Papa."

"Let us go and meet him half way."

They walked out from beneath the tree and joined Papa in the field.

At dinner that night, Papa had some good news. "I hear gasoline rationing is going to end on August the fifteenth. Good news for everyone. As Roosevelt used to say, happy days are here again."

Henrik smiled. "That means that soon the war with Japan will be over."

"I appears so. There's already talk of surrender."

"That is good. Peace has been a long time in coming."

"Looks like I won't be going in the army then," David said.

Papa nodded. "I guess not. I think you're stuck with sloppin' pigs and doing hard labor for the rest of your life."

"That's okay with me."

"Believe me," Henrik said. "You wouldn't want to go and fight in a war. It is the most horrible thing you could ever imagine."

"Okay," Clara said. "Enough talk of war. When will we begin harvesting the oats?"

"In about a week," Papa said. "Maxwell is getting the rig ready now. We'll do the Hasselberg farm first, and then come here. We'll finish up at the Hortl place third, and then go over to the Jagger farm last. We should be finished by the end of the month."

Henrik threw a quick glance in Elsa's direction. She smiled.

"This is a good time of the year," Papa said. "Hard work, plenty of sweat, good crops, good food, enough to make a man fat if he didn't work it off the next day." Then he looked at Henrik. "I talked with Mr. Lewis down at the camp, and he said you'd be coming up here for as long as we needed you. There'll be some other prisoners working for the Hasselberg's, and another for George Jagger. You'll have some friends on the crew. The only thing you'll have to bring is a good appetite. These farm gals are going to feed us like we were kings."

Henrik smiled. "I will be able to handle that."

"Good." Papa slapped his thighs and reached for his pipe. "Now while I light up and sit in the easy chair for a while, why don't you and David go out to the haymow and throw down some feed for the cattle. I'll take you back as soon as you're finished. No sense in wasting another good hour doin' nothing. Is that okay with you, Henrik?"

"Let's go," he said, excusing himself from the table, smiling at Elsa one last time before he and David left the house. Outside the sky was already gray with dusk. The yard was smothered in its softness. When the screen door slammed the chickens began clucking, and in the warm, evening air the barn bats swirled and darted, feasting on mosquitoes. Halfway to the barn, Henrik put his arm around David's shoulders.

"I'm going to miss you when I'm gone," he said.

"No more than I'm gonna miss you."

"You have become like a brother to me."

"Yea, you too. Ain't there some way you can stay?"

Henrik pulled him closer as they walked. "No. Miracles aren't meant for prisoners of war. We go where we're told to go. Freedom is for people like you."

"It ain't fair."

"Well, not much in life is fair."

They went into the barn, past wooden columns festooned with spider webs, into the warm, moist scent of cows and stale milk, sweet hay and fermenting silage, cow urine and manure. They climbed the ladder up to the haymow and in the dim light David began pitching hay down to the cow stalls. It was a one-man job, so Henrik watched, and when David was finished they both stood quietly. David wiped sweat from his forehead and then said something that had been on his mind for some time.

"I think you're gonna miss my sister more than me," he said.

Henrik accepted the question with raised eyebrows. "I will miss the both of you. But maybe her just a little bit more. I will miss your whole family very much."

"Corina tells me she's been cryin' sometimes at night."

"Oh, why is that?"

"Corina thinks she's in love with you."

Henrik pushed the comment aside as if it were unimportant. "I cry sometimes, too, and so will you when everything seems to bunch up on you. No one is exempt from sadness."

"Yea, but Corina says she mentions your name when she cries."

"Ah, it is just a fancy."

David stood very still, his eyes straight on Henrik. "I don't know nothin' about love, but I heard about it. It's when a boy and a girl get to wanting each other so bad they can't think of anything else. Is that right?"

"What does your father say?"

"We don't talk about that stuff. It's just what some of my other friends say when their brothers or sisters get into a mood, they get strange sometimes."

"Is Elsa strange now?"

"Yea, sometimes. I noticed her a couple of times just gazin' into the sky when there was nothin' there, like she's lookin' at something far off."

"I have done that."

"I just thought you'd want to know," David replied.

David speared the pitchfork into the hay pile and climbed back down the ladder. He slapped at a cow or two, and then spread the hay into their troughs, enough to satisfy them until morning. Then he and Henrik started back toward the house, stopping first at the pump to bring up some ice cold, iron-tasting water. They both drank from the old metal dipper that hung on a wire alongside the spout. It tasted good.

"Best water in the world," David said.

"Has your father said anything about Elsa and me?"

David shook his head. "Nah. Just Corina. She and I talk about stuff once in a while when we have time."

"Well, don't worry about it. I'm sure whatever it is that's troubling Elsa will soon be over. Things like that always pass."

David made a fist and punched Henrik on the arm. "Well, I still think she's in love with you. But I promise, I won't say anything. I'm trustworthy."

"Well, that's good to know, Mr. Trustworthy. Then I have nothing to worry about."

"I guess I won't be seeing you until we start cuttin'."

"I guess not."

David slapped at his arm, once, twice. "Well, let's get inside before these damn mosquitoes start eatin' us alive."

Henrik didn't see Elsa again that day. As they approached the porch, Papa came out of the house waving his car keys. "Let's go," he shouted.

THE THRESHING MACHINE WAS PUT TO WORK when the fields were all brown and gold, and faces were happy with pride. It was a time for the exhilarating blend of power and sweat, when exhaustion was savored as something to be content with, for the instinct to preserve oneself through work was inbred in the farmers as much as it was in a hawk that scanned the fields for its food.

Each homestead contributed two two-bundle teams, David and Henrik being one, Albert and another prisoner from the camp being the other, one on each end of the feeder trough.

The separator was placed in a feedlot where the leftover straw could be used for winter bedding. The separator itself was a giant machine that ate up bundles like a hungry predator. It was propelled by an eighty-foot belt that stretched between it and the flywheel of a powerful tractor. Hayracks loaded with bundles of grain were driven parallel to the spinning belt, and from there the bundles were pitched evenly onto the feeder that drove them into the hungry jaws of the machine. The noise was deafening, the slapping of the belt, the grinding, the blowing, the constant movement, the whir of motors, the calls of men, the screaming of chains and pulleys and the grinding of gears. And then there were the shouts, and the warnings as the feeder's crossbars conveyed the bundles into chopping knives that cut the twine and impelled the grain into the grinding cylinder teeth of the separator. Spikers stood high in their hayracks awaiting their time to unload, going from wagon to wagon, pitching bundles, resting a bit when driving to and from the thresher. Henrik and David were both spikers.

A stacker stood head down at the discharge end of the machine, amid the hail of chaff being expelled from the metal monster's mouth, like golden snow in August. His job was to level the cascading straw. The augured grain drizzled into a wagon, where a farmer would occasionally test its heft by running it through his fingers.

Henrik saw what might happen to someone if they fell onto the belt or into the feeder. One of the men, who had been fortunate enough to escape a fatal injury, had only one arm. Another was missing a hand. Several were missing a finger or two. Cycle bars, whirling belts, spinning pulleys, pitchforks or even ropes were dangerous devices if one happened to be careless, or in a hurry, or just plain unlucky.

The noon meal was a feast beyond anything Henrik had anticipated. The table was laden with plates of beef, mounds of pork, slabs of ham, and brown, crisp chicken. Bowls were mounded high with mashed potatoes and sweet potatoes. Containers of cabbage salad and squash, parsnips and peas were emptied in order, and behind those were carrots, pickles, jams and jellies. And just when the men could pack no more into their stomachs, a quartet of pies arrived.

When all the food had been devoured, the men began smoking and joking and belching as the women cleared the tables. They went outside then and found a chair or a step, or a patch of grass. They lounged and told jokes, laughed, picked their teeth with wooden matchsticks, and hurried to the outhouse or to the grove if the outhouse was filled to capacity. They drowsed in the mood of the noon sun, and found peace in rest.

Then, when their conversations became muted and their bodies strengthened, they arose and went back into the field until the sun drifted down to late afternoon. Then they went each to their own home, to do their daily chores and to wait for tomorrow when they would do it all over again.

Albert brought the prisoners back to the camp each night, right on time, and picked them up the following morning. After they cleared the Hasselburg field in three days, it was back to Albert's farm for another three days of grinding work.

HENRIK AND ELSA SAW LITTLE OF ONE another during the harvest. They exchanged glances at mealtime, and whenever she was assigned to carry food to the field. Henrik was with the men, and she was with the women; their places in the scheme of things.

It wasn't until the second day into work at the Sommer farm that they got together in a most dramatic way.

Henrik was bringing his load of bundles toward the threshing machine when a snake frightened the team of horses pulling the wagon. He was walking alongside, holding onto one of the braces when the horses reared, and bolted. The sudden movement pulled him off balance and he tumbled to the ground, his arms spreading out to break his fall. He knew instantly that the wheel was close, but before he could withdraw, it had driven his arm into the ground, cutting it open just behind the wrist. He yowled with pain as David pulled the wagon to a stop, shouting at the top of his voice. "Got a man down over here. Hurry! Hurry!"

When David got to him, Henrik was already on his feet, holding his forearm tight. The skin just behind his wrist was split open. Blood oozed from the wound. Henrik was quick to apply pressure to his forearm to stem the blood flow. He was dizzy, and within seconds he drifted to the ground and sat stunned. David came up and dropped to his side.

"Is it bad?" he asked,

"The skin is broken open. Fortunately the wheel ran over the back of the arm and not the front where the major blood vessels are."

David turned. "Here comes Papa. He'll know what to do."

"I know what to do. I just have to get to the farm."

"Did you break it?"

"No, I don't think so. I can move my wrist. I think the ground was soft enough. The wheel just pressed my arm into it."

"Better than gettin' it caught in the feeder."

Henrik rose to his feet as Papa dashed around the back of the wagon. "What happened here?" he shouted.

"Henrik fell and the wheel ran over his arm. But he's okay."

Harold knelt at his side and took a cursory look at the arm. "You got a good one there," he said. "But it's fixable. Don't look broken."

"It's not broken," Henrik confirmed.

Harold took charge immediately. "David, you go and get a stick, a bit over a foot long, there, in the woods. I got some twine here in my pocket. We'll patch this up good enough to get you back home. Then the women can fix you up, good as new, and for a day or two they'll spoil you rotten." He nodded. "Could have been worse. Now you just hold still until David gets back. One thing's for sure. You won't be pitchin' bundles for a couple of days."

"I don't want to go back to the camp."

"You ain't gonna. I'll tell camp commander that I need ya, and that's final. Hell, as long as they make their money they won't care where you are. We'll get this patched up and bandaged, but in the meantime you'll rest a bit."

"Thank you, Mr. Sommer."

"No need to thank me. You been working hard, and you got hurt. That's all there is to it."

David came with the stick. Harold positioned it on the backside of Henrik's wrist, from palm to forearm, then tied it tight with twine, fashioning a makeshift tourniquet. When he was finished he helped Henrik to his feet. "Now you keep this arm up. The farm ain't more than a half mile away. You know where it is. Walkin' isn't gonna hurt you. The women'll know what to do when you get there."

"Again, thank you."

"Save your words and get goin'. As for the rest of us, we got work to do."

Henrik walked back to the farm, holding his arm up, thinking all the while what Elsa would do. She would want to be with him, for sure, but would she make a scene about it?

The day was warm, without a hint of rain, and so he walked slowly, using his energy wisely. He came into the barnyard whistling an old German tune. The dog greeted him at the gate. He went up the porch steps and entered the back door to the scent of food and the gaggling of women busy at the stove and table. Clara turned, saw his arm, and gasped. "Oh my God, Henrik's hurt."

Everyone turned at once. Elsa was at the sink, her hands in the water. When she saw him her mouth widened in shock at the sight of blood. She dropped what she was doing, scrubbed her hands dry on her apron, and walked boldly forward. "What happened to you?" she said

"A wagon wheel ran over me."

Clara pressed toward him. "Let me see," she said, pushing ahead of Elsa.

Bunching together, Clara began untying the twine. Carefully, she removed the stick. Immediately, blood began draining from the fissure. "Hold it tight up here," she said, pressing her hand to his arm, just beneath his elbow.

Elsa pushed in close, looking into his eyes. She saw no sign of pain. In fact, he was smiling, perhaps to put them at ease.

"It is not as bad as it looks," Clara remarked. "I have some cotton pads and gauze upstairs. You know where it is, Elsa. Go and get some and bring them here. I'll wash this off, and we'll see if it needs any stitches."

Clara had stitched up Papa's arm once, and his leg as well. She knew what to do. She had all the necessary items. Stitching up wounds was part of a woman's life on the farm. Elsa ran off the get the dressings that Clara kept in a small cabinet in her room. In the meantime, Henrik was ushered to the sink, where Clara cleansed the wound, and examined it further. "You'll not need to be stitched," she said. "I think we can press this together and wrap it tight. It should start healing right away. Sometimes wounds look much worse than they really are. But then, you already know that, don't you?"

"Yes, ma'm. I have seen a few wounds, some of my own."

"I am sure you have."

Within twenty minutes the wound had been cleansed, compressed, dressed and taped, and as the women returned to their work, Henrik went out on the porch and sat in Papa's chair. He elevated his arm while listening to the muted grunting of hogs in the sty and the cackle of chickens in the roost. Within minutes his eyes closed and he dredged up some of his worst memories, shellfire and smoke, shouting and running . . . then peace. He dozed as the sun worked its way across the sky. About a half hour later Elsa came through the door. He jerked awake as the door slammed, smiling as she approached.

"I had to just about sell my soul to come out here," she said. "Mama finally gave me permission. I told her I had to check on the patient." She sat down in a chair beside him and touched his arm. "Does it hurt?"

"No."

"You wouldn't tell me if it did, would you?"

"No."

Her hand moved from his arm to his shoulder, then to his face. She stroked his cheek briefly with the tips of her fingers. "It's lunch time soon. We'll be feeding you right here on the porch. Mama is making an egg sandwich for you."

"Papa said you will spoil me rotten."

She looked at him with mock defiance. "Well, if I had my way about it you'd get right back to work."

"No, you wouldn't," he teased.

"Then what would I do?"

"Well, you might sit with me and let me say sweet things to you."

"Like what sweet things?"

"That you are pretty, and wonderful, and delightful, and," he whispered the last words, "crazy in love with me."

She pulled back from him in mock surprise. "Is that what you think?"

"Yes."

Her expression became smug. "Well, if that's what you think, you are wrong."

"Why am I wrong?"

"Because," she said, whispering in his ear. "Because, to phrase it correctly, I'm desperately in love with you."

With that she sprang out of her chair and hustled into the kitchen. Moments later she returned with a plate of food. She ate lunch with him on the porch until it was time to resume her work. When she left him she kissed him quickly on the cheek.

As for Henrik, well, he slept part of the afternoon away and sometime later, walked down the road where he and Elsa had walked that evening when he had pointed out Epsilon. And during the walk, he wished he could stay there forever.

THIRTY-ONE

New Ulm, Minnesota, August 1945

B Y THE TIME THEY FINISHED HARVESTING at the Sommer's farm, Henrik was able to return to the field. Six days would pass before he saw Elsa again. During that time Clara would sometimes find her sadly gazing off into the sky with nothing apparent in sight. At other times she would sit by herself in the living room, as if in another world, and listen to records on the Victrola, over and over, love songs mostly, content within her own little world. Soon Clara came to realize the true meaning of her apparent detachment so one day she sat down beside her.

"It's Henrik, isn't it?" she began.

"What do you mean?"

Clara looked at her with pronounced authority. "Don't deny it. I've watched you for days. You're detached and sullen, and nothing seems to interest you any more. I know what that is. I've seen it before."

"What is it then?"

The reply was delicate, yet forceful. "Why it's love, or the beginning of love. It's obvious, you know."

Elsa shook her head. "No, I don't know."

Clara's apparent cajoling mood darkened slightly. "Now don't be obstinate. You know as well as I, that Henrik is at the base of your thoughts these days."

Elsa sank into a mood, "I think about him sometimes."

Clara was direct. "You think about him more than sometimes. You think about him at work, at the dinner table, here in this room, and, why even Corina says you hardly talk to her anymore. And even David has questioned your silence."

"Alright then. I think about him a lot."

Clara sat back and tapped Elsa's leg. "Now we're getting somewhere."

Elsa knew better than to get stubborn, or angry, or impossible to deal with. If she did, Papa would find out and Henrik would be banished from the farm, and she'd never see him again. Papa was hard that way. His punishment was never cruel, but always effective. He had never struck any of the children, but his commands were always brusque and intimidating, which was enough to deter any negative response. Obedience was a quality that had been instilled in the Sommer children from the moment of their birth.

"Tell me about it," Clara asked gently.

Elsa shifted, squirmed a bit, sat up straighter, and then looked directly at her mother as if to seek assurance. "You know how he is, always so kind and gentle and heartwarming. I'm going to miss him."

Clara nodded. "Yes, before another month is over, he'll be gone."

The statement brought a tear to Elsa's eye. Quickly, she wiped it away. "It'll be like losing my best friend."

"I know. Perhaps even worse."

Compelled by doubt, Elsa reached out and grasped Clara's hand. "Oh, mother, you don't really believe I'm in love with him, do you?"

Clara's head tilted as she smiled. "I guess only you can answer that."

"Well, I'm not."

Clara took a deep breath. "I know why you're saying that. I know that if you tell me the truth you're afraid that Papa will never bring him back here, that he'll go back to Algona without seeing you again. Am I right?"

Elsa was forthright. "I don't want him to leave." Then the tears came again, one after the other, expelled by sobs.

"Your tears tell me a lot of things," Clara said.

"He's been so nice to me."

"As he has to all of us."

"He's made me feel like . . . like . . . someone I've never been before."

Clara patted Elsa's hand again. "I know the feeling. We women all go through it at one time or another.

Elsa sat up hurriedly, brushing away the tears. "Don't say anything to Papa."

"I won't, unless . . ."

"Unless what?"

Clara faced her with a strict schoolmaster expression. "You two haven't done anything improper, have you?"

Elsa shook her head rapidly. "Never. He wouldn't do that. Never. He's a perfect gentleman. That's more than I can say about a lot of the boys at school."

"Okay, enough said." Then Clara's expression mellowed. "You know, Papa has been watching the two of you also. He told me I had better have a talk with you."

"So Papa put you up to this?"

"It was mutual. I suspected something. The way you look at him is clear enough.

Again, the plea, direct from Elsa's heart. "Please, Mama, he has only another month here at most. Don't send him away now."

"Don't worry, your father has taken a liking to him as well. I don't think he'll be sending him away any time soon."

As Elsa breathed a sigh of relief, Mama continued. "Just so you know. Papa will be keeping an eye on him. Watch what you do."

"I will. We will. Thanks, Mama."

Clara slapped her thighs and rose from the couch. "Okay, talk time is over. Now get up on your feet and do something, Keep busy. The best cure for heartache is work, so get to it."

Elsa tried one last denial. "I don't have heartache."

Clara spoke back over her shoulder as she headed toward the kitchen. "Don't tell me what you have or don't have. I'm a woman, too. I know what you've got."

THAT NIGHT AFTER THE CHILDREN WERE IN BED, Clara and Harold sat on the front porch for a while, both resting from the day's labor, much in need of solitude. The mosquitoes were few. The females of the species had been either eaten up by the bats, or they were out searching for water on which to lay their eggs. The moon was brillant, nearly full, and casting light across the farmyard, deepening the shadows. Howard was smoking his pipe. Neither or them were in the mood for talking, but talking was needed. Clara spoke first.

"I talked to Elsa today."

"And?"

"She and Henrik are close."

He took a long puff on the pipe and blew the smoke skyward. "How close?"

"It's nothing to worry about. Puppy love, mostly."

"Huh!" he grumbled. "Puppies grow up."

"I know. But they're only testing the water now. There won't be time for anything more. You know as well as I do, that he'll be gone soon."

"Ya, next month, when the leaves start turning, he'll be gone."

"Then there's not much time left."

"Not much."

A cricket chirped nearby, and from a distance came the creak of the windmill turning slowly. "He's a fine lad, Henrik is. Every day when I watch him workin' I think how grand it would be if he stayed here. I could use him on the farm."

"And what does David think about him?"

"David? He's like a brother to him, always trailin' alongside, always talkin'. David will be hurt when he leaves. He told me so."

"Is there anything we can do to keep him here, in America?"

Harold shook his head. "Nothing. I already spoke to Mr. Lewis down at the camp. He said if anybody is going to stay behind its engineers and doctors, those who can make a difference one way or another. Everyone else goes back."

"Back to what?"

"Strife and worry, I expect. Nothin' left over there but wreckage."

Silence again, longer this time, as if the stillness would breed words. It was so quiet they could hear the leaves move out in the grove, a whisper so faint as to be nearly unheard. Then Harold said. "If he and Elsa get out of hand I'll not hesitate to ship him back where he belongs."

"But they're never alone, and if they are, it's within view, or not for very long. Nothing will happen, Howard."

"Humph! I know how a man can get when he gets the urge."

"And I know how a woman can get."

Harold laughed. "Ya, I guess we know."

"Don't worry. I keep my eye on them when they're here, and you keep your eyes on them when they're with you. I think Elsa's wise enough to know that there's no future with him. She would resist if it ever came to anything sexual."

Howard grumbled. "You think so. Well, a lot can happen in five minutes."

"Nothing will happen, Harold."

"I will hold you to that."

She shrugged. "Hold me to it then. I know my daughter, and so should you. She is trustworthy, and so is he. So bury your worry."

The aroma from his pipe drifted across the porch. "I am not worried."

"Good, then let's go to bed. It's late enough."

T HE NEXT DAY, WHEN THE FIELDWORK WAS finished, the men returned to the farm earlier than expected. Dinner was not yet ready. The women were still in the kitchen, preparing food. With no wind outside, and the windows wide open, the kitchen was hot and the air thick with humidity. A few flies buzzed near the door. The dog groaned as it heard footsteps on the porch, then lumbered out onto the porch as the door opened.

Sweat beaded on Henrik's face, as he entered. He smiled broadly. "Hello ladies," he said,

All three women, Elsa, Clara and Corina, looked up and grinned. "You are early today," Clara remarked, wiping her hands on her apron.

His eyes went straight to Elsa. Her smile was magnetic.

"We have finished early. I have come for a drink of water. Do you have some for a thirty farmhand?"

Without pause, Elsa hurried to the sink, reached for a glass, filled it, and brought it to Henrik who waited patiently in the entry. As he took the glass his eyes danced freely over her face. He drank immediately, and then returned the empty glass to her.

"It is delicious," he said, wiping his lips. "But don't let me take you away from your work. I will go and wash up at the tank, and maybe take a short walk to improve my appetite. Now go back to work. Good day, ladies."

Elsa returned to the sink as he left. She watched him for a while through the window as he sauntered toward the water tank where a towel hung. Her heart trembled as her eyes matched his stride, and for a moment she was caught in an imaginary embrace, with the thought of his arms around her, his cheek on hers, his body tight in her arms. It was enough to make her shudder, and in that instant she wanted him more than imagination could supply. She might have run after him, had the impulse lingered, but her mother's voice dashed the longing in an instant when she said, "Alright, enough gazing. Now get back to work."

Henrik washed up at the tank, the ice cold water bathing him from head to waist as his shirt dried in the sunlight. Then, refreshed, he drank from the dipper and slipped into the shirt. Alone, with no one in sight, he stood momentarily against one of the windmill braces and gazed across the farmyard, into the garden, along the fence, past the sheds and cattle pens, then to the barn and through the grove, a panorama of peacefulness. Then he glanced at the house where Elsa was. He felt a pressure in his chest and a tightening in his thighs, to a point where his penis began to stiffen. No, he told himself, do not be foolish. Nothing will come of this. After tomorrow I will be gone from here again until the corn requires harvesting, and after that it will be ended and we will be sent back to Algona, and all this will be given to memory, and I will, once again, become a prisoner.

Walking, Henrik went past the house and up the road, to where the fields trembled to the eye, to where the sky rolled out in all directions to grasp horizons, to where the fresh breath of autumn tingled the air with a scent different than the week before. He walked slowly; wanting to take it all in, wanting to remember it, for only in memory could he return here whenever the need to revisit became unbearable

As he walked, his senses brought up new emotions, a longing to stay, a desire to make this place his home, the need to love a girl he could not have, and as the emotions crested, tears came to his eyes. This was a dream world, he thought, as unreal as those conjured up in a deep sleep. He knew, as certain as the sky was blue, that soon he would awaken to reality. Before another month was gone he would be back in Algona to begin repatriation, to eventually return to his battered country. It was difficult for him to think of that, and each time he did, he tore the images away and gazed again across the fields, to where the corn plants marched like a resplendently green army, and to where the pheasants paraded through the stubble field, seemingly without a care, unleashing a long, drawling cadence of birds and insects.

Henrik could do nothing, of course. Fate had sealed his future and he was bound to accept its machinations. He thought, amid his perplexity, that perhaps he could return some day, to her, here. But then, as quickly, he saw the years ahead of him rolled out like an open scroll, and on it were etched the difficulties, and the impossibilities, and the turmoil that his shattered life would confront, and the dream he so desperately desired faded in a crush of hopelessness.

He breathed the air, deeply, so as to carry it with him, to store it up for another day, when thoughts would return him here.

Walking on, he felt freed now and then from his disturbed manner, and as he reached the end of the road he looked up into the sky where Epsilon would be, come dark. He hoped she would look into the night sky and remember him when he was far away in another land, so distant from her that memory might not prevail. He wanted this so desperately, this freedom, the feeling of accomplishment he had felt during the harvesting, the hard work, the joy, the comfort of a home, the pleasure of friends, the wanting of love, and something else, the softness of a woman's body tight against him in his bed at night.

Turning, he began his return walk toward the farm. At this short distance away it appeared so imaginary; the house trembling in a wave of heat, the woods silent and still, the windmill vanes unmoving, a calmness so perfect that it seemed illusory. As he approached the yard, his dreams began to fade into reality. At that point he saw Elsa headed toward the barn, a pail in her hand. He was just entering the yard when she disappeared behind the door.

He glanced around, saw no one, slowed his pace, and then stopped dead in his tracks. Something told him not to interfere, to cease and resist his impulse. Walk over to the water tank and wait, a voice said within him. But his anticipation to see her overcame his judgment, and despite his best intentions, he continued on and entered the barn.

Henrik walked into the hot interior that was mingled with scents of hay and livestock. The air was thick and heavy with heat, the area dim, lit only by the sunlight slanting in through the line of small windows set in front of the stanchions. Where had she gone? He moved cautiously into the interior, pausing, trying to hear a sound, but nothing came to him. Had she gone out another door? Had she climbed up into the haymow? He began sweating. beads of moisture formed on his forehead. No breeze to alter the oppressive heat. Time to go, he thought. But the intense uneasiness of the moment, and the desire to see her only intensified his eagerness. Even though she was gone, the sense of her presence compelled him to stay just a moment longer, to hope for her appearance. Then he heard a sound, metal on metal, distinctly, coming from the direction of the separator room. His heart leaped, and in a moment of extreme desire he turned toward the sound, just as she emerged.

At first she didn't see him, but as she turned toward the barn door he made a move. "Elsa." he said softly

Abruptly she stopped and turned toward him, her eyes wide with wonder. Then she smiled and lowered the bucket and took a step or two forward.

"I saw you enter the barn," he said. "I was tempted to follow you here."

Slowly she walked toward him, her eyes set on his face. She took a deep breath, as her breasts lifted beneath her coarse pair of overalls. He saw something else in her he had not seen before, a sense of longing, the way her footsteps drifted over the floor, the way she held herself, in a soft and sensitive manner, her arms weak to her sides.

"I was just thinking of you," she whispered, stopping within an arm's reach of him.

Elsa's face was so sensitive, so expressionless, so alluring that it scrambled his thoughts. He had all he could do to keep from reaching out to her, to take her into his arms. A pressure unlike anything he had felt before invaded his chest. A sudden weakness nearly collapsed his knees, and a desire within him all but destroyed his caution. He wanted to say something but his lips would not respond. Only his eyes moved, as if to study her through all of eternity.

Her breath quickened, and in that long and sensitive moment, he reached out to her and she placed her hand in his as he drew her one step closer. She gasped. Her breath came hard. Her eyes closed against her will. Her shoulders settled like the closing of a flower. A second later she reached up and stroked a bead of sweat from his cheek, and her fingers glided over his skin as if touching a treasure she had searched for her entire life. A moment later she was in his arms.

Henrick felt her there, deep in his embrace, and all his worries and all his concerns, and all the grand and glorious dreams he had ever envisioned challenged to be recognized. He drew her in, tight against his body, felt her breasts soft against his chest, her arms snug around his neck, her cheek supple and warm against his own, and in that, their first moment of expressive love, he felt invincible, as if nothing in the world could harm him. They came together, tightly, body against body, thigh against thigh, their arms in a full embrace.

Her leg rose against his. He felt the pressure of it trembling against his thigh. "I love you," she breathed. "I love you."

He was unable to respond, for then her lips were on his, tight and pliant, soft and expressive, and she moved against him with a passion she had never experienced, a total release of her emotions, a flood of euphoria.

His hand rose up. He touched her breast. He heard her gasp.

"ELSA!" The sound of Papa's voice roared through the barn.

Immediately she pulled away. Her face went ashen, and tears came as her body seemed to shrink within itself.

"Come over here at once!" Papa shouted, his face red with anger.

She glanced quickly at Henrik. He did not move. He stood rigid with fear.

"GET OVER HERE!" Papa shouted again.

Elsa moved quickly in response to his command. "Papa, it's not what you think," she cried.

"I have eyes," he said, pulling her toward him as his arm clamped her wrist. Papa's eyes leveled at Henrik like a beam of unseen light. "I trusted you!" he shouted.

Henrik knew at once that his honesty, his dedication, his grand ambition, and his dreams, had all been crushed in that one single embrace. He said the only thing that might free him from certain condemnation.

"I am in love with your daughter," he said, straightforward and direct. He stood his ground proudly, without any sign of submission.

"And I'm in love with him," Elsa said instantly.

Papa pushed Elsa away, toward the barn door. "Go to the house. I will take care of this."

"No," she screamed. "It was not Henrik's fault. It was me. ME! Please, Papa, do not hurt him."

"Get to the house," he repeated, his face reddening.

She saw Papa's fists, curled tight, his knuckles white with pressure, his lips drawn forcefully against his teeth. Henrik would be no match for him. Pleading, she grabbed at his coveralls.

"Listen to me, Papa. It was me. I went to him. Please hear me? I love him."

He turned on her. His arm shot out. His pointed finger trembled toward the door. "I will not say this again. GO TO THE HOUSE!"

"Papa, NO!" Her voice screamed out.

"I will not say it again. Have you not heard me?"

"But, Papa. It was not Henrik who did this. IT WAS ME! ME!"

Desperately she looked at Henrik, her eyes pleading silently. Tears washed across her face. She took a step, almost collapsed, then took another. Then she was out the door. The sound of her crying echoed back until it was swallowed by distance.

The two men stood apart from one another, their eyes locked in a standoff. Neither of them moved. Their thoughts were almost vocal.

"I am disappointed in you," Papa said, his voice mellowing slightly. "I brought you onto my farm because I trusted you. Now you humiliate me, and take advantage of my daughter. I accepted you almost like a son. LIKE A SON!"

Henrik stood flatfooted. He would not fight Harold, not even in self-defense. He was already beaten. It appeared certain that no amount of reasoning would change Harold's opinion of him. Anything he said would be useless in his defense. Words would be powerless. He had no choice but to take his punishment. Then, as if prodded, he said. "I am in love with Elsa."

Harold stood like a stone effigy, his jaw flexing, his eyes riveted. He took one step forward, saw Henrik stiffen. Then he paused. "I do not think you know what love is. You could not know love in a matter of days."

"I know how I feel," Henrik replied sharply.

"And I know how I feel. I think we'll go to the car now, and I'll take you back to the camp. If we stay here, eye-to-eye, I think I'll fight you. I don't want to do that."

"Nor do I. But I would take your beating, and do nothing to stop it."

Henrik saw Harold relax. His shoulders came down as the tightness in his jaw gave way to a more natural appearance. His fists unclenched.

"I am saddened by this," Papa said.

"I am also."

Papa motioned toward the door. "Go! Get into the car. I'll be along in a minute or two. No more words now, unless I forget that we are gentlemen."

Henrik sighed. He felt as if the world around him had disappeared, as if he had never met the man standing in front of him. Compelled forward, he walked past Harold, and into the sunlight. He went directly to the car, stepped into its hot interior, and wiped his tears away with a vicious swipe of his hand. For a moment he felt as if he was sitting in an execution chamber.

Harold was unprepared for the scene in the kitchen. Clara was standing near the sink, holding Elsa tight to her body. Corina stood in the doorway leading to the dining room, tears rolling down her face. When she saw Papa she turned and ran. The sobs coming from Elsa were loud, uncontrolled, guttural. The moment Clara saw him she held out her arm, palm forward as if to stall his forward progress. Then Elsa pulled away from Clara and swung on him.

"It was not Henrik," she sobbed, her face awash with tears. "It was me. ME! I came onto him. I forced him to kiss me. It was not Henrik. It was me. Please! Please! Don't send him back. Please, Papa, don't."

She collapsed into her mother's arms. Her legs nearly gave way beneath her. Clara hugged her close, shook her head in response to Harold's fiery expression, and glared at him with unforgiving eyes.

"We are going back to the camp," he said sternly.

"No! No!" Elsa tried to pull away from her mother again, but she was held tight. "Please, Papa. It was me. Don't you understand? IT WAS ME!" She turned on him then, forcing away from her mother's arms. Her face was red from weeping. Her mouth gasped for air. Her words stuttered. "I love him...Papa. Please, do not blame him."

Papa's hands trembled. For a moment he felt compassion welling up inside him. Whenever one of his children cried, it made him vulnerable. He would do anything for his family. Anything. He would even die for them. But this incident required toughening.

"I am leaving now," he said, the tone of his voice unchanged. "Nothing you say will change my mind."

As Elsa made a move toward him, Clara dragged her back. Her mother's arms refused to yield. "I love him," Elsa shouted. "I love him. Can't you see that? Oh, my God, please don't take him back." Her face was red with anguish, flooded with tears. Her words came out between lips, blubbering and soulful. "Papa. PLEASE! Don't take . . ." She then collapsed into her mother's arms, who tried desperately to comfort her, Harold turned and left the house, the sound of his daughter's tears tearing him apart inside.

A father had to do what was right, he told himself. He had to uphold the integrity of his family. He had to balance right from wrong. He had to be firm in the face of adversity. He walked straight toward the car, saw Henrik sitting erect and undaunted, like a man determined to take his punishment. Without pause, he opened the door and entered the car, and without a glance at Henrik, he drove forward.

Henrik took one last look at the farmhouse as they headed down the dirt road. He realized how their embrace must have appeared, but he chose not to comment. The farmyard drifted from his sight. He had never felt so desolate, so alone, so devastated, and as they drove he hung his head, for he could not force himself to do otherwise. Still, amid all his anguish, he felt vindicated, for he had accepted the guilt to save her from possible punishment.

Papa drove with his eyes straight ahead. Neither of them spoke for a while. Then Henrik felt obligated to say something. He cleared his throat and sat up straight. "You have been good to me," he said. "I would do anything to change what has happened, but I cannot. I would say only one last time that Elsa did nothing improper. I was so taken by her that I could not resist her. Please, show her no disfavor. It is I who must take the blame, not her."

"You have violated my trust in you," Harold said straight out.

"I have, yes. I will admit that I was wrong."

"Yes, you were, to the fullest."

"What more can I say, except that I have fallen in love with her."

Harold's jaw tightened. His hands gripped the wheel tighter. "No excuse will change what has happened. I'm going to send you back to Algona. That's all I will say about the matter."

Harold didn't say any more. He drove straight on, his face unturned. He remembered what Elsa had said in the kitchen, that it was she, and not Henrik, who were to blame. Was that so? Was he, in fact, blameless? No! Any decent man would have avoided the contact. Any decent man would have turned away. But he thought back on the early days when he had first met Clara? Would he have backed away from love?

Now he was faced with a new dilemma, one that might force him to reconsider his actions, but it took him only a moment to reaffirm his decision. He would hold Elsa blameless, and punish the German soldier who had invaded his home. Damn that incident of love. How quickly it had turned trust and admiration into chaos.

Henrik remained silent. The car quickly ate up the miles. It seemed like only minutes had passed since they had left the farm, and now they were turning onto the dirt road leading down through the ravine toward the camp, toward the Cottonwood River, where he and Elsa had talked that warm afternoon, that first time they had been together. He breathed hard, and the extreme weight of sadness was so strong he could hardly think. He felt as though life was not worth living any more, and for a while he wished he had died on the bricks in Aachen, so he did not have to live these moments. Then they were there. Harold parked the car. They both got out and walked together toward the camp office.

"You can go to your barrack now," Harold said tersely.

Henrik turned and walked slowly away while Harold watched. Then, for reasons he could never explain, Harold called after him. "Wait," he said.

Henrik stopped, turned around, and watched Harold approach him. So, this is it, he thought, his one last chance to chastise me, to say something I will never forget. He waited patiently, ready for the discharge, his eyes riveted with firmness on the man he so admired.

Harold stopped a stride away and held out his hand. "I do not want you to think I am a spiteful man," he said.

Henrik reached out and grasped his tough, leathery palm.

"We have been close, you and I," Harold continued. "I want you to know that I wish you God's speed on your return journey home. I hope you find what you want back in Germany."

Henrik nodded. He felt an immediate compassion for the man. He nodded in response.

"You have given me a new chance at life. Your kindness is appreciated."

"I wish this had ended differently."

"As do I." Then Henrik said the only thing he could. "You must tell Elsa that I hold her blameless for this. And I want you to know, that although I will go now, back to Germany, my heart will stay here, with her. Will you tell her that?'

Harold took a deep breath, turned his head away, felt a swell of emotion just behind his eyes. "I will tell her," he said.

When they looked at one another for a moment, Henrik saw a spark of genuine compassion in Harold's eyes. Then Harold nodded, turned, and headed back toward the building, the coarse cloth of his overalls scuffing in the silence.

Harold turned one last time to watch Henrik disappear behind one of the structures, and for a moment he regretted his actions in the barn. After all, Henrik and Elsa were both young, both filled with desire, as he had been when he was their age. He remembered clearly the times he had wanted Clara so much he could scarcely control himself in her presence. Still, a man had to know his place. A man had to be capable of defending himself against lust, especially a man who was a guest in his house, a prisoner who had no place to go but home to Germany. He placed his foot on the first of two steps and rapped on the door. A voice from within shouted, "Kommen!"

Harold opened the door and stepped inside.

Mr. Lewis looked up from his desk. "Mr. Sommer. I am surprised to see you at this hour. What can I do for you?"

"I have brought Henrik back."

Lewis nodded. "Will you be needing him tomorrow?"

Harold shook his head. "No, I'm finished with him."

"Sorry to hear that. He's a fine lad."

Harold's composure stiffened. "I caught him kissing my daughter," he said straight out. "I want him gone from here so there'll be no more problems."

"So, it has come to that," Mr. Lewis mumbled. "I am sorry. I thought he could be trusted. I will have him placed under confinement immediately, on bread and water also."

"No!" Harold countered. "I want him gone."

"You want him gone?"

"That's what I said. Gone! I want him sent back to Algona."

Mr. Lewis considered the request for only a moment. "Well, yes, we could arrange that. I have a courier driving down there tomorrow morning. I could have Henrik go with him."

"That would be sufficient. I want no more problems."

"Sorry, Mr. Sommer. Nor do we. I will see that it's done."

"Good. Then I'll go back home. I don't want any more help from this camp."

"Understood, Mr. Sommer."

"Good day, then."

"Have a good day as well, Mr. Sommer."

Harold went outside. For a moment he looked toward the camp buildings, saw some of the men sitting on the grass, smoking, others down on the soccer field kicking the ball around. He swallowed hard, felt an imaginary lump in his throat, then turned, and went back to his car. He sat in the warm interior for a while, mulling over the incident. He was satisfied that he had done the right thing. He had protected his daughter as a parent should. Any man would have done the same. Then he started the car and turned it around and headed back up through the ravine.

The ride back home was riddled with concern. He dreaded the thought of facing Elsa.

WHEN HAROLD ENTERED THE HOUSE UPON his return, he found only Clara there, sitting in a chair, waiting for him. He went directly to her and placed his hands on her shoulders "I did what I had to do," he said.

Clara nodded, turned, and looked straight at him. He could see that she had also been crying. "She is in love with him. I believe it. I could see it in her."

He nodded. "Where is she now?"

"Up in her room, with Corina. I don't think she wants to see you right now."

"Will she be okay by supper?"

"I think so. She has enough sense not to make a scene."

He rubbed the base of her neck with his thumbs. "If it is true, then he should have been man enough to resist her."

Clara turned on him. She had fire in her eyes. "Don't be foolish to think that the mind is stronger than emotion."

"But she has known him for only a few weeks. It is not enough time for a girl to fall in love."

She shook her head. Her eyes were sharp with memory. "You will never know a woman's mind. I was taken with you from the first moment we met. I want you to remember back, to when we were their age."

He did look back then, to the time they first met, how his senses were aroused just looking at her, how her voice sounded, how it felt just to touch her. They had just finished eating, and had walked outside into a cool twilight. She had shivered slightly and had taken refuge in his half embrace. And he remembered how she had felt against him, as if a dream had enveloped them both, and how the world seemed to have disappeared, leaving only the two of them together on a strange, yet familiar street. Yes, he remembered.

"It was a good time for us," he said wistfully.

"And it is a good time for them. I'm sorry to see him go, Harold. You shouldn't have been so forceful. You should have thought it over."

Harold sighed. "It's done now. Right or wrong, it's done. He'll be returning to Algona tomorrow. He will be out of our life."

"Then you'll not give him another chance?'

"No," he replied tersely. "What's done is done."

"And she will be saddened even more."

"No. She'll be all right. She'll think it over and come to her senses."

Clara nodded. "Perhaps she will. Time and distance will melt their passion."

"Passion?"

"Yes, passion. Love has a way of arousing passion."

"Hmmm. I seem to remember that also."

"Then leave her alone. Let her come out of this in her own way. Go now, and do your work, and leave us women to settle this in our own way. You'd be best to just keep silent from now on. You've done your duty."

He stepped back away from her, then kissed the back of her neck. "I'll be in the barn."

"David is out there. He didn't want to witness the tears."

"He and I will finish the work. The girls are free for the rest of the day."

"I'll call you for supper."

Harold took her hand. "Be good to her," he said.

"You also."

"I will." Then, as an afterthought, he said. "When I left him, he said one thing. He wanted Elsa to know that when he goes, his heart will stay here with her. Will you tell her that for me?"

"Certainly. She may not want to hear that from you."

He grunted, then turned. Having nothing more to say, he left the house and headed for the barn.

Clara sat for a while, head in hands. She had not told him how devastated Elsa had been, how terribly she had cried, how much she had pleaded. Papa would never know her anguish, would never know her pain. He would just go about his business and find comfort in work, to pack away his worries. Men were fortunate that way. They could find escape in everyday tasks, in exertion and hard labor, in anything that would take the mind away from reality.

Dinner that night was quiet, strained. Henrik was not mentioned, but his presence was felt by the empty chair where he had sat, in the lack of his voice, and in the absence of laughter he had shared with them. Papa recalled the only thing David had said to him when finding out about his return. "Gee, dad, I was just beginning to think of him as my brother."

They all went to bed that night with Henrik on their minds. Harold and Clara talked for a while in bed, their voices low, heard only as muffled sounds by the others who shared rooms close to theirs. Within a half hour Elsa heard Papa's low snoring.

Until that moment Elsa had sat by the window, fully dressed, unwilling to go to sleep, lest her memory of him would fade. Outside, the farmyard was bathed in moonlight. The skies were festooned with stars, a billion glimmering spots of dust marking the Milky Way. She yearned to see Epsilon, but it was nowhere in sight, not from where she sat. She thought of nothing else but Henrik, of their times together, of the final embrace, and of the days and months and possibly years ahead, of a bleak future without him at her side.

When it was near eleven o'clock, she stood up and boldly walked to the door of her room. She listened intently. No sounds. Not even a breath of wind outside.

She moved forward, cautiously, softly, passing her parents' bedroom, hoping that a board would not creak, that the sound of her passing would go unheard. She reached the main staircase and gripped the banister. The fourth step down would give off a sound, right in its center. She knew that from years of travel up and down its length. Reaching it, she stepped to the left, tight to the wall. No squeak. Again, the second step from the bottom would growl. When reaching it she grasped the railing tightly and stepped over it, down to the next one. No sound. Perfect.

Elsa tiptoed into the kitchen, then into the entry to where Papa kept his car keys on a hook near the door. She reached for them. They were gone. She gasped, then settled down and thought, what will I do now? Only one decision was possible; she would walk all the way to New Ulm, to where the Cottonwood River flowed through a culvert beneath the road. From there she would find the path that led to the dam beneath Shell's Brewery, and then take the footpath to the fence and to the camp where Henrik was, and from there...only fate would decide.

Carefully, she opened the screen door, and stepped out onto the porch. The dog labored up and brushed against her, its tail wagging. "Quiet, boy," she whispered. "Lay down."

The dog obeyed. It slumped down at her feet and gave off a moan of disappointment. Then, with only moonlight to guide her, she walked to the gate, opened it, and began her long trek toward town, an eight-mile journey through the dark of night. She reckoned that if she walked cautiously and calmly she could reach the Cottonwood in about four or five hours. No need to hurry. If she saw a car coming in either direction she would head for the ditch until it passed. She didn't expect to see any traffic on the roads, not at this time of night.

Elsa walked up the farm road and glanced at Cassiopeia, saw Epsilon bright and clear against the black sky. The sight of it gave her hope. She squeezed the small bit of paper in her dress pocket, the one containing her address, and a note she had written, a note she hoped would someday bring him back to her.

Defiantly, and with her purpose well set, she paced off along the roadway toward New Ulm, confident that the night, or the new day, would end in success. Nothing would deter her. Nothing. Her destination and her determination were rock solid, and she would succeed. She no longer felt like a girl. She felt like a woman, with her purpose well-defined. She would find the man she loved, and she would set herself deep into his soul, so he would never, ever, forget her.

By two o'clock she had walked almost four of the eight miles. She had seen only one car in the distance, but it had turned off the road long before it would have reached her. Being a farm girl, her legs were strong, but her body craved sleep. She had not slept in over twenty hours and fatigue was beginning to slow her down. Still, she plodded along, her destination well set, her determination stronger than ever. She would see him again, and tell him what was in her heart. She would plead with him to be patient, to remember her across the miles, and to come back to her some day. No other man would do for her now. Her mind was set on Henrik, and that was that. Men could come and go and attest their love, but she would never shrink from her unspoken promise, to bring him back, even if it took years.

The night sky seemed brighter now, glowing and content, without disturbance. She trekked on, foot after foot, yard after yard, section after section, until the lights of New Ulm glowed low to the horizon.

Twice she crouched in the ditch to avoid cars coming toward her. She did not want to be caught alone on the highway, although a lift into town would have been welcomed. Her feet were sore now, and her legs ached. Fatigue was beginning to eat away at her. Still, she labored forward, undeterred, knowing what waited for her at the end of her journey. She would see him again, unless she was injured, or unless a guard prevented her from entering the camp, or unless Papa came up from behind, knowing where she had gone, his lights off, his eyes searching the road. He could practically guess the distance she had traveled by the time of day. Papa would not be fooled. At best, he would sleep until five o'clock, then he and Mama would be up to face the new day. She would peer into the room to see if everything was all right, and she would discover her gone. By six, if not before, Papa would be in his car, headed for New Ulm. He would know where she had gone. He had the eyes of a hawk and the will of a bear. He would track her down for sure. The thought made her increase her pace. Another hour and she would reach the Cottonwood River. The camp was only fifteen minutes beyond that, unless, unless . . . unless. The sounds of her footfalls were like whispers on the road. Stay with it, she told herself, stay with it.

Before Elsa reached the top of the bluff above the town, the sun had begun rising over her right shoulder. It would be at full light before she reached the camp. She began to descend the grade, walking on the shoulder of the road. Ahead of her the spires of New Ulm rose above the trees. Somewhere farther on, the Cottonwood would reveal its snaking course, although it was mostly dried up now because of the dam situated below the brewery. She should be able to walk the path without fear of falling. Daylight would guide her.

She was extremely tired now. Her eyes drifted shut, and then snapped open again as her feet shuffled across the gravel. Stay with it, she repeated. You are almost there. Traffic was increasing. More cars were coming up the grade. The sounds of their motors hummed through the morning stillness. No one paid attention to her. One driver waved, then went on his way.

She descended from the top of the bluff, deeper into the depression where the water flowed, to where the Cottonwood snaked away from the dam site, between the bluffs and past the brewery. She paused, breathed steadily, looked away into the tangle of trees that crowded the banks, saw the narrow trail threading into them.

Elsa didn't wait any longer than necessary. She caught her breath, and then looked to see if anyone was near. Confident she would not be seen, she descended the embankment. An instant later she crossed the stream on the small footbridge that the prisoners had built. The river gurgled ahead of her, somewhere between the trees.

The trail took her in, winding its way between the cottonwoods and the elms and the jack-pine rearing up from the valley floor between them all, nearly hidden in the maze of foliage. A short distance later she passed the August Shell Brewery situated on the bank above her, up beyond its icehouse on the river's edge. The sun caught its roofs and turned them golden, and just then the path opened up to her and she walked hurriedly toward the small dam that had created Lake Flandreau.

Pausing to rest, Elsa caught her breath. The sun cast deep shadows into the forest. Across the river the crown of trees atop the bluff erupted in light, trembling in a breeze that swept across the upper banks. She moved on, cautiously, and then increased her pace as the dam came into sight. Seeing no one about, she crossed it and stepped onto the dirt trail leading directly to the camp. Her heart pounded softly, beating in time with her footfalls. Then the barrier came into view, its large white sign pinned to the fence: Warning! Keep out. Prisoner of War Camp.

The fence was only a dressing. It kept few people out. The path turned right around it and headed off into the distance, to where it curved to the left, into the campsite. Strengthening herself with resolve, she stepped around it and continued on, knowing that her moment of destiny was fast approaching. She looked to her left, to where she and Henrik had talked on those two Sunday afternoons. The place was hidden in darkness.

The call of a mourning dove's coo, coo, coo, matched her footfalls for a while until she made a turn. The camp buildings came into sight all too quickly, and she paused, unsure of what her next move should be. A tendril of white smoke drifted from one of the chimneys, the kitchen she assumed. Other than the movement of the smoke, the camp was utterly motionless, not a sound except for the cooing of the dove. The sunbeams came in streaks now, shafts of golden light spreading to the opposite bluff, burnishing the treetops. She moved on, silently, toward the building where Henrik was housed, one of four nearest her. Her heart rapped in her chest. Her breath stuttered. Slowly and deliberately she made her way closer to the barrack.

Just then someone strode out from between the barracks, directly in front of her. It was a man dressed in a uniform, a dark-haired American soldier, a guard wearing a sidearm. She drew to a halt, gasped, and then froze in a standing position, studying him. He was no more than twenty feet away, smoking. She watched his exhale drift away with the breeze. Fearful that she would make a sound, she stood erect. Her heart rapped incessantly.

The guard smoked for another minute, casting his eyes toward the lake. Then he flipped the cigarette away, yawned, stretched his arms, flexed his shoulders and took one step forward as his face turned in her direction. He saw her, and stopped immediately. His expression hardened.

"What are you doing here?" he snapped. He took two steps toward her, and then paused. His voice was exceptionally loud in the silence of morning. "I asked you. What are you doing here?"

Her entire body trembled, and in a moment of weakness she was unable to speak Then, as he came toward her, the words tumbled from her mouth. "I have come to see Henrik Arndt."

The guard halted. A small grin surfaced on his otherwise stolid expression. "Henrik Arndt is unable to talk to anyone. He is in confinement. Now go. Just turn around and go. You have no business here."

No! She had walked the entire night to see him, and nothing would deter her now. He was here, close by, and neither the guard, nor the entire military, would prevent her from completing her mission. She stiffened, her jaw tightening with determination. Her shoulders went back, proudly. "I have come to see Henrik. You will not turn me away."

"Oh, yes I will, miss. Now get back to where you came from."

"I will not."

"We'll see about that."

He came toward her, but she was faster. She dashed to the right, toward the trees.

He was heaver than she was, and she would bet that her legs were stronger. She scampered quickly, outracing him, her voice calling out as loud as possible. "Henrik! Henrik Arndt! HENRIK! HENRIK!"

The guard called from behind her. "Stop, goddam it! Stop!"

She ran around a building, stopped momentarily and rapped on the window. "Henrik! Henrik!" she called.

Then she ran again, to the next building, where lights had already come on. "Henrik! It is Elsa."

"Damn you!" the guard shouted. "Get back here!"

"I have to see him," she shouted.

"You ain't seein' nobody."

"HENRIK!" she screamed. "HENRIK!"

She pulled to a stop and turned on the guard. She was panting now, like a cornered animal. Her breath came hard and fast. The guard approached her slowly, his hand on the sidearm.

Elsa sneered at him. "Don't you dare...touch me. If you do . . . I'll see that uniform...stripped from your body."

He paused, breathing deeply. His voice was softer, more consoling. "Now look, lady," he said. "You got no business here. None of these prisoners is going to see you. Now, please, just turn around and head for home."

"I came to see . . . the man I love."

The guard laughed. "Now ain't that a fine one."

She looked again toward the buildings. Then she screamed again, as loud as she could. "HENRIK! IT IS ELSA."

Then one of the doors opened. A man came out. He was dressed in pants and an undershirt. It was Henrik. Her heart skipped as tears welled to her eyes.

"Henrik!" she shouted. "Here! I am here!"

He dashed down the two steps and ran toward her. The guard stepped into his path. Again, his hand went to his sidearm. Henrik pulled up short of him.

"Now get the hell back," the guard shouted.

Henrik looked past him, at Elsa. She stood, slightly bent from exhaustion, waiting for him. His face hardened. "I will not go back. I have to see this woman."

"NO! Now turn around." The guard's hand tightened on the sidearm.

Henrik rose up full height, his chest thrust forward. "Are you going to shoot me Come on then! SHOOT ME! Because if you do not, then I'm going to her, and nothing you will do can stop me."

The guard's hand tightened on the gun. He made a slight motion to lift it from its holster, but then he hesitated.

"I am going to her now," Henrik said.

The guard stepped aside. "Oh, what the hell. Go ahead and talk. But after that, you're goin' back to Algona, and she's goin' home where she belongs. And I'll be right here watchin' you."

By this time a dozen other prisoners had formed on the barrack steps. One of them shouted encouragement. The guard stepped back.

Henrik walked past the guard, nudging him with his shoulder. He walked straight to where Elsa stood, as if rooted to the ground. Tears flooded her face. Henrik stepped up to her, took her gently into his arms and eased her forward, tight to his chest, and in that singular moment he felt a love so strong that no power on earth could have pulled him away. Her eyes looked up at him with an expression so warm that he could feel the heat of it. He kissed her with a tenderness that came directly from his heart, a heart beating with rapture, an emotion he had never know.

"I had to see you . . . again," Elsa muttered.

"Yes, I know."

"I had to tell you . . . how much I love you . . . before they take you . . . away."

"You are my beloved," he said. His face drifted to her neck, where it rested in the perfume of her body.

She cleared her throat then and stood up straight before him. The morning light lay bright on her cheek. "I must get serious now," she said, wiping a tear. "Before they take you away."

"Go on. Oh, God, I love you."

She reached into the pocket of her dress. "My address is written on this paper. I want you to write to me, to tell me where you are. I want you to know that I will do everything in my power to bring you back here . . . to me. Do you want to come back to me, Henrik?"

Crushing her tighter to his body. "Oh, yes, yes."

Taking the note from her, he cupped it in his hand, as he would a golden coin. But this was much more valuable than money. The paper was his future.

"I will find a way to come back," he said.

"We can do it together. There will be a way."

"I will find it."

She looked him directly in the eye. He brushed away her tears. Her face took on a new expression, one of determination, one of purpose.

"I love you, Henrik Arndt. I always will."

"And I love you, Elsa Sommer."

"Promise me that you'll return. Promise me that we'll someday be together again."

He held her tightly in his strong arms. She could feel his love, pressing on her, comforting her, with no need for words.

"I will come back to you," he said. "If it takes my whole life."

"And I will wait, and pray, and hope."

"I love you."

"And I love you."

The guard's voice broke their emotions like a knife cut. "Okay, that's enough, Romeo. Now you get back home, lady. And you, Henrik, get back to your cabin. Fun's over."

Henrik stepped back, holding her hands. He took one last look at her face, to endear her to memory, and then he released her.

"How did you get here?" Henrik asked.

"I walked."

"Oh, God," he muttered. "You must love me very much."

Elsa smiled, and then laughed, to send him away with joy instead of sorrow. "You come back to me, Henrik Arndt. I will show you then how much I love you."

A few of the prisoners cheered, and catcalls came from the men on the steps.

He turned and walked away. Halfway to his cabin he spun around, and waved. And then he was gone.

The guard came up, shaking his head. "Quite a show, lady. Now it's time to get back home."

Her expression was firm and challenging. "Do you have a telephone here?"

"Yea, we do."

"I want to call my father, so he can come and get me."

"Fair enough."

Elsa did not have to use the telephone. On their way to the administration cabin, a car sped down the ravine and slid to a stop on the road adjacent to the camp. She knew at once that it was Papa. She paused, saw him get out and start toward her. She waited beside the guard, proud and erect, her hands folded in front of her. She no longer felt like a girl. She was grown up now, full of pride and confidence. As her father came closer, she smiled at him, presenting an expression of unmistakable happiness.

As he approached her, she knew what she had to do. He had always said to them; for every action there is a reaction, or, what you reap you will sow. She knew, now, at this critical point in her life, that those lessons were vital to bringing Henrik back to America. If she confronted her father in anger, he would not support her when support was needed. So, she had to be cautious, and thoughtful of his reaction. Anything else, anything said in anger, would jeopardize her plans for the future.

Stopping in front of her, and without saying a word, he nodded.

She spoke only once before stepping toward the car. "Good morning, Papa. You can take me home now."

He nodded and motioned to the car.

She walked ahead of him, without saying another word. As soon as the car was headed up the hill, Elsa calmly spoke, "I had to do it, Papa. There was no way I'd let him go without seeing him again."

"Then it's done."

She was firm in her reply. "No. It has just begun. I will do everything in my power to bring him back here some day. Whatever it takes."

"You are serious, I think."

"I have never been more serious."

"Then we'll see what happens."

Papa drove on with his eyes straight on the road

Elsa sniffled. "I want you to know that I'm not angry at you any more. I had to say good-bye to him in a proper way. I hope you understand. If I had not done this, my life would forever be confusing."

"So. What now?"

"So I'll be patient, and see where fate takes me, again."

Harold wiped his brow and then sighed. "I just want you to know that I did what I did because of what I had told him one day. When he first came to the farm I told him to keep away from you so as not to cause problems. I told him if he ever stepped out of line I'd send him back to Iowa."

Elsa sniffled. "You always were a man of your word."

"Aye. And sometimes that can get a man in trouble."

She sat back and thought of Henrik again, how he looked before he drifted from her sight, and how he sounded when he said he loved her. As they drove, she stiffened her resolve, confident that some day, somehow, she would see him again, to take up where they left off, in each others arms, eye to eye, breast to breast.

When she arrived home she went directly to the living room. Mama told the other kids to leave her alone, to give her privacy. Papa went to the barn while Clara prepared lunch. Elsa put a record onto the turntable of the Victrola, a new one by Jo Stafford and as it began playing she curled up on the sofa and listened as the words filled the room:

> *Hide your heart from sight*
> *Lock your dreams at night . . .*
> *It could happen to you.*

As the music played, she remembered that first day she had seen him on the porch, his hair all a mess, his eyes the color of clouds and blue sky, his smile as warm as a summer morning. He had looked at her, surprised to see her there, as if he had seen her before, perhaps in a dream. And she remembered how she felt then, rigid and staring, as if he had materialized from nowhere. And she remembered how her breath had hushed.

Don't count stars, or you might stumble.
Someone drops a sigh, and down you tumble.

And she remembered him in the field, his skin bronzing in the sun, with chaff clinging to his body, his clothing, his face, his hair. And again, his smile, as pure and fresh as daylight, his words as clear and ringing as a bird's song. The way he looked at her was magic at best, glances of wonderment, stares of delight, making her breathless at times.

Keep an eye on spring.
Run when church bells ring.
It could happen to you.

Henrik said to her, I love you, and even now his voice was present, and she heard it again, and again, and again, as the record went round and round, as the words mingled with dreams yet to be fulfilled.

All I did was wonder
How his arms would be . . .
And it happened to me.

The embrace in the barn came back to her then, and she recalled the pressure of his lips, the tenderness of his arms around her, the pure pleasure of his body against hers, the enchantment of the moment, so much so that her body trembled, and for a moment, just for a moment, she thought he was there.

Then the music stopped and the needle drifted into the final grooves of the record. She sighed, got up, put it back to the beginning, and listened to it once more, and again, and again, and again, until she was called to the kitchen.

THIRTY-TWO

Back to Algona, Iowa, August 1945

THE CAR THAT WAS TO BEAR HENRIK back to Algona came at ten o'clock the next day. Henrik had been told to have his belongings ready by then, and right on time he stepped out of the cabin. He had said his good-bye to Emil much earlier, had explained the entire story to him, having said nothing to him until Elsa had appeared in the camp, shouting for him. Some in the camp were appalled, others jealous. Most were indifferent. Henrik didn't care. They could think whatever they wished. He walked out to the car with his head high, confident that he would return some day, to see this camp again, and to remember the morning he vowed to keep his pledge to the woman he loved.

He stepped into the car. The driver came right behind him, with an envelope in his hand, a report, no doubt. As soon as the driver stepped into the car, he said, "Hey, I remember you. I brought you up here earlier this year, right around April."

"Yes. Me and one other."

"Yea, where is he now?

"Back in one of the cabins. I am going alone this time."

The driver started the car, ground it into gear and turned toward the grade. "Yea, I heard you had a problem with a local gal. Got yourself into a bit of a fix, didn't you?"

"I fell in love with her."

The driver laughed. "Well, hell, distance will cure that. They're already sending guys back home from Algona. Word has it that this camp will be empty before the end of October. I'm beginning to wonder what they'll do with the place once it's empty. They'll probably tear it down and turn it back into farmland. Just for your information, they took about five hundred prisoners out of Algona last week, sent 'em on to one of the Eastern ports in Virginia, Norfolk, I guess."

Henrik settled back in his seat. The interior of the car reeked of cigarette smoke and age. The dashboard hadn't been dusted in about a year by the looks of it. Henrik ran his finger through the layer, drawing a line. The guard merely laughed. "Everything gets dirty out on the prairie this time of year," he said.

The familiar roads were behind him now, leaving nothing but hills and farmland and prairie ahead. Only the purr of the motor and the bumps in the road interrupted the monotony that came on quickly. Soon Henrik wanted to talk, to keep his mind busy and to end the loneliness that had crept into his thoughts. He wanted to think about Elsa, to relieve the pain of separation, so he looked over toward the driver and said, "It doesn't matter where I go when I get out of here. I'll be back some day."

The driver snickered. "Some of the other prisoners have said the same thing. But I doubt if they'll be back. Too much red tape. Once they get home they'll forget about the good ol' USA."

"Not me. I will marry this woman."

The driver laughed again. "Shit, man. You're just a kid. You got plenty of time to think about settlin' down. With the war over you'll have the whole of Europe to choose from? With all those soldiers dead and gone, hell, the women'll be clamoring for you guys."

"I've already selected my woman."

"The one back there? Hell, man, she'll be dancing before the weekend is over. Trust me."

Henrik didn't like the tone of his voice. He had heard others describe him as a smart ass. Even so, he did not want to cause trouble, so he kept his opinion to himself.

The driver continued talking. "Surefire thing, love, until it fades away. Hell, I've been in love three times. Each time was better than the last. I'll bet that you'll find a good fraulein and settle down in Germany like all the others. I'll bet you a ten spot on that."

"No, I won't."

The driver just laughed and lit up another cigarette. Henrik rolled down his window and breathed the scented air of the farmlands, felt the wind through his hair as he thought back to those days of sunshine and budding love, when Elsa was near.

They drove on for a while, through a countryside laced with cultivated fields and endless stretches of corn already tasseled. They passed farm after farm, and hills stretching to the horizon, and fields of cows languishing in the sun, and silos reaching skyward. Henrik was glad the conversation had ebbed. His thoughts were elsewhere. The fact that she had walked all the way from the farm, just to see him, was enough to convince him that she would wait for a while. For a while, yes, but how long beyond that? Months? A year? If someone else came along, would she remember the young German boy who had spent a couple of month on their farm? Would her memory of him last beyond the year? Would her love last beyond two? Questions persisted until the driver spoke again.

"Bet you didn't know what happened yesterday. Japan surrendered. Guess they got tired of losing their cities to our A-bombs." He laughed again, as if the war had been a funny event. "They signed the surrender papers on one of our battleships, the Big Mo, with McArthur lookin' right over their shoulders. Lots of celebrations in the cities. I guess I can look forward to goin' home now. Hey, we both got something to cheer about. We're both goin' home."

"I am glad it's over."

"Sure as hell. This lousy war's been wastin' too many lives for nothin'. It took too long for us to get rid of both those son's of bitches, Hitler and Tojo. I don't care what you think about your dead Führer. That's the way I feel. I pray for the day when everyone's got the same freedoms we have. Then there won't be any more wars."

"There will always be wars. Someone will always want more than they have."

"Yeah, I guess you're right. People never learn."

The conversation ebbed away and Henrik closed his eyes. The road and the wind soon lulled him to sleep and in those silent moments he dreamed of Elsa walking across the field, her eyes bright with sunlight, and the smile on her face beckoning and meaningful as if meant only for him.

Welcome to Iowa. Henrik awoke when they crossed the border. He knew that Algona was only a short distance away. He braced himself for the inevitable. Would he be punished for his misconduct? Would he be sent home immediately? Would he be denied pencil and paper on which to write a letter addressed to the slip of paper in his pocket, an address he had already committed to memory. Actually, he didn't care. He just wanted to get on with it, to go home, to eat up the days and months that lay ahead, and to find the right time when he could return…if she still wanted him. God, that is a terrible thought, he said to himself. Nothing could be worse. Put it out of you mind, he said, over and over. She will be loyal. She is in love with you. She will not abandon you.

Sooner than expected, the Algona prison camp came into view, row upon row of barracks and wire fences, the sweeping prairie, the guard towers, all the same. It is so desolate, he thought. Then, as they approached the main gate, he closed his eyes again and willed himself back to the field where Elsa's laughter sang in the wind.

THIRTY-THREE

New Ulm, Minnesota, September 1945

JUST BEFORE ELSA BEGAN HER SENIOR year of high school, the tomatoes were picked and canned. The kitchen was a very busy place that time of year. Later in the month the ear corn was harvested on a bright, rain-free weekend using Papa's two-row picker that had thankfully replaced hand husking. After picking, the corn was hoisted into the slatted crib aside the barn where it was kept dry throughout the winter when it would be fed to the hogs and the cows after being put through a hammer mill that David loved to operate.

Erica had remained silent about Elsa's sojourn with Henrik, nor was anything said about it at school. Right from the start Carlyle kept his distance. She just ignored him. For a few days after Henrik's departure she had been somber and withdrawn. Papa had said nothing. Mother understood. Corina prodded her for information. David ignored her.

Before the week was over she was back to her usual self, pitching in, humming, helping whenever she could, but never forgetting about the man she loved. She wrote him letters in the evening but did not know where to send them. She had not heard from him for two weeks, but she knew a letter would come soon. She had a strong faith in Henrik. He would not disappoint her. Monday evening, the third week in September, when the family sat down to dinner, her wish was answered. When the meal was finished, Papa leaned back and lit his pipe and blew his smoke skyward and the rest of them waited for him to speak.

"We received two letters today," he said, his eyes widening. His gaze went directly to Elsa. "Both of them were from Henrik."

Elsa leaped out of her chair and danced as if struck by a golden wand. "Really!" she screamed. "Honestly? Oh, Papa, let me see them."

"One is for you; the other is for the family. Now you just sit down, and I'll read ours first. Then you can take yours to some private place and read your own. Is it a deal?"

"Oh, yes," Elsa said, regaining her seat. She could hardly sit still. Her anticipation was wild.

"Now sit and be quiet," Papa said. "Here's what he writes to us." He read slowly so the words would be clearly understood.

> *"My Dear Family Sommer, It is hard for me to say how much I miss all of you. I must express my gratitude for your kindness and generosity to me during the time I worked on your farm. You were all like a second family to me. I must also express my apology for the way I behaved. It was unworthy of me. I am now in Algona, preparing for repatriation to Germany. I believe they will be sending me through France. If I can be so bold, I would like to keep in touch with all of you, with your permission. Give my best to David, my new brother, and to Corina, my new sister. Elsa will receive a letter of her own. God bless you all. Be safe in His arms.*
>
> *Your friend, Henrik.*

Corina hugged her tightly as tears rolled down Elsa's cheeks. Mother had a hand to her mouth, censoring a sigh. David looked down at the table. Not a word from any of them, only compassion for a lost friend.

"Here is yours," Papa said, handing her an envelope. She accepted it willingly and scrubbed the tears from her cheeks.

"Can I read it privately?" she asked.

"Yes. Go. It is your letter."

"May I be excused then?"

"You may be excused."

She took it from his hand and went up the stairs to her bedroom and sat beside the window and opened it. She withdrew the paper with trembling fingers and unfolded it. It was the first time she had seen his handwriting. She touched her quivering lips and read:

> *Dearest Elsa, my love,*
> *These might be my last words to you for a while. I am about to leave Algona to return home. Everything is fast here. My luggage is packed and tagged to be sent to the International Red Cross in Geneva, as I am unsure if I still have a home in Bergheim. I have new clothes, U.S. Army uniforms dyed black, with no PW on the back. When I leave, my personal belongings will be returned to me in a sealed bag. I cannot take American currency with me, although I do have some. All repatriates will receive a government check for the amount*

saved, so I will have some money when I reach Germany. I will leave in two days. By the time you receive this I will be on the train.

Now for us. I can never convey in words how much I love you, my darling Elsa, and I can see us together again some day, at home in America. The times I have spent with you, however few, have strengthened me and have given me hope for the future. My love is strong, and it will survive anything that lies ahead for me. I will write when I can, and will give you an address when I arrive in Bergheim. My blessing to you, my love. God is on our side. He will give us strength to wait for the day when we can once again hold each other. Until then, keep me in your heart. I am forever yours.

Love, Henrik.

Elsa carefully folded the letter and held it tight, then looked outside into the farmyard where they had once stood side by side beneath the summer sun, then to the windmill where they had drank from the same dipper, and across the yard where he had chased her and Corina, when his laughter had filled the air. She heard his laugh again, loud and clear, and felt a flutter in her heart as memory stirred her blood. "You are everything to me," she whispered. "I will wait for you until the end of time. Just come back to me. Come back to me." She cried again, and held the letter to her breast, and felt the nearness of him even though he was not there.

THIRTY-FOUR

At Sea, October 1945

BEFORE HENRIK LEFT FOR EUROPE HE was issued a barrack's bag, several woolen blankets, a first aid kit, and eating utensils. The remainder of his belongings were boxed and shipped to Nuremberg via the Red Cross. Henrik never saw the box again.

He spent his days looking out to sea from the deck of the liner, one of the many still in service to transport prisoners back to war-ravaged Europe. The ocean brought him both sadness and comfort, depending on its mood, for in its pure and endless desolation it carried him farther and farther away from America and closer to uncertainty. On the other hand, if the sun settled just right on its waves, it appeared to be something enlightening. Its broad expanse, sketched with sunlight and clouds and blue sky, often gave him hope, and in its unblemished purity he found a calmness that sometimes bridged the gap between him and the small farm near New Ulm.

Daily he wrote to Elsa, sometimes on the same paper but with a new date. He told her only good things, nothing of the crowded conditions, or the meager food, or the tight quarters shared by so many confused and angry men whose world had been damaged by war. He wrote about memories, those days in the fields, the night beneath the stars, the hours wherein he had dreamed of her, the dreams that sustained him. And with each and every day he pledged to himself that he would return. Somehow he would find a way,

One day he wrote:

> There is a place on one of the top decks where I can stand against the rail and look out over the bow of the ship. And when I am there, with the sea wind in my face, I close my eyes and see you, so plainly that my body quivers at the sight of you. It is a magical place, where I can put my future in order and find you standing beside me. It is so real, and if I move just a little I can feel your shoulder against mine. Sometimes I can stand there for an hour and let my imagination bring you to me. You are always beside me.

Henrick missed Emil. He was alone in the world, surrounded by thousands of men who were not searching for friends. Most all of them just wanted to go home, to whatever awaited them, to begin a new life amid the wreckage of war. The future to them was a big question mark, nothing permanent, everything vague. Young and old, they were all the same, and for some it was a voyage into madness. Suicides continued, those who knew their homes were gone, their families dead, their futures nothing more than an empty plate to a very hungry man. And so they took their lives. The ocean swallowed them up and no one missed them.

All these men would be going to France, to the same port he left on his way to America. From there it was anyone's guess. He hoped, as they all did, that the French would send them straight back to Germany, to search out their loved ones. But there were rumors. Some said the French would never forget the rape of their land. They would keep them as prisoners, to begin reconstruction, to work in the mines, or to clean off the wreckage of war that lay scattered across their country. The French could be tough taskmasters, brutal at times.

So it went, day after day, increasing the distance away from her. He clutched at hope, that fragile and irreplaceable dream that kept him going. He watched the sea go by, endless in its many moods. On November 16th he celebrated his eighteenth birthday, alone. It was raining. The ship pitched heavily, its decks creaking with the strain. He stayed below amid the cigarette smoke, the cursing and the vomiting.

THIRTY-FIVE

New Ulm, Minnesota, October 1945

THE CELEBRATION OF "HERMANNSCHLACT," or Herman's Slaughter was over. The observance commemorated the victory of a Roman-trained son of a Cheruscan chief in 9 A.D. who had organized the German tribes in the Black Forest near Kalkreis. His forces had massacred three Roman legions. The victory had stopped further encroachment of the Roman Empire into areas east of the Rhine.

The celebration was another reason to drink beer, and eat sauerkraut.

Also, because New Ulm didn't have a local radio station, the panel truck from Alwin's Electric cruised the streets with its loudspeaker blaring from the roof, "It's basketball tonight at the high school, Gaylord versus New Ulm."

Autumn had settled in, and on most evenings smoke from burning leaves drifted through the temperate twilight air, signaling the coming of snow, ice, and cold. Across the length and breath of the river town, the foliage had turned red and golden and a shade of light brown. The winds from Canada brought out sweaters and jackets and headgear on some days, mittens or gloves on others. All of Minnesota, New Ulm included, began buttoning down for the shorter days of winter.

Clara, Elsa and Corina had finished canning peaches about three in the afternoon. Corina had gone upstairs. Before beginning supper, Elsa and Clara went out onto the porch to rest for a while. It was cool there. A light breeze puffed in from the west, and in the yard the dry leaves swirled and danced before piling up along the fence.

Clara sat in the large rocker whenever Harold was not in it. She wiped her forehead. Her tired eyes peered out as if wishing for nightfall. It was the perfect time for Elsa to bring up a notion that had been occupying her mind since the day before when she and Erica had walked down Minnesota Street after school. During the walk Elsa had noticed a sign in Earl's shop window. They were seeking a part-time server behind the soda bar, and were paying the minimum wage of forty cents per hour. Curiosity had drawn her into the store.

Hesitantly at first, not knowing what her mother's response would be, she spoke, "They're hiring for a part-time worker at Earl's," she said, keeping her voice low.

What for?" Clara asked.

"They want someone to tend the soda bar, and they're paying minimum wage."

"That's nice," she said, continuing her rocking as if no one had spoken. She awaited the inevitable statement.

"I want your permission to take the job. Winter is coming. I'll have some spare time on my hands. Besides, I have a reason."

The rocker stopped moving. Clara turned her head. "I can only guess," she said. "Does this have anything to do with Henrik?"

"It does."

"What is it?"

"He tells me over and over in his letters that he wants to come back here, to me. He wants to start up a farm, and he wants me for his wife. I want to save up enough money so I can sponsor him. There is a way, but I'll need to finance the trip. Please say yes, Mama."

Clara turned her head. "You're really taken by him, aren't you?"

"You know I am."

"And what will this passage cost?"

"Somewhere around three or four hundred dollars I guess."

"You guess? Have you looked into it?"

"Not yet."

Clara swung around in her chair, exasperation masking her face. "Do you know how downright silly that sounds, wanting to bring a boy back here who worked for your father only a few weeks, a boy who might want to stay in Germany once he finds his family? Elsa, you can do better than that."

"I love him, Mama."

Clara turned away. "You are no more than a grown child."

Elsa's voice strained. "You were my age once, right?"

"What's that got to do with it?"

"You said you were only eighteen when Papa came along. You said you knew he was the man for you the instant you looked into his eyes. Well, I felt the same way when I looked at Henrik."

"You were just reliving the story I told you."

"No. It was more than that, and you know it."

Clara sighed. "Okay, so it was. But do you know how crazy it is to imagine he'll be back, a German prisoner, repatriated to his own country, with parents there, with mountains of work to be done. He'll never come back, Elsa. And your father shares the same opinion. He was a nice boy, and you had your fun, but now you've got to forget him. After graduation next year you'll be going on to college, and from there, who knows. Keep your mind on the future, dear, and forget the few days you had with Henrik this past summer. It's foolish to keep his memory alive."

Elsa stiffened. She felt like a river flowing into a great gulf, where she would be disbursed amid a million miles of water, straining to find an unseen shore somewhere beyond.

She had been taught not to argue with her mother, and she wouldn't, not even now when forces were gathered against her, but she had to go on.

"I know how you and Papa feel. But you both have to listen to me at some time, because I am going to take that job, like it or not. I'm seventeen now, and I know where I'm going. If I get the job I'll work Saturday for eight hours, and Sunday for four hours after church, and I'll save my money . . . just in case."

Clara nodded. "Okay, I think you should take the job. It'll at least put you on a path of your own choosing. If it works out, then fine. If it doesn't, well you'll have some money for college. I don't think your father will object."

"Good, because that's what I'm going to do."

Clara faced her again, reached out and took her hand. "I know about love, Elsa. I know what it can do to a woman. It can turn out to be wonderful and exciting, and in the end, a lot of work for little compensation. Or it can fail. The good part about failure is that you can start all over again, only on a different path."

"Did you take psychology or something?"

Clara laughed. "No, we call it the school of hard knocks."

"Okay, then tell me this. How long would you have waited for Papa if he had gone away, to war, or something?"

She waved the question away, but then answered. "Why, I would have waited forever. And I bet that answer suits you just fine."

"I start next Saturday," Elsa said.

"So, you already took the job."

"Yes."

"Playing a little game with me then, weren't you?"

"I had to find out."

"Pretty mischievous, if you ask me."

"Do you think Papa will approve?"

"It's winter. There's little work here on weekends. But answer this. How will you get to and from work? It's a long way to New Ulm."

"I'll pay Papa a dollar a week for gasoline. It should be enough. He can take me in when he goes for supplies on Saturday morning. Hopefully he'll pick me up on Saturday afternoon. I can start on Sunday after church. Four hours later he can pick me up. That's only two extra trips for him."

"You've got it all figured out, haven't you?"

"You taught me to think ahead."

"Yes, I guess I did. I figured sooner or later those lessons would come in handy, only I didn't know it would have something to do with a German boy five thousand miles away."

Elsa left her chair and took two strides to where Mama sat. She leaned over and wrapped her arms around her neck, then kissed her on the cheek. "I love you, Mama. I knew you'd see it my way."

"Well, the job is one thing. Henrik is another. We'll just have to wait a while to see how it all works out. By the way, what did he say in his last letter?"

"He's landed in France. I haven't heard anything since then. He said he would write the minute he's settled, hopefully back in Bergheim."

"Do you want to tell your father about this when he comes in?"

Elsa squirmed a bit. "Can you tell him for me?"

"No, it's your show. You do the work."

"Okay. I'll charm him."

Mama laughed again. "Yea, you do that. He's a pushover for charm."

Just then Harold appeared in the yard, coming from the barn. Clara chuckled. "Well, here he comes. Let's see how your down-home charm works on a hard-working farmer who sent your boyfriend back home. Are you ready for him?"

Elsa stood up straight and took a deep breath. "Ready as I'll ever be."

She was bit nervous as Papa came through the gate. He gave them both his usual warm smile as he took the steps one at a time. Elsa stood up and met him face to face on the landing.

"Elsa has something to tell you," Clara said.

"What is it?" he asked, leveling his eyes at Elsa.

"I've got a job, Papa," she said straight out.

He nodded as a half grin spread across his face. "A job?"

"Yes, at Earl's, in town, on Saturday's and Sunday's. Minimum wage."

He glanced over to where Clara sat as questions formed. She nodded, giving him the lead. "And why do you need a job?"

She fumbled for words. Her hands twisted nervously. "I want to save up some money."

"What for?"

She looked at Clara for help, but found none. "I want money enough to bring Henrik back here."

The silence seemed to go on forever. Eyes met, shifted, met again, hers to Clara, his to the kitchen door and beyond. "That is a noble thing to do," he said at length. "But, if I must say, it seems a bit foolish given the circumstances."

"I know."

Then Papa took a deep breath and nodded. "But who am I to stand in the way of romance? I guess I had something to do with his leaving so suddenly. And, I must admit, I miss the lad."

She relaxed as the tension eased away, and then went into his arms, her face tight against his chest.

"How much money will you need?" he asked.

"About four hundred dollars."

"Let's see, at forty cents an hour . . ." he calculated quickly in his head. "If my mathematics is right, it'll take you about a year and a half to earn that much, well past the end of school. I won't have it interrupting your college."

"I should be done earning by first semester, depending on where I go."

"Okay. So be it. I'll drive you when necessary, and no need to pay for gasoline. Rationing is gone."

Elsa beamed, "I love you, Papa."

"Well, what is a father to do when his daughter has eyes for a handsome young man?"

"Thank you, Papa."

His expression mellowed, and then turned somber, as it always did when dispensing wisdom. "It was never a plan of ours to tell our children what road they had to follow in life. You'll choose your own course. We only hope that, through good sense and reason, you'll choose the right one and make the best of it, until another crossroad comes. There will be crossroads, mind you, there always are. We can only hope that you'll choose your course wisely, this one being no exception. Now go, and start supper. I'll talk to your mother about this."

Elsa kissed him on the cheek and went into the kitchen. Together, Harold and Clara left the porch and took a little walk across the farmyard, hand in hand.

"Well, what do you think of your daughter's plan?" Clara asked him outright.

"It's a bit reckless. Henrik will have his hands full over there. Unless he's very dedicated, he might lose faith. It'll be hell for him in Germany."

"And then again, he might persevere."

"True, he might. But I rather doubt that we'll see him again. Still, it's no reason to refuse her. She'll have to learn about the road of life for herself."

"And if she does save the money, and if she does sponsor him, what then?"

Harold paused and took up Clara's hands into his own. "Well, if it must be, then I expect we'll go along with it. If he's man enough to remember her, and man enough to cross oceans for her, and man enough to want her for a wife, well, any man who can do that is worth his salt. If they can both persevere that long, then maybe they'll have a life together. But no word of this to her. She can choose her own course, in her own way."

"I understand."

He looked longingly at her. His eyes studied the calmness of her face. "I remember us some years back, the struggles we overcame, the difficulties, and how sure we were of one another. She's a bit like you that way, tough and determined. I would say that if she and Henrik ever get together, he's a very lucky man."

He kissed her then and held the embrace longer than either of them had expected.

Then, as she headed for the house, he washed up at the tank.

THIRTY-SIX

France, October 1945

THE SHIP EASED UP TO THE PIER on a cold day in late October when the sky was near black with rain. The harbor was still littered with sunken ships, masts jutting above the water, superstructures canted, debris still floating on the oil-slicked surface, the smell of ruin still in the air. Many of the harbor buildings were damaged or under repair. On the sea wall ahead of the bow someone had scrawled a message in German that read: "Welcome Home, Nazi Swine." The port appeared sullen and broken, desolate in the rain that came just as they were descending the gangplanks to a waiting train, a dirty gray line of old coaches and boxcars so long they could not see its end.

The French guards who stood with rifles and machine pistols were deliberate in their hate for the German soldiers, some of whom had fought in France, others who might have occupied Paris; some who might have made love to French women. They pushed and shoved and sometimes kicked the men in line, saying things like: Get going Nazi pigs. You will not see Paris this time. We have a more appropriate place for you now. Or, you, son of a Hitler bastard, get in line. When they saw a man wearing a watch they stopped him and took it off and slid it onto their own wrist, then prodded him along with the barrel of a rifle. The prisoners were allowed to keep the envelopes containing their identification, money, and personal effects. All else was confiscated.

The railroad cars they entered were filthy with dirt and mud. They were made to stand so more could get packed in. One of the guards shouted; now you know how the Jews felt. When the cars were full, the doors were slid shut and locked. Inside, shoulder to shoulder, the men could hardly move. Everyone cursed. Some of the men peed in their trousers. Some defecated. The stench was horrible. Never had Henrik been treated in such a way, surely not in America. The two situations were beyond comparison. All they could do was obey, and wait, and hope for the best. It was an hour before the train moved with a sudden jerk, shifting the mass of men backwards like a huge tidal wave. Water was in short supply. Some of the guards had taken away their canteens. The guards had also stripped off the prisoners' long coats. Everyone wore the same clothing, the black shirts and trousers they had been issued in Algona.

"Where are we going?" someone asked.

"We are going to Hell," another replied.

"We are already there. How worse could Hell be?"

The train pulled out of Brest as darkness moved in across the port city. They traveled for hours, sleeping on their feet, their bodies aching, their lungs crying for air, their mouths finding only saliva, and little of that. Whenever a man slid down within the mass, others pulled him back to his feet. Occasionally a man would cry, and someone would inevitably say: Stiffen up, you are not a baby, you are a German soldier. Others coughed. All of them strengthened themselves mentally for the ordeal ahead. They expected nothing better from the French.

Henrik stood lodged between a young boy from Munich, another older man from Dresden. They didn't say much, only where they were from; too many ears around. The young boy shivered a lot, and sometime during the night he cried on Henrik's shoulder. Henrik put his arm around him and held him.

He thought of Elsa much of the time, how she looked that day in the field with the wind in her hair, and her smile as bright as the sky. And he felt her against him, as he had that day in the barn, her arms tight around his neck, her impassioned lips pressing warmly to his, moving with a tenderness that had brought his breath to a standstill. The vision of her kept him going through the long night, when he thought his legs would surely collapse beneath him, when his mouth was so dry he could scarcely breathe. She kept him going that night, when the world was black and cold, when rainwater drizzled through the top of the car onto their heads, and when the press of bodies became almost unbearable. He spoke her name a thousand times to himself, in time with the clacking of the steel wheels against the tracks. Elsa. Elsa. Elsa. Elsa.

The train stopped sometime near dawn, and then they waited impatiently as those outside commanded others. The prisoners inside could hear trucks moving, getting in line to take them someplace else, to a more humane place they hoped. Then, as tensions mounted, the doors opened and cool, fresh air blew in like the breath of an angel. They gulped it freely, anxious to leave the living crypt. Then, upon command, the entire group moved forward toward the open door. They jumped out, several at a time, and shifted into line as instructed, under the watchful eyes of mounted machine gunners atop risers not far from the line of cars.

The trailer trucks came up, one at a time, from a long line of trucks once used for hauling cattle. They were dirty and rusted. The interiors were littered with straw and dried dung and scattered paper. They climbed into the trucks and pressed themselves together. Then they started out, over an uneven narrow dirt road that shook them and shook them and shook them. Only the press of bodies kept them upright.

They came to a huge open field, as flat as the land in Iowa. The area was divided into sections, each bordered by rolls of barbed wire. Each section contained hundreds, if not thousands of men. Once out of the truck they were herded into lines and were assembled behind the barbed wire. Watchtowers stood at intervals, each one manned by machine gunners. The Germans who were already there told them to get some rest, anywhere, on the ground still wet with rain if necessary, because they would need their strength for the days ahead, when the interrogations began, when they would learn how to survive.

The newcomers from the train soon learned that space was limited, and food was unavailable, and that latrines would have to be dug by hand out near the wire. The stench of earthen toilets already permeated the area.

Thankfully, on that first day, the rains stopped, but the ground was nothing but mud. The grass, if there had been any, was totally gone. Sit in the mud, or lie in the mud. They only had two choices. Writing a letter would be impossible. He had no paper, no pencil, and no postage. All he could do was wait, and hope to be processed quickly, so he could begin his journey home. In the meantime he would pray for deliverance.

Just before dark the searchlights came on. He did not sleep well that night. The most he could manage was two or three hours, then he was awake, shivering, his body cold to the bone. Throughout the night as many as thirty or forty percent of the men wandered aimlessly, trying not to step on those who were trying to sleep. They had nowhere to go but around in circles, heads low, shoulders hunched, like beggars on a lonely street.

The rain had soaked through Henrik's clothing. Whenever he turned, the mud squished beneath him. Late in the night someone curled up close to him, to seek his body heat, of which there was little. Many men were coughing. None had anything to cover themselves with. Some of the men said it would be days before the French got to them. There was a pecking order, first come, first served. And there were thousands of them waiting. The French watchmen said there was no place else to put them because there were so many. They were doing the best they could under the circumstances. But it was obvious that the French took some delight in watching the supermen suffer. The men from the Wehrmacht did not look so tough, or so superior, when sleeping in mud.

The next day they received their first food, a spoonful of raw beans, another of sugar, a meager helping of raw wheat and powdered milk. They ate like starved men. Some could not keep their food down. They received water from a single spigot, drank from their dirty hands. Then they stood in the sun and warmed themselves, and removed their clothes and stockings to dry them on the barbed wire. The stench in the camp reeked of human waste despite daily efforts to reduce it by sprinkling the trenches with ample doses of lye.

The days were always the same, waking, waiting, hurrying for food rations, waiting again, resting when possible, and waiting. Each day the prisoners carried their dead to the gate and placed them in line. Then the trucks came and took them away while the others prisoners looked on, sallow faced and angry because of the horrible treatment they had received.

Henrik remembered the New Ulm camp, the dark wood barracks, the clean beds, the shower rooms, toilets, and warm interiors, and the meals made by the camp cooks; plates of steaming food, cakes for desert, water in abundance, grass and trees overhead, the lake to swim in, to fish in, fillets of fish for dinner, games afterwards, music and laughter, lights and happiness. When he told some of the others about New Ulm, they didn't believe him. So he stopped telling them.

The next day they lined up for their first ration of bread, one loaf for ten men. Sharing became a frenzy. Some got more, others less.

Sleeping on the ground became a dreadful routine, even when it was not raining. Not only did their clothing begin to rot, but their minds did as well. Some never stood. They just lay there and died and were carried out the next morning.

After a week of suffering, Henrik was moved to a smaller enclosure containing about a hundred men. From there they would be interrogated. His papers and money, enclosed in a waterproof wrapping, were his most precious possession. Late in the afternoon he was told they would be processed the following day. He slept soundly that night for the first time in a week.

The next morning ten of them were moved to a small enclosure adjacent to a series of large tents. They waited about an hour, talking among themselves about homes and destinations.

Occasionally groups of men would be herded into the tents. About an hour later they were taken out and marched away to waiting trucks. From there they would be taken to a place where they would be released, probably to the German border, so they thought.

Toward mid-morning Henrik and nine others were taken to one of the tents. The Frenchman who sat in line with ten others, behind old wooden tables, spoke fluent German. When Henrik came up the Frenchman asked for his papers. He took the envelope and spoke without looking up. "Your name is Henrik Arndt?"

"Yes."

"And you are from Bergheim?"

"Yes.

He counted through the small amount of scrip Henrik was carrying. "This currency will be confiscated to help pay for your keep," he said, stuffing the notes into a wooden box beside his chair.

"But . . ."

"Silence. You have no rights here."

"But, the money . . ."

"Do you want to go back behind the wire for another week?"

"No."

"Then keep your mouth shut."

When motioned to, a doctor came over and looked in his mouth, put a stethoscope to his chest, his back, asked him a few questions, and then nodded. Passed.

"Go and stand over there," the Frenchman said.

Henrik went over and stood with four others. None of them spoke. All had hope in their eyes. One of them smiled. Soon it would be over, they thought. They waited about a half hour, inside the warm tent. It felt good there, better than behind the wire. "Soon they will take us to the border," one of them whispered. Five more came to join them, ten in all. Again they waited.

Then a French soldier came in and ushered them outdoors to a waiting truck. They all climbed aboard. Their faces showed signs of both comfort and delight. Henrik counted the days before he would be back in Bergheim, three or maybe four depending on how quickly they processed him through. If he could get a ride, it might be as soon as three days. Then he would begin planning his future.

The back gate was closed and locked. As the truck started out, a jeep bearing three French soldiers and a mounted machine gun pulled in behind them.

One of the Germans said, "Where are they taking us?"

"It's just an escort, "another replied. We are going to the border."

"I'm not so sure. Perhaps they will shoot us."

There was a small window between the cab of the truck and the box. The man who had raised the questioned rapped on the glass. "Where are we going?" he shouted.

The driver turned his head briefly. "Why, hell, all you German bastards are going to Merlebach. You're gonna do a little coal mining for us, in payment for the good treatment we gave you back there." He laughed.

Henrik knew of Merlebach. The town rested on the same coal vein that ran all the way up into the Ruhr valley, to where the German mines were located, but well back from the border. Not that far though. Thirty, or forty miles perhaps. On the German side of the border the land was festooned with farmland and villages, and the city of Ulm. Beyond that, to the north and east–Bergheim. He could walk that far. All he would have to do was escape the mines.

To some in the truck, Merlebach sounded like another prison. To Henrik it sounded like a sure way home, provided he could escape, make it to the border without being apprehended, cross over, and walk the distance. But winter was coming. He would have to prepare for that. He would have to escape the French, if the mines did not kill him first.

Merlebach. Perhaps when he arrived there he could write another letter to Elsa. Perhaps there he could do a good job for the French, and earn their respect, as he had in America when working for Harold Sommer. And when he had their respect, and when their guard was down, perhaps then he would strike out for the border, praying he would not be shot on the way.

It all sounded so easy in thought, but he knew any attempt at escape would be met with gunfire. The French would not just let him walk away. Also, the thought of working in a mine sent shivers through his body. Stuffed in a narrow shaft underground, in darkness, and breathing coal dust all day would wear him down within weeks, and as his strength ebbed, so would his determination. He knew he would have to act sooner than later, if he had any chance at all of returning to Bergheim.

As the realization became unmistakably clear, the men began talking.

"They will work us to death," one of them said.

"When I was younger I hated to be in enclosed spaces. It even bothered me to crawl into a foxhole. What will I do in a mine? I will go crazy in there."

"I will not go down. I will fight them."

"And you will lose."

One of them who had been with the Panzergrenadier-Lehr Regiment 901 at Remagen looked at Henrik. "What will you do?" he asked outright.

Henrik took a deep breath and gritted his teeth. "I will work in the mines. I will do what they tell me to do until I can find a way to escape. I will die if I remain there too long. I cannot waste time working there. I will find a way out as soon as I can."

"Good. Then let us, together, say one thing. We are still fighting the French."

In unison, they either nodded, or said. "Aye, we are still fighting."

The truck rolled on toward the German border even as night fell. To the man, they sprawled out on the floor and amid the jostling and bumping they found a few moments of sleep.

They skirted Paris the next day, and headed out for Lorraine. During the trip, when he could not sleep, Henrik's mind filled with deep remorse. How long would he be in Merlebach? Would he survive the mines? Would Elsa wait for him? How soon would he be able to write another letter to her, to strengthen her love? How would he ever return to America? He had nothing. No money. No clothing, except for the black pants and shirt he wore. Why would she wait for a man who had nothing to offer except love? Yet, all the way, in the constant, miserable rocking of the vehicle and the incessant noise, and the terrible weight of the unknown, Henrik silently promised Elsa that he would do everything in his power to come back to her.

Thirty-Seven

New Ulm, Minnesota, November 1945

A FULL MOON BRIGHTENED THE NIGHT sky as Harold and Clara crawled into their bed, weary from the day's work. Thanksgiving was only three days away. Preparations had been constant. Anticipations, however, were less than normal, especially for Elsa, who suffered every day, not knowing where Henrik was, not knowing if he was alive or dead.

Harold rolled toward his woman beneath the single wool blanket that covered them, slid his arm around her and touched the softness of her breast. She nuzzled against him. She had bathed, and her skin was fresh and scented. He was warm and comforting against her. They lay there for a while, finding solace in their soft embrace. He kissed her shoulder.

This was a peaceful time for both of them, the moments before sleep when they could, by touch alone, display the affection they felt for one another. On some nights, if they were not too weary, and if the mood was right, they would make love slowly, to extend the passion, to absorb the love. On this night, however, after the initial embrace, they faced one another in the semi-darkness and whispered softly.

"Elsa is so worried," Clara began.

"Yes, I know. I can see it on her face. She wears her anxiety like a mask."

"She has not heard from Henrik in over a month. What do you think is wrong?"

"He's on French soil. Who knows what they have done with him."

"Could they be holding him?"

"Yes. He could still be a prisoner."

"That would be horrible."

"It would. They are short of manpower, just like we were last summer. They could have him working anywhere, in a factory, on the docks, under the gun."

Clara sniffled. "To think of him that way makes me tremble."

They were silent for a while. The owl in the grove started his nightly callings. The wind, stronger than usual, brushed through the treetops like a long-issued sigh.

"I found her crying this afternoon," Clara said.

"And?"

"I comforted her. I told her he was probably in a place where postal service was unavailable, because of the war. I told her to be patient." She squeezed Harold's arm. "She said to me, you don't know how much I miss him. I said, I did. I told her I knew how much the heart can hurt. She thanked me for caring. She plays her record. You know the one."

"If he doesn't write again, do you think she'll forget him?"

"It'll take a long while. She's so in love with him. I see it, you don't."

"It takes a woman to know."

"Yes, precisely."

"I still find it hard to believe that she'd fall in love so quickly, in such a short time."

"I don't."

He hugged his wife closer. "You speak from experience."

"Yes."

"Then I hope for her sake that he's still all right."

Clara took his hand and held it tightly beneath her chin. "What are we to do if he does write again? Her expectations and hopes will be uncontrollable."

"We do nothing, until she is sure of him."

"She is already sure."

"Ha, it's desire whispering in her ear. If he comes back, then we'll see."

"She's saving her money."

"How much now?"

"Only sixteen dollars."

"That's a long way from the hundreds she'll need, and with no word from him, she's goin' on hope alone."

"Still, she has determination."

"Yes, you've given her that much, I'll say."

She worked her bended knee in between his legs and rested it there. "If he does write again, and if things are okay between them, and if she still wants him to come back, will you help her?"

The question took him by surprise. She felt him stiffen a bit, felt his body tense up, heard his breath stall. He said nothing for a while. She knew he was thinking. It was his way, to respond only when he was certain of his answer.

"She is my daughter," he said. "I will help her."

She squeezed him in a soft embrace, pleased with his reply. "You are a saint, Mr. Sommer," she said.

"I ain't a saint. I'm just a father who wants his children to be happy."

"Would you help her sponsor him then?"

"If need be. She might not be able to do it on her own."

"And suppose we're successful in bringing him back, what then?"

He did not hesitate. "Well, then they'll get married, right off. I won't have him taking up space if she's not his wife."

"And then what?"

Again, the pause, the working of his mind, and then the reply. "Well, if he comes home soon, the Schroeder place is still for sale He's got no taker yet, but he's anxious to sell, to move to Colorado where his son is. Schroeder's seventy-two-years old now, too old to keep on going, he told me."

"You'd buy it then?"

"I'd take the mortgage only long enough to get them started. Then they can go it on their own."

"What if they don't want the farm?"

"The cities need workers too. There's a big need now that the war's over. They can do whatever they want. I know he's aggressive. He'll do whatever's necessary to succeed. I saw that much in him."

"Thank you," she said.

"Don't tell Elsa yet. Wait until the letters come again. We need proof that he's okay, and if his fire still burns in her heart."

She nuzzled him. "Oh, Harold, you can be so poetic at times."

He pinched her cheek as a sign of affection. "Now you're being flattering."

The moonlight slanted through the window, bathing one wall with light. She snuggled closer to him, happy with his response, content with his willingness to help if help was needed. She loved him so, even now, after the struggle and the children and the years of hard work. She hoped that Elsa would feel the same someday.

"Lay on your back," she whispered. "I want you tonight."

He shifted, and then drew her over him, and within seconds he was ready for her. She straddled him and settled down to feel him inside her, and as the owl hooted out in the grove, and as she felt his breath upon her, she immersed herself in his silent passion.

THIRTY-EIGHT

Merlebach, France, November 1945

THE PRISONERS' TRUCK ROLLED INTO Merlebach when the sun was at its zenith. Exhausted and cramped from the bone-jarring ride and the raw cold, Henrik eased his way out of the truck with the others and waited in a loose formation at the rear of vehicle. Three Frenchmen stood at a distance, armed with rifles. Their faces turned one by one to examine the Germans with stern and indolent expressions, as if they were looking at animals instead of humans. Then one of them pointed in the direction they would go and said, *"Schnell. Schnell,"* and then they walked single file up a hard-packed dirt road toward a shabby cluster of weather-worn Nissen huts that had been erected during the war. Each of the huts was constructed of sheet metal bent into half cylinder shapes and anchored into the ground with its axis horizontal. Three small windows on either side provided light during the daylight hours.

Entering through the only door into a dim interior, the door was closed behind them. At that point, Henrik was as forlorn as he had ever been. Not only was he facing a bleak and uncertain future in a French camp, but his longing for Elsa consumed his every thought. The dismal hut only intensified his need for her.

His first impression of the space was startling. The walls of the hut rested on a concrete foundation. He estimated the structure was about thirty feet long. A quick count of the angle-iron bunks slatted with wood and inch-thick mattresses indicated a compliment of twenty men, double-decked. On one end of the room a single three-faucet pipe brought in water from somewhere outside. A wooden shelf housed soaps and towels. A drain trough carried the used water outside. A single toilet, unshielded, accommodated everyone.

The only other man in the room came toward them through the haze of light. He was a tall man, a German, who had a tight mouth and tighter eyes, and a look of authority about him. He walked erect, with the obvious demeanor of an officer. His footfalls were the only sound in the room. He stopped in front of them and folded his arms. He did not salute. "I am Alfred Kleinen," he said. His eyes scanned each man individually. "Welcome to Hell," he said. His lips barely moved when he spoke. "So there are ten of you, all looking scared and uncertain as to what lies ahead. But you will not wait long to find out. Tomorrow morning you will be down in the mine, shoveling coal for France."

No one said a word.

Alfred continued. "From here to the German border it is just 14 kilometers. Not very far. But just yesterday we lost three men, one in the shaft, another two last night when they attempted to climb the slagheap. So if you want to strike out for Germany, you do so at your own peril. Few have escaped. This place, my friends, is worse than trying to dodge American bullets. At least in the war, we were given some food now and then. Here, well, the food is not the best of fare. We do our work. We eat. We work some more, and when the French taskmasters are ready to release us, then we will go home."

Smiling slightly, he then shifted his feet to an at-ease position and rubbed his hands together. "There is only one door and it is always guarded by a machine gun, a new guard every eight hours. At night the compound is illuminated by floodlights. But there are no fences, no barbed wire, nothing to prevent you from escaping, except for the danger itself." He waited for a reply, but none was given. "Outside this pleasant little compound, and beyond the rail yard, the French miners and their families live in rows of cheaply built nineteenth century houses called "corons." The gracious French company owners rent them to the miners. Parents and children and even grandparents live crowded together in these places that none of us would want to live in. They have very little furniture and are offered few comforts. It is the best the miners can get from the greedy French owners. The miners live and die here. The streets are hard-beaten earth in the summer and muddy paths in the winter. Other than the houses, there are few facilities. The money-hungry shareholders think only of themselves. When a miner is hurt, or killed, the survivors lose their house, as well as their income. We are more fortunate than they are. We lose only our lives. The French call this place "les Pays Noirs,"–the Black Country. Outsiders rarely visit. On the far side of the camp there is an ugly, black slag pile. Beyond it the German border awaits those who are fortunate enough, and bold enough, to escape. Now, are there any questions before you settle into your comfortable quarters?"

"How long have you been here," one of the ten asked.

"For me, three months."

"Not long."

Alfred grinned, revealing yellowed and chipped teeth. "Three months is like an eternity. You will see. In three months you will feel like an animal."

Henrik looked at the man beside him, whose face was stark and fearful.

Alfred stood up straight, nearly at attention, his mouth terse, his eyes piercing. "I will say one other thing. None of us planned on being here, but here we are. I must remind you that you are still German soldiers even though we are not in uniform. Therefore, I expect all of you to act accordingly. We were not trained to dishonor our country, and we will not do so now. We must show our French captors that we are firm in our resolve to always do our best, regardless of the situation. Do you understand me?"

All nodded in unison. Alfred's statement was clearly understood.

"Now go and find a place to rest on one of the empty bunks. You have the afternoon, and a meal ahead of you, if you can call it one. And try to sleep tonight. Tomorrow you will go down into the bowels of the earth."

Henrik spoke up. "Can I get some writing material, paper and pen?"

"We have some, yes."

"Can I get a letter forwarded?"

"It can be arranged, for a price. The French guards are known to give a favor for a favor."

"But I have no money."

"None of us do. We are paid only with sweat."

"What favors then?"

"They will let you know. Maybe you will shine their boots. Some will ask you to drop your pants."

No one replied. Someone snickered. It was becoming very clear to them that Merlebach was not a castle on the Rhine. It was, they imagined, a place where men's souls were devoured.

As they filed off to find a bunk, Henrik addressed the officer. "Where do I get paper and pencil?"

"I have some. It is limited."

"Can I have it now?

"Yes, follow me. I have it at my bunk." He spoke louder so everyone could hear him. "I am the one you will see for this sort of thing. I try to accommodate everyone here. It is all I can do to make life easier for us."

Henrik followed Alfred to his bunk where he removed a small box from beneath his cot. Opening it, he handed Henrik a small piece of paper.

"Is this all you have?" Henrik asked.

"It is adequate. We must limit. To get paper is very difficult."

"How can I write on such a small piece?'

"You will learn to squeeze your words. Write small and legibly."

"And the pencil?"

"Here." He dug into the box and removed pencil stub no more than two inches in length. "Once again. Make every word count. When you are finished, bring it back to me. I have small envelopes as well. As for posting it, well, you'll have to take care of that yourself. You will find a way."

"Thank you."

"A word of warning. Don't mention where you are, and don't say anything about your treatment, or your disfavor with the French. If you do, your letter will be destroyed. I will look it over for you. I know what they will, or will not, post. Take my advice."

Henrik went to his bunk that was covered with a single, woolen blanket, and the farthest away from the toilet. The air inside the hut was rank and chilly, and they had no heater. It would be a cold night and a colder winter, he thought. He found a hard surface and began to write on the piece of paper measuring no larger than four inches by six inches, those words he had wanted to write for the past month.

> *Dearest Elsa,*
>
> *Forgive me for not writing sooner. Paper and pencil were unavailable.*
>
> *I am in good health, and well fed. I have a small job in a French city in order that I might earn some money. I will be heading home soon. I miss you and your family. You are always on my mind, day and night, and I want you to know that I love you, and always will, despite the distance between us. Have faith in me, Elsa. I will come home to you as soon as I can, and we will start a new life together. My only wish is to be with you again. You are my life and my future, and my reason for living now. Hold me close to your heart.*
>
> *My love always, Henrik*
>
> *Give my regards to the others.*

He took the letter to Alfred who read it, nodded, and folded it in half. "You have big dreams," he said.

"My only dream is getting back to her?"

"And where is this place."

"In America. I was a prisoner there, in a town named New Ulm. I fell in love with her there."

"You were a prisoner, and you fell in love?"

"I was an easy thing to do."

"Well, then, here is the envelope. Address it. I will do what I can for you, to get it to the right guard. I know one who is willing to help now and then."

"Thank you."

Alfred nodded. "I have dreams of my own. I hope we both can find a way to realize them. Now get some sleep. Tomorrow will be a busy day for you."

THE NEXT MORNING THEY WERE GIVEN breakfast in a small building adjacent to the Nissen huts, some potatoes, and a gruel consisting of thick oat meal and bits of dark bread. The water tasted of chlorine. They were issued trousers, shirts, a helmet with a battery light, a pair of knee-high rubber boots, and a small bucket for a lunch that consisted of a half sandwich, a pickle, and a small apple. After breakfast most of the men from Henrik's shelter were marched to the mine.

Some of the near eighty Germans who were at Merlebach during the last days of November worked in the machine shop, a large structure where lorries were lubricated and repaired. Others worked atop the slagheap where rocks and other debris from the mine were dumped. All of them were under constant watch.

The mine entrance was carved into the side of a hill festooned with tall, slender pine trees. It was a small entrance, large enough to accommodate the height of a man and a horse. Constructed with large rocks and a huge headstone, it appeared like the mouth of the devil, ready to swallow them up in its black maw, never to spit them out. An air tube jutted out from one corner of the mine's mouth.

They entered in line, led by a Frenchman who didn't utter a word. They walked down the center of the track line, between narrow, rusted rails. The floor slanted downward, going ever deeper. Immediately, the darkness closed in on them and they turned on their battery-operated helmets in order to see. The light beams drifted ghostlike across the walls and ceiling, creating a glowing path that guided them inward. An occasional battery-operated lantern, spaced at intervals along the shaft, provided additional light. As they made their way down the shaft, Henri realized that Alfred's description had been accurate; it was like descending into an all-engulfing and frightful hellhole.

The ceiling beams were just inches above their heads. The tallest men had to duck frequently to avoid striking them with their helmets. The supports and headers, hewn from ragged pine trunks, were spaced about six feet apart. Rail tracks that guided the coal cars in and out of the mine to be emptied and reloaded were spiked to the center of the shaft, paralleled by pneumatic air lines. Horses pulled the coal cars up and out to wherever they were dumped. The horses were housed inside the mine where they were fed oats and water. The men passed theirs stalls, dark openings carved into the side walls. The horses stood head in, rump out, their tails swishing as the men plodded past them.

One of the men beside Henrik said softly. "I will go crazy in here. I do not do well in enclosed spaces. My head wants to explode."

"You will get used to it."

"No. I will not. I can feel it already, creeping in on me like some kind of demon."

"Oh, my God," someone yelled. "There are god damn rats in here."

Rats, big ones, ran down the side of the shaft, a string of them, scurrying along the uneven floor in a seemingly unbroken line. One of the men, who had a shovel in his hands, swung it at them.

"I hate rats," he shouted, his voice dulled by the black, engulfing walls.

In time the prisoners would learn to ignore the rats, and the Merlebach mine had many. They would learn later that the lubricants in the mine were stored in large oilcans near the horse stalls. Not only did the rats feed on the oats given to the horses, they also fed on a paste comprised of coal dust and oil residue. The rats ate anything.

When they came to the side shafts, one of the men pulled Henrik aside. "You, come with me. We are partners today. I will show you how to mine coal."

Dug into the side walls of the main shaft, the smaller tunnels led into the pitch blackness of the coal seam. The only items running into them were narrow belt lines and air lines. "My name is Karl Ehlers," the man said. "I was once an Oberleutnant, but now I am a mole. Come, we will go in. Here." He took a shovel from just inside the entrance and thrust it into Henrik's hands "I will dig, and you will shovel. Consider it good exercise and you will make it through the day."

Karl led the way, standing at first until they were about twenty feet inside the black hole. Then he bent down, hunched over at first. Then he dropped to his knees. In the light of their lamps, Henrik saw him pick up a pneumatic drill and punch its point into the black coal seam directly ahead of him.

"I will break off the coal with the hammer, and you will shovel it onto the belt. The belt will carry it to the main shaft, where others there will load it into the demand cars. From there it will be horse drawn to the surface. We will dig coal for three hours, and then we will eat our lunches."

Henrik looked at him blankly. "I do not think I will last for three hours."

"You will. But we will rest now and then, to gather our strength."

Henrik got down on his knees and crawled into the space. His lamp glowed on the rough, black wall of coal ahead of him. He drew the shovel toward him and looked back to where the belt was, to where he would deposit the coal, shovel full after shovel full, after shovel full. He shivered. The temperature in the mine was low, about fifty degrees he estimated. But soon he would be sweating. Three hours seemed then like an eternity. He took a deep breath as Karl started the hammer.

The noise was a deafening rap, rap, rap rap. The coal splintered away. Chunks and dust and specks rained down on him like shrapnel. He closed his eyes and felt the power of the hammer stutter throughout his body, shaking him, roaring in his ears. It would deafen him for sure. He thought: in a week I will be unable to hear. In two I will be crippled. In a month I will be dead. He did not think he would be able to keep this up. Then the hammer stopped and he jammed his shovel forward into the heap of loose coal Karl had broken away from the seam. Scooping it up, he drew it backwards and dumped it onto the belt. The belt shivered like a broad, black snake, carrying the coal away. He shoveled again, and again, clearing the space. Then Karl started the hammer again—rap, rap, rap. Shovel, shovel, shovel.

Before the first hour was over, Henrik's face had blackened. His shoulders screamed for relief. Every muscle in his body ached. He thought he would never be able to stand again. He remembered the last time he had laid on his belly, on the brick pile in Aachen, on the day he was captured. The brick pile had been much better. At least there he had room enough to move. At least there he had light. At least there he had cleaner air to breathe. They worked steadily, hammering and shoveling, before they took their first rest. Breathing hard, Henrik rolled over against the coal wall and sighed.

"I will not last the day," he breathed, his lips peppered with coal dust.

"We will go back a ways, and stand up. It will ease your discomfort."

They crawled back to where the shaft height allowed them to stand, and there Henrik pressed his back against one of the support beams. The pain of working on his stomach crept through him like some ravenous beast intent on devouring him from the inside out. He squirmed in retaliation.

Karl stood quietly in the light of his lamp. All Henrik could see of him were the whites of his eyes. Then Karl said. "I would like very much to have a smoke now, but we are not allowed matches down here. A spark could set off an explosion"

Henrik took in shallow breaths, afraid to breathe in the coal dust. "How can you take this, day after day?"

"We learn to endure. The war is over. I would rather wait to be released than to take a bullet now. Many have tried to go home. Some have made it, other have not. I also know that my town is gone, and my wife is dead. I have no home to return to, so I work and wait for the day they will release me."

"Alfred said the border is only fourteen kilometers away."

"Yes, it is close."

Henrik's chest swelled. "Then I will try for it."

"Your life is a big price to pay. This mining will not last forever. When we have done our job, the French will let us go."

"I cannot wait."

Alfred nodded. "Yes, you are the one with the American sweetheart."

"I am. How did you know that?"

"Everyone knows it. Word spreads fast in our little hutch. I wish you luck, my good friend. Very few of us have a goal in mind. Starvation is widespread in Germany now, and there is no work there. So, we stay with the French for a while. At least here we eat three times a day."

Henrik looked back into the black hole where they would go and he shivered. "What happens if the roof falls down?" he asked.

"Well, if one of us is still alive, we take that long pin of the hammer, or the shovel, and rap it on the air pipe. They will hear it up there on the surface, and then they will come down to dig us out, if we are still alive."

"And if we are?"

"Then they will load us on the oil lorry and take us out. From there they will take us to the hospital for treatment, or to the carpenter shop for a casket."

"Where is the hospital?"

"By the company houses."

Henrik did not reply. He tried to put the information into perspective. He knew the corons were positioned along the northern perimeter of the mine, at the edge of the slagheap, beyond the rail yard. He would learn more as the days came and went. Eventually he would work out a plan, a means of escape, and then he would go, bullets or no bullets.

"Come," Alfred said. "We have to get back to work before they start shouting at us. We have to keep the lorries filled. You will see the hospital in time. When the lice get the best of you and you cannot sleep, you will go there to be sprayed with DDT on the head, under the arms, between the legs, all over your body. Then you will sleep better."

They worked together for another hour, rested a bit, listened to the horses as they were hitched up to the coal cars, the wooden lorries three feet high and six feet long, that carried the coal up and out of the dungeon.

At noon in the light of their lamps, they ate lunch, just enough food to keep them going, not enough to nourish them. The rats came, as if on cue, and watched them from a distance, ready to fight for any scraps thrown their way. The rats were greasy looking things with small, sinister eyes. They crouched and scurried like miniature wolves, their evil figures colored just slightly lighter than the coal seam. Sometimes, if the men were quick and accurate enough, they killed one of them with a lump of coal, or a stone. The carcasses were thrown on the belt where they were shoveled into the lorries. The dead ones ended up on the slagheap. In time, the men learned to ignore the rats. In time the men leaned to ignore many things–fatigue and darkness, dampness and chills, coal dust and anger, hunger and pain. The discomfort and the fear and the darkness were all part of the mine; payback for the invasion and rape of a country other than their own.

At the end of the first week Henrik received his second scrap of paper. He wrote the following.

> *My dearest Elsa and family. I pray you will receive this before Christmas as it is the only gift I can give you. I am still in France, but when I am finished here I will go back to Bergheim to see my parents. From there I will find a way to come back to America. Christ's blessing to all of you. Keep a candle lit for me. Dear Elsa, my love for you is stronger than ever. Distance has only strengthened my hope. I talk to you nightly and hear your voice as I did when we were together. Pray for me this Christmas and keep me in your heart.*
> *Your beloved, Henrik*

> *The only address I can give you is this; Henrik Arndt, German compound, Merlebach, France. Write to me. Hopefully I will receive it.*

The letters were taken, read, sealed and posted by the guard who said he expected nothing more from the Germans than obedience and hard work.

Henrik went back to the mine day after day until it became routine. In time the pain ceased, and he became accustomed to working on his stomach in near darkness, with rats and cold, and with the French, who still held hatred deep in their hearts. He learned the layout of the grounds around him, and the placement of the guards, and the streets less traveled, and he was encouraged when one of their group left early one morning before sunrise, never to be seen again. They assumed he had made it free of the mining area because no one had heard gunfire, nor had they seen a body being returned. This gave those who were planning to flea an added element of hope.

The fields of Lorraine were covered with snow as the December winds swept down from the north. Temperatures fell. The Nissen huts became colder. Additional blankets were given to the men. The mines felt warmer then, and the tunnels in which they worked became havens from the fierce winter days. News from Germany was scarce. The French were adept at sealing off the world.

The only thing that kept Henrik from breaking under the strain were memories of Elsa, those halcyon days in the field, and visions of the family together at the table, when the world outside seemed distant and nearly forgotten.

THIRTY-NINE

New Ulm, Minnesota, Christmas 1945

ELSA RECEIVED ONLY TWO LETTERS from Henrik in December, the last one only two days before Christmas, on a day when fresh snow had fallen, and when the sky was crystal blue and dazzling enough to make her spirits soar in memory of him. She took it from the mailbox and ran all the way back to the house, to her room, where she read it twenty times, until it became emblazoned in her mind. Then she secured it in her secret place, until Christmas day when she took it out again and read it almost from memory.

Corina and Elsa had adorned the Christmas table with pine boughs and confetti and white candles, six in all, five for each of them, and another for Henrik. They had gone into church and had returned by noon, filled with anticipation. At five o'-clock sharp they sat down to dinner, still dressed in their finery, the girls in dresses, Papa in a dark blue suit, mother in a white blouse emblazoned with colored snowflakes, David wore long pants, a white shirt and bowtie.

Before the meal began they lit the candles, all except one. Then, as she and her mother had planned, Elsa leaned forward and lit the sixth, the one closest to her. "This one is for Henrik," she said. "He is here with us today, not just in thought alone. This candle represents his presence at our table. Now let's give thanks, for ourselves, and for him on this day of our Savior's birth."

They prayed in silence, hands folded, heads bowed, and about a minute later Papa said, "Amen." They ate ham and sweet potatoes, a Jell-O salad and green beans, hot rolls and butter, cake for desert, and when everyone had their fill it was time for talking. Papa began, as usual, after filling his pipe and savoring the tobacco taste. He blew the smoke out the side of his mouth, away from the table. It was Tuesday. School had let out on the Friday before. It would not convene again until after New Year's Day.

"Elsa," he said. "You seem fidgety today. Have you any news for us?"

"Yes, I do," she said proudly. "I have been chosen to help with the publication of our yearbook."

Papa beamed. "Good. Good for you. And what will your role be?"

"I'll help with the page layouts."

"Anything else?"

"Whatever needs to be done. We're entitling it, "The Keys to the Kingdom.""

"Appropriate."

"And the cover will be brown with the NU emblem on top, along with the year, '45. We voted on several designs and that one was selected as the most appropriate."

"And?"

Elsa snickered. "In it, we're referring to the faculty as 'The Master Race.'"

Papa blew a stream of smoke. "Ah, citing your German heritage, are you. Well, some might very well be offended by that, given that we just fought a war to rid the world of the master race."

"We thought about that. But it was selected just the same. We thought it would be humorous, and we're hoping that everyone will understand that it's just a play on words. After all, the faculty are the masters of the school, and they will approve the final layouts."

Papa brushed a spec from the lapel of his suit and grinned. His broad smile relaxed them all. "Six more months to go, Elsa. Have you thought about college yet?"

Elsa's eyes drifted to the tabletop. "I have."

Papa's gaze focused on Clara, as if to seek permission for further questions. Something in her silent reply told him to continue. "And?" he asked.

"I haven't made up my mind. I may want to continue on with Journalism."

"To be a writer?"

"Or a news reporter."

"That's a challenging job."

"I like challenges."

Papa chewed on the pipe stem. Again, his eyes drifted to Clara. The children followed his gaze, wondering what he would say next. He held them in suspense for a full minute. "I hear that you have received another letter from Henrik. Do you want to share it with us?"

Elsa glanced at her mother. She was rewarded with a slight smile and a nod of her head. "I would," she said.

"Well then, tell us what he had to say."

"The letter is upstairs."

He laughed. "You mean to tell me you can't remember his words. You must have read them a million times by now."

Elsa shrugged timidly. "Well, I guess I can."

"Then out with them. He's as much at this table as you are. Six candles, five people here. The one that's flickering is surely him."

"It is."

"Then we have to hear from him. Go ahead; tell us what he wrote about."

Elsa cleared her throat as the letter formed in her head. "Well, he's still in France in a town named Merlebach, but soon he'll be heading back to Bergheim, to his hometown. Once he gets there, he'll try to find his parents, and then he'll begin planning to come back to America, here, to New Ulm. I have an address for him at last."

"And what will he do here?"

She appeared exasperated. "Well, Papa, you know. We'll be married."

"Ah," he said, his face lighting up. "So we'll have a wedding then?"

Elsa's frustration became obvious. Clara merely smiled. "You can't expect anything else from your father," she said. "He's always a tease."

"Papa," Elsa remarked. "You know I plan on marrying him. And if he doesn't come back over here, then I'll go over there. One way or another, we'll be together."

Papa nodded. "Well, that's the first I've heard about you going over there."

"It's only as a last resort. If I can't provide passage for him, or if he can't work his way through all the red tape, then maybe I'll have to go to him."

Papa scratched the back of his head. "It's a long way to a Germany that isn't much of a country any more."

She looked at him proudly. "Then he and I will just have to rebuild it."

"One brick at a time?"

"If that's what it takes, yes."

Papa cocked his head. "You're determined, aren't you?"

She rose up proudly. "I'm in love with him, Papa."

His expression mellowed. His smile was sympathetic and tender. "I hear what you're saying. But now's not the time to talk about love. I think David has something to say, and then Corina. After that it's time to open presents. So let's get on with it."

Corina talked about the doll she was making out of old cloth, cotton stuffing and doilies, for a daughter of a serviceman who had been killed in action during the final moments of World War Two.

David talked about the fishing trip he and his friend had planned, going out onto Lake Flandreau when the weather was decent, in hopes of catching enough fish for an evening meal. His friend Bruce and his father were taking him along. He loved to go ice fishing, provided he was dressed warmly enough.

Papa completed the conversations with a bit of news that brought a tinge of nostalgia to the table. "They're closing the prison camp on the Cottonwood this December thirty-first. It'll be the end of an era, a time none of us will ever forget." Then he pushed back his chair and stood up, stretching his arms "Now, let's open the presents."

They had two presents each. Corina handed them out, one at a time, as the others watched each one being opened. Elsa received a new stone necklace from her mother, and a record from Papa; songs by Frank Sinatra. Hugs and kisses followed each opening.

It was a happy and festive time, with popcorn on the table, sweetmeats in bowls, eggnog to drink, festive music on the Victrola, the scent of pine needles in the room, fragrance from Papa's pipe, and the comforting scent of wood burning in the fireplace. When all the presents had been opened, and the room was silent with the warmth of family, Papa stood up and cleared his throat.

"We've eaten our fill and have celebrated, and now I think it's is time to give a present to someone who's not with us today."

Elsa looked up as his gaze settled directly on her.

"Our good friend, Henrik is a long distance off, in a country not of his own, wishing, I am sure, that he were here."

Elsa sat back in the couch and drew her legs up beneath her. Almost at once the softness of Papa's voice brought tears to her eyes, and the sound of Henrik's name being mentioned warmed her throughout.

"Mother and I have been talking," he said. "And I think it would be appropriate this Christmas to give Henrik a gift."

Elsa sat up straight on the couch, her face aghast. Something secret was about to be revealed, and it was about Henrik. Her full attention riveted on Papa as his smile broadened.

"Now, Elsa, we know you've been working hard to earn enough money to bring Henrik back here some day, to be your husband." He hesitated, expanding her curiosity. She felt the intensity of his words running through her like a river, exciting her, weakening her.

"And we know how long you're going to have to work in order to make your dream possible. Many months. Maybe years."

She knew something important was about to be said, and she leaned forward, toward Papa, her mouth agape, her senses keen and focused.

"Your mother and David and Corina and I have been talking behind your back. I wanted to get their permission to do something before this gift was given to him. They have all agreed that it's right and proper."

He hesitated, heightening Elsa's curiosity.

She could not bear the delay. "What?" she asked. "What?"

"Well, we've decided, unanimously, to help you bring him home."

She leaped off the couch and stood flatfooted on the rug. Her hands twisted together like a knot. She stiffened head to foot, unable to control her mounting curiosity.

"We all thought it would be okay if, when the time is right, if we all helped you financially, to provide enough money to bring him back to America."

Elsa didn't move. She stood quietly as her tears flooded her face. She bent forward on quaking knees and caught the warm tears in her hands as Papa moved forward and wrapped her in an embrace. "Now, now," he said in a soft voice. "Everything's going to be all right."

She cried for a while longer, clinging to Papa's body, her arms wrapped around him, her face buried into the bend of his shoulder. Then when she had fully absorbed the wonderful news, she stepped back and wiped the tears away and looked at her family, all of them smiling, her mother weeping, drying her own tears. Papa arose, firm and quiet, as if nothing could break his solitary determination to stand like a man. Corina pranced as if listening to music only she could hear.

"What can I say," Elsa said. "You have made me so happy. Now I can tell Henrik the good news, and he can plan to come home when he is ready. Oh, thank you so much, so very much. No one has a more wonderful family than I."

Her family came, in turn, to embrace her. Papa held her the longest. She smelled the pipe scent on his clothes as he pulled her tight against him. "If it's God's wish," he said. "We'll bring him back to you."

"It's the best Christmas present I've ever received," Elsa said, sniffling.

"Well, he's a lost and lonely boy who needs our help now."

She looked up at papa. "He's a man, father."

"Yes, he's a man for sure."

"And he'll be my husband."

Papa smiled. "Ya, that too."

The remainder of the day was filled with laughter, food, music, and gaiety, and about five o'clock, when most of them were resting, Elsa went upstairs to write a letter to him, to give him the good news, and to tell him he was loved.

She wrote:

My dearest Henrik. I received your wonderful letter two days before Christmas. It was the best gift ever. We lit a candle for you at our table, and earlier that morning, in church, I prayed for your safety and for your quick return. My family has given you a gift for Christmas. They will provide the money to bring you home to me. Whenever you are ready, please let us know. We will wire to you whatever is needed, and I will once again hold you in my arms, to love you always and always.

More words of endearment, sentences filled with emotion and love and hope, filled the page. When she finished she folded it and placed it in an envelope and addressed it to Merlebach. The next day she mailed it from New Ulm.

Henrik would never receive the letter.

His time in Merlebach was running out.

FORTY

Merelbach, France, Janruary 1946

THE MINE SEEMED DARKER AND colder than ever before, and the rats more prevalent. Outside, a new snow had blanketed the mining town, turning its dull and depressing appearance into something cleaner, blanketing the slagheap, and the bleak buildings into shapes more appealing to the eye.

Inside the mine, however, everything was the same. Cold and dismal, and as black as coal could be, it sucked the endurance out of a man and depressed his soul so thoroughly that thought was limited to the task alone, to the grinding and the shoveling and the twisting on one's stomach, and to the fear that rose just above them in the ebony vein of coal that yawned like an open mouth ready to devour them. The grinding of the air hammer and the scraping of the shovel were the only sounds heard, and when they stopped, the silence came in as if to squeeze their breath away, and were it not for the meager light of their helmets, they would have thought themselves as swallowed in a living death.

Henrik had worked in the mine now for twenty-two days with only Sunday off to rest and to write another letter to Elsa. He had lost nearly twelve pounds to the constant work, had slept hard, until the lice found him. He had to go to the hospital then, to be deloused. After that his sleep was better, though never good. He would fall asleep in the mine sometimes after eating his lunch, oblivious of the rats that came to eat the crumbs and scamper across his legs. He had killed four rats just last week.

Late in the afternoon when the sun was already low, they left the mine and went to the hut to clean themselves with harsh soap and cold water, to wash away the stain of coal dust. Then they would eat whatever the French gave them. Sometimes it was adequate enough to quench their hunger, often it was not. Vegetables mostly. Meat was scarce. Meat was saved for the French. They ate a lot of potatoes those days, and whatever else the cooks could scrape together. In winter there would be less food, but the work would be the same. Henrik figured he would lose another twelve pounds before spring came, before he could plan his escape back to Germany, over those long and dangerous fourteen kilometers.

On a Thursday, Henrik went into the mine with twelve others, down the incline, between the tracks, into the black mouth. He had a cough that day, a cold coming on. All the French gave them for colds was aspirin, or something like it, in pill form, no liquid. Seldom were they released from working. If they could stand, they worked. He descended slowly with the men grouped around him. No one talked. When they arrived at their designated shaft, one of the men pulled him aside by the arm. "We go here today," he said. Together they walked into the shaft, past the upright timbers and head braces that held up the ceiling, into the yawning hole thirty feet deep now. Darkness settled in on them. Their lamps cast a dim light forward until the beams were swallowed by distance. Then came the vein, narrowing. They bent down and crawled in deeper to where the ceiling was, inches above their heads, low enough to keep them kneeling, not high enough to brace with timbers lying next to the discharge belt that carried the coal away to the rail carts.

"Do you want the hammer or the shovel today?" the other man asked. Henrik had learned to operate the hammer the week before, and now they took turns driving it into the vein, knocking down the coal.

Henrik coughed, spat out some phlegm and cleared his throat. His head began aching. "You start, I'll shovel. Later we can switch."

The other man grunted and shifted closer to the vein. He struggled to hoist the hammer forward to spike it into the coal. Henrik crouched down, pushing the shovel ahead of him, ready to receive the fallout. The hammer roared to life, *rap, rap, rap* against the jagged wall. The coal rained down, chunk after chunk. Henrik began shoveling, thrusting the blade into the loose coal, drawing it back, depositing it onto the jerking belt. Again and again and again, thrust and pull, shift and dump, rap, rap, rap, the noise like a barking, rabid dog in his ears, rap, rap, rap. One hour, two hours, rest, rap, rap, rap again, movement without thought, repetition, shoveling, shifting, faces blackening, no words between them, only work, endlessly and without letup.

CRACK!

Henrik had not heard that sound before, but when he did, he froze. Instantly, the hammer man shouted, "Back! Back! Get back!"

Henrik shifted quickly. His hands drew away from the shovel, but not before he heard the crack again, a roar this time.

WHOOSH!

A split second later the ceiling came down in a cloud of dust, burying the man and the hammer beneath a mass of jagged black coal. Fear gripped Henrik so tightly he could scarcely move. He lay frozen as the black cloud settled around him. When he tried to pull his arm back, away from the shovel, he could not move. Frantically, he tried to ease his arm away from the shovel handle, but it was pinned tight between the handle and the ragged floor beneath it. The only movement came from the buried man. His legs thrashed in the final throes of death, his rubber boots pounding against the floor of the shaft. Then he was still.

Henrik tried to move again, to free his arm, but to no avail. The light from his helmet was the only light in the tunnel. He turned the beam to where his arm disappeared beneath the handle, tight against his wrist. He shuddered, then panicked. He heard the coal seam groan and felt its weight against him, knowing it could collapse again. Then he took a deep breath and began to think rationally, realizing that time was running out, that he might be the next one trapped beneath the coal.

The steel pick attached to the air hammer had been buried with the dead man. He had nothing to pound against the air pipe that lay just beyond his reach. Directing the beam of his light against the coal pile, he tried to pull his arm free, but pain was already beginning to cripple his strength. Soon his arm would swell and turn white. If not released soon he might lose it. He thought of cutting his way free, of severing his arm just below the elbow, as they sometimes did during the harvests when caught in the auger, but he had nothing to cut with, no tool of any kind. He had only his voice.

"Help! Help!" he shouted.

No reply.

"Help me! Cave in! Cave in! One dead in here!"

All he could hear was the dragging of the belt that carried the coal out of the shaft. He moved his leg and stretched it toward the belt, placed his heel against it and pounded it with his foot. He was sure the noise would be heard.

"Help! Help!" he shouted. "I am trapped in here."

Over and over, minute after minute, he continued shouting until a voice replied. "We are coming. Hold on."

He saw the lights bobbing through the shaft, men coming toward him, three of them. Soon they were there beside him.

"My arm is caught. I cannot remove it," Henrik said.

"Bring up the handpick," one of them said. Then, to Henrik, "We will get you out. The other man is finished."

CRACK!

The sound startled the men, and they moved backwards as if they were one body. The sound was swallowed up by silence. The man closest to him tapped Henrik on the shoulder. "Lay still. I have a handpick. I will free you."

He brought the pick in and began hammering at the coal atop the shovel handle. Bit by bit the coal separated. He dragged it away, all the while easing the load pressing down on the handle.

The pain in Henrik's arm had reached his shoulder, and now his back, and he wanted to scream, but he held it back. Chink! Chink! Chink! The hammer continued to pound away at the coal. Slowly, he felt the pressure on his arm ease, and then, suddenly, he felt blood surge into his hand. Slowly, he tugged free from the coal. His wrist and hand pounded as blood seeped from the torn skin.

"You are a lucky one," the miner said. "Now, let's get out of here. We'll let the French come in and clean up this mess. As for him," he nodded toward the dead man. "He'll find peace in heaven this night."

Crawling until they were able to stand, they then walked out of the shaft. In the main shaft, Henrik had the first look at his arm, split open just above the wrist, blood oozing out. The man who had rescued him pulled one of the others over. "You! Apply pressure here to stop the bleeding. I'll go and find a horse. Make a tourniquet out of something, anything, and tie it across his forearm. As for you," he said to Henrik. "You'll be spending a day or two in the hospital. They'll fix you up quick so you can go back to work. They waste no time with us. You'll be on your feet in another day, back to work in two." He tapped Henrik on the shoulder. "You were a lucky man today. Had you been on the hammer you'd be talking to angels now."

"Thank you," Henrik replied. "I am a not yet ready for angels."

Sitting down, he held his arm tightly, slowing the blood flow. He remembered the day when he had fallen beneath the wagon in New Ulm, the day Elsa had bandaged his arm, the day they had sat together on the porch. Then a man came with a piece of rope and tied it firmly around his forearm, reducing the flow of blood.

Henrik had cheated death, he thought, by a second or two. Had he been deeper, pulling out coal, he would have been trapped. Had he been on the hammer, he would be dead now, and his dream to return to America would have died with him. He trembled, not from fear or pain, but from relief. He had been saved by a twist of fate, or by a miracle, or by his quick action. It didn't matter what had saved him. He was thankful to be alive, thankful that his dream was still intact.

Closing his eyes as tears welled inside his eyelids, he saw again the pounding of the man's legs as the life eased out of him, felt the terrible weight of the coal against his arm, felt the terrible pressure in his heart, felt weakness now throughout his body as he lapsed into semi-consciousness.

He could scarcely remember the horse coming down, the men picking him up and laying him on the oil lorry, nor could he recall the long ride to the entrance. There, he was placed on a wagon and pulled down past the railyard to the small hospital adjacent to the living quarters where the French families were housed.

When he arrived at the hospital he was undressed and cleaned, and his arm was examined and redressed. He was then given a coarse, white hospital gown and placed in a room where a single light dangled from a ceiling cord. There he went to sleep, a long, deep sleep that brought him back to New Ulm for a while, to where the sunlight glistened on Flandreau Lake, to where the fields stretched like golden carpets to the horizons, to where Elsa waited for him, her arms outstretched.

Henrik awoke the following morning to the sound of a train whistle close by. The first thing he felt was pain in his arm, a throbbing there, awakening his memory of the cave in, and the quaking legs of the dying man, and the fear of what might have happened to him had he been tending the hammer.

He was in a large room with eight beds, four on each side. Three other men were in the ward, one two beds away, the others across the narrow aisle. Two windows lighted the room, one on each end of the room. One faced the rail yard. He could see a chimney from where he lay. He glanced again at the other patients. All of them appeared to be sleeping. He turned and looked around, to the single door leading to a hallway, to the hooks beside his bed where his clothing hung, discolored with coal dust. His rubber boots stood beside the chair. His stockings lay haphazard across its seat. Through the window he could see snow falling, lightly now. Straining, he could make out the roof of a nearby building. The snow appeared to be about six inches deep. It would be another cold day in the mine.

Peering at the ceiling, Henrik laid there for a while, looking at the light shade above him, watching a fly alight and circle, alight and circle, as if distance would bring it into uncharted territory. The episode in the mine kept returning to him, and he felt the fear and the terrible weight of death again, and he knew then that he would never return to the mine. He would refuse his French taskmasters and take his punishment, whatever it might be. He coughed. His chest heaved. His mind was all tangled up now, trapped up in a war of indecision, like the fly on the light shade. Could he stand? Could he walk? Other than the pain in his arm he felt rather good, except for the heaviness in his chest and the tightness in his head from the cold he still carried. Turning in the bed, Henrik placed his feet on the cold, wooden floor. Slowly, he stood up, and as the swirling in his head abated, he placed one foot cautiously ahead of the other and walked slowly toward the single door. He tried the knob. It turned. Carefully, he cracked the door open and peered through the aperture. A hallway, albeit a short one, led to a flight of stairs. He was on a second floor then, with no one in sight. Carefully, he stepped out into the hallway and walked to a window. He stopped, heard nothing, and then looked outside. He saw the rail yard stretching out in both directions, and house smoke rising from several chimneys. Beyond that, a field covered in white snow, and a fence, and a structure, perhaps a storage shed. Snow was still falling, limiting his vision. He could only guess as to what lay beyond, but he knew one thing for sure. The German border was just fourteen kilometers away, and at that moment the border was like a magnet. He could feel its pull, a force he could not resist.

Someone was coming up the stairs, squeaking the steps. He scurried to the door, dashed inside, closed it silently, and crawled into his bed. His heart was beating so fast, he almost forgot the pain in his arm. No sooner had he settled down than the door opened. A Frenchman entered, stopped, and peered across the room. Then he slapped his hands together, and shouted in German. "It is time to wake up. No more sleeping now. Breakfast is coming." He glanced at Henrik, a long and questioning stare, his face like a mask, unmoving and without expression. Then he turned and exited. Within five minutes their breakfast was delivered by a short, fat nurse. Henrik sat up and ate with his left hand. The fingers on his right hand were swollen and red. Pain began its relentless throbbing again. He ate slowly, one hard boiled egg, a piece of black bread with some sort of jam, a small amount of milk in a thin metal cup. Just enough food to quell the uneasiness in his stomach.

Henrik lay there for about two hours, heard movement in the hallway, voices distant, some low, an occasional shout of sorts, an order or a call to someone. He did not understand French. Near mid-morning someone came into his room and examined his arm, unwound the dressing, probed at the wound, stitched together now. A new dressing was applied. He was given some pills, pain pills he thought. Then they left him alone with his thoughts.

Because his right arm had been damaged, Henrik would not be able to write a letter this week, or perhaps the next. Even if he had paper, he could not write left-handed. So, Elsa would wait and wonder what had happened to him. She would be concerned, or possibly frightened by the sudden lack of communication. He might be able to hold a pencil between his swollen fingers but what would the writing look like scrawls, unintelligible words, a definite indication that he had been injured.

Think!

Shifting, he swung his feet out, and sat on the edge of his bed. The man across from him stared with the expression of a dead man. He looked at him, slack-faced and disinterested, his little mustache balanced like a caterpillar atop his upper lip. Then he turned his head.

Henrik stood up again and went to the door. No sounds outside. He cracked it open again, and stepped into the hallway. He walked quickly to the stairs and peered down. He saw a door leading outside. There had to be an office there, near the door, with an attendant inside. Perhaps it was unoccupied at night. Perhaps the door was also locked. Perhaps. Perhaps. His mind began working faster, just as a voice sounded behind him.

"What are you doing out of your bed?"

He turned. A nurse, thin, black haired and stern-faced, stood like a ramrod.

He said the first thing that came to his mind. "I am looking for a toilet, and if I don't find one soon I will wet this covering."

"The bathroom is at the end of your room. Now get back there at once or I'll call a guard."

"I had to piss," he said, walking past her as if she was non-existent, retracing his steps to the door.

Henrik knew that the bathroom was at the end of the room, just as she said, to his left, on the same wall as his bed. He had used it before. He went in and relieved himself, then returned to his bed under her watchful eye. She covered him up without as much as a glance at his face. Then she walked hastily to the door. Before exiting, she turned. Her German was understandable. "You will not leave this bed again. If you do, I will report you to the authorities."

He lay there in bed, alone with his thoughts.

So there is a door downstairs. It may, or may not be locked at night. Chances are it would be unlocked if there was an attendant downstairs, in case someone needed to be admitted, although chances were few that anyone would be admitted at night. The French are in their homes. The mines are unoccupied during the dark hours. Chances are there would be no one upstairs to tend the four men in this room, at least not until morning. After the supper hour most of the staff will leave, with only a limited few left on the premises. The building will be dimly lit, except in an emergency. If he could dress himself and get to the door without being seen, and exit silently, he could begin his journey northward. But he would be dressed in dark clothing, his mining clothes, and his rubber boots. He would be seen immediately against the white snow. Any guard alert enough to spot him would sound an alarm, and if he did not stop they would fire upon him. Even if he made it to the fence, the searchlights could follow him. A bullet could find him up to four hundred yards away. He could be dead before Merlebach was out of sight. But if he took his white blanket with him, draped it over his head so that it covered his body and his clothing and his boots, he might be able to camouflage himself with the help of the snow, making it more difficult to see him, making it more difficult to fire an accurate shot.

As the pain in his arm intensified, he trembled. He needed another pill, something to kill the pain. He leaned out of his bed and picked up the wooden chair. His stockings fell against his boots. He pounded the chair on the floor and waited. Three minutes later the tall, thin-faced nurse came into the room. "What do you want?" she asked.

"I need something for the pain. It's bad."

"Then wait a minute."

She left. About five minutes later she was back with a glass of water and three white pills in her hand. "Swallow these and then be quiet. We don't need noise here." He did not reply. He took the pills and tossed them into his mouth, swallowed them down with the water and handed the glass back to her.

So it would be tonight, he thought. No waiting. No delay. As soon as they think I am well enough to move, they'll have me out of here, possibly tomorrow, back to the German complex where guards waited twenty-four hours day to catch a prisoner foolish enough to try for the border. They'd like nothing better than to bring him down. Perhaps they even kept score. The drinks are on me, they might say. I got another German today.

No, it had to be tonight, or he'd be down in the mine again within days. It had to be tonight.

THE DOCTOR CAME IN LATER IN THE DAY and examined Henrik's arm, nodded, said nothing to him. By then the pain had subsided. The dressing the doctor applied was much smaller than the first. Henrik was certain there would be no reason to keep him in the hospital beyond the following day.

Greedily he ate supper, every crumb, enough food to last him a day or two, possibly more. At ten o'clock the lights went out and his room was plunged into darkness. The windows high on the wall offered the only light, limited at best. The sky was dark, still filled with snow clouds, although snow did not seem to be falling. Moonlight was scarce, much to his liking.

Careful not to fall asleep, he kept his mind busy thinking about Elsa and what they would do when he returned to New Ulm. He wondered how he would begin the process of obtaining new identification when he returned to Bergheim, if anyone there would still know him, if the legal process would be up and running, if his family's farm were intact, if his parents were still alive. A hundred things kept him alert.

Near midnight he stood up and got out of his bed and listened for the slightest sound. Hearing none, he moved silently toward the door. The stillness was all engulfing. He waited, listening. He could not make a mistake. This was his one and only chance. Every tick of the clock, every second, made his movements more and more dangerous.

Ten minutes later he returned to his bed and slipped out of his hospital gown, then worked his feet into the stockings. He managed to get his bandaged arm into his shirtsleeve, drew it around him, worked his other arm in, and then buttoned it with the fingers of his left hand. It took him five minutes to slip into his pants and button them securely. Then he eased his feet into the boots. As a final precaution, he slipped the hospital gown around him. He was dressed, and with the gown on, he was nearly white to the floor. Careful, so as not to wake the others, he rolled up the wool blanket, tucked it beneath his arm and walked cautiously to the door. He opened it silently and stepped into the hallway.

Listening, he heard nothing. Inching his way toward the stairway, he placed his foot on the top step, pressing down lightly. No squeak. Breathing harder, he took another, then another, his progress cautious and deliberate. Pausing at the landing, he leaned over, glancing down the hallway, past an open area that usually housed an orderly. The space was empty, the only chair unoccupied.

Henrik then continued down the second set of steps until he reached the bottom. Looking in both directions, he moved to the door, grasped the knob and turned it. The door responded. His heart leaped. He drew it open without making a sound. Stepping outside, he latched it behind him. He felt the cold immediately. It swept across the ground as if to challenge his presence. He stood for a moment to get his bearings. His eyes scanned right, then left. Across the street, a line of homes stretched off into distance. To his left, a short street slanted off northward toward a snow-covered field that disappeared into darkness. He saw no movement, nothing to indicate the presence of people.

By now it was close to one o'clock, an hour into the new day. He knew he could not remain on the steps. Carefully, he opened the blanket, and then drew one end of it tightly across the top of his head. He cupped it securely beneath his chin with his good hand, allowing the remainder of it to trail behind him. Then he stepped off into the snow and moved ahead toward the street. His head pulsed with a soft drumbeat. His breath fogged in the air. His heart rapped like an air hammer in his chest, rap, rap, rap. He knew that within minutes, he would either cross the field and begin his long walk toward the German border, or he might possibly be dead, taken down by a French sniper. As his senses peaked, his hands began shaking. Without further pause he stepped down and headed directly toward the field.

With the blanket trailing behind him, he was all but invisible in the darkness. He walked twenty paces, then twenty-five, counting them off as he went. Thirty, thirty-five. He rounded the corner and headed toward the field. Forty. He could see the fence ahead. When he reached it he would have to abandon the blanket momentarily to climb it. He kept on going, face forward, as if the field ahead of him was magnetic, drawing him onward, drawing him closer, pulling him home. He prayed all the way, asking God to deliver him from evil. The fog of his breath intensified with each step he took. He did not look back.

Then he was at the fence. Fortunately, it was only four feet high, a post and rail fence with enough room between the rails to allow him passage. He would have to get through it using only one arm. He thought for a moment, realizing he was now a target for any alert Frenchman with a rifle. The cold began working its way into his body, chilling him. Hurriedly, he removed the blanket, rolled it up and tossed it over the fence. Then, gathering what he could of the hospital gown, he lifted one leg up and over the bottom rail and began squeezing through. At that moment he saw a searchlight beam behind him, coming his way. Frantically, he pushed through the rails, stood up, grasped the blanket, unrolled it and drew it over his head.

The searchlight followed his tracks in the snow. A second later it was full on him, casting his long shadow across the field. He heard distant shouting, then a shot. A bullet cracked against one of the rails as he took off running. He knew he could not outrun a bullet, so he began zigzagging, first one way, and then another. Again, a shot. If he was hit he hoped it would be a clean kill. He did not want to suffer another day at the hands of the French. He dashed on, weaving across the field, kicking snow. Two more shots. He heard the whine of a bullet, close, but missing. The searchlight followed him like a dog on scent. Another shot, wild. He was certain to leave a path that could be followed in darkness or daylight. He would need luck if the French took after him. If they had dogs he would be brought down quickly.

Henrik ran on. He listened for more shots. He heard none. Maybe he was out of range. The light beam had faded. Perhaps the French had just given up. After all, there were plenty more Germans where he came from. He dashed through the snow, across a field where a crop had been planted. It was uneven and furrowed. He stumbled several times but didn't fall. Fear ran along with him. The hope of freedom, kept him going, until his breath ran out. He paused, wheezing. He leaned forward, sucking air, hoping he had not gone in a circle, hoping he was still going straight toward the border. He placed his good hand on one knee and leaned into it for support. He drew in the cold air. It pained his throat, breath after breath, until he was able to breath naturally. Minutes later, he glanced back at his path, saw it running straight. Confident he was going in the right direction, he continued, running slower now to conserve his energy.

Eventually, when he thought the situation safe enough, he slowed to a walk. Foot after foot, he plodded on, looking back occasionally to make sure his direction was straight. He picked out a landmark far ahead, a grove of trees. He headed toward them. How would he be able to walk a straight line in woods? He thought if he veered right, or left, he could avoid the trees. They appeared wide and thick and impenetrable. But as he closed the distance, they became less formidable, a windbreak of sorts. He constantly looked back to see if he was being pursued. He saw no one, heard nothing, so he kept on going.

Alfred had said it was fourteen kilometers to the border. If he remembered correctly, there were three-thousand-two-hundred-and-eighty feet to a kilometer, and if his pace were two feet to a stride, it would take him one-thousand-and-forty strides to complete one kilometer. It would be daylight before he reached the road that would lead him to Germany, to the town of Auersmacher, just across the border. But if the French had an airplane in the sky by then, they would surely find him. And if he held up in a barn, or a ditch, or a culvert, his tracks would lead them directly to him. So, he decided it was best to keep going, and wait for sunrise, to find the road, and hope the French were too tired, or too disinterested to pursue him. Better to remain in their warm beds than to chase a runaway German.

Plodding on, tiring as he went, one foot following the other, Henrik scuffed his way through the snow layer, making progress, praying and hoping, while saying Elsa's name out loud to further his determination. The cold was penetrating, the air heavy with winter. His stitched arm ached severely, a creeping, unrelenting pain. His eyes, mere slits now, gazed out at his new destination, a farm building deep in the distance. He kept on going, forcing himself forward. Thoughts of the coal mine, and the dead man lying beneath the caved ceiling, urged him on. I will soon be in Germany, he thought, and then I will go home, and I will find what I am looking for there, and after that I will return to America, and I will marry the woman I love, and we will raise children and I will think back on this as only a bad dream.

Henrik walked on through the cold darkness until the sky began to brighten. Then it began snowing again, large flakes straight out of the north, some landing directly onto his face. Occasionally he would wipe the moisture away and hunker down beneath the blanket and pray that the snow would not intensify. It did not. Within an hour it had ceased, and when the sun was about ready to break the horizon, he climbed up an embankment and found the road he was looking for running east and west. Relieved, and thankful, he clutched the blanket tightly around him. His body shivered uncontrollably. He tightened his jaw as best he could, and retraced his steps until he was well back from the road. Then he began walking east, toward the sunrise, keeping the road in sight, but not traveling upon it, even though there was no traffic.

He figured he was halfway now. By the time the sun was above him, he would be at, or near, the border. Not knowing what awaited him there, he walked faster, buoyed by his success thus far, hoping a French chase car would not come along and sweep him up. Merlebach was behind him, and he felt confident in his ability to keep on going, despite the hardship, despite the uncertainty, and despite his lingering fear, and despite the numbing cold.

He hummed Lili Marlene as he walked. It was one of his favorite tunes, and it kept him going.

FORTY-ONE

ALMOST A MONTH HAD PASSED since Christmas, without a word from Henrik, and day by longer day Elsa's worries intensified. She tried not to appear sullen, but with every passing hour she fell deeper and deeper into a pit of sadness, and soon it began showing on her face. Clara spoke to her often, to perk her up, to give her hope. Clara saw the concern, hidden secretly in her lack-luster movements, her quiet moods, and the disappointment that came whenever the mail failed to bring a letter addressed to her.

"He's just fine," Clara would say. "He's in a difficult world now and it will take time to put things in order." Or. "When he gets to Bergheim things will become clear to him. Just watch. He'll be able to write more often." Or, "Be patient. If he's as dedicated to you as you are to him, he'll find a way through his problems. Think of what it must be like over there."

Nothing worked of course. She hung onto his memory with the greediness of a miser, day in, day out, night after night, in her dreams, and in the visions of him that came without notice, on the sunniest of days and on the days when it snowed so hard one couldn't see the barn from the house. Each day, no mail. It was enough to challenge her sanity. But despite her sadness, she never put his memory aside. He was always with her, and she intended to keep it that way. So each day she walked to the mailbox, and prayed that a letter would be there. And when there was none, she felt as if the earth had dropped away beneath her feet.

On those days the way back to the farmhouse was a long and lonely journey, down the dirt road where Henrik and Elsa had walked together.

FORTY-TWO

Auersmacher, Germany, February 1946

THE SUN WAS HIGH WHEN THE ROAD took an abrupt turn to the south. Henrik paused behind some trees and looked across the road. He saw a canal, about a hundred feet across, and beyond that a town. Auersmacher. He had reached Germany. He was certain of it, and for a moment he gripped his teeth tight together in a moment of triumph. In the space of two minutes, a few trucks and a single car went by. He knew he couldn't wait, so he threw the blanket aside, stripped off the hospital gown and ran quickly across the roadway.

To his disappointment, the canal water was unfrozen. As a last resort, he would swim across, but for now he began walking its shoreline toward the town still some distance away. He had gone only about a hundred yards when a figure appeared on the opposite bank.

"You, there" Henrik shouted. "I need help."

The man hesitated, and then walked toward him. "Who are you?" he shouted.

"I am a German soldier . . . who was being held by the French . . . in Merlebach."

"You are German?"

"Yes. I have walked all the way . . . from Merlebach, from the mines there."

"Do you have papers?"

"I have none. The French . . . took them all."

"Where did you live before the war?"

"I lived in Bergheim."

The man came closer. He was an old man, dressed in shabby clothing. He had a small cap on his head that did not seem to fit him. His face was bearded. He walked hunched over, with a noticeable limp.

"I can help you," the man said. "But you have to walk down that way." He pointed southward. "There is a small boat further down the canal. I can row over to you, and bring you across. Follow me, and I will help you get home."

He followed the old man's progress along the canal bank. God, he was cold. His fingers, his legs, his entire body screamed for warmth. His feet were like ice. I hope I am not frostbitten, he thought, or they might amputate my toes. I would be hospitalized for a long time. He shivered so hard he could not walk fast. The man on the other side had to slow his pace to keep abreast of him.

"I cannot . . . go much . . . farther," Henrik shouted. "I am freezing."

"It is close now. When I bring you across I will take you to my house. There you can rest and get warm. My wife is an excellent cook. She can make anything out of nothing." He laughed. The laughter sounded good.

Henrik saw the boat resting on the opposite bank. It was a small weather-beaten thing, scarcely large enough for one man and a passenger. When the old man arrived there he eased himself down the embankment and picked up the rope tied to the boat's bow hook and released it from an anchorage on the bank.

"Hold on," he shouted. "I have crossed before, but not in the winter. If this old scow does not leak I will reach you, otherwise you will have to swim."

The man got into the boat and pushed off with a single oar. With careful maneuvering, he made the crossing. Henrik beached the bow, and as the stranger held the boat steady, he got inside. The boat settled into the water, nearly swamping. Both men sat absolutely still. "We must be careful," the stranger said. Then Henrik pushed away from the bank.

Minutes later they touched the other bank, then pulled the boat ashore, tipping it over to empty an inch or two of water that had seeped in through the hull. "Another minute and we would have sunk," the stranger said. Then he reached over and grasped Henrik's hand and helped him up the bank.

Henrik Arndt was on German ground.

"You are a sad mess," the old man said.

"Yes, I am."

In the distance, Auersmacher appeared like a white jewel, its roofs dusted with snow, smoke whirls rising from its houses, a church steeple rising grandly from its midst. Henrik held his emotions in check as the old man took hold of his shoulder

"You are a lucky man," he said.

Henrik nodded. His jaw shivered. "I never thought . . . fourteen kilometers could be so long. I can never . . . thank you enough," he added.

The old man nodded. "You have thanked me already. You have fought for our country. That is thanks enough. I know how it was. I fought at the Somme. That is why I limp like an old cow. Come now, we go home."

Henrik could hardly remember walking the distance to the old man's house. When they arrived there, the man introduced him to his wife, who warmed some milk for him after he had stripped off his black clothes in the small bathroom where he washed with warm water. He was given some of the old man's clothing to wear even though they were too large for him. While he was changing, the woman brought some bread to the table, and a jar of preserves, some strudel and cheese, not much, but enough. He ate until the food was gone. The heated milk warmed him inside. Then his eyes began closing and the woman led him to a bed and covered him with blankets. He slept the remainder of the day and the next night. When he awoke, sunrise had already brightened the room.

He sat at the table with his new benefactors, Herman and Marie, and ate porridge and sliced apple, and he drank more hot milk. The woman waited on him as if he were her son. When the conversation began between the two men, she went on with her work.

"You said you were from Bergheim," Herman began.

"Yes, we have a farm there."

"We were not touched here during the war. Most of the fighting was to the north, in the Ruhr, and to the east with the Russians. Terrible. Terrible."

"I was captured in Aachen."

Herman nodded. "We are beginning to rebuild. Most of the large cities are still in ruin. Everything is difficult in Germany now. No food. No work. Everyone is a beggar in one way or another. Whatever is loose, one takes."

"I hope my parents are still alive."

"For your sake, I hope they are. I lost a boy in Poland, another in Italy. Marie I are the only ones left. Our daughter is somewhere, but we don't know where. We have not heard from her for over a year now."

"Can I get transportation to Bergheim?"

"I think you can. Trucks are running again. Many are going north, if not to Bergheim, then close enough so you can walk, or get another ride. I will begin asking today, while you rest. You will need to regain your strength. Many like you are coming home again. When the trains go through the villages, the people crowd around them searching for their sons, or fathers or brothers. Some give bread to the men who had been prisoners. It is a terrible thing. So many good men with no place to go."

"You are kind to me."

"And why not. You are one of us." Herman looked out the window then, and for a while he said nothing. Then he turned back. "What was it like for you, the war I mean?"

He told them about his capture in Aachen, and the trainride to France and about the crossing to New York. Then, as he ate more, he told them about Algona and New Ulm and his treatment there, and about Elsa, and their plans to reunite if he could earn enough to return to America. And he told them about Merlebach and the mines and his escape. And when he was finished, Marie came and hugged him around the neck and told him he was a fine boy.

He rested that day, slept some of the time, and spent most of the afternoon writing a letter to Elsa on a full sheet of paper, with a fine pen. He told her he was safe in Germany, looking for transportation to Bergheim. He mentioned the mine in Merlebach, but gave no detail, and throughout the letter he told her how much he loved her, and that soon, if God would favor it, he would make arrangements to return to America, after he had earned enough money for passage. Then he folded the paper and put it in an envelope and addressed it, and gave it to Herman, explaining that he did not have any money for postage.

"There is a postal station here," Herman replied. "I will see that it gets on its way. As for you, sleep again, and get strong. Tomorrow I will seek passage to Bergheim for you."

Marie gave him four sheets of paper and a stub pencil to take with him, to write on whenever he wanted to send another letter to his woman. Then he slept again, and ate the evening meal with them, and they talked for hours afterwards. Then he went to bed, and in the calm of the night, when fears had gone their way, he dreamt of Elsa again.

On the following day he accompanied Herman into the town, and within an hour they found a truck bound for Duren, a city in Westphalia on the river Rur, east of Aachen. From there a road ran directly to Cologne, another north toward Bergheim. The driver said Henrik was sure to find a ride from there.

The truck left Auersmacher late in the morning. The driver's name was Fritz Haushman, a man about forty, a man who could not sit still behind the wheel. His shoulders were in constant motion. Henrik was sure he had a disease of some kind by the way he moved. He had the lowest voice Henrik had ever heard, a foghorn sound, even when he laughed, which was seldom. The truck was carrying cement for use in Duren.

"We are rebuilding there," Fritz remarked soon after they started north. "The Americans bombed the hell out of Duren during the war. They destroyed everything. We lost over three thousand people there. The rest evacuated. There was no one left when the war ended. But now they are slowly coming back, and we find what we need anywhere we can."

Actually there was little talk. Fritz was content to remain silent. He moved and shifted constantly, like a machine, his eyes glued to the roadway, his legs rocking back and forth. Henrik was content to rest.

The ravages of war became more and more evident the farther north they went. Here an overturned truck. There a downed aircraft bent and twisted, a bomber, a burned fuselage, then a dead tank. Shell holes appeared alongside the road in increasing numbers, then an overturned wagon, a battered car riddled with bullet holes, a black scar on the countryside where fire had raged. The dead, the people and animals, had all been buried or burned. The smaller towns seemed intact, though an occasional house or building was either flattened or roofless. The roads had been patched, but only enough to allow for traffic. The going was slow, tedious, through rolling hills whitened with snow, and towns bleak and deserted, each bearing the marks of conflict.

Henrik slept in the truck the first night, with the driver who was cramped in a seated position with his head bent forward, his right arm propped against his chest. Henrik woke up four times, went to sleep again, and was fully awake when Fritz came around, yawning like a fog horn. They didn't eat breakfast. They kept on going.

Henrik was horrified at the scene when they reached Duren late on the second day. Nothing remained. Most all of the buildings were down, houses destroyed or burned. In the center of the city, bricks were stacked in piles, to be reused. The streets had mostly been cleared. Some of the structures were beginning to rise again. The people were ragged, unkempt, like moving scarecrows. Duren, which had once been one of Europe's richest cities, was now more like a dumping ground.

That evening he found refuge in the basement of a bombed-out building and the next morning he begged food from a women who was cooking outside her shattered building, on a piece of metal supported by bricks. She had plenty of fuel. All she had to do was rummage the wreckage.

That morning Henrik walked to the edge of the city and started northward toward Bergheim, through a battered countrywide littered with the wreckage of war. His spirits were low because he didn't know what awaited him there, or beyond the next turn, or over the next hill. There were scavengers about, ready and willing to steal anything they could, to kill if necessary to stay alive. He had been warned to remain alert. Soon the cold wind chilled him to his bones, and walking became difficult again. His feet were sore, his legs tight. He walked with his shoulders hunched, his head down, his hands pressed into his armpits. Toward midday he was fortunate enough to get a ride on a horse-drawn wagon. He slept for a while despite the weaving and bumping, crowding in beside whatever the driver was carrying beneath its wraps. It was near dark when the wagon stopped and he got out. He found refuge in a barn where the hay smelled of dampness and decay. But he burrowed beneath it to where it was dry and there he found some warmth and fell asleep again.

The next day, early in the morning, he got a ride from a middle-aged woman dressed in long pants and a leather coat. She was a smoker. Her cigarettes were held in a long purple holder that she balanced between her fingers. She puffed on the cigarette without inhaling. The smoke bothered him, but he said nothing. He was grateful for the ride. She hardly talked. She kept her narrow eyes on the road and never glanced his way. When she had stopped to pick him up he told her he was going to Bergheim. She only nodded, said get in, and from then on she remained silent. She appeared to be one who had been in the BDM, Hitler's program for young girls. Her demeanor was very military. She would know quite well how to take care of a man if he got out of hand. For all he knew, she had a loaded Luger on her hip. So he ignored her and nodded the time away until she was near the city. Then in one breath she told him to get out, and she drove away. He walked into Bergheim late in the day.

Like Duren, the town had been ravaged. Nothing was as he remembered it. The few people there were working in the rubble, scavenging materials, beginning to rebuild. There would be work here, he thought, if he were to stay, without pay, unless the monetary system was back up and running, and if businesses were beginning to recover.

Henrik now walked directly through the town and down the road leading into the countryside. Soon he began to pick up familiar landmarks, the barn to his left, the small bridge to his right, the hillside heavy with trees where he had hunted fox once, the valley, deep in snow now, but recognizable still. He saw no cattle, no movements. Everything was different.

It would be another hour before he reached his family's farm. The sun was settling, its color fading into pink, and all at once he felt the need to run, to close the distance, to see his farm again, to rest the night within the house, and to hug his dog again, the way he did two years past, before the Volkstrum had thrust the Panzerfaust into his arms and pushed him into Aachen to die.

Then before he knew it, the farm was there, and his eyes ached as the tears came. The barn, where the horses had been stalled, was flat to the ground, its remains covered with snow. The house, partly damaged, swayed to one side, crippled by ruin. There were no sounds, nothing to give him hope that anyone was there. He moved on slowly. He reached the fence he used to climb on, and then he called out. "Papa! Papa!"

No answer, only silence, a deep, sad silence that wrenched his heart in a grip tighter than death. He walked to where the door had been. He kicked aside some fallen wood, part of a chair, an unbroken cup. His mother's apron, the one she always wore, the one with a yellow rose sewn to its pocket, lay in a heap beneath the shattered table. Not even the snow could hide its demise. He pushed his way into the room where they used to sit and talk, where the fireplace was, its stones still upright, the hearth still filled with ash. Most of the furniture was gone, taken by scavengers. The pieces that remained were damaged beyond use. The room he had slept in was still intact though its windows were shattered. Snow had blown in. The bed was broken, the mattress gone, the blankets missing. The only thing remaining was death and decay, and broken memories.

Henrik returned to the fireplace, cleared the debris away from the hearthstone, and sat down. He remembered the times they had gathered together in front of the fire, talking about the day, the dog curled up beside him, its head in his lap, his mother darning or sewing in the big chair alongside the sofa. The room had always been cheerful; a place where one could forget the problems of the day and concentrate on the happiness that dwelled there. He could see it all again, as if time had erased the violent years and had taken him back. But then he opened his eyes and saw the ruins and instantly the memories faded, and the cold moved in on him, and he cried.

Henrik Arndt had returned home, to Bergheim, to nothing but ruin.

FORTY-THREE

New Ulm, Minnesota, February 1946

THE LETTER FROM AUERSMACHER ARRIVED, and when Elsa removed it from the mailbox she shouted so loud that she was sure her voice could be heard throughout all of Brown County. She kissed it and then dashed down the road, as fast as she could go, her words soaring high in the clear air, "Henrik, Henrik, Henrik, I love you, I love you."

She ran into the house waving the letter, startling the dog. "A letter from Henrik," she shouted. "At last. At last."

Breathless and excited, she slid into a chair at the kitchen table. Clara wiped her hands on a dishtowel and said, "Finally. I'm so happy for you."

Elsa picked up a knife and slit the envelope open, removed the letter as it if were a sheet of gold, and began reading. "He's in Germany," she shouted. She could hardly restrain herself. Her body trembled with giddiness. "He's well, and seeking transportation to Bergheim." Her eyes came up, tearful. Clara handed the dishtowel to her. "That means he'll be home soon."

Then she read more, the endearing words, those passionate phrases he wrote so well, and her lips quivered. "He was working in a French coal mine for a while. I'm sure it was to make some money. When he gets to Bergheim I'll have a new address. Then I can write him again, and he'll be able to tell me what he intends to do. Oh, mother, I'm so happy. Pretty soon we can start making plans. When he finds out about sponsorship, so many questions will be answered."

Her words ended with silent questions. What would he do when he arrived back in Bergheim? Would his parents still be alive? Would he choose to remain with them? Would he forget about her? Would he start a new life there, with someone else? Even if he did want to come back, would it be possible for him to return to America?

Placing the letter on the table with trembling fingers, Elsa turned to her mother. Her eyes spoke of her concerns even before he words came out. "Oh, mother, what's going to happen now?"

Clara nodded. She tapped Elsa's hand lightly with her fingers. "Things will be just fine. If you want him bad enough, he'll come back. Just keep the faith, and keep on praying."

"You make it sound so easy."

Clara shook her head slowly. "Life is never easy, but it is manageable. Keep your mind focused on the goal. I know how determined you can be, once you set your mind to something."

"But this is so different."

"Every new challenge is different. But your resolve must be strong."

Elsa sighed, wiped a tear away, She glanced at the letter again, at the familiar handwriting sketched on paper, his handwriting, his words, his promise, and she felt encouraged just looking at it.

"I'm going to my room." Elsa said, folding the letter carefully.

Clara stood up, smiling. "You go now. I won't need you for a while."

Elsa climbed the stairs and sat once again by the window in her room where his vision came to her so clearly sometimes. She held the letter tight in her hands and read it at intervals, and each time her emotions swelled to near breaking and her resolve strengthened. He would come back. She would make certain of it. If only he held on. If only he held on. If only his love remained strong. If only his memory of her continued on through all the days and weeks of decision.

Five months had passed since the day he left New Ulm, five months of wondering, hoping, praying, and questioning. But now he was in Germany, and soon everything would fall into place, and conclusions would be drawn. Soon she would know if he still held a place in her future. Soon she would know if his love was strong enough to survive.

Holding the letter close, Elsa looked out at a sky leaning toward dusk. The yard was mostly clear of snow. The wind scarcely moved the tree branches near the house. Life is manageable, her mother had said. Well, she had some managing to do. In the short periods of time they had together, she had never really told Henrik what she wanted from a man, had never made love to him, not in the deep sense, nor had they begun planning a future. Obviously there were things about him she didn't know. Was he honest? Was he spiteful? Was he as loving as he appeared to be? Was he sexually perfect for her? Did he want children? Was he the sort of man she wanted for the rest of her life? Did he really love her, or were the words he had spoken to her just buttery to present a good impression, to keep him coming back to the farm as a means of escaping the prison camp in which he lived?

Elsa did sense a deep love for him, but was it artificial, was it true, would it stand the test of years and the moments of disagreement or conflict? There were thing she had to know, and there were things he had to know, especially now, when he was approaching his home in Bergheim, especially now when the pull of family and country could alter former pledges, especially now when his love for her might already be waning. This was a time for reflection, for looking deeply into the future, to begin building a foundation she could construct a life upon.

She could do nothing but write it all down in a letter. She could not call him, nor could he call her. The written word was all they had now, words scrawled on paper, thoughts converted to sentences, hopefully clear and concise enough to be correctly understood by the receiver. She knew quite well that thoughts on paper could be misinterpreted. What a writer meant to say, and what the receiver perceived, could be quite different. So what was she to do? If he were standing in front of her, what would she say? If he were listening, what would he want to hear? Life is manageable, her mother had said. So, begin managing it.

Elsa would have to construct it carefully, would have to write it down, perhaps several times, until it made perfect sense to her, until she was confident he would interpret it correctly. So what would she say?

First of all, he had to know point blank that she would never allow a man to determine how she would conduct her life, be it physical or intellectual. She would want him to honor her body and her soul, and to be respectful of her opinions. And she would want him to know that she would leave any man cruel enough to ruin her life.

Conversely, she would tell him that she would never prevent him from doing whatever was right and healthy and respectful in regard to the personal things he enjoyed doing, nor would she ever let her own fears stand in his way. How she would write it all, she didn't know, but now was the time to do it. She would be honest and forceful and direct, to let him know that she was committed to a life with him, hoping his reply would mirror her sentiments.

Life was manageable, her mother had said.

At her small desk, she removed several sheets of blank paper from the drawer, sat down, picked up her pen, and began writing. She rewrote the letter a dozen times—and after she had read it over a dozen times—she folded it carefully and inserted it into an envelope. She would mail it as soon as she received an address. Soon now, she thought, soon now I will have answers that will, or will not, establish a course for the rest of my life.

Tomorrow she would tell Erica the good news.

That night, in the darkness of her room, she prayed for him again, as she did every night, and to seek assurance that the letter she had written would be interpreted correctly.

That night, Elsa laid awake for some time, listening to the wind outside the window and Corina's soft breathing above her, until a vision of him came to gently close her eyes.

FORTY-FOUR

Bergheim, Germany, February 1946

WHEN HENRIK AWOKE THE following morning he searched the shattered remains of his family home for any scrap of food he could find. Nothing remained. The scavengers had stripped the cupboards clean. He went outside to urinate near the barn where the sun had melted away the snow, where tank treads had left their impression on the ground, and where several spent cartridges lay. He wondered what had happened there, how fierce the battle had been, if his mother and father had been involved, or if they had fled like thousands of others as the armies clashed.

Henrik's immediate concern was that he needed something more than the clothing he wore, something warm, to take the chill away. He went back inside and searched for any remnant of clothing he might have overlooked. After digging through the rubble for a while he found his father's old trunk buried beneath some rafters. He worked it out and opened it. Inside he found a wool sweater, two pairs of woolen stockings, a jacket belonging to his father, some of his mother's clothing, an old blanket he had used as a boy, and a jar containing forty-five Reichmarks. It was the first money he had held since entering France. He pulled the sweater on over his dirty shirt, and then stuffed the money into his pants pocket. He was fortunate enough to find some matches in a small kitchen container. Outside, he kindled some dry wood, lit it, and when the flames were hot enough he took off his shoes and suspended them over the heat. His feet were a mess, calloused, bleeding between the toes, white and wrinkled from dampness. He dried his feet near the fire, and when the shoes were dry and warm, he pulled on a clean pair of stocking and then the shoes. Better. He sat by the fire for almost two hours, warming himself, thinking about what he should do next. Where would he go? Who could help him?

Henrik looked out over the dormant cropland where he and his father used to work. He saw three shell holes not far away, more beyond that where the land rose up. The battle had gone right through here, he thought, straight toward Berlin. He wondered if the neighbors were still alive, if their property was still intact. He remembered that he could see the Schroeder place from his own barn, and so he stood and walked to where the door had been. Yes, there it was, covered with snow, upright and intact. Herr Schroeder and his father had been good friends. Their son, Otto, and he had hunted together until the Jugend came and swept them away. Otto, who was probably dead now, once had visions of becoming a Luftwaffe pilot, but wishes usually had a way of dying, just as flesh did. The Schroeder farm was the first place he would go.

He still had his rubber boots from Merlebach, but the soles were worn through. They would not keep out the water he might have to walk through. So he tossed them aside and eased his feet inside the dry shoes. Almost at once he felt the pain that had accompanied him on his flight to the border. He knew he couldn't walk far that way, not for long, and so he took them off again and rubbed his feet while looking at the fire that was slowly falling to ash. No, wait, he thought. I can do better. He pulled on the rubber boots again and went into the wreckage of the house and probed through the kitchen. He uncovered a bent tin pail that could still hold water. He straightened it out as best he could, and filled it with snow. He rekindled the fire and suspended the pail over it, and when the melted snow was hot enough, and ample enough, he removed it, took off his boots and stockings and slid his feet into the warmth. He soaked his feet for well over an hour, first one, then the other, until they were soft again. Then he rubbed them with a small amount of vegetable oil he had found in the kitchen. Satisfied, he put the stockings and shoes back on, and started out for the Schroeder farm with the sun on his face.

The stone-faced house appeared unoccupied as Henrik approached it. The area around the house was punctuated by more shell holes and tank tracks. The property appeared to be intact except for some broken fences and a flattened shed. It was as he remembered it, picturesque beneath its shade trees, quiet and homelike in its simplicity. He walked slowly toward the house, thinking that if it was unoccupied he might put up residence there. But then he saw a movement inside, and a light. He stopped short as the door opened. The man who stepped out had a pistol in his hand.

"Keep going," he shouted, the weapon pointed directly at him. "You have no business here."

Henrik held up his arms, a customary surrender. The man was tall and slender, his hair a wiry gray, his eyes deep and contemplative. He recognized him by more than voice alone. The man was Paul Schroeder. He was relieved to see a friend.

"It is Henrik Arndt, Herr Schroeder. Do you remember me?"

The pistol lowered. Schroeder's eyes squinted. The barrel of the gun went down. "Henrik? Is that you?"

"Yes, Herr Schroeder. I have a beard now, and I am worn out a bit, but it is me."

The pistol descended to Schroeder's side as he stepped down onto the dirt path outside the door. He walked quickly to Henrik, stood for a moment and studied him, then stepped forward and embraced him as he would have embraced his own son. "You have come home," he said.

"Yes, it has been a long journey."

Schroeder stepped back and looked at him while trying to match the present with the past. Then his eyes twinkled as the gruffness in his voice modified. "You have changed," he said. "When you left here you were just a boy. Now look at you. You are a man now."

"It has not been that long."

"I know. But war can make a man look older than he is. Look at me. I have aged ten years in the past five. But enough of that. Come in, come in. You remember my wife, don't you?"

"Yes, of course I remember Mrs. Schroeder, Mabel."

"Come she will fix you something to eat. We have chickens in the barn who are still good layers. We have eggs, and a small amount of bacon. My biggest talent now is knowing where and how to get food. Come and eat. You must be starved."

"I am hungry, yes."

They walked the short distance to the house. As Schroeder opened the door, he shouted. "Mabel, come quickly. It is Henrik Arndt. He is home. And he is hungry."

Mabel rushed in from another room, her hands waving, a broad smile sketched across her face. She was two years older than her husband yet she appeared to have aged even more by comparison. She was attired in a long dress covered with a plain white, unadorned apron. She walked with a slight hitch in her step. Her face, lightly wrinkled, failed to hide the accumulated grief of past years. Her chin was as he remembered it, round and ball shaped, as if the Creator had been placed it there as a last minute effort. Her hair was gray. She smiled broadly as she embraced him.

"Welcome home, Henrik," she said, enfolding him in arms reminiscent of his mother's own embrace.

It was a good moment, the three of them together, as if they had suddenly returned to a time before the war, when laughter had been plentiful, and trust was as common as sunshine. She kissed him on the cheek, as if he were her own boy, and then sat him down to the table with her husband. "Now you two talk while I fix you something to eat. You have been on the road too long. Look at you. You are famished. We are some of the lucky ones who still have food enough to eat."

Henrik was a bit nervous as he sat down at the table. It was unlike him to seek favors without some sort of remuneration.

Karl Schroeder must have seen the expression on his face, because when he reached over to clasp Henrik's hand, he said, "You make yourself at home here now. I have seen your place. It is not fit to live in. You will stay here now, until you decide what to do."

"I appreciate your offer, Herr Schroeder."

Karl scoffed. "Herr Schroeder is incorrect now. You will call me Karl, the same as everyone else."

Henrik nodded. He felt for a moment as if he were home, surrounded by those he knew and admired, in a place where he had played as a boy, in a home that had always resonated with love. They were so much like his parents, the same tough exterior, the same soft interior, their love and tenderness just out of sight. His first question was one he didn't want to ask.

"Where is Otto now?"

Karl sat back and rubbed his chin. He looked beyond Henrik to something on the wall, a picture perhaps, or just to the wall itself. His eyes lingered there momentarily. His reply was slow in coming. "The last we heard from him he was in Italy at a place named Anzio. When the Americans invaded there his letters stopped coming. We do not think Otto will be coming home."

Henrik hung his head. His best friend was gone. The dirty war had taken him. "I am sorry," he said.

"The war was a terrible thing. When we fled from here, to go south, we thought there would be nothing left when we returned. We were more fortunate than most, much more fortunate than your parents. Other than all the windows out, and everything upturned, and part of our shed missing, we were untouched."

"You were lucky."

Then Karl's face saddened. "We learned later, when the Americans were advancing, that your parents had gone to Cologne. It was heavily bombed. They would be back by now, if . . ."

Henrik nodded, understanding their grief. He looked out the window as if to distance himself from reality. "I thought as much," he said, his jaw tightening.

Karl tried at once to lighten the conversation. "But now you are here. So tell me, where have you been all this time?"

Henrik took a deep breath as Mabel turned to smile at him, her face a veil of contentment. Then he began. He told them of Aachen, his capture, his period of time in France, his transportation to America, of his train ride to Algona and his eventual transfer to New Ulm. And he told them about Elsa.

By the time he spoke about her the breakfast was ready. Mabel sat down with them. They ate; and all the while he spoke about Elsa in ways that made their eyes spark. Grins appeared in answer to his descriptions of the times he and Elsa had been together. Then he told them of France, and his days in the mine, and of his eventual escape back to Germany. The moment he stopped talking, Karl sat up straight in his chair, and in a firm voice, he said. "You will stay here now. This is your home."

"But . . ."

Karl waved a finger in reply. "No objections now. You have been through enough. You will stay here with us. We have Otto's clothing for you, and the bed he slept in. We will take the place of your parents, and you will take the place of Otto. It is the logical thing to do."

"My wish is to return to America."

"I understand, and we will help you get there when the time is right. But now is not the time. Refugees are pouring in from all over Europe, to the many camps the allied armies have set up across Germany. You will have to go to one of them if you want any chance of getting back."

Henrik shook his head. "I will not stay in another camp. Not here in my own country."

"Then you do not know. Germany is no longer a country of its own. It has been divided into four sectors, French, American, British, and Russian. Berlin is also the same. There are four Berlins now. If you didn't know, the sector we are now in is being handled by the French."

"The French?"

"Aye, the French."

"I am not in good favor with the French. They have all my papers, my money, my belongings. I have nothing. If they find out who I am they will probably ship me back to Merlebach. I will not go there again."

"Then you will be Otto Schroeder. My son would want it that way. If the French come calling, you are our son."

Henrik nodded. "Thank you."

Karl sat back and patted his stomach. "We are fortunate to have food. There is nothing in Germany now. All the major cities are in ruins. There is no government. We have not planted a crop in two years. The Reichmark is practically useless. Most everything is bought on the black market. I don't know if we will ever get back to anything normal again."

"Tell me. Are any of these people in the camps being resettled?"

"I believe the Allies are working hard to do that."

"Is there anyplace else I can go to find out?"

"Certainly not here in the French sector. Perhaps to Wiesbaden, in the American zone, in Hessen, north of the Rhine. Some day we will go there to find out."

Henrik nodded. "Then I will go to Wiesbaden."

"The city was bombed for over two months. There is practically nothing left in Wiesbaden. The city is almost empty. Many homes were lost. Thousands lost their lives. When the Americans entered the city they captured almost a thousand of our soldiers, and also," he laughed–"four-thousand cases of champagne."

"They had a good celebration then," Henrik grinned.

"I suppose they did."

As Mabel cleared the table, silence came once again. All Henrik heard was the rattle of dishes, and the clink of tableware, as it had been in his own home when the meal was over. Then Karl said, "There is a trial going on in Nuremberg. War trials they call it. The Americans will be hanging all of the German High Command when it is over."

Henrik nodded. "They deserve to be hanged," he said.

"Did you know they have found concentration camps all over Germany, where the Jews were being held?"

"I heard of them in America."

"And did you know that the Nazi's had gassed many of the Jews and had burned their bodies in crematoriums, thousands of them, women and children and..."

Mabel's voice came sharply. "Karl, stop it. There is no need for that."

"I was just telling him."

"Then go outside and tell him, not in this house."

Henrik's voice came softly. "There is no need to tell me of the horror. I would just as soon concentrate on the future."

Karl's mood changed immediately. "Aha, the future. Come, my young man, I will show you the future."

They stood, and as Mabel shook her head, they went outside. Karl led him toward the barn. "I must show you how I earn money and food now. You can be my assistant."

The barn was empty except for several dozen chickens, two cows, a horse, and one goat. Other than the small number of livestock, the farm was as he remembered it when Otto had been there. Karl still had much of his equipment. Henrik was led through the center of the barn to a small room secured with a padlock. Karl removed a key from his pants and unlocked the clasp.

"Welcome to my business," he said, ushering Henrik inside.

The only thing in the room was a homemade contraption built of old wood and copper tubing. Behind it, on a bench, were a hand press, an old metal stove and a collection of pails. Henrik recognized it immediately. It was a homemade still.

"This is my workplace," Karl boasted.

"You make schnapps?"

"Yes. I am what you would call in America, a bootlegger."

"How?"

Karl explained. "Well, first we find our sugar beets. The fields are full of them, if you know where to look. I take them usually in the night, and if they are frozen I thaw them and clean them, here, in the buckets. My well is still working, so I have plenty of water. When they are cleaned, I press out the juice and then cook what is left until the water is gone. What remains is a brown mash. Then I add yeast to the mash and allow it to ferment for several weeks, and when the stew is ready I cook it again. See here. The steam is evaporated through the copper pipe, and alcohol comes out. Then I pour it into bottles and bury the mash in the back field, and start all over again."

"And what do you do with the schnapps?"

"Ah, that is the best part. I have customers in many places, in Elsdorf and as far as Bedburg, and in the south to Kerpen. A big estate there has survived the war. Other places also. I take the product there. They give me food in return so we can eat, and sometimes money so we can buy what we need from the black market. I make schnapps, they drink the schnapps, and we live as best we can."

"And how do you get it to them."

"I have a bicycle. It is not the best, but it gets me to where I want to go."

Henrik nodded. "And where do I fit in?"

"Ah, it is difficult for me to make the schnapps and deliver it also. Time is precious and I must make the best of it. If I had someone to deliver it for me, I could keep on making the product. And the more I make, the better we live. Now, do you want to be my assistant? Half of what we make will be yours."

Henrik laughed. Already he was in business for himself. "Ya, I will be your partner."

"Then we shake hands on it," Karl said, holding out his hand to Henrik. "It is good to have you home again," Karl said. "You are so much like Otto. Now come, we will go back to the house and get you settled."

"What if the French come and find your still?"

"They have stopped by a couple of times. They do not look around. They are too busy going somewhere else. They are lazy. They do only what they have to do."

"Then it is safe?"

"Ya."

On the way back to the house, Henrik said. "I must write a letter to Elsa. Do you have paper and envelopes?"

"We do. Many of them remain, after we stopped hearing from Otto. They are yours. You can write at his desk."

"I must let Elsa know where I am."

"There is a postal in Bergheim. It is up and operating. Neither you nor your Elsa will have trouble getting a letter through. Some things still work in Germany."

"Thank you."

They went inside. Karl brought him to Otto's room and showed him where the paper was, and when Karl left he sat down to the desk and wrote.

My dearest Elsa.

First of all, my love to you. How much I miss you. Forever I am grateful for our meeting, and for the times we were together. I am in Bergheim now, staying with my neighbor. My parents are both gone. My home is demolished by shellfire. I will be here for some time instead of going to a refugee camp. Herr Schroeder has allowed me to live with him and his wife, Mabel. They are a fine couple. You can write to me here as soon as you can. There is a postal station in Bergheim. I want to hear from you as soon as possible. So much has happened to me, but now is not the time to tell you about it.

You must know that I think of you always, and I pray for the day when we can be together again in America. I will soon be finding out how I can apply for immigration, but to do so I must go to Wiesbaden, which is in the American sector of Germany. I will go as soon as I can. Until then, my darling, keep me in your heart, and remember always that I love you for all times. Send me your love in the mail so I will know you are all right. Bless you and your family. I will write whenever I can. You are so precious to me. You are the only one I have left. Keep me always in that special place where love abounds.

Henrik

He sealed the envelope, complete with his new address, and then took it to Karl. "I have to mail this," he said. He dug in his pocket and took out the few Reichmarks he had.

Karl waved him off. "Keep your money. It is practically worthless anyway. We will walk together into Bergheim tomorrow so you can see what it has become. We will mail your letter."

"I don't know how to thank you."

"Now that is enough. Thanks are no longer accepted here. We are together, and you are my partner now. Come with me. We will start working."

They finished the day by repairing a section of the barn. That evening just before dark, they walked about a half-mile to a field where they dug beets out of the ground and carried them back in gunnysacks. It was late before they went to bed.

Henrik had not been warm since the day he left the home in Auersmacher, but now, with soft blankets around him, and a good mattress below him, he breathed a sigh of pure contentment. He turned and twisted in the bed, unaccustomed to comfort, and all he could do at first was inhale the cleanliness of it. Then he rested with his face to the ceiling, and he thought of what it would be like to have Elsa beside him, with her body warm against his, with her arms fastened tight around him and her breath soft on his neck. He thought so hard he could almost feel her presence. Someday it will be so, he thought. Then he prayed, and even before the prayer was ended he fell asleep with the blankets tight around his neck, with Elsa's name still on his lips.

FORTY-FIVE

New Ulm, Minnesota, March 1946

THE WINTER SNOWS MELTED SLOWLY away toward the end of March, and just when the spring sun began to brighten the awakening landscape, snow came again to coat the farm with whiteness.

Snow wasn't the only thing to arrive in March. Just about the time Elsa began worrying deeply about Henrik, his first letter arrived from Bergheim, bringing with it new hope and expectation. Overpowered by her eagerness to read it, Elsa stood on the road, and with the wind in her hair, and with her heart pounding, she carefully opened it and read. Then, overjoyed, she ran to the house, into the kitchen still heavy with a scent of fresh baked cornbread, and into her mother's arms.

Elsa read the letter out loud, up to the place where it became private, and then sped to her room to address the envelope that had awaited his address. Just as quickly she ran back out to the road and deposited it into the mailbox, lifted the red flag and returned to the house. She went immediately to her room and began writing another letter. Shortly thereafter Corina entered the room.

"Are you writing to Henrik?" she asked.

Elsa didn't look up. "Of course. He's the only one I write to."

The letters from Kenny had stopped coming. Elsa was worried that something bad had happened to him. The last she had heard he was in the Philippine Islands. Nothing had been written about him in the newspaper, and she didn't want to call his parents for fear the news would be terrible. So, she waited for another letter, but none came.

Corina was gleeful. "Mama says he got home okay."

"Yes," Elsa sighed. She lifted her head and smiled. "He's in Bergheim."

"That's his hometown, isn't it?"

"Yes."

"I wish he would write me a letter. I've never had a letter."

"I'll ask him to write one."

Corina climbed up into her bed and sat there looking down at Elsa. "I hope he comes back," she said.

"I do, too. And I'm going to do all I can to make sure he does."

"Like what?"

"Like writing letters to the Department of the Army, and to the Immigration Bureau, and to the War Department, to anybody who'll be able to help me."

"What will you say to them?"

Elsa shifted in the chair and relaxed. Her voice carried easily to the top bunk.

"I'll tell you at the supper table. I've got one of them done already, the one to the Immigration Bureau. If Mama and Papa think its okay, then I'll mail it out and write some more to other government departments."

"You're smart, Elsa."

Elsa snickered. "I'm not as smart as I am desperate. I've got to find a way to get him back."

"So you can get married?"

"That would be a splendid idea. I'm glad you thought of it."

"Now you're foolin' me."

"How would you like to be my flower girl?"

"No. I want to be a bridesmaid."

"You're too young to be a bridesmaid."

"No, I'm not."

"Well, we'll see. It might just work out."

"Read the letter to me."

Elsa shook her head. "I told you. I'll read it at dinner. I want Mama and Papa to approve."

"They will."

"I think so, too."

Corina was quiet for a while as Elsa continued writing.

***

THE SMOKE FROM PAPA'S PIPE HUNG LOW that evening, creeping through the center of the room as if it had nowhere else to go. When they cleared the last plate from the table Elsa took her place. Papa's eyes went directly to her. "You've been nervous tonight, Elsa. Is something on your mind?"

She sat up straight in her chair. "Yes, Papa. I have written a letter."

"To Henrik?"

"No. To our government."

Papa bit down on the pipe stem as his gaze shifted to Clara. "Well now. What could that be about?" Elsa's eyes also traveled to Mama who remained silent. The only movement from her was a slight nod of approval, a gesture to continue.

"I'm writing them to find out what we have to do in order to begin the immigration process to get Henrik back to America."

Papa blew a smoke ring. "Well now, that seems a bit bold."

"I don't know what else to do. No one in New Ulm knows a thing about present-day immigration. It's the only way I know of to help him."

"And what will you say to the Department of Immigration."

"I'm not only going to write to them. I'll write to the President if I have to."

"That's your privilege. I'm sure Truman will read it."

Elsa appeared to be a bit irritated. "Please, Papa. Don't make fun of me."

He nodded. Apology given. "So, what will you say?"

"I've already written the letter. I'd like to read it to you.

"Let's hear it."

Elsa removed the letter from her apron pocket and unfolded it. She cleared her throat and read aloud.

"Dear Sirs,
In the summer of 1946 we had a German Prisoner of War working at our
farm from the POW camp in New Ulm, Minnesota. He was a fine boy, and
when he was here he expressed a desire to someday return to America. Our
family has discussed this, and we have all agreed that we would like to sponsor
his return. Can you provide us with information that will allow us to begin
the immigration process to return a former POW to America? His name is
Henrik Arndt. Upon arrival to the United States he was transported to the
Algona, Iowa POW camp, until his transfer to New Ulm. He is presently in
Bergheim, Germany. He is also seeking help from the authorities there. He will
make a fine U.S. citizen.

Sincerely yours, Elsa Sommer."

Papa puffed again, and then turned his head away to cough lightly into his hand. "It is a fine letter," he said. "I would mail it if I were you."

"Then you approve?"

"Of course. We said we would help you, and this is a beginning. The sooner we begin, the sooner we'll see him again."

Elsa's smile lit up the room.

"I was hoping you'd say that," David said.

"Thanks Papa," Corina echoed.

Papa clicked the pipe stem against his teeth. "He's taken a long time getting back to his home. And now his parents are gone. Sad thing. Tell him what you're doing for him, and tell him we all wish him well. Hopefully he'll be back here before the next Christmas."

"Sooner than that, I hope," Elsa said.

Papa expression mollified. "Things like this take time. Be prepared for a long wait. I'm sure the government has many things to do. Returning a POW might not be high on their list. Be patient, Elsa. That's all I'm saying."

Elsa's expression was firm with resolve. "I'll wait no matter how long it takes. He'll be back here, you just wait and see."

"Then do what you have to do," Papa said. "We will help you when the time comes."

Elsa mailed three letters that week. And then began her long wait.

Forty-Four

Bergheim, Germany, May 1946

KARL AND HENRIK MADE AS MUCH schnapps as they could that spring, and after it was sip tested, and bottled, Henrik loaded it into the wooden basket Karl had tied to the handlebars of a bicycle. The bicycle was old but reliable, except for the tread-thin tires. Henrik kept a patch kit in the basket in case one of the tires went flat. A hand pump was fastened to the stabilizing bar between the seat and the steering column. The inner tube that serviced the front tire already had half-dozen patches on it.

Henrik delivered the product in every direction from their farm, exchanging it for bread, or non-perishable canned goods, or sometimes for articles of clothing. If he received a chicken, he would cram it into the basket and tie the cover down with string. He became experienced at bartering; often receiving more than he should have once he realized how dependent his customers were on alcohol. In May he and Karl began planting a new crop of beets. On weekends Henrik went back to his own home and began rebuilding it, piece by piece. Elsa's letter, telling him what she expected of a man, had arrived. He wrote back and assured her that if she ever stopped loving him, for any reason, he would be man enough to simply walk away. Then he told her she was right in questioning him, that she was the perfect woman for him, and that he was ready to accept the role of husband in a new country, with her, and to dedicate his life to whatever else came their way.

Spring was in the air. Trees had erupted with new life. As soon as the frost went out they began filling up the shell holes in the fields. They shot a deer back in the woods on a clear, sunny day and gutted it out. Henrik had his first lesson in field dressing, cutting from backbone to anus, removing the urinary bladder and tract, rolling out the internal organs, cutting through the edge of the diaphragm to where it met the ribs, and cleaning the body cavity. Karl said it was something he needed to know in case he was lost in the woods some day. The animal was then left to Mabel. They would have venison for a while, and jerky later on. Karl had been wise enough to haul ice in from the river during the winter months. He stored it in the barn beneath a tarpaulin and straw. The meat would keep for a while. The venison was a welcome change to their usual diet of fruits, vegetables, and an occasional chicken.

Henrik learned the delivery route rather quickly. He was pleased that the weather was turning warm. The winter snow and freezing winds had slowed him down considerably during the few deliveries he had made in late March. Also, there were still occasional marauders about who would kill for just about anything of use, so Henrik carried a sidearm just in case. Karl was happy to assign that part of the business to Henrik.

The apple trees were in bloom when he delivered his first jar of schnapps to the big estate in Kerpen on a weekend when French patrols were busy on the road. They stopped him twice to see his papers, the new ones he had acquired in Bergheim. The French merely looked at them without bothering to examine his basket. Satisfied, they sent him on his way.

Later that same day, just before he arrived in Kerpen, a thin, gaunt-faced soldier with a sharp little mouth, who looked famished enough to search for food, asked him to open his basket. "My food is gone," Henrik said immediately. "I carry my own water. I get thirsty riding this bicycle, especially when I cough a lot because of my sickness." The soldier was about to open the schnapps bottle when Henrik coughed up some imaginary spittle and wiped his mouth clean on the back of his hand. The Frenchman then sneered at him, thought twice about drinking from the jar, and put it back where he had found it. Henrik delivered the product about four in the afternoon. Then, with a loaf of warm bread, two jars of canned chicken, and a bag of potatoes safely stashed in his basket, he started off toward Bergheim, eager for a hot bath, a good meal, and the taste of warm milk. But first he would have to pedal three hours, on a road roughened by the war.

Two hours out of Kerpen, the sun began going down across fields still pock-marked with shell holes. The road was nearly empty, except for a few plodders who seemed intent on traveling through the night. He was content. His trip had been successful. Karl and Mabel would be pleased. She would give him a good meal before he scrubbed down with hot water and slid into clean underwear and went to bed in the soft warmth of clean blankets. He would dream again of Elsa, he thought. Maybe this night he would kiss her, as he had several times before. His dreams were more prevalent as of late, clear and visual, physically intense at times, arousing him fully. He hated to awaken on those days, and when he did he laid there still immersed in her presence, his shorts still damp with his discharge. He thought only of going back to her, to where the veined fields and the woodland birds rejoiced beneath the sun. Visions of her and the farm continued to strengthen his resolve.

Henrik saw the lone man well ahead of him, just a spot on the road at first, before the distance closed between them. He thought it would be wise to steer to the other side of the road, but the man appeared small and harmless and so he kept going straight. The man was hunched over, his eyes apparently looking at the road, his arms clasped behind him. For whatever the reason, Henrik decided to increase his speed, to pass him as quickly as possible. He didn't trust anyone on the road. So he sped up a bit just before he passed the man.

Time seemed to end just then.

As he sped past, the man's arm shot out. Henrik had no time to maneuver. The man was holding something in his outstretched hand, a branch, or a board of some kind. It came up quickly, before he could react. It caught him straight across the neck. The blow was hard enough to pitch him backwards off the bike, into a cartwheel. He had only a flash of time in which to realize his danger, but by then he had struck the road, first with his right foot, then with his arm. He tumbled three times before coming to a stop. The bike flattened on the roadway and slid into some bushes before coming to a halt. He sensed numbness, distant but distinct, and then the board came down again hard on his head and he drifted off into oblivion.

Waking up sometime later, pain was the first thing he felt, hard violent pain, vicious enough to halt any progress he was capable of making. He drew up tight, sucking air through his dry throat. His eyes swam open, and then closed as his mind began reviewing the incident on the roadway, the man, the stick, the black out. He tried hard to peer through the darkness that surrounded him. He saw nothing except for a black, ominous slate. Immersed in pain, he groaned and shifted, felt dirt beneath him, or was it mud? He slid a bit to one side, then moved his arm and grasped a handful of soil. He realized he was lying askew, his head elevated. His legs were slanted downward to where most of the pain was centered. He shifted his leg, and then issued a silent scream as the pain intensified.

Remaining absolutely still, he tried to determine where he was. As his head cleared, and as his senses returned, he realized he was in a shell hole somewhere beside the road.

He remembered then.

The stranger had struck him with a board. He had seen it come up suddenly from behind his back, and before he had time to react, it had made contact with his neck. He felt his neck, found it swollen and sticky. Blood, off to one side. Nothing serious. It had already clotted, probably because he had been lying on it. Why? What could the man have possibly gained by striking him down? The bicycle, yes. He had been tired of walking. He needed transportation. He had been desperate enough to take a life for it. So the man had struck him down, and had dragged him to one of the many shell holes, and had thrown him in, hoping he would be dead before any-one found him.

Shifting again, Henrik gasped as pain roared through his leg. He moved his right foot, felt it slide across the ground. He tried to move his left, where the pain was centered. It would not move. His only sensation was one of excruciating pain, a charge sensitive enough make him gasp, and bring flashes of lightening to his eyes. He knew at once that his leg was broken, probably his tibia, the bone that supported body weight. He knew that weakened bones could easily be broken. Any amount of force put on a weakened bone was sufficient enough to break it. When he struck the pavement, it had snapped.

He remained in a motionless position, assessing his odds. He could scream. Someone might hear him. He turned his head, tried to locate the moon, but it was not to be seen. The sky was utterly black, no stars showing, no glow. As if to answer his question, he heard the growling of thunder, not far away. It would soon rain, and the longer it rained, the more difficult it would be to crawl out of the hole. The soil around him would turn to mud.

Henrik took a breath, coughed up a bloody mass of spittle and spat it out. Pain erupted in his neck. He gasped, tried to shout. The sound came out no louder than a wheeze. Don't try to call out again, he told himself. Wait until daybreak. Give your throat a rest. You can do nothing until there is light enough to see. You could be ten feet off the road, or you could be a hundred feet off the road, depending on how far he had been dragged. Use your head now. Don't panic. Above all, hold the broken bone still, to decrease the pain and to limit the swelling. He knew that swelling could get so severe that it could cut off blood flow to the leg.

Amputation! The word chilled him. He imagined himself with only one leg. How could he farm with only one leg? What would Elsa do with a one-legged man, except pity him? Try not to aggravate the injury. Elevate the leg if possible. But he was in a shell hole, with his leg facing downward. How could he elevate it?

Reaching forward with his arms, he found the lip of the crater, no more than two feet above his head. He thought: if he could use his right leg for leverage, to push with, and his arms to pull with, he might be able to drag himself over the edge and find some way to elevate the broken one. Movement of any kind would be painful, but he would have to try.

The thunder sounded nearer now. Soon it would rain. If it rained and the ground turned to mud, getting out of the hole might be impossible. He would have to do it now while the ground was firm. Slowly, he eased his right leg forward and planted the toe of his boot firmly into the ground. Then, clawing his outstretched hands into the soil he eased his body forward and upward as pain roared through him. He moved about one foot. But it was enough to give him hope. One foot at a time. Six more tries and he would be out of the hole.

Waiting until the pain eased away, he then repeated the process. With each attempt, he waited a bit longer, gaining strength and determination. It took him about twenty minutes to crawl the six or seven feet, but eventually he lay prone on the ground, his left foot slightly elevated on the lip of the crater. Then, as the rain began, he cupped his hand and caught the drops in his palm, and drank.

He knew he would be found now. If he had not returned within the allotted time, Karl would have missed him. He might even be out on the road looking for him.

Where was the road? He peered out into the dark distance and saw nothing but indistinct shapes lurking behind the rainfall like a fleet of ogres waiting to pounce on him. Where are you Karl? Was he already on the road, looking for him, or would he have sense enough to wait until morning? No, he would be out there somewhere, in the rain, walking both sides of the roadway, calling for him, hoping he would not find him dead. Karl was not the type of man to wait until the sun came up.

The rain continued, soaking him through, pelting, pelting, pelting him for hours. He drank more rainwater and then laid his head on his hands and prayed as the cold crept in. Alone and unable to move, panic seized him tightly until his body shivered and his teeth chattered. He trembled, head to foot. His hands clawed into the mud. At one point he felt a stone beneath his fingers and he dug it out and allowed the rain to wash it clean. Then he searched for another, knowing he would need them in the morning. He found a second one not far from the first and again he washed it clean and placed the two stones side by side. Then he shivered again. For a while the pain in his leg subsided.

Henrik was in and out of sleep during the night, drifting into pain, awakening to periods of uncertainty when he would see images of Elsa, there, ahead of him in the storm. She urged him to be still, to give patience its sway, to wait until sunrise. Then she would disappear and he would succumb to his pain until his mind rested again.

Toward morning, just before the sun began to lighten the sky, the rain stopped. Henrik was unaware of the time until he awoke an hour later. He looked out across the landscape. The field was steaming in the morning sun. A few birds skittered through the sky, calling out. He tried to move, but the pain was intense, and so he paused. He knew in his gut that Karl would come, but if he did not come by noon, when the sun was high above him, he would have to crawl out by himself and hope for the best. He had crawled six feet the night before. He could crawl farther if he willed himself to do so. His only fear then was that the French might find him. If they did there would be questioning. They would bring him to a hospital and patch him up, and find out who he was. And when he healed he would have a debt to pay, perhaps years in the mines again, this time deeper into France so he could not possibly walk away.

So he lay there and thought of America, and Elsa, and the bountiful fields filled with grain, and the laughter and the wonderful food Clara had made, and the time Elsa had kissed him in the barn. What would Elsa think if she saw him now? He did not find an answer amid his stress. His agony continued unabated.

Soon the sun warmed his back and he closed his eyes. He drifted into sleep again against his will, and in an agony of dreams he thought again of Aachen, of the firefight and the explosion, and of the old man's arm lying in the street, its fingers twitching as if it were alive. And he dreamt of Algona and the barbed wire and the terrible face of Hauptmann Schmidt jeering at him, saying over and over, Heil Hitler, Heil Hitler, Heil Hitler, until it became a drone in his head, a never-ending sea of misery that send angry breakers crashing against his brain in an endless cascade of despair.

He was jarred awake by the sound of his name. "Henrik! Henrik!"

The sound came from his right, not far off, there, beyond the small copse of trees that hung dead still in the breathless air. He opened his mouth to shout back, but his throat would not respond. He could hardly make a sound. The rocks! He remembered the rocks he had unearthed the night before. He reached for them and took one in each hand. He clapped them together, hard. The sound spread out across the field like a dull gunshot. Clack! Clack! Clack! The clear, distinct sound would carry a distance.

"Henrik!"

He pounded the rocks together again.

Almost at once he heard a rushing through the tall grass to his right. He sighed, relieved that his ordeal was almost over. Turning his head, he saw Karl dashing past the trees through the high weeds. Within seconds he was at Henrik's side.

His words came in spurts. "What happened to you? You did not come home. We were worried. I was out most of the night looking for you. But I could do nothing in the rain. Thank God I have found you. What happened?"

Henrik grinned. His voice wheezed. "My left leg is broken below the knee. You will have to be careful with me."

Karl examined him, and then nodded. "It is twisted just above the ankle."

Henrik tried talking again. "A man struck me with a board when I was riding the bicycle. He dragged me here. I don't suppose you found the bicycle."

"It is gone."

"My neck is swollen. It is difficult for me to talk."

"Then remain silent. I will take care of you now."

Henrik groaned. "You will need a splint. Perhaps the board is still on the road."

"Lay still. I will see."

Karl left quickly while Henrik warmed in the sunlight. When he returned he said, "I have found it. It is sturdy. Now lay still, and I'll try to stabilize your leg. It's going to hurt a bit, so bite down on your teeth."

Karl rolled him over on his back. Henrik tried not to cry out, but the pain was severe. He yelped like a wounded dog. When he was face up, Karl straightened his leg and bound the board tight to his calf with strips of cloth he tore from his shirt. The entire effort took about an hour. When Karl was finished he eased Henrik to his feet. They stood together in the sun, resting.

"Our business is gone," Henrik said. "We have nothing with which to deliver our product."

"I will get a new bike."

"Where?"

"There is a man in Bergheim who repairs bicycles that people have found in the rubble. He has many bikes. More bikes than people are willing to buy. Perhaps he will take a bottle of schnapps in trade."

"I am sorry, Karl. I should have been more alert."

"It is not your fault."

"You are understanding."

"If I had been on the bicycle, you would do the same."

"Yes, I suppose I would."

"Alright now. Put your arm around my shoulder and bear your weight to me. I will be your crutch. We have about three kilometers to go. When you are tired, we will rest. Are you ready?"

"I am ready."

"So here we go."

They walked out of the field and onto the road. It took only a few steps for Henrik to realize how difficult the passage would be. With every stride his leg pounded. With every stride his weight became more and more difficult for Karl to handle. They rested five times before the wagon came along, a husband and wife and two children bound for Bergheim, who gave them a ride.

They went into Bergheim and found the hospital, what was left of it. A doctor set his leg and made a cast for him. Henrik remained there for the night while Karl returned to his home. Karl said his neighbor had a car. He would arrange for him to pick Henrik up the next day.

A French administrator came by later that night and asked him a few questions about his leg. Henrik told him he had fallen from a ladder while repairing their barn. The Frenchman seemed satisfied with the explanation, but not before glancing at Henrik with a questioning stare. They had crowded him into a small room with a dozen other patients. He spent a rather restless night, hoping that the French authorities would find him unimportant enough to ignore. The following morning Karl returned and took him back to the farm.

The first thing he did was to embrace Mabel. The second was to eat a good meal. The third was to write Elsa a letter.

Dear Elsa, my love. You were so close to me last night I could almost hear you breathing. You comforted me. I have broken my left leg on a fall from the barn. It is now in a cast and will take about two months to heal, so I will have plenty of time to write to you. I have decided that when I can walk again I will go directly to the American Zone to the city of Wiesbaden. There I hope to speak to someone about immigration. I will not go to the French because they have no programs available, unless one would give up their life to become a servant of their country. I must rely upon the Americans, and you, to bring me back.

Heinrick

He went on to tell her about the wonderful care he was receiving from Karl and Mabel, who had become his surrogate parents. And he told her in detail how much he loved her.

Karl fashioned a pair of crutches for him out of poles he found in the barn. He covered the supports with layers of old soft blankets, and attached a hand brace to the center of it. It gave Henrik mobility, allowing him to move about the farm with regularity.

Karl bartered for another bicycle, schnapps for wheels. Soon they were making product again. Karl did the delivering.

Henrik continued to write, and with time on his hands, he began crafting his future.

FORTY-FIVE

New Ulm, Minnesota, June 1946

ELSA AND ERICA SAT TOGETHER ON THE beach at Flandreau Lake, a short distance away from the vacated POW camp that now stood idle and forlorn in its emptiness. The day was beautifully warm and fragrant. New foliage rustled contentedly through the trees sheltering the camp buildings. The sun scattered diamond patterns across the water like ripples of winter frost. Birds called in the distance. Everything was peaceful in the valley.

It was a Saturday afternoon. Erica had picked Elsa up after work and, acting upon Elsa's suggestion, they had driven down to the campsite and had spread a blanket on the shoreline. There, amid the pure and inviting setting, they continued their conversation.

"I don't know how you do it," Erica said, while picking at the grass alongside the blanket. "It's been almost a year now. How do you keep focused on him?"

"Through our letters. He writes me often now, whenever he can get postage. He said things are very tight over there. Everything is scarce. Some of the people don't have clothing, and wear only rags. There are no shoes available, and no place to live. Many of them are in camps. He said it rained so hard last spring that most of the new crops were flooded. He tries to be positive, but I know he's sorrowful at the way things are. Yesterday I received a picture of him, one that Mr. Schroeder took." She dug into her small purse and extracted an envelope containing Henrik's photo, showing him with a broad smile, a mustache and a short beard. It had been taken in front of the house. "Here, look at him."

Erica gasped in surprise. "Oh, my gosh. He looks so different."

"He looks scrumptious."

"Yes, he does."

Elsa pressed the photo to her chest. "Now I can see him every day."

She showed Elsa three other photos, one of Mr. and Mrs. Schroeder, another of Henrik on crutches, and a third of the house. He had written on the bottom, "This is where I live now."

"I sent him my graduation picture," Elsa said.

"So," Erica replied. "You're going to wait for him then, no matter how long it takes. Right?"

Elsa nodded. "I will."

"But what about school?"

"I haven't heard yet. Papa wants me to go to Mankato, to Bethany Lutheran. He said it would be the best school for me."

Erica shrugged, tossed a handful of grass to the wind. "Well, I'm not going anywhere. My average was only seventy-nine-point-three, not good enough for even taking an entrance exam."

"Mine was just good enough, eighty-two." Elsa sighed. "I should have spent more time studying and less time chasing around."

"Don't worry. You'll get there."

"Naw. I'll probably slop hogs for the rest of my life."

They looked out over the shimmering surface of the Flandreau and for a moment their thoughts surrendered to the beauty of the place, to the absolute contentment of the land, to the skittering light patterns that glistened on the surface. For a moment Elsa found her way back to the past, and as she looked at Henrik's picture in her hands, she remembered the day she had said good-bye to him, at the place just over her right shoulder.

She turned then, and looked there, to where the trees rose up, to where the shade patterned the grass, to where the abandoned cabins stood as a stark reminder to that day. "I said good-bye to him, right over there," she said.

"I know."

"God, I'll never forget that day."

Erica grinned. "You were quite the brave one, walking all that way."

"It was the only thing I could do. If I hadn't done it, I wouldn't be looking at his picture now."

"You're really in love, aren't you?"

Elsa sighed. "As deep as I'll ever be. I'll wait for him 'till the suns stops shining."

Erica lay down on her back and stretched her arms over her head. "I envy you sometimes, finding him like you did."

"When I think about it, it was a miracle, a gift from God, a billion-to-one shot."

Erica nodded, took Elsa's hand in her own, and squeezed it. "Have you heard anything from the government?"

"Just from the Department of Immigration. They said they have no definite plans to immigrate German nationals just yet. But they said they're working on it."

"Did they say how long it would take?"

"They were unsure. Maybe a year. Maybe two."

Erica covered her face, muffling her voice. "Holy cow! Two years. That's an eternity almost. How can you wait that long?"

"I have to. I promised."

"Yea, I'll bet. When you're in college the boys will pester you silly. You'll probably forget Henrik in a heartbeat."

"Not on your life. Never."

Erica sat up quickly. "Elsa, my dear friend, are you going to waste away a couple of years on hope alone? Why, in two years he might just change his mind. He might find some sweet little delicacy over there and settle down."

Elsa gazed out at the lake. "I'm not listening."

"Okay, so you're not listening. All I can say is, I have to give you credit for your tenacity. I don't think I could wait that long for a man on just a whim."

"It's not a whim. I love him."

"Could be you're just throwing away some of the best years of your life."

"No way."

"This love of his could be just a flash in the pan."

Elsa nudged her hard in the side. "And it could be that I'm just planting seeds that'll bring me a bountiful harvest some day."

"Now you're talking like a farmer's daughter."

"I am a farmer's daughter."

"A patient one, I might add."

A flash of red caught her eye. A cardinal winged past, then another. She looked around at the cottonwoods that moved in an almost magical way, their leaves glistening, all silvery and alive, and she knew, she just knew, that someday she and Henrik would be together again, right here, sharing a day just like this one, with their hands clasped, with their love intact. All the days of waiting and wondering and wishing would be over and they would have nothing ahead of them but seasons and years of planning, a promising future, and the raising of children who would surely brighten their lives.

Elsa closed her eyes and envisioned it clearly. She dreamed of the house and the romping children, and of the glee on their faces, and of his bronzed figure striding in from the rows of green plants, with pride on his face, and the children racing toward him, hugging his legs, grasping his hand, pulling him homeward, and he, lifting them up toward the sun and laughing in their faces, and then putting them down to whisk her into his arms.

That was how it would be, and nothing would change her dream.

FORTY-SIX

Wiesbaden, Germany, July 1946

ENRIK'S LEG HAD HEALED WELL, and after two weeks of careful exercise it had strengthened to the point where he felt confident enough to travel the distance to Wiesbaden, in the American Zone. He would travel on Karl's bicycle, and he would take little more than expectations with him

Wiesbaden was a hundred and twenty kilometers from Bergheim. If he were fortunate enough to make sixty kilometers a day, it would require two days of travel to get there. Mabel had packed him enough food, mostly vegetables, dried meat and fruit, to last him for six days if he ate sparingly. He would carry the supplies in a small container attached to the handlebars, along with a single blanket rolled into a tight bundle tied with cord. Karl had given him a rubber raincoat for protection.

Early June was unpredictable when it came to weather. His feet were soft now and well healed for travel. He would carry several changes of stockings, one additional shirt, an extra pair of shorts, and a light jacket. He and Karl had plotted a travel route south to Kerpen, then to Bonn. From there he would take the Rhine road to Remagen. Then he would cut east to Wiesbaden, which lay west of Frankfurt. Two days down, and two days back. He hoped he would have no trouble with the French. His papers said he was Otto Schroeder. If Henrik Arndt's name did appear on any list of theirs, it would not matter.

On the night before he left, he sat down at the kitchen table with Mabel and Karl. Karl scratched his three-day growth of whiskers. "So, now you begin your journey back to America. Good luck, my friend."

Henrik nodded. "I hope the trip will be useful. It is, as they say, a shot in the dark."

"You will go to the Lutheran Market Church. It has many tall Gothic towers, six in all, I believe, the main one reaching ninety-two meters high. You cannot miss it. You should be able to see it from the hillside as you approach the city. The church borders the market square where the government buildings are, the parliament and the city hall. If they are still there."

"You know the place well."

"I was there twice, before the war. Perhaps much of it is gone now. Hopefully the church remains. You can see the pastor there. He should be able to give you the information you need. If all is good, he might be able to introduce you the American authorities."

Henrik snickered. "I will take better care of your bicycle this time."

"Ha, if you don't I will spank you soundly."

Henrik and Mabel laughed together. Karl's words were reminiscent of his own father's advice. They were much alike, those two, raised in the same crucible, rural fathers who had little to do with political machinations.

"So, I will leave tomorrow morning. Thank you both for your kindness. I hope to return with good news."

"Just take care of yourself. Much can happen during seventy-five miles of travel, as you well know. Remember the man with the stick who sent you flying. I would give you a gun, but the French might take it at the checkpoint. You will be better off unarmed this time."

"I will be careful."

"Then God go with you."

Henrik slept uneasily that night. His mind was on the journey, and on Elsa, back and forth, back and forth between the two, settling at last on Elsa just before he went to sleep.

She was there for him, her face aglow in the darkness, assuring him, cautioning him, whispering words of love. Her image was the last thing he saw before he fell asleep.

Just after sunup he left, heading for the low hills south of Bergheim. Far to the east a murmur of rain growled in the sky above the city. He hoped the rain would not come his way. He pedaled fast at first, wanting to put miles behind him, but then he eased up, sensing the need to conserve energy. He coasted down the hills and pedaled up the inclines, walking sometimes to take the pressure off his rear end. The bicycle seat was small for him, offering little in the way of comfort. Even so, his spirits were high, his expectations broad. Nothing would deter him from his goal.

With no cloud cover, by noon the sun was hot and bright. Rain had not materialized. A slight breeze drifted across the land. By midmorning he had rolled up his sleeves and opened his shirt, and by noon he was sweating. He passed burned fields and weedy fields still recovering from the war, saw wreckage at times, a burned half-track far out near the trees, a row of shell holes, the road beneath him patched with dirt. Many of the farm buildings had survived. Some were abandoned. Others had occupants, none of whom waved at his passing. Everyone was involved in his own survival. Occasionally he passed groups of people, a horse pulling a wagon, a truck or two now and then, and few cars. He stopped frequently and drank water from the jar, rested, then resumed his trip. By noon he had reached the road paralleling the Rhine where shaded areas cooled him and the smell of water replaced the dry, arid scent of land. He found a small waterfall cascading down the hillside, and there he filled his jar. He would not drink out of the Rhine, despite its pristine appearance.

He took his lunch at the side of the road in a cool place where the sun could not find him, in a shelter of trees overlooking the river. He was comfortable there. After he ate he rested, sleeping lightly for a half hour. The sound of a truck awoke him. Then he was on the road again, headed toward Remagen.

The bridge at Remagen had collapsed into the Rhine in March of 1945 shortly after the American forces had crossed. All that remained of it were the four towers guarding its banks, two on the east, and two on the west. A pontoon bridge carried all the traffic. Henrik arrived there late in the afternoon, and waited his turn.

That night he took refuge in the front seat of an abandoned car, on a crossroad somewhere east of the bridge. He crawled in the back seat after tying his bicycle tightly to the door handle, just in case. He was on the edge of a forest, up beyond the cliffs that dominated the Rhine. The brittle darkness was profound, even though the small bit of moonlight evaded the clouds. He was uncomfortable in the back seat. He tossed, unable to will himself to sleep. He ended up outside on the ground with the blanket tight around him, wishing he was back in the Schroeder's bed where Elsa's photograph was only a glance away. After midnight the chill worked its way through his blanket and he shivered for a while until sleep took him. After sleeping only four hours, he awoke as the dawn was just breaking through the trees.

The first thing he saw was the dog, about ten yards away from him, hunched down in the grass, its eyes bearing on him with unwavering intensity, as if he were prey. When he moved, the dog moved. It stood up on its paws and backed away slowly, its eyes glaring.

"Come here, boy," Henrik said. The dog did not move.

"I have some food for you," he said. He reached slowly into the box containing his food and removed a small portion of dried venison. The moment the dog caught the scent, its head came up.

"For you," Henrik said, holding out the morsel.

The dog was white and black, a sheepdog by the looks of it. It came on to him hesitantly, its eyes intent on the venison. When it was within arm's reach, Henrik tossed the meat toward him. The dog caught it in mid air and devoured it instantly. The dog moved in closer. Henrik pulled off another small piece of venison and held it out in his fingers. The dog came on without pause and nipped it away. It held its ground long enough for Henrik to pet it between the ears.

"If you come with me, I will call you Remagen, so we will both remember this day."

The dog cocked its head. It dropped to the ground contentedly, as if it had found a new master. An hour later they were on their way to Wiesbaden.

Leaving the river behind, Henrik pedaled into higher country where hills and valleys dominated the landscape. The dog kept pace with him. He loved dogs and was glad the dog had come his way. His own had been a constant companion before the war.

Traffic on the road was slight, trucks mostly, or an occasional car. Many of the people he passed were on foot. He was clear headed and excited about his destination. He came upon a small pond early in the afternoon, so he took the dog there, washed it, and picked it clean, tried his best to untangle some of its fur. The dog was obedient enough. It made no effort to snap at him, choosing to lick him instead. By that afternoon they were good friends, and it appeared that Remagen would remain with him throughout the journey.

As they approached the hills they came to the French checkpoint. The cross through was simple enough. They examined his papers, asked him where he was going. He told them he was headed into Wiesbaden to visit his uncle. They looked him over, and then passed him through. As twilight pressed down, they descended the high ground and entered the city. The church was easy to see. Its tall, gothic towers rose proudly above the ruins. He went directly to the church and wheeled his bicycle in through its large front doors. Remagen stayed outdoors, obediently reserving his own place beside the door. Henrik was surprised to find the nave occupied by groups of people, obviously refugees, some of whom were sleeping on the pews. He headed toward the chancellery and found the office occupied by an elderly man in street dress. He knocked. The man looked up across the top of his glasses and waved him in.

"Another one," he said with a smile. "Come. Come. There's always room for one more."

Henrik entered. He bowed slightly, his hands clasped together. "I am not seeking shelter," he said. "I am seeking advice."

"Advice? Well, that I can supply, provided it has something to do with God."

Henrik grinned. "I am afraid not. I am seeking legal advice. I was told to come here, that you may be able to direct me to the proper authorities."

The man stood up and extended his hand. "My name is Harold Kruger. I am the acting pastor. My predecessor was killed during the war. I am attempting to rebuild here and help the people as much as possible. How can I help you?"

"My name is Henrik Arndt. I am from Bergheim, in the French Zone."

"Ah, I know of Bergheim."

"I am seeking information regarding immigration proceedings to the United States. I was a prisoner of war there, and I wish to return. The people I worked for there are ready to sponsor me, if and when it is possible."

Kruger nodded. "Ah, you are one of the fortunate ones." He motioned Henrik to a chair and the two sat down. "I am no authority on immigration. All I can do is direct you to someone who might help you. I know an American Colonel who is working in the city hall across from the marketplace. His name is George Weir. He is of German descent. I can direct you there."

"I would appreciate that, Herr Kruger."

"He is not there now. Tomorrow morning, perhaps."

"Tomorrow would be fine."

"I will go with you. He is always willing to talk with me. You will find him to be a very considerate officer who has been placed here to help us."

"Thank you."

Kruger arose again and took Henrik by the shoulder. "Come now. If you need a place to sleep tonight, you can find a pew that is unoccupied. We have food in the basement, and a place to clean up. We do what we can. Our city is on the rise again but it will take some years before it is complete."

"I have a bicycle outside."

"Then bring it in. There are still thieves around who will take anything."

"And I have a dog."

Kruger laughed. "The dog will stay outdoors. You can tether it."

Henrik found a pew that night. He folded his blanket up and used it as a cushion on the hard wooden seat. Despite his discomfort, he slept well.

The following morning, after a breakfast of bread and porridge, Harold Kruger walked with him across the cobblestone marketplace to the reconstructed city hall, and there he was introduced to Colonel George Weir.

Weir was a heavy-set man with a strict military manner. His keen eyes were penetrating, his mouth tight set, even when talking. But despite his disciplined exterior he was kind and respectful. Henrik felt genuine concern in his handshake even before he began speaking. He thanked Kruger for the introduction. Then he and Henrik sat down together on two chairs, facing one another. The colonel was the first to speak.

"First of all, I have been assigned to this city for one reason, to help its people in any way I can, and to be of assistance in rebuilding its infrastructure. I and my staff will do anything to assist in that effort. You may have noticed that the rebuild ing effort is in full swing. Our lumberyard is operating again, as is the brick factory Our schools have reopened. At least one of the hospitals is taking patients. German and American doctors are tending to the sick, and people are going to church again But those are the big issues. Now, what can we do for you? If its work you are look ing for, I think we can help."

Henrik cleared his throat, sat back, and began. He told the colonel about his background in Bergheim, of being forced into the Volkstrum, of his near-death ex perience in Aachen, the field hospital, the voyage to America, Algona, New Ulm and about the Sommer family, his return to France, the mine, his travels back to Bergheim. He omitted any mention of his brief affair with Elsa. He concluded by saying, "The Sommer family knows about my strong desire to return to America They have offered to sponsor me. It is why I am here in Wiesbaden, to find out what I must do to begin the process of immigration."

The colonel sat straight in his chair. "Well now, that presents a bit of a problem mainly because there are no regulations in place for immigrating German citizens to America."

Henrik frowned. The news struck him hard. The expression on his face was ap parent to the colonel. "But don't despair," the colonel said. "The American govern ment is well aware of the problems facing Germany. They're working on legislation right now that might pave the way for immigration, especially for someone who has a willing sponsor. In that regard, you might be one of the lucky ones." He went on. "We have displaced persons (DPs) camps throughout Germany already, to han dle the eleven to twenty million people who have no place else to go. Many of them were victims of the Nazi concentration camps. Now it's up to our military and civil ian authorities to resolve the problem of displaced persons. Monumental, I must say. We're classifying them as fast as we can, war or political refugees, forced or vol untary workers, former soldiers under German command, deportees, intruded per sons, extruded persons, civilian internees, stateless persons, and ex-prisoners of war like yourself. The list goes on. Millions."

The colonel brushed back his hair and then breathed deeply. "Right after the war our plan was to repatriate them to their countries of origin as quickly as possi ble. The American, French, British and Soviet forces tended to their immediate needs as best they could. Nearly all of the DPs were malnourished. A great number were ill; some were close to dying. Shelter was often improvised. We used former military barracks, hotels, castles, hospitals, private homes, and even partly destroyed structures to house them. Most all of them experienced some sort of hardship, including a constant fear for their lives, or neglect, or abuse, or torture. There were even instances of attempted murder. We provided shelter wherever we could, fed them diets of less than 1,500 calories a day, and improved the sanitary conditions whenever possible. There was minimal medical care. As a result many of them suffered from malnutrition, and a variety of diseases. They were often unclean, lice-ridden and prone to illness. It wasn't a pretty picture. To top it all off, many were apprehensive around the authorities that tried to help them. Many were depressed and traumatized. Can you see the picture, Henrik?"

"Yes, it is terrible."

"It is terrible, of course. But we are coming out of it, slowly but surely."

"As for me?"

"Well, you have a home in Bergheim, and willing sponsors. All you need is a law permitting you to resettle in American. It'll come, but when I don't know. I do know that it will probably be handled through organizations such as the Lutheran World Federation, or the International Red Cross. I would suggest at this point that you notify your sponsors and tell them to put pressure on the Congress to adopt an immigration policy for displaced German personnel. We're already doing that. Here in Germany, we are the ones who understand the problem more than they do. Believe me, we're doing all we can."

"So, I must wait."

"Unfortunately, yes. A law is needed. Then we can proceed."

"So, until then, what can I do?"

"Be patient. Go back to Bergheim. You'll have to get new papers when the time is near. You'll have to become Henrik Arndt again, and hope the French don't interfere."

"And if they do?"

"That's for them to decide. You're in their jurisdiction. I would suggest that you relocate before then, perhaps here to Weisbaden. We can find work for you here and shelter as well, if you give us fair notice. You are fortunate in that you can be easily classified."

"That is some satisfaction."

The colonel gestured affirmatively. "That's all I can give you at this time. I'll turn you over to my clerk now. He'll take all the information about you and place it in record. Keep in touch with us. We'll help you when the time comes. Until then, you'll just have to wait and be patient, like so many others."

"Thank you, colonel. You have given me hope."

The colonel nodded. "Hope. This country's so full of hope that it's almost over-flowing. Sometimes I think taking care of all these people is a far greater challenge than winning the war." Then he directed Henrik to another room filled with eight desks. They approached a man busy at a typewriter. "This is Sergeant O'Halloran," the colonel said. "He'll take the information. For now, good day, Mr. Arndt. My best wishes for a safe return to Bergheim. We will see you again, sometime soon, I hope."

"Thank you for your courtesy, Colonel."

"My pleasure."

Henrik sat down in a chair beside the desk and spent the next half hour giving the Sergeant the information he required. Then he went outside into the city, where countless people, machines, and equipment had started to raise Weisbaden from the dead.

Two days later Henrik was back in Bergheim His letter to Elsa read:

> *My Dearest Elsa, my love. I have just returned from Wiesbaden in the American Zone. I learned there that no law exists to help German POWs return to America. The Colonel I spoke with told me that I can only wait. He also told me that it would be kind of you to keep putting pressure on the Immigration Department to pass a law providing for the return of German POWs to America under sponsorship. My dear Elsa, I yearn for the day I can set foot on the farm again, to take you in my arms, and to tell you face to face how much I love you. For us, please, keep writing the Immigration people. It will help us. Be patient, my love, for there is much we have to gain when the new law goes into effect. I have . . ."*

The letter went on, expressing himself in the words he felt in his heart. All he and Elsa could do was wait, and hope.

FORTY-SEVEN

New Ulm, Minnesota, September 1946

A T CHURCH THAT SUNDAY IN SEPTEMBER, Elsa had prayed harder and longer than she ever had before. She prayed for Henrik, and their eventual reunion, and for a long life together, and for a new immigration law that would enable it all. She shed a tear when the hymns were played, when the choir sang, and when she took communion. She prayed also for her near future, for on the following morning Papa would load her belongings into the car and would drive her to Mankato to begin her first semester at Bethany Lutheran College. Not only would she be away from Henrik, but from her family as well. The thought of it brought sadness and a deep sense of separation. A new experience awaited her, being alone with strangers, learning to manage on her own, studying long hours by a lamp, finding new friends, planning for a future albeit an uncertain one, in the feverish world of business, or with the man she loved. She prayed long and hard that day.

Elsa's suitcases were all packed, on the porch, ready to load into the car. She had said her farewell to Erica. More tears. All that morning she saw the veiled melancholy in her mothers' eyes, just above the forced smile. Her lips trembled imperceptibly whenever she spoke. David had hugged her. He had never done that before. Corina, sweet Corina, had picked flowers for her, and had given her a note that read: Don't stay away too long. I will miss you. You are my only sister. I love you so. The bedroom will be lonely without you. Elsa had cried when Corina gave it to her. She had hugged her with a passion neither of them had ever experienced before. The time of separation came quickly. The family had eaten their last Sunday dinner together, and while the others finished dishes, Elsa excused herself and walked outside into the bright daylight, and stood on the porch where she first laid eyes on Henrik Arndt, that day he had come in from the field after helping Papa with the fence. Again the tears came. So she walked down the steps and went into the barn and stood in breathless silence at the spot where she and Henrik had embraced.

So much had happened since that day. They were both alone now, he in Germany, and she in Minnesota, about to go off to college to a new and different lifestyle. It came to her then, in a moment of deep thought that she needed to be away from the farm for a while, away from the memories secreted in its buildings and within its yard, and in the very air that covered it. And so she began walking. She went up the dirt road away from the farmyard, past the place where he had pointed out Epsilon, that night they had been alone, their eyes on the heavens, on their star. She walked out onto the main road and passed the field embraced by the old wooden fence. A soft wind brushed her hair. Fall leaves rustled their muted song in the grove. The sky, a fresh blue, seemed to be nothing more than a delicate coverlet on the flowered meadow. Overhead a flock of blackbirds darted past her, winging over the herd in the north pasture. She scuffed along, kicking at the pebbles on the road. The gravel crunched underfoot. The warmth of the day rested on her shoulders like a treasured friend, comforting her, easing her thoughts. The breeze, fresh with sunlight, whirled her yellow dress around her legs.

The destination she sought was just over a mile away. Bracken's Creek. She didn't know why the place drew her toward it that day, but she knew she had to go there, and only when she came close to it did she recognize its pull on her. There, on the bank above the stream, the approach was covered with a profusion of wildflowers.

Elsa went down into the ditch and began picking them, white alyssum, some yellow buttercups, several blue phlox, and the bright red Indian Paintbrush. The scent of the field enraptured her. Then she walked to the bridge and leaned over its railing and gazed into the waters, remembering, remembering, remembering.

She gazed at the flowers in her hands, and then in a moment of extreme emotion, she casually separated the few white alyssum from the rest, studied their simplicity for a moment and then released them. They cartwheeled slowly downward into the water. The stream carried them away. Instinctively, she remembered the reef of white clouds that had occupied the sky on the first day she had seen Henrik.

The yellow buttercups were next, reminding her of the sunshine on his face that hot day in the field, when a bead of sweat had crossed his cheek to intercept his broad, magnetic smile. The buttercups fell straight down. Their stems pierced the water, causing a bend in the current, a smile in itself.

The blue phlox were, of course, his eyes, large and piercing and garnished with tenderness, so unlike those of a warrior. She looked at them longingly, as she had looked into his eyes, wondering what thoughts lay behind them, wondering if any of his thoughts were of her, then, later, learning that his eyes were indeed a path to his soul. She released the phlox hesitantly, saddened by their fall.

The Indian Paintbrush was last, as red as the blood that had flowed from his arm that day he had been injured in the field. He had said it was nothing. But she had felt his pain, even though his voice had been comforting. The last of them fell from her hand and disappeared beneath the bridge.

The moment was, to her, a promise for the future. For on that day she knew that she would wait for him, no matter how long it took.

The flowers in the water carried her memories downstream toward the Cottonwood, and as she walked the gravel road back toward the farm, she prayed that God would keep him safe, wherever he was, wherever he would go.

All the way home, Elsa's tears were the only things that kept her company.

That night, alone in her bed, as a full moon garnished the sky, she prayed again, and sobbed for a while. The silence of the night was broken only by the breeze and the touch of leaves against the roof above her head.

Elsa woke up to the first pale light of morning, amid the lonesome sound of the morning doves. The hours that morning were mostly a blur, and at just a few minutes before two o'clock she said good-bye to her family, got into the car, and rode with Papa to Mankato

FORTY-EIGHT

Bergheim, Germany, December 1947

KARL SCHROEDER AND HENRIK BROUGHT in their first harvest the fall of that year, not as bountiful as desired, but worthy of their effort. They planted corn and wheat, and, of course, sugar beets. Karl had acquired a horse, two goats, and four cows. The place was beginning to look like a farm again. When the winter months came, the still turned out tongue-numbing schnapps that became high in demand. Henrik delivered it to their customers on a regular basis, without mishap.

The correspondence between him and Elsa had continued on a weekly basis. He was kept up to date on her schooling, on her parents, on the bountiful harvest, and of course on her continuing, stalwart love. He was disappointed, however, in the seemingly slow effort in Washington to establish an immigration policy for those of German ethnic background, and there were times when he felt unable to vision the future despite his strong desire to do so. Only the letters kept his hope alive, each of them strengthened by Elsa's continuing pressure on Washington and the Immigration Department to hurry their work. He was sure, by now, they knew her name quite well. Perhaps her persistence would pay off when the task was finished and Congress gave their approval. So he waited, and prayed, and hoped for the day that seemed so long in coming.

Henrik was twenty years old now, strong and muscular, handsome and fully developed, his beard close clipped, his face bold and smooth like a granite sculpture, his smile full and self-assured, a true product of his Aryan heritage. He had several photos taken for Elsa, on film he had purchased in Kerpen from a man who had been a photographer before the war, who was now beginning to rebuild his business. And as he continued to reconstruct his own house, he had found his mother's locket, one given to her by his father on their tenth anniversary. He had boxed both the photograph and the locket together and had sent them to Elsa with a long letter for the family.

Just before Christmas he received a box from them. In it were items of clothing, shirts, trousers, stockings underclothes, sweaters, photos of the family, a striking photo of Elsa, food in the form of canned Spam, cookies from the Sommer kitchen, dried fruit, a jar of Mrs. Sommer's grape jam wrapped safely in towels, and more. Also included were letters from David, Corina, Clara and Papa. He cried when he ead them, for every word was poignant, every sentence one of hope, every paragraph filled with their desire to have him return. Oh, how he yearned to see them again, to sing Christmas songs with them, to taste a bit of wine, to smile and dance, to laugh around the tree that glistened with lights and hand-made treasures, to experience the tenderness of family again.

Henrick and Karl drank a bit of schnapps on Christmas, and they did what they could to relive the good days, when the holiday had been ripe with family, cheerful with their laughter, tender with their love for one another. But Henrik's parents were gone, as were the Schroeder's two boys. Only the three of them remained. In the warm comfort of the Schroeder living room, as the old hymns played, Henrik saw the tears in Mabel's eyes, and the almost imperceptible tremble on Karl's lips, and the longing in their eyes for the boys they had once held dear.

Henrik traveled twice back to Wiesbaden to visit the Colonel. Both times he was greeted warmly. Both times the news was disturbing, no progress being the only news from the states.

Remagen was part of the family now. The dog followed Henrik everywhere and occasionally ran with him to deliver schnapps, trotting alongside him with his tongue hanging out, never tiring, laying with him whenever they stopped, his head across Henrik's stomach, his eyes begging for food or a bit of water, or a hand to scratch his ears. He would hate to leave Remagen. He wished there were some way he could bring him to America.

The days, though filled with work, were bleak sometimes. He could not dismiss the feeling of despair whenever his dreams seemed to vanish, whenever his hopes were squeezed paper thin by the endless frustration of waiting. How he longed for Elsa then, when passion stilled his breath, when thoughts of her languished in a bed of despair, like warm ashes turning cold beneath a gentle rain. But the remorse was never long lasting. Whenever he felt it coming on, he paused in his work and allowed it to drift away, and somehow he resurrected an image, be it small or large, from his meager collection of memories, and he allowed it to carry him through until he could get back to his room and look into her eyes and feel her love inside him like a wellspring.

The colonel in Wiesbaden had prepared new papers for him. He was Henrik Arndt again. He was ready for the time when the immigration policy was passed into law. He would be one of the first to take advantage of it.

Neither he nor Karl saw much of the French. Even in Bergheim they were almost invisible. The Germans had taken back the city. It was humming with new construction now, and food was more prevalent. Stores were opening again. Water was flowing. There was so much to do, but so few to do it. Work was prevalent. The Reichmark was beginning to recover its purchasing power, with rumors of a new currency being considered. If one listened carefully, one could hear the laughter of children again, even amid the rubble. Hope for the future was stirring, as the rubble gave way to progress.

So he and Elsa waited, and despite the time lag and the loneliness and the occasional loss of desire, they never lost hope.

On Christmas Day that year the Sommer family lit a special candle for Henrik and all of them prayed together for his safe keeping and for his eventual return.

FORTY-NINE

New Ulm, Minnesota, June 1947

E LSA HAD COMPLETED HER FIRST YEAR of advanced education in Mankato, and on the tenth of the month Papa picked her up and drove her back home. What a wonderful day it was, the family together, laughter again across the table, the farm full of love and memories.

Elsa's first year in college had been good for her. She had blossomed from a simple farm girl into a fine woman, near twenty, with a fresh approach to life, eagerness abounding. She had never lost faith with Henrik despite several attempts by the boys to whisk her away into their own world. One, a handsome, dashing young man from Saint Peter, who aspired to be a teacher, had come close to breaking the barrier she had erected, but she never relented in her love for Henrik. They had dated twice, had dined together, had danced in a ballroom filled with whirling lights and soft music and an ambience for romance, but she had convincingly thwarted his attempt to extend their relationship beyond that of friendship. She didn't tell him about Henrik. No one at the school knew of her association with a German prisoner of war.

No sooner had she settled back into her old routines when a newspaper came. David had brought it in, and, as usual, he had deposited it on the kitchen table where it stayed for most of the day until Papa picked it up at lunch after returning from the field for a period of rest. He paged through the paper as he always did, turning the pages slowly, scanning the columns, reading, going on, all the while puffing on his pipe. No one saw him pause. No one saw the pipe slip from his mouth. No one saw the widening expression on his face. No one saw his smile. But they all heard his voice.

"Look here, in the paper. Do you know what it says today?" His question turned Clara's head, Elsa's also. The others did not appear interested.

"Tell us, Papa," Elsa said.

"I will read it slowly, so listen carefully" he said, his smile broadening. "On June 25, President Harry Truman signed the first displaced persons act into law. The program will allow for the relocation of 200,000 persons of German ethnic origin born in Czechoslovakia, Estonia, Hungary or Yugoslavia, and in Germany to apply for relocation to the United States."

Papa did not read more. He didn't have to. He looked up as Elsa shouted and hugged her mother. David rose up from his chair, his face blank as the words sank in. Corina looked amazed as the full meaning brought her anxiously to her feet.

"They have done it," Elsa shouted as tears of joy streamed down her face. "They have done it. Oh, my God, Henrik will be coming home." She cried then, unabashedly, her hands all aflutter, her body weak with emotion as the grand news unleashed her joy.

"What do I do now?" she screamed, seeking advice. "What do I do now?"

Papa sucked his pipe, blew a smoke ring. "Well, it says here that anyone who is interested must contact the Immigration Department immediately. "If I'm not mistaken, I think you already have the name of an official there. I suggest you write your letter immediately, today, now. Not a minute to spare, my darling."

Elsa dashed to where Papa sat and hugged him tightly. "Oh, Papa, I love you so. Thank you. Thank you."

He embraced her strongly, and then said jokingly. "I think you have to thank the U.S. Congress and the President. It was they who did all the work."

"But it was you who made it all possible." She fled to her room then, to begin the work that would bring the man she loved back home to her.

TWO WEEKS LATER THE INSTRUCTIONS CAME, pages of them. In effect the law stated that, according to Section 12 of the Displaced Persons Act of 1948, in order for a person of German ethnic origin to be considered for immigration to the United States, assurance had to be submitted in his behalf by either a U.S. citizen or a recognized voluntary agency residing or established in the United States, to the Displaced Persons Commission, Washington 25, D.C. It went on to say, that if submitted by a U. S. citizen, the assurance had to be in notarized affidavit form, in quadruplicate, and that the assurance had to specify that the benefactor wished to sponsor a German ethnic person, name and address given, for immigration to the United States under the DP act. Assurance also had to be given stating that the sponsor would provide safe and sanitary housing accommodations, without displacing any other persons from such accommodations. Also, that suitable employment would be furnished at prevailing wages, without displacing another worker. Also, that the person sponsored would be met upon arrival and that all transportation costs from the port of debarkation in the United States to his final destination would be borne by the sponsor. Proof was also needed to assure the commission hat the sponsored person would not become a public charge. All assurances had to be mailed to the headquarters in Washington.

After they were approved they would then be forwarded to the appropriate European office. On the other hand, Henrik would have to apply for immigration to any of the Commission's European offices, hopefully the one in Wiesbaden. He would then wait until his case was ready for review.

All of it signaled another agonizing period of waiting for both Elsa and Henrik, made more difficult because of time itself. Hours and days and weeks would extend beyond the norm, and time itself would seem incapable of moving. It would be an unbearable period with the waiting, the wondering, the expectations, and the mental stress.

Elsa, with the help of her parents, did everything that was expected of her. The forms were obtained, completed, and mailed, and by mid July all she could do was wait. She had told Henrik what his task was. She had mailed copies of their petition to him, so he knew how sincere they were. He had gone back to Wiesbaden, to do what was necessary there. For both of them, the waiting was almost over.

Then the doubt, the nagging questions, and the uncertainty of it all began to surface. Would he be the same man today as he was two years earlier? Would she see him in the same light? Had the years changed their love to the point where it could be fractured? Would the family want him there on a permanent basis? Would she respect him for the man he had become? What unknown issues stood in their way? Would they be compatible sexually? Did either of them have a limited temperament? Neither had seen the other one angry, or disgruntled, nor upset. How would they individually, or jointly, handle a crisis? Would their personalities put an end to love?

There were no answers of course, but neither of them faltered. They continued on with whatever had to be done, hoping that the future would answer all their questions favorably.

FIFTY

Bergheim, Germany, August 1948

Toward the end of August, Henrik said good-bye to Karl and Mabel Schroeder. He signed the deed for his farm over to them, and on a warm morning, after he had eaten, and after he had said good-bye to Remagen, he stood on the porch with both of them. It was a bittersweet moment, he going off to recapture his dream, they saying good-bye to a man who had taken the place of their own sons. Mabel cried. Karl held out his hand.

"You go and find your dream now," he said.

"I will."

"And when you get to America you must write to us."

"I will. Certainly I will."

"And you must not forget us, nor will we forget you. You are part of us now."

"I will never forget what you have done for me."

Karl laughed. "And now Remagen and I will have to deliver the schnapps. He will keep me company on the road."

Henrik stepped back, felt a lump in his throat, and for a moment his words could not find release. He swallowed and looked away, until his sadness disintegrated. Then he said quietly. "My parents have gone, but you have taken their place. You have both made me a happy man. But now I go to meet still other parents, those of the woman I will marry. I will send you a photo of our wedding. And when our children are born, the boy will be named Karl, and the girl will be named Mabel."

The two said nothing. Their gaze went beyond him, to the sky, to the fields, to the trees. Eventually their eyes drifted back to him and rested soulfully on his face. He saw tears in Mabel's eyes, and a sense of pride in Karl.

Then Henrick turned, and without another word he stepped onto the path leading to the road and hurriedly walked there. The dog whined behind him, and then barked. By the time he was out of sight, Remagen was tugging at his rope.

Looking back only once, he saw the two of them wave. Then he turned and began his long trek to Wiesbaden, to pass through a new door, into a life he had only dreamed of.

FIFTY-ONE

New Ulm, Minnesota, September 1948

H is letter read:

My dearest Elsa and family Sommer. By the time you read this I will be in Bremen. I have been passed through. All of the formalities are over. The questioning and the approvals have been given, and they will be putting me on a bus tomorrow morning. When I reach Bremen I will embark on a ship headed for Boston. The crossing will take us approximately eleven days. I cannot wait to set foot in America. When we reach Boston the Red Cross will be waiting for us. There are thirty-two of us, some families, some soldiers. When I arrive, the Red Cross will put me on a train to Minneapolis. Think of it. I will be home again, with all of you, before the month is gone. The threshing will be over, but I am sure you will have work for me. How can I say how grateful I am? How can I say how much I love you all? How can I express my gratitude? Surely, not in words alone. I must express them by being everything you expect of me. You will see how thankful a German boy can be when I come home. We are in a hurry now. There is much to do. I send my love to all of you. To you, Elsa, I pledge my devotion for all time. I wish you all good health. Yours, Henrik.

Elsa folded the letter and crushed it to her breast. Her breath stuttered

Corina had watched her from across the room, and now she walked slowly toward her on stocking feet, careful not to alarm her. Elsa's eyes were closed. They did not open until Corina touched her on the shoulder.

"Oh," Elsa remarked. "I didn't hear you."

Corina appeared solemn. "What does he say in the letter?" she asked.

Elsa smiled and pulled her close. "He's coming home. He's on his way to Bremen."

"Where is Bremen?"

"It's a harbor in Germany. He'll be on a boat for eleven days crossing the Atlantic. When he is in Boston, he'll be put on a train to Minneapolis. Think of it, Corina. He's coming home."

They both smiled radiantly. Corina skipped a couple of steps, her glee emitted in laughter, in unconcealed happiness. "I am so happy for you," she said.

"You'll have a new brother-in-law. I expect we'll be married."

"Do you really think so?"

Elsa tweaked her nose. "Why else would he come back? He's going to be my husband."

Corina nodded. "I knew it all along."

"Come," Elsa said, leaping to her feet. "Let's go and tell the rest of the family."

THEY SAT AROUND THE TABLE THAT NIGHT, talking and planning, making arrangements for Henrik's arrival. Most of the discussion was directed at Elsa.

Papa said, "He'll be sharing the room with David, until the timing's right, until you and he decide what you're going to do. If it turns out okay, there'll be a wedding at the church, and a reception right here at the house. Twenty or thirty people I suppose."

"There will be a wedding," Elsa stated.

"Time will tell. And we'll be talking about where the two of you will go, to the city, or to the farm next door. I already talked to them. They're itching to sell the place. You'll both have to work off the mortgage if that's what you want."

"Henrik will decide what we're going to do."

Papa cocked his head. "Well, looks like he'll be making the decisions then."

"He will."

"But not always," he joked.

"I'll have my say," Elsa replied, laughing.

"And I'm sure mother'll have a few things to talk to you about also. If you were a son, I'd do the talking."

"Oh, Papa."

"Oh, papa, nothin'. It's a big adventure ahead of you. You're going to need all the advice a family can give you, and that includes your mother."

"I'll listen, Papa."

"Good." He was busy with his pipe, puffing, and chewing, scattering smoke. "I got it all figured out how he can help us around here, meaning David and me. There's more work here than two men can handle, so he'll be puttin' in a full day until the two of you move on. But take your time with movin' on. Be sure of yourself, in everything."

"I will, Papa. I'm twenty years old now. I know quite a bit about the world already. I'm not like an ostrich. I haven't had my head buried in the sand."

"I know. I know. But a father's got to talk once in a while, and this is the time."

"You sound like an old pioneer, Papa. This is the twentieth century."

He bit at his lip. "I know what century it is. I also know that a woman has to be careful about the man she marries. You haven't been with him long enough to know his wants or desires."

"We have been writing for two years. I haven't shared all his letters with you."

"Letters are one thing. Bring right there in the face of hardship is another. Time's gonna tell if you're right for one another."

"There won't be much time until the wedding."

He brushed off the statement. "I hope you're right with your decision, darlin'."

They talked for about an hour, each having their say, each putting dibs on Henrik for one thing or another. David wanted him to go hunting deer before the snows set in. Corina wanted him to help her with homework. Mama wanted him to have a good hearty appetite. In the end, all had their say.

NEAR THE END OF SEPTEMBER, HENRIK ARNDT arrived in Boston. The Red Cross workers met the German contingent at the pier and gave them all a good meal. Then they separated each family and individuals, and escorted them to their assigned trains, to take their final ride into a new country where the promise of freedom awaited them.

Henrik was placed on a train bound for Minnesota, and in a late evening hour it pulled out of Boston and clacked its way along the rails in a slow but methodical rhythm, singing its metallic song, beat by endless beat. He sat by himself in a dimly lit half empty coach and recalled his first trip across America in a car filled with German soldiers on their way to the Algona camp in Iowa. He remembered all the details. This time, however, his destination was clear, his purpose well set, his future painted like a magnificent canvas positioned right before his eyes. He saw it all, the endless sky, the fields, the farm, and the faces, especially the faces, those he yearned to see again.

He watched the lights go by, saw the roads teeming with cars, and he sighed as the city melted into countryside where the night seemed to stretch on forever. He fell asleep then, impatient for morning.

FIFTY TWO

Minneapolis, Minnesota, September 1948

EVERY MEMBER OF THE SOMMER family had piled into the car, David in front with Papa, mother in back with Elsa and Corina. They had left New Ulm around ten Wednesday morning, and were now headed toward Minneapolis along the winding Minnesota River, where the trees had acquired their autumn colors, sparkling silver greens, browns and ambers, reds and gold. Their spirit were high. Henrik was due to arrive at the depot at four o'clock. They had allowed plenty of time for stops along the way and for lunch in Shakopee.

Elsa was nervous, but in control. Corina spent most of the time gazing out the window. She loved riding in a car. Up front, Papa and David looked straight ahead without saying much, their eyes on the road. The ride gave Elsa time to reflect on a conversation she and her mother had the following night out on the porch.

"This is going to be a trying time for the both of you," Clara had said.

"Are you going to lecture me, mother? "

"I wouldn't dream of it. You have a mind of your own. You'll make your own decisions. The right ones I hope."

Elsa had reached over and tapped her mother's hands, lovingly. "You've raised me right, mama. Don't worry. I won't do anything to dishonor you or Papa."

"I know that."

"I think Henrik and I both realize that there'll be moments of trial. We're going to form a life together, and that will mean discord and questioning and learning how to reach common ground. We've settled much of it through our letters. We've both learned how the other thinks. We've done our homework, so to say."

"But there's one thing you haven't covered yet."

"That is?" Mama's voice had drifted into a more instructive tone. "You haven't been to bed with him yet."

Two years earlier mama's statement would have shocked Elsa. But not now Elsa had accepted the comment like a woman and not like a child. "We'll be careful." she had replied.

"I know how two young hearts beat when passions are aroused. Sometimes there isn't time for thought."

"Oh, mother, please."

"I'm just saying, think before you act. Papa and I don't want any babies coming along before the wedding."

"There won't be any babies. I'm prepared to be safe, if it comes to that. Remember, I work in a drug store. We will take precautions."

Clara had grinned. "I'm just a mother talking."

"I know. I wouldn't want it any other way."

"There's a big world ahead of you. I wouldn't want you to step into it burdened down with problems."

"We'll be just fine, mother."

The landscape had been nothing but a blur during the time she had relived the conversation, but now everything came into focus again, the trees, the hills, the roadside. In several hours she and Henrik would be together, and their new life would begin. What course would it take? How would an unexpected meeting on the bank of the Cottonwood transform their lives? Where would they be one, five, ten years from now? Would they grow old together?

Elsa pondered the questions over and over again until they drove down Hennepin Avenue into the heart of the city and parked their car alongside the depot that rose grandly beside the Minnesota River. They entered the cavernous concourse that filled them all with a bit of wonder, well ahead of the train's arrival, and as the tension in Elsa's body continued to rise and rise and rise, she prayed like she had never prayed before.

As THE TRAIN ROLLED INTO THE STATION, Henrik adjusted the Red Cross band on his arm, the one he would use to identify himself to the authorities when he stepped out onto the platform. His attention, however, was on the city, at the collection of buildings and roadways that bordered the tracks. Minneapolis. His body tingled. The hairs on his arms seemed to crawl like an army of ants. His mouth was dry. He felt uneasiness in his legs, as if they wanted to take him to his destination faster than he could walk. He examined himself. His clothing was fresh, given to him at the point of debarkation, a gray shirt, and dark trousers. He had washed in the restroom, and had combed his hair. He thought he looked presentable. As the train jerked to a final stop, he took a deep breath. Outside the window, on the platform he could see the Red Cross personnel, two men and a woman, waiting for him. As they scanned his window, he flashed his armband quickly. The woman saw him and motioned. The others straightened and nodded. Then he took his bag, the one with the Red Cross on it. He left his seat, walked down the aisle and stepped out into a waiting handshake.

"You have come a long way, Mr. Arndt," one of the men said.

"Yes, a long way."

The woman smiled. "Welcome to Minnesota. We have met your sponsors. They are all together awaiting you in the concourse. You are a very fortunate man, Mr. Arndt."

"Yes I am."

"Right this way, please."

They began walking alongside the train, through the noise and the crowd, toward the staircase that would take them up and into the concourse. Suddenly he felt impatient, as if his legs would not walk fast enough, as if the attendants were walking too slowly, as if time had slowed down. The woman was talking.

"The Sommer family is anxious to see you again," she said.

"I cannot wait," he replied. He did not want to talk. He wanted only to hurry.

The woman spoke. "Before we meet them there are some papers you have to sign. It will only take a moment."

"More papers?"

"For the records, Mr. Arndt."

"Ah, yes, the records."

They went up the stairs and entered a small office. The papers were all ready for him. They explained what they were for. He signed his name. Some of the people there grinned at him. Others did not. He felt for a moment as if he was trapped, but the uneasiness left him as they took the papers away and ushered him to the door.

"We'll accompany you, Mr. Arndt. It won't be long now."

Everything became surreal then, the crowds, the noise, the surroundings, his own movement, the pace with which he walked. His sight reached out ahead of him, searching, searching for a recognizable face, for Elsa's face, and in those moments he felt as if he wanted to fly, to reach her ahead of himself. He could not believe where he was, back in America, about to embrace the woman he loved, about to begin a new future. His breath stuttered. He could not feel his feet touching the tile floor.

Then Henrik saw her, standing with the rest of them, and he drifted to a stop as she stepped toward him, away from the others. The bag he was holding fell to his feet. His face seemed to shrink into itself as his emotions crested. He felt incapable of taking that final step toward her. His legs would not move. He felt only a warmth that enveloped him like a shroud. His tears came quickly, all at once, as she stepped into his arms. Then all he could do was hold her, to feel her against him, to see the others through his veil of tears, coming toward him with smiles on their faces. Elsa's arms tightened around him. Her voice choked "Welcome home, my love. Welcome home."

Then the others surrounded him, Papa and Mama, David and Corina, all seeking his hand, his embrace, enveloping him with love. He wiped his tears away and hugged them all, while Elsa clutched him tight to her body. And when they had said all the small, but important words, and when his tears had dried, Papa said to him. "Come now. Let's all go home."

ON THE FOLLOWING DAY HENRIK SAT alone in his bedroom and wrote a letter to Bergheim. It read:

Dear Karl and Mabel.
I have arrived in New Ulm, and am now with my new family, and with my future wife, my love, Elsa. I cannot tell you how happy I am. Good fortune had smiled on me, and God has fulfilled my wishes. How could a young German boy, who almost died in battle, have been as fortunate as I? Now I must thank you for caring for me when my past had disappeared. You have been more than friends, more than neighbors. You have been my keepers, and I ask God to bless the both of you. I wish you well. My prayers will carry your names. Karl, don't work so hard in the barn, if you know what I mean. And, Mabel, take good care of him, for he is the best there is. And when you can, give Remagen a bone or two from me, and scratch his ear from time to time, for he likes that very much. I will write more later, after I have settled into my new life in America. Until then, my love and affection to you both.
Henrik.

FOUR DAYS PASSED, DAYS FILLED WITH laughter, talk, eating, planning, and a bit of working. Henrik had reunited with the family. He had erased the years between his going and coming. His acceptance was total. Within the four days he felt as if he were indeed a member of the family.

It was not until the evening of the fourth day that he and Elsa found time in which to be alone. They had walked outside and up the road, on a night when the sky was filled with stars. They were happy and carefree. Her hand was tight in his. Her cheek pressed softly against his shoulder. They paused to look up at Epsilon and she was propelled unconsciously into his arms, into swirls of rapture. He crushed her into his body, rocking her in an embrace that seemed to lift them skyward. Her lips burned on his neck, pulverizing his heart in a moment of ecstasy.

She moaned in his ear, hasty words spoken through her kiss, sounds expelled by the frantic pounding of her heart.

"You are here now," she muttered, "and nothing will take you away."

"I will never leave you," he replied.

She felt secure in his embrace, sure of herself, confident of their future. He trembled in her arms, absorbed in the fleeting seconds that distanced the world, immersed in an infinity of time as broad as lands, as wide as seas. He felt a strange pang in his chest. He kissed her, fueling his embrace with a desire that flowed along his veins like streams of pure fire. Her hands moved over him, touching, feeling, clutching, holding him, as if he were a treasure found after years of searching.

Elsa whispered, "Come," as the embrace ended.

She took him by the hand and led him toward a place she had selected that same day, to the place where they would make love. She had taken a blanket there several hours before, had prepared the ground, and had spread the blanket full out in the warm sun.

Now the waiting was over. Two years had vanished beneath the flash of his eyes. The waiting and wondering and worry were like nails being pulled from the wood of her past concerns. She led him toward the grove, impelled by the excitement that drove her on. He followed breathlessly, along the moon-ghosted path between the towering black trees, into the woods smothered by night. Moonlight splashed like gossamer waves through the branches, making shadows of every living thing. The wind whispered, guiding them, silvering her hair, leading them into the warm, tolerant silence coveted by trees, into the comforting shadows. Henrik walked freely, filled with a solemn mood. He felt like hugging strangers.

The place was a small clearing where she had often played as a child. Tonight she would use it to kindle their passion, to discover fully, the extent of his love. She would submit to him, and implore him for more, and find her way into the future. She was prepared. Now was the time for discovery.

Then they were there, where the moonlight lay like a satin fleece upon the grass. She stopped, and turned toward him, leaning into his kiss. They didn't speak. Words were unnecessary. Instead, their bodies moved and shifted like warm coils beginning to heat.

He understood her need.

Her tongue moved sinuously along his lips.

His breath flared with a sudden petulance as his hands tugged at the buttons on her blouse. He fumbled like a boy attempting love for the first time, frightened at what he would find beneath the clothing, yet anxious to receive the ultimate reward. As he undid the garment he was rewarded by her warm and wonderful approval, her fingers grasping at his belt.

She unfastened her bra as his hands glided over her breasts, whimpered as his fingers brushed her hardening nipples.

Then their movements became hasty, almost clumsy, as if they were sensing time as an enemy. His shirt was stripped and flung. Her skirt fluttered to the ground. She drifted into him like a moth in graceful flight. He nestled into her, into the most intense pleasure he had ever know.

She hesitated, and then bent down to search through the pocket of her blouse. She came up with a packet and pressed it into his hand. "Please," she said. "Use this."

He looked down, nodded, and then together they brushed their clothing aside and sank down onto the blanket. Nervously, he prepared himself.

Then she felt him enter her, a slight shock, a brief spasm of ecstasy and pain. Within seconds, the shock of his penetration gave way to fluid thrusts, and her body writhed like a warm, pulsing cocoon. She gasped as if her head were floating in the crowns of the oaks, as if she were drawing life through their roots into the trunk of her body. Elevating her knees, she became accustomed to the size of him, his fruit, his ripeness.

It was her first time, as it was his, her initiation to intercourse, and as her natural fluids responded to the motion, she began a slow, deliberate undulation that drove her to the depth of happiness. Like gliding silk, her hands swept over the surface of his buttocks, and with quick, synchronous tugs, she urged him inward.

Soon the scent of the woods and the grass were overpowered by the musky odor of their bodies. Delirious with passion, she lunged to meet his every cadent drive, accepting in return, the soul-pounding convulsions within herself that brought her to the brink of pleasure.

Then he strained. His breath ignited in her ear. He gasped with quick, lurching spasms as her hips swelled upward to assist in his release.

Elsa felt no climax of her own, but it didn't matter. His fulfillment was all she cared about. There would be many more days, many more nights. Her mouth opened onto his hard muscled shoulder. Her teeth closed on his skin. His passion vibrated through her lips, into her very soul, until his straining ended. Then, expended, he drifted down like a weary cloud and casually removed the condom.

They rolled as one, onto their sides. Her hands glided along his back, caressing him. His body trembled in the wake of his ejaculation. She kissed his heated cheek, his eyes, his forehead, his fiery lips, then slipped her hand across his thigh, onto the warm, damp copse of pubic hair that held his softening penis. He shuddered.

"I have waited a long time," he whispered.

Tears softened her words. "You have come back to me, as you said you would."

"Now we are together. We will always be together. Nothing will separate us."

"Oh, Henrik, hold me."

She felt an inflowing of happiness, as if it were meant to solemnize the moment. Giddy with the pleasure of his voice, she muttered, "I love you. I love you. I love you."

"And I love you," he replied, his hot breath warming her ear.

She trembled as he kissed her, as the early night chill roamed across their naked bodies.

"Are you cold?" he asked.

"No."

"Let me cover you."

"I am not cold. You're the one who is cold. I haven't warmed you enough."

He kissed her quickly. "You have warmed me more than fire."

"I will warm you more." Her hand trailed across his stomach, onto his genitals. She looked down at him and laughed. "You are white and naked, like a baby. No wonder you're cold."

He pulled her body tight to his own. "Then build me a fire."

"I am your fire."

"Yes, you are."

"I will warm you forever."

"Yes, forever."

Her happiness was pure, like a mountain stream. There was much to say, but she would say nothing this night. She would only love him, to satisfy his every need. The past was insignificant now. All that mattered was the future, the two of them together.

He kissed the soft curve of her neck.

She embraced him wantonly, clamping her leg over his. Her senses stirred like new life, reeling with half-visions of tomorrow and promises of all the days ahead.

His eyes misted in the moonlight.

She lay still, soothed by the pleasure of his hands, in an embrace that wrapped her with a magnificent, fulfilling silence.

He melted into her. For a time there was no wind, no world, no universe. Only the two of them.

And when their passion had burned away they dressed and walked hand in hand out toward the dirt road that led to the farmyard. And all she could hear in her head were the last words of her favorite song.

All I did was wonder how his arms would be.
And it happened to me.

FINIS

Elsa Sommer and Henrik Arndt were married in the spring of 1949. The bride wore a gown of white marquisette trimmed with lace and fashioned with a fitted bodice and lace peplum. Her finger-tip length veil edged in lace was held in place by a coronet of lace. The necklace, which had once belonged to Henrik's mother, was her only jewelry. She carried a bouquet of white roses, lilies of the valley and stephanotis with ribbon streamers.

They took residence in the farm adjacent to the Sommer place.

Their first child, a boy, was named Karl.

Their second child, a girl, was named Mabelle.

Their love for one another never dimmed.

THE END

REFERENCE MATERIALS

Signs of Life: Lebenszeichen, Michael Luick-Thrams, author
Memories of Times Past, Ideal Publications
A Boyhood Revisited , Otto W. Benjamin, author
Swords into Plowshares, Dean B. Simmons, author
The Dictators, Richard Overy, author
Behind Barbed Wire , Anita Albrecht Buck, author
Stalag Wisconsin, Betty Cowley, author
Nazi Prisoners of War in America, Arnold Krammer, author
POW research materials, letters, articles and documents, Brown County Historical
Museum